La Mia Sorella

(MY SISTER)

KIKI PRZEWLOCKI

Relax. Read. Repeat.

LA MIA SORELLA (MY SISTER)
By Kiki Przewlocki
Published by TouchPoint Press
Brookland, AR 72417
www.touchpointpress.com

ISBN-13: 978-1-952816-83-3

Editor: Kimberly Coghlan
Cover Design: ColbieMyles.com
Cover Images: Kiki Przewlocki

Visit the author's website at http://kikiprzewlocki.com/

First Edition

Printed in the United States of America

For my mother and her mother,
Her mother's sister
and mine,
And all those who
Seek to uphold the heart

PROLOGUE

I REMEMBER THAT DAY IN THE KITCHEN WITH MAMA. It was one of those momentous days that had me pivoting from present-day to future ponderings—a day I contemplated big concepts about relationships and behaviors, understanding how people "worked" one moment and then stewing in a pot of confusion the next (so it is when the little girl begins to outgrow her child's skin).

Mama seemed to be in a trance of sorts—not happy, not sad. Something had happened within the *famiglia* that I could almost read in the green fields of her eyes, but it remained just beyond my reach. It was not unlike that dream where you see the end of the road, and though you walk toward it, the road stretches out endlessly, forever in front of you. I opened my mouth to add another round of inquires—words as tools to dig around and root out the truth, but something stopped me. Maybe some part of the future me understood what she was saying yet didn't want to acknowledge it.

Mama tried to teach me about people through her stories of our ancestors and current tales of those in our village. She spoke of the human psyche, of the needs of the heart, of interpersonal relationships. Her focus always *famiglia*—promoting, maintaining, supporting the structure of *family*, for family, in Italy, is everything. Throughout the entirety of her story-filled lessons, she gave clues, road maps—keys on how it is and how it should be— ideologies that would have knocked any other acquiescing human to the ground. Alas, I was not one of them.

Mama continued in her sermon-like way, spewing concepts like betrayal, greed, and heartbreak as I continued my chore of sweeping the *cucina* floor. I brushed away the debris from under the braided rug in our *kitchen*—crumbs from Mama's rosemary bread, soil from the rows of basil, oregano, arnica, and other medicinal plants of our garden, dirt from the rocky shore of the Mediterranean Sea just outside our door. I recognized that a lot of pertinent life was being lived and breathed right there in that kitchen. I marveled at the room's importance where everyday meals, conversations, and milestone celebrations happened—where the stories of the past intersected with the tales of the future, and I wondered how people could inhabit this warm, loving place and be anything but perfect in their love for one another. As I continued to sweep, to move myself and the debris around the floor, I became a bit more willing to grasp Mama's disconcerting presage.

"People fail one another, Arabella. It is a fact of life," she stated matter-of-factly.

"What 'people'?

"Most people."

"But not us, not the Mandarinos."

She snorted. Mama, my well-mannered mama, snorted like a pig!

"Mama?"

"We must be realistic, Arabella. No one is exempt."

"Mama, you are talking about *our family*."

"Yes, Arabella, I'm afraid I am," she whispered, a tinge of sadness in her voice.

"But we're different," I insisted.

"Arabella, *different* does not exclude us from disappointment."

"But Mama, I think you are wrong." It was the first time I ever thought that and the first time I said it aloud.

"Well, you are entitled to your opinion, Arabella, but it is the opinion of a child."

Every member of our household knew there was no use arguing with Mama. She was a woman who stood firm as an ancient fir tree. I felt all jumbled up like when my sister's yarn balls were not properly rolled and put away (like when her little sister got into them and tangled the colors and textures into knots). Somehow, on that day, within that conversation, the past and future collided in fuzzy tones of gray. Was I trying to brush away the future failings of my family before they grew into hills of disaster without even realizing it? Perhaps I sensed a family can be a tangled mess of knots— just like my sister's yarns.

I was a girl of innumerable questions (tending to exasperate most people), but I wondered this: Do most mothers sense what the future holds for their children? Do they know, like fortune-tellers peering into crystal balls, the future of their family? Do all families crumble beneath the weight of time and troubles?

Even that day as I swept the floor of our *cucina*, I believe Mama knew that two sisters who were so perfectly attuned like radio frequencies on the same wavelength could end up on discordant ends of the same song.

I wish she could have foreseen whether hearts can endure the devastation of perfidy.

PART 1

Paola, Italy
1913-1923

LA MIA SORELLA, MY SISTER, DREW ME TO earth from the lap of God, calling me down from heaven. It was *mia sorella*, Filomena, who knew me before I was even a thought, let alone, a form. She spent a good deal of her nine years imploring God to bring me to her—asking Mary, Mother of God, to intercede on her behalf. Her persistence night after prayerful night must have kept God awake!

When a relationship begins in such a way, it is destined to be one of immeasurable love. Filomena is my best friend, second mama, and sister all rolled into one! She is my lifeline to all that is good in this world, to all that is wholesome and pure.

There is a kindred, compatible connection between all the women in my family that is easy and flowing. Those who possess this type of *simpatico* relationship with another recognize the blessing and responsibility of it. At thirteen years old, I know this to be true. I cherish all my relationships—with my Papa, brothers, grandfather, and uncles, but it is with the women in my life that I feel a kind of elemental, alchemical love—the kind that keeps this Earth in orbit, aligns the course of celestial bodies, keeps time for the ocean's rhythmic dance, the waxing and waning of the cyclical light of the moon. Without a doubt, men can love deeply, but the bond of women marks the longitude and latitude of love. We are born benefactresses of the heart, with the capabilities to extend the fullness of love to others.

Like Mary, Mother of God, we are the cartographers of the heart, mapping out the byways where love will endure, charting the crossroads where compassion kindles kindness, navigating the seas of forgiveness to set sail upon—instinctively aware of auspicious winds to carry us to destinations of the heart. It is our love that demonstrates possibilities.

My mother extended that love to me on 2 April 1900, when in an exhausting twelve hours of labor, she brought me safely into the Mandarino family. And she extended that love to *mia sorella*, Filomena, who declared that though my mother birthed me, I belonged to her! She informed the *famiglia* that my name would be *Arabella*, which means "answered prayer."

It was a momentous day to be born in our village—I was born on the same day of the same month that our village's patron saint died. That could be viewed as *malocchio* or *bad luck*. Signora Tuttobi used to shake her crooked finger at me when I was younger and ominously announce I was cursed because of my birthday. But Mama claims it a high blessing to be associated in *any* way with a saint's coming into or leaving this world. I say it is all a matter of perspective: what is a blessing can seem like a curse and vice versa. Being associated with Francesco di Paola, our patron saint, due to his profound impact on our village's past, present, and God willing, our future, is indeed a blessing. This extraordinary man dedicated his life to communicating with the divine through devotional prayer, and he healed the physical and mental ailments of hundreds of people. His honored sanctuary houses rows upon rows of crutches, braces, and canes that the once afflicted no longer need. He and I share a similarity or two—like my interest in healing. Though, rest assured, I have no miraculous powers, just an eager, able mind, which is studying the healing properties of herbs and herbal concoctions for everything from coughs and bellyaches to burns and croup. I study herbology with Signora Ruffino, our village *erborista* or *healer*, who is the mother of Gregorio, my soon-to-be brother-in-law. In this small village, many of us are related through marriage. I am so blessed that the wonderful Gregorio is not only going to become part of our family but will remain my tutor in the study of mathematics, literature, and the arts.

And though I do not wish to hide away in a cave and renounce the ways of the world through silent prayer like San Francesco di Paola, I do enjoy the luxury of being alone to think my thoughts and ponder ever-present curiosities of this living, breathing world I reside in. There are many beautiful, natural settings here in the exquisite "*Mezzogiorno*" or *southern provinces* of Italy to engage in such reflective thought: majestic, verdant mountains, symmetrical groves of olive and lemon trees, meadows of chamomile and gurgling streams, but my favorite place is the expansive shore of the sapphire blue Mediterranean we call the *lungomare*. This vast stretch of water and shoreline I consider part of my home, as our villa sits not fifty paces away from the gentle, lapping blue waters.

I can hear the song of the sea in my imagination like a Viennese waltz luring me to it. I can summon its salty breath by filling my lungs with a slow four-count. It is there I wish to be, in fact, alone—skirt hiked up over my ankles to stroll barefoot on the worn pebbles of its shore. Instead, I am with the other inhabitants of Paola held in the sacred womb of the cave-like sanctuary. A hundred candles bounce shadows on the earthen floor as voices sing in celebration of San Francesco di Paola's Ascension Day. Padre Busardo recounts the extraordinary life of our patron saint: impoverished boy, prayerful monk, healer. Padre gestures to hundreds of canes and crutches lining the north wall, proof that what is broken can be repaired with faith.

The church fills with musky incense—smoky tufts of gray-white clouds as Padre carries the censer and boat down the center aisle. He swings the contraption back and forth like a pendulum, pausing at our pew to give me a special birthday blessing.

Now it is time for the *festa di San Francesco di Paola*! We all gather in the *piazza*, the *meeting place* in the center of the village, to do what we Italianos do best: cook, eat, make music, and dance! The smell of roasting pigs and goats stuffed with prosciutto and garlic, bubbling tomato sauce, wood-fired pizza, sizzling sausage, and fried dough mingles with the spring breezes wafting down from the mountains. Italians live by these words: *Quando mangiamo, bevanda e siamo felici! When we eat and drink, we are merry!*

Already, the musicians' song is gathering momentum like a sled down the high hills in winter. The guitarist's hand is steady and vigorous as our house helper, Pina, scrubbing our clothes up and down, up and down on the washboard. It doesn't take the crowd more than a few bars of the song to totally throw themselves into the music. The more the audience claps to the steady beat and hollers, "*Bravo, bravo*," the more intense the music swells. The accordion exhales its melody into the group of dancers spinning with unencumbered joy. A piccolo adds a magic texture of wing fluttering lightness to the full pulsing song. Signore Oballo's deep voice bellows the lyrics.

Benvenuto a mare, il bello mare, libero e felice, il mare, il mare, e una benedizione per tutti. Viene, viene, si povero si stanca, viene, a mare.

Welcome the sea, the beautiful sea, free and happy, the sea, the sea, a blessing for all. Come, come if you're tired or sad, come, come to the sea.

As invigorating and heartwarming as this scene is with all the Paolians joined in a common celebration, leaving behind any troubles within themselves (or their family, their village, their country), the song of the sea continues to beckon me. It is my birthday, and I wish to spend some time by myself on my beloved *lungomare* before my family joins around the table for my birthday dinner. As usual, Filomena demonstrates her love for me by leaving the singing and dancing and her betrothed, Gregorio, to help prepare my favorite meal: *ravioli di quattro formaggio*. *Ravioli with four cheeses* is a grand affair with the delicate mixing of the pasta dough, shaping, and perfect blending of the cheeses. Mama, Pina, and Filomena are home working on the masterpiece! My eldest brother, Octavio, gives me *lira* to buy one of Emelia Salerno's *zeppole* or *fried dough*. I thank Octavio, and he nods his solemn head. He's engaged in conversation with Papa and some other men about the perfect soil of Brazil. I skip over to the table where my best friend, Antonio, helps his nonna Emelia Salerno sell the scrumptious treat.

"*Ciao* Antonio," I say as I step up to their table.

"*Ciao*," he replies, his smile like the sun bursting onto the sky.

"Arabella, *buon compleanno, happy birthday*," Emelia Salerno sings as she hands me a *zeppole*, refusing my money.

"*Grazie*," I answer and step away to allow the others their chance to savor Emelia's pastries.

"See you tonight, Antonio," I remind him as I saunter away scanning the crowd in search of my other *fratello*, Marco. He's with Gregorio. I smile, thinking how like pastry they are, *dolce, sweet* on the outside with layers of airy warmth on the inside.

"*Ciao!*" I greet the *simpatico, kindred* spirits.

"*Ciao,* "they echo back.

"Are you enjoying the *festa*, little one?" asks my brother Marco.

"Do not call her 'little one' any longer," teases Gregorio. "This young lady is thirteen years old today."

"*Grazie tanti*," *A thousand thanks*, I respond. "It is a fine feast, but you two know where I'd rather be right now?"

Together, they chime, "*Illungomare!*"

"Go on, little one-er, my apologies-young lady." Marco winks. "We will tell Papa and brother Octavio you were escorted home."

I hug them both, grateful for their confidence in me to be alone, unescorted, and free. Turning from the throng of people toward home, I must at least appear ladylike strolling down the hundred steps that will take me closer to the Mediterranean Sea. I play a game where I place an invisible shield around me protecting me from a conversation with Signora or Signore-So-and-So about why I am alone, the whereabouts of Mama and Filomena, "*Papiagetti, how nice to meet* your niece who is visiting from Naples" or some other polite notion. In a village as small as ours, any ill manners would certainly be communicated to my parents, and I would suffer the consequences of such behavior! Fortunately, I make it all the way through to the lower part of the village where the *lungomare* begins without so much as anyone even noticing me. Perhaps my invisible game is more than just a game. Do I possess mystical powers like Francesco di Paola or the Queen of Sheba? "Shhh! Arabella," I admonish myself, "that kind of talk is bordering on blasphemy!"

I reverently approach the water's edge as I would the cathedral door of Francesco di Paola's church. Slipping my boots off on the gray and white mottled rocks of the shore, I inhale the perfume of the breeze. Some people require a dose of chamomile and valerian root tea for relaxation (and some a few swigs of anisette or whiskey), but under the spell of the sea, I settle into a state of peace, slowly breathing its essence deep into my soul. It fills me like a bellow fueling the fire in a hearth. *Breathe in, breathe out. Inspira, espira.*

And, ah, *grazie Dio, thank God,* I am gloriously alone allowing my bare feet to strike the butter-smooth surface with measured tenderness, marveling at being thirteen years- old but an infinitesimal drop in the vast sea of existence. I think of my life now, rich in the love of family, of studious learning, of comfort and opportunity. I think of my life in the future and wonder what thirteen more years will bring and thirteen after that. Will I continue studying and become a *professora* much like Gregorio who is learning in his travels to San Lucido and Rome? Oh, how I would love a life of scholarly discussions, readings, and writings and imparting that knowledge to others! It is 1913, and the world is changing for women—well, for women in cosmopolitan places like London and New York City. Will Paola catch up to that evolving mentality where women teach, heal, travel and lecture? One can only hope and keep working daily to become all that life is calling her to be.

I step into the chilly water at the shore's edge where slender flashes of green and blue dash by. Anchovies are so rich and plentiful, we eat them daily. Tonight, Pina will serve them as *crispeddi, little fried treats* sprinkled with oregano from our garden. I test my knowledge of the health benefits of anchovies. Hmm, they're abundant in protein, which the body needs to build muscle and tissue; they are full of minerals like calcium and iron that contribute to strong bones and marrow. And hmm, what else? I take a big breath of sea air waiting for my memory to click in, but my stomach gurgles, and I can't recall anything else. Exasperated, I put my hands on my face. Ah! There is so much to remember about the healing properties of foods! As fingers melt into my face, I recall something else—they are good for glowing skin!

After splashing about in the shallow quiet of the sea for a while, I stroll toward home to see how the birthday feast is unfolding. Just thinking of the food stirs my appetite. Well, quite honestly, it doesn't take much to get my mouth salivating when it comes to food! I love to eat, like a good Italiana girl. Prosciutto-wrapped figs stuffed with fresh mozzarella, *polpetta melenzanes* (eggplant meatballs that you don't even know are vegetables!), and then my favorite, ravioli. My appetite is undiscerning especially when it comes to Mama's cooking.

I come to the imposing front door with its etched glass lily panels and carved vine woodwork. It is a substantial piece of wood for a substantial palatial home. For all its grandeur, it is a most inviting entryway to a most hospitable home. The brass doorknob was on my mother's childhood home and is warm and smooth to the touch. The back plate of tooled flowers was made by my mother's grandfather as a wedding gift for his wife.

I open the door to an aroma as pleasing as the sea: Mama's sauce. It is the smell of home, of warmth, of love, of nourishment, of safety, of mouth-watering delight! In it is the garlic grown in the garden alongside the oregano and the basil, my *uncle, zio* Benito's red *vino*, the shank simmering in the tomatoes canned from last summer-comingling in this jewel of a sauce.

This birthday dinner will be a work of edible art! The ravioli is crafted like a fine ceramic platter using flour from our mill. Mama scooped out a well in the middle of a mountain of flour and dropped three eggs in its center. Then *whip, whip, whip* hands moved as fast as a tornado funnel to mix the dough. Then slowly, like a potter working her clay, it was kneaded and tossed, kneaded and tossed until its elastic perfection was separated into two balls. It was allowed to rest for thirty minutes or so, like a *sonnellino, nap*, no? Next, the dough was rolled out into two flattened sheets that looked as square as the window in my bedroom. One square is for the bottom of the ravioli, the other for the top. The ravioli stuffing of four delicious cheeses—Parmigiana-Reggiano, ricotta, Romano, and Asiago tossed with flat parsley and egg—are blended to creamy perfection. Some children long to lick the *biscotti cookie* batter bowl but I prefer the *formaggio* bowl! Mmm, tangy, creamy *cheese*. Mama broke another egg into a bowl with a little water. She "washed" the dough with this mixture. Now the *formaggio* could stick to the dough. Then *plop, plop, plop* perfect piles of the cheese mixture were lined up like fruitful cotton plants all in a row.

I come into the kitchen just as Mama is filling the ravioli with the cheese.

"Mama," I inquire. "How do you know where to place the cheese? Will you use a ruler to measure it out?"

"No, Arabella." She smiles. "One's hands learn how to space the cheese from many years of practice. You will learn too, just like my Mama taught me."

Filomena laughs and rolls her eyes playfully. She knows me too well! I am clumsy in the kitchen, as I would rather be outside splashing in the sea or climbing an olive tree, yet she knows how much I love to eat! I am sent out of the *cucina* to go study for a while before dinner. I am happy to oblige.

I enter the room smelling of the richness of story, of days gone by, of people I'd wish to know, of leather and print. Papa's study is lined ceiling to floor with books of every kind, some in various languages from Homer and Socrates to William Shakespeare. I am nearly as happy here as I am in the peacefulness of nature. I pick up a Signore Shakespeare's sonnets and begin reading number 137 aloud, "' *Thou blind fool, Love, what dost thou to mine eyes-*'"

Marco enters and begins to recite with me, "*that they behold and see not what they see?*'" I smile at him, and he pats my back lovingly.

"Marco," I inquire, "do people really love so disastrously?"

"Love comes with its heartache, Arabella. As heart-wrenching as it may be, it is equally as blissful."

"But *la famiglia* is full of love, and it isn't like that."

"Ah, well, *families* are different than lovers, but they too can have their heart burdened by the clashing of viewpoints."

"Does our family have such burdens of the heart?" I ask innocently enough.

He smiles, but I detect sadness in it. He stands with lively aplomb and declares, "I will look forward to continuing this conversation with you another day, my dear, but it is your birthday, and we must prepare both the body and the spirit for such an important occasion! "

He takes my hands over my head and spins me about.

"I'll call Pina to prepare your bath, your majesty," he says as he bows.

Perhaps I should examine his statement regarding families more closely, but today of all days, I do not wish to see with the acute vision of adulthood.

THE MANDARINOS SIT AROUND THE chestnut table my Babbo hand-hewn for his family decades ago. Papa and my brothers don their best wool suits, Mama looks ravishing in her rose-colored gown with cranberry lace she and Filomena wove like intricate spider webs. Filomena is breathtaking in the celery green gown that crisscrosses at the neckline. My fanciful dress is pale blue with a bodice of green netting and two long ribbon panels down the front. Mama's father and brother enter: Babbo Piero, cane in hand, and Zio Benito, accordion in hand! Pina serves the *crispeddi* as we congenially talk of the *festa* of San Francesco di Paola and the glorious winds of spring. Next, Pina serves us a steaming bowl of *pastina*: tiny-starred *pasta* with dark broth, spinach, and lots of fresh butter. I drink it all up as I know what comes next is the platter of ravioli!

Mama, Papa, Babbo, my two brothers, sister, and uncle fill their glasses with zio's ruby red vino and pour me a taste in an *aperitif* glass. We take turns chinking the crystal to life as we exclaim, "*Salute, cheers!*" Pina serves the next course, and now, I really do feel like I am in heaven as I devour the best part of my birthday dinner: the *quattro formaggio* ravioli. It disappears like a raindrop in a pond—a perfect match.

Marco teases, "Arabella, I don't know what happened to you. You used to be such a pert, pretty baby with your sea-blue eyes and curls as tight as a gift's ribbons. But somewhere along the way, you seemed to like the *pantaloni* of boys more comfortable."

"*Basta, Stop*" Mama chides. "Your sister does not wear pants."

Pina delivers another tray of food, this time whole trout seared and roasted in garlic and rosemary.

Filomena sighs dramatically and joins the teasing, "Ah, yes, I miss dressing my sweet young Arabella in little lacy dresses. That was before she could beat her friend Antonio in a foot race!"

"Or a boxing match," chimes Marco.

I giggle behind my napkin. The momentum is building like an avalanche of naughty behavior. Their playful banter is one of my favorite parts of mealtime.

"Tsk, tsk, we must watch her closely. Acting too much like a boy will never get her a husband," chimes Marco. "Who will marry Arabella?" he sing-songs.

"I am thirteen. Old enough to marry Gregorio!"

We all laugh as we know my tutor Gregorio and Filomena are betrothed.

"She has eyes for her best friend, Antonio," jests Filomena.

Octavio is silent but observant as Papa makes a sound like a low growl and commands, "*Basta. Enough.*"

Marco's earlier comment about families knocks presciently at the back door of my mind. We're uncomfortably silent until Filomena saves the day; she could coax sunlight from a blackened sky.

"Marco." She smiles. "This might be a perfect time for your composition."

Zio Benito lifts his pearl-buttoned, black accordion and begins to play a lively melody that beckons the feet to tap and the body to sway. Marco stands and sings in his strong alto voice,

Our family treasure, our darling one,
A prayer from heaven, a ray of the sun,
Joy you bring to a parched, thirsty earth
We celebrate you and the day of your birth.
Your smile erases any trace of gloom,
your beguiling beauty like the
light of the moon.

Papa hands me a crimson-red velvet box, my birthday regalo. They all gather around me, and I gingerly open the box, knowing by the shape and size of it that it is jewelry.

I am anxious and excited at the same time. The top snaps open, a sound like the trap that catches a small *ratto*! But there is no *rodent* in this box—only the shimmer and strength of *oro—pure gold*: a delicate chain with an intricately etched cross dangling from its center rests within. Mama helps fasten the clasp around my neck, and I reach my hand up to stroke the cross lying perfectly at my throat. I make the sign of the cross and thank God for everything good in my life.

I throw my arms around Mama and Papa, Filomena, Octavio, Marco,

Babbo Piero, and Zio Benito. I feel so blessed! They clap their hands and chant, "*Bella Arabella, salute!*"

"Is it time for my birthday story?" I ask excitedly.

"Arabella, I'm surprised that a thirteen-year-old still wants to hear it."

"But it's *my* story." I try to sound mature, but it comes out as a whine.

More ruby red vino pours into crystal goblets sparkling in the candlelight.

Zio Benito taps out a lilting lullaby on his accordion as Filomena begins, "*La mia sorella*, it was I called who you down from heaven." She smiles, entranced by her own tale. "It took nine years of praying on my bony knees, begging God to bring you to me."

She pauses. Together we chant, "Knock, knock on the door of heaven."

"What happened next?" I ask.

Mama continues the tale, "It took most of the night, but as the stars faded into dawn, you were delivered safely into our arms. "

"And then?"

"I thanked our mother for birthing you, declared you would be Arabella, and that you belonged to me," recounts Filomena.

"*Vero*," states Papa, sipping his wine, "*true.*"

My favorite part comes next.

Marco continues, "Filomena sprinted down the *lungomare*, her obsidian black curls bobbing over her shoulders like springs, half singing, half shouting to anyone and everyone, 'She's here! She's finally arrived, *la mia sorella*, my sister, is here!'"

We all clap our hands and join in my favorite lullaby, "*Farfallina, bella e bianc, vola, mai si stanca gira qua, e gira la, poi si resta spra un fiore, e poi si resta spora un fiore. Ecco, ecco, a trovata, biana e rosa, colorata, gira qua, poi e gira la.*"

"*The butterfly, beautiful and white, flies and flies, never gets tired, runs here, and turns, remains on a flower, remains on a flower. Behold, behold, white and pink colored, turns here, then spins.*"

Mama tells Pina to brew the espresso; Papa pours the whiskey for the men. The knock on the door announces Gregorio, looking like one of

Michelangelo's statues, and my friend Antonio, a shoo-in for one of Botticelli's angels carrying a box of Nonna Emelia's confections. They are both so handsome I think as the blush rises on my cheeks. Trying to right myself, I hand the box of pastries filled with *sfogliatelle, zeppole,* and anise *biscotti* to Mama.

"Here you are. "Gregorio smiles as he hands me a package. "No studying required!"

"Thank goodness," sighs Filomena. "Tonight, you are *famiglia,* not *professore.*"

I rip open the box to find a handmade azure blue and burnished gold *aquilone.* Gregorio has written my name across it in elegant letters. Satin ribbons hang like the braid down a girl's back.

"*Grazie,* Gregorio," I exclaim. "It's the most beautiful *kite* I have ever seen! Mama, Papa, may I be excused to go fly my new *aquilone?*"

They nod their agreement as Antonio and I steal our way out the door, leaving the adults to their espresso, whiskey, cigars, and Nonna Emelia Salerno's desserts.

I must hike up my dress to race down the *lungomare* with Antonio. I throw off my shoes—now I'm free. This is our world: the air, our tonic, the rhythmic slap of water on the rocky shore, our melody. Here, we are snorting *cavallos,* neighing as we rip across an open field, exotic jaguars traversing the mysterious rainforests, gazelles leaping freely across the savannah. Most of all, we are the happiest of friends. There is nothing here of want or fear, only cool breezes, and camaraderie.

Antonio helps me prepare the kite for flight. Soon, it is sky-bound. I watch it rise then close my eyes and speak to God. "It's me, Arabella Rosa Mandarino, waving hello to you, God. Do you see my name on the paper bird, written large enough for you and the angels to read?"

The hair on the back of my neck rises, and I turn to see if someone is behind me. I blink at a flash of light before seeing a parade of relatives strolling down the *lungomare* back toward the *festa.* Babbo Piero, zio, my brothers, Filomena, and Gregorio all bid us goodnight. Sunset melts into hues of peach, lavender, and coral over the edge of the sea. My friend and I sit on the shoreline in perfect, companionable silence. I could stay like this forever (especially if I were in *pantaloni* like Antonio). I daydream about us being together, but the reality of our differences interferes. His good family works the land, seasonably traveling from town to town to plant and harvest various crops. When they're in Paola, they all work with Emelia, making and selling confections at the market and *festas*. The whole *famiglia* including Nonna Emelia, his three brothers, sister, mama, and papa share but three small, rented rooms. The taxes consume them Papa says. This hard life seems so unfair. In conversations with Marco and Gregorio, I've come to see there are no easy answers to why we have so much and others have so little.

"Thank you for celebrating my birthday, Antonio." I smile as we say goodnight.

"My pleasure," he states as he takes a theatrical bow, "to be in the presence of such a lady."

We both burst into laughter, but the way he's regarding me makes me look away.

"Oh, I almost forgot," he says. "I made you a little something." He hands me a gift wrapped in a lace embroidered hankie.

Unwrapping the white linen, there's a Madonna—serene, smooth, and sacred carved from an olive branch.

"Oh, Antonio, the Virgin Mary! She is the absolutely—perfect," I say.

"I'm pleased you like it. I carved it from the olive branch you couldn't take your eyes off of the last time we were in the grove. Do you recall how taken you were by a stick?"

We both laugh. I had indeed turned the branch over and over again, commenting on its shades of gray and its smoothness.

"It will be one of my treasures for life," I exclaim with sincerity.

We say goodbye and make plans to meet soon. I take my time getting home, dragging my bare toes along the stretch of wet, cold sand. Arriving back at the house, the windows look like the moon is filling square pockets of inky sky. Several rooms are aglow with the village's first electric light.

I have a naughty thought to eavesdrop on my parents' conversation. I duck under the long, open window of the main room, quiet as a sunflower in a field. I could never be a saint like San Francesco!

"Vittorio, please tell me you are not considering this match."

It is my Mama's serious voice. I know that tone. My stomach flip-flops, a tumbling leaf blown across the road.

"Carmella, you know these arrangements are made when the girl is young."

"I know how it works, Vittorio. Do you think I've forgotten that *our* marriage was arranged?"

It can be risky for a woman to speak this way to her husband, for such a tone could result in a backhand slap across the face—or worse, but my Mama and Papa are different, more modern.

"Please, Carmella, do not interfere in matters of business. The taxes of Cavour on our land, the flour mill, and even the grain our animals eat whittle away our earnings. Your family's flour mill barely makes enough to keep it operating. Expanding our business through this match will be the difference between thriving and simply surviving. We'll have more land to graze our animals and increase our herd. It can open up new possibilities for us."

"Possibilities for *you*, you mean!"

I have never heard such rage in my mother's voice.

"Possibilities for *us*, for all of us," he tries to console, "and they are investing in the coffee plantation in Brazil as well. It is business."

"Business?" She gains more fuel, fuming like Vesuvius. "Arabella is a spirited, brilliant girl. You should have consulted me about the 'business' of her! How dare you make this decision without me!" Her voice shatters in her throat like broken glass.

The delicious birthday dinner is roiling about my stomach like linguine boiling in the pasta pot.

"It is done, Carmella." He doesn't sound comforting now. He sounds like a king issuing a decree. "At nineteen years of age, our daughter will wed. It is a good match that both families will announce when Arabella is sixteen."

A sound splits the night like lightning. Mama's primal scream jars me to the enormity of this decision. I hear her hands on her thighs and chest like the sad, slow beating of tom-toms.

I sink to the dirt beneath the window of that once-cherished room that will now be the dungeon of future gloom. My father has leveraged the family's future on the shoulders of my betrothal. This happens every day to a girl in Italy. It should come as no surprise. But Mama is tormented, and that is not a good sign. With Mama's cries as a backdrop, I fall asleep.

I awaken, my hand clutched around my gold cross, Marco hugging me close to him. "We've all been out searching for you, Arabella. You had us scared half to death!"

"Marco, what is going on? I heard Mama crying. I heard something about my betrothal and—"

"Shh, no need to worry now."

"I heard Mama's reaction. It must be a terrible match! Tell me."

"I will tell you that life works itself out, Arabella. I only know this: you are deeply loved."

With that, he ushers me inside where Mama looks stricken but relieved to see me.

I attempt to speak but my voice is a squeaky mouse, then a croaking frog. "Mama? Papa? *Che cosa c`e? What's going on?*" I look from one parent to the other, but neither answers me. Papa reads his book; Mama goes back to pounding her body with her hands. Maybe they cannot understand the language of their daughter whose voice was stolen by squeaky mice and croaking frogs. Maybe I am here in spirit but not here in person. But I am here, rooted in my childhood, willing my world to remain the same. It's clear, however, that everything about my world has been displaced.

Filomena enters the front door. Her smile tingles with the memory of

Gregorio's goodnight kiss but takes one look around and worriedly asks what's happened.

I run to her and babble about a match, a secret, and how upset Mama is. Papa barks at me to go to bed. Filomena nods for me to obey, and I heave myself one foot in front of the other to my room.

There are ghostly whisperings in my dreams. Words I don't understand. Voices I do not recognize. Lace veils fill the air like kites before descending on my body with the weight of rocks.

IT IS ONE THING TO KNOW YOUR fate is sealed and quite another to accept it. I have implored Filomena to tell me what she knows about my betrothal, but she insists she's trying to find out more. She asks me to be patient (might as well tell a lion not to hunt).

"I know I am to marry someone associated with Papa's many new business partners, but who?" I inquire.

I ask my parents.

As Mama and I walk to morning Mass, I decide to be more direct.

"What is it about my betrothal that upsets you?"

"Your future is being discussed by Papa and me, Arabella,"

I frown. Under my breath, I mutter, "You and Papa but it's *my* future."

"Arabella, if you are going to speak, speak clearly. Enunciate."

I clear my throat. "Because this decision concerns my future, I should be a part of it."

"When the time is right, you will be informed." Mama's tone is firm.

"Informed? So, it is decided then? How could you?" I blurt like a broken bottle spewing its contents.

"*Basta* Arabella! *Stop!* You are acting like a spoiled child with no self-control!"

Heat emanates from my skin like a flash fire. Maybe I should dunk my head in the *Fontana di Paola* to cool off. Mama will reveal nothing. I try a different angle with Papa as we ride the wagon up the mountain one day.

"Papa?"

"Si, *figlia?*"

"I can be someone when I grow up, si?"

Clearing his throat, he answers, "What do you mean?"

"I mean—" I take a big gulp of air. "I can be a doctor and heal. Or teach like Maria Montessori. Or both." I pause again. "I can be *something*, si?"

He glances at me then puts his attention back on the road. I am nothing if not persistent.

"It is the 20th century Papa. It's 1913. Women are making a difference."

"What 'women'?"

"Well, there's Millicent Fawcett and Emmeline Pankhurst—"

"The women in Great Britain who were arrested?"

"These Suffragettes were talking to Signori Churchill and Grey about women casting their votes on important issues. The men got angry and had them arrested for obstructing a meeting! *Pazzo, si?*"

It feels good to talk to Papa about *crazy* injustices. I take his silence as a sign that he wants me to continue.

"And the assault charge Papa? It was a 'technical assault.' What does that even mean?" I'm so excited, I have to stop to take a breath. "Do you know the American women are joining in the fight? "

Papa clears his throat. The mountain mist enfolds us. "Arabella, it is good to be informed, but there is a fine line between informed and obsessed. These issues have little to do with Paola."

"They are fighting for women everywhere, Papa. They —"

"Arabella, enough!" he shouts. "Lofty plans to join the Suffragettes or

Maria Montessori or anyone else outside this village are not in your future. You will be someone: a mother."

My bullheaded, *testa dura* nature is unstoppable. "Yes, a mama and a wife but also a doctor or *la professora*, *si* Papa? Just think what I could do with the education you have given me!"

"It is true that your mind is keen and sharp." He pauses. "If you had been born a son, you'd have made an excellent businessman."

My heart stops, and my stomach lurches. Did he just pity me for my *gender?* My Papa? I must have misunderstood his meaning. I continue with the force of a sail harnessing the wind's fullness. "But that is what I am telling you. The world is waking up to the fact that women can do what men do."

He jerks the reins so hard, we jolt to a stop. My teeth rattle. He looks at me directly in the eyes with a sternness I had previously not encountered in fourteen and a half years.

"Men do not have children, Arabella. You are a Mandarino with duties to your *famiglia*. You will marry, be a good wife, and give us grandchildren. God willing, you will live a long life here in Paola. We need you here as daughter and wife. *Capisce?*"

I swallow. The mouse and the frog return to capture my voice. "*Ho capito*, Papa. *I understand*," I answer, lying to him for the first time in my life and wondering how many times he has lied to me.

"GREGORIO, IF YOU KNEW INFORMATION my family was keeping from me, would you tell me?"

"Do not speak hypothetically around in circles Arabella. What are you getting at?"

"My betrothal."

"Arabella, let's not be consumed by the future."

"But it is *my* future, Gregorio. What do you know?" I am poised for information I'm certain he will give me.

"Even if I knew, you would put me in an awkward position to reveal it."

"They are going to marry me off to some wealthy old man, aren't they?"

"Arabella, your family loves you. They wouldn't do anything to harm you."

"I'm not sure anymore. Mama instructed me to silence my tongue, and Papa told me I will be a mother and give him grandchildren—period! I know I will gain more herbal knowledge from your mama, but think what else I could, if given a chance. "

"*Si*, I agree. But for now, let us consider another Italian who probably felt as frustrated by hindrances as you do."

He puts a book in front of me.

"Machiavelli?" I whine. "His concepts are too confusing, Gregorio."

"*Prego, please*, do not play imbecile with me."

"But I can barely pronounce his name, let alone understand his politics," I protest.

He smirks. "And how do you know of his interest in politics?"

I am caught. "His work is laborious to read. I don't want to."

"*Va bene. Very well.*" If you've no interest in the banned words of those labeled "dangerous, forward thinkers" let's skip Machiavelli."

Banned, dangerous, forward thinker? I am hooked, and he knows it.

"He, like you, dear Arabella, was a person who was always questioning the way things were and what they could be."

Despite the glaring factual difference of gender, I plunge into Machiavelli's writings officially banned by the church in 1564. I feel a bit of a rebel, charged with enthusiasm. My tongue does not need silencing here, with my beloved tutor, my future brother-in-law, Gregorio. He nods his head, and before I know it, the afternoon has slipped into dusk.

TAP, TAP, TAP PAUSE TAP, TAP. The special knock gives the knocker a count of sixty before I can scurry to find him in our cat-and-mouse adventure. I grab my shoes hurriedly, counting aloud. Mama gives me a disapproving look, but she doesn't understand that the sooner I get to the door, the less time Antonio Salerno has to hide. The fast, slippery eel is already zigzagging to the grove!

"Arabella, your behavior is unladylike!" Mama admonishes.

"Let her go play, Mama. She'll work harder on her studies."

"But with a boy? She is not a child anymore and I worry—"

"*Non ti preoccupare, Mama. No need to worry.* Arabella is a good girl."

"*Grazie tanti, sorella,*" I whisper as I rush out the door. I'll give my *sorella* an extra hug when I return. But right now, my attention is on the whereabouts of my good friend, Antonio Salerno. Which grove will he choose today? I try the one near Zio Benito's, near the Campenello's, and then the citrus grove just past the Gambinis. Once there, I pause to inhale the intoxicating scent of lemon and orange blossoms intermingling like a fine perfume. Quieting my rapid breath, I listen to the hypnotic bees buzz their way in and around the thick, white blossoms. Do they put the flowers under their spell so they offer up their pollen? Do they speak poetry the flowers long to hear? I close my eyes, swaying to the melody of the starling's wings on the wind. The sunlight taps silent shadows on my face.

I wait for a clue that Antonio is in the grove, as patient as the lioness in the bush. *Snap!* Too loud for a little furry grove dweller; it must be a clumsy human! Quick as a deer, I spring in the direction of the breaking twig. Keen eyes scan the grove of trunks, some thick enough to shelter three children, others too narrow to hide a mouse. Antonio attempts to flatten himself as if he were a walking stick bug aligning its narrow body on a limb.

"Antonio!" I yell, a playful smile of conquest on my face. "There you are!"

"*Allora, So,* I am found," he laments with a laugh.

Together, we walk through the mottled shadows in comfortable silence. We both notice a rabbit at the same time, and like practiced soldiers, we stop in unison. It hops a few inches, scrunches its wet nose, and then out from behind another tree, a second rabbit joins the first one. They are perfect together. *Like us.*

"Nature is simple and sweet," I say.

"*Si,*" he answers, bobbing his head in agreement.

"If humans observed nature more closely, we'd live happier lives," I profess.

"*Si,* "he nods. "Working in nature feeds us."

I nod, but inside I flinch. There is such a discrepancy between his way of life and ours.

He continues, "The growing seasons are like the stars that sailors use to chart their course; we know where we will be and what we will be doing not by the name of the day or the month but by the fruit ready to plant or the vegetables to harvest. In a way, field workers belong to the earth itself."

But more so to the landowners and the tax man. Another pang of guilt rises. My family does not ever have to pack its belongings and travel to other places to survive. We are not at the beck and call of others who own our time through the taxing of wages or rented homes. My hands are soft, my clothes freshly pressed by Pina, my mind sharpened by the study of the classics, not dulled by long hours toiling in the blistering sun. I sigh. Antonio's mind is not that way! Now I am confused. Maybe time in the fields is like an empty canvas awaiting creation.

"Antonio, do you ever begrudge your lot in life?"

He looks at me, his eyes full of mirth. "With you to always beat me in our games?"

"Be serious, Antonio. I want to know."

"No, Arabella. I am not resentful. This life is a gift, and I'm going to make the most of it! Today, I am here in this beautiful *mezzogiorgno* with you; tomorrow it may be Sicilia, next season San Lucido, and then, who knows?"

"What do you mean?"

"Possibility is everywhere—even when it doesn't seem to be. I intend to find it."

"But, how can you? You are poor—"

Oh, *Dio mio, my God,* there goes my runaway tongue. A look of horror flushes my face.

"Antonio, forgive me. This tongue of mine is like a frog spotting a fly."

"I respect you because you look for *and* speak the truth!"

But my bluntness seems hurtful. "I did not mean to imply that your family is poor. The Salernos are rich in—"

"No, Arabella. You don't have to mask the truth. I *am* poor, but only for now. *Capisce? You understand.* For now, I will work in the fields alongside my family and help Nonna Emelia bake, but only for now. You watch, Arabella. I will make something of my life!"

He speaks with such passion the hair on my arms stands up to salute his ambition.

"I believe you, Antonio Salerno!"

"And you?" he asks.

"Me? Even my standing in life doesn't allow me to make something of my life that is my own choosing. I am a female." I shrug, but a well of tears threatens to burst.

"That is what is unjust, Arabella. You of all people could be anything you set your mind to."

He takes my hand. It's what I imagine an electric current feels like. My skin is flushed red by the voltage coursing through me.

"Come on," he invites. "Nonna Emelia is baking some of *zeppole* this morning. Let's get them fresh out of the oven."

I drop his hand. I must or I will transform into a solid beam of lightning, flash and disappear. He doesn't seem to notice my flushed expression nor can he hear the triple beat of my heart. He sprints off, and I join him happily. Side by side, we traverse the groves into the village *piazza*, past the *Fontana di Paola*, and down the back alleys toward his home. The sweet, buttery scent of Nonna Emelia's pastries hits us like a blast of sunshine through clouds.

THAT VERDANT HILLSIDE NEAR where Antonio and I played is busy today with the activity of creatures as small as my thumb and as large as my arm. Butterflies, hoverflies, and dragonflies—black woodpeckers and peregrine falcons hammer and screech. The sun covers me like a fine, golden gown as I take in the view of the mountain before me and the dip of the Mediterranean's sapphire waters below. Back to the task at hand, I search for the plant Signora Ruffino has instructed me to find. I have little Maria Ruffino at my side. She toddles after me like I am the Pied Piper of Hamlin.

"I think I've found some fennel in bloom. *Guarda, look* here." I am staring at a grayish-green plant with soft lacy leaves and a head of swollen flowers.

"Ah, you have a good eye, Arabella. It does appear to be fennel with its branching stem system and flattened heads of little flowers," she says scooping Maria into her arms.

I am smiling and very proud of myself.

"However, "she begins in a tone that indicates my identification is wrong, "this is where the eye of the healer must be extra cautious." She points out that what I mistook for fennel is actually poisonous hemlock, a major difference being the white flowers of the hemlock versus the yellow flowers of the fennel.

Dio mio! My God. I sigh a little louder than I intended.

"Arabella," my kind teacher says. "The study of plants will be lifelong, *capisce, understand?* There are thousands of plants to identify. Paying attention to every detail is important. Do not be discouraged. Make a note and a drawing in your *libro,* and then we'll continue our search of the aromatic seeds waiting for us at the end of the umbels."

She sings a song to Maria while I open my notebook and sketch the specific details of this poisonous plant, making note of every part of it. I close my *book* and look at my teacher.

"Now then, "she says as we continue walking the mountainside. "Tell me some of the other useful plants that are part of the *Umbelliferae* family."

I hear the word family, and in the sunshine of the afternoon on the mountainside, the woozy laziness of a daydream blooms. I see the Ruffino family and the Mandarino family together at our home's long dining table, laughing and toasting each happy occasion that will grow like these plants on the mountain. She and I are going to be related soon enough when Gregorio Ruffino and Filomena will be married. Signora Ruffino will be Filomena's mother-in-law, Gregorio, my brother-in-law, and little Maria my—hmm, what will she be to me? Related, somehow, just like herbs and vegetable families.

A dragonfly flits near me awakening me from my reverie. I see that *signora* is waiting for my reply, and I do not want her to think I am confused or without the answer. "Let's see, parsley is part of this family, and chervil." I pause, going through my memory like a deck of cards. "Oh, yes, and also angelica."

"*Brava* Arabella, *brava.*"

"There are vegetables that belong in this family too," I continue, as Signora Ruffino nods her head. "They are carrots and parsnips."

"In the herbal family, there is also *Myrrhis odorata*," she continues, "or sweet cicely."

She enjoys a good laugh like me, so I make an attempt at humor. "Sweet Sicily? Like the island further south?" I feign confusion.

Her mirth explodes, and she rests herself on the grassy knoll of the hillside. "Arabella, you are a joy to be with." She laughs. "Always remain light-hearted," she says, patting my hand.

Maria smiles and looks from one to the other not really understanding the reason for our humor but laughs too. I tickle her toddler belly. She squeals with delight.

"Back to work," Signora Ruffino winks at me and quizzes me on the different systems of the body and which ones the *Embellifers* are best for.

"Well, firstly, we use them for the digestive system, along with licorice root, garlic, and barley grass. Hand in hand with the digestive system are the eliminative systems. I'd use the *Embellifers* for the health and maintenance of the colon."

"*Si*, very good. Now, you've mentioned licorice root and garlic. What other organs or systems benefit from these?"

"Hmm, of course, garlic is the key to the overall health of our bodies. It is good for the cardio-pulmonary system, the digestive system, liver health, lung health, lymph glands, ears and, and, there's something else." I am racking my brain, "Oh yes, our nails!" I wiggle my fingers in front of me.

"*Si! Brava, figlia, brava.*"

Signora Ruffino has called me her *daughter* without hesitation. I am grateful to be apprentice-daughter to the *erborista* of Paola. I will study more and make her proud! I tell Signora Ruffino how I have commandeered a part of Mama's garden for the cultivation of my own herb garden.

She nods and pats my hand again. We continue strolling the brush on the hillside. The midwife from San Lucido has written to ask Signora for some *Atropa belladonna*. We make certain we have the hand of little Maria as we traverse the underbrush for the shiny-black berries, attractive to the eye but fatal. We locate a patch of the tall branching plant. From a few steps away, Signora directs me as I gather the oval leaves, greenish-black berries, and some roots. I place them carefully in a special pouch.

"Once you prepare the plant, we will get them to the midwife. You will dry the leaves, roots, and some of the berries in a dark, dry place before storing them in an airtight jar. Mash 4-5 fresh berries and float them in a jar of some of your zio's vino."

"Of course," I respond. "Drinking the steeped herb will make for quicker assimilation." As I take notes in my book I ask, "What is the dosage for say, the pain of a twisted ankle or back?"

"An adult may take up to the equivalent of ten berries, but no more. We would give the injured a dose of three and observe for an hour. After that, if needed, they can be given one more at a time." She seems to read my thoughts. "Arabella, this is a powerful plant. It can be lethal."

I step back from the plant that is growing wild on the mountainside. I make the sign of the cross.

"It is good to respect nature. *Attento, careful,*" she warns.

Maria is trying to waddle over to me, but signora keeps her at her side.

"Two or three of these berries are enough to kill a child."

I am anxious to complete the gathering of something so powerful.

MOST PAOLIANS LACK THE RESOURCES to live comfortably, but *tutti devono mangiare! Everyone must eat.* Mama's family started the flour mill a generation ago, and Papa's business provides meat. He is a fair businessman. He could plunge the villagers into further debt by charging high prices, but he doesn't. He touts his wisdom to his sons like a priest at his pulpit: fair prices and good product yields loyalty. Depending on the day of the week, Papa and his business partners—the Basillios and the Spognas—choose a cow, pig, goat, or sheep to butcher into varying portions. Next, they load the meat on a wagon ingeniously equipped with a cold box to keep the meat fresh as possible (save the delicacies of tongues and feet, which go immediately into a brine water solution). From the homes along the *lungomare* to the winding roads that lead to Francesco di Paola's cathedral, and all the way to the alpine-like mountain top, Papa and his partners deliver fresh meat to the denizens of Paola and their mountain cousins.

Tonight, Pina has cooked tripe with an unusual sauce of olives, onion, garlic, cinnamon, vanilla, pancetta, and Mama's marinara sauce. Pina prepared this delicacy of healthy cow's stomach lining with great care.

Papa shakes his head and announces, "Carlo Carbonara has seen how lucrative our business is and has taken to the streets with a cartload of tainted meat."

"Spoiled meat?" says Mama appalled. "What can come of that but sickness?"

"Don't forget profit," a disgusted Marco explains. "He probably gets his meat for near to nothing from the farm owners like the Frescattas who'll stop at nothing to make a profit. Let us presume a cow dies giving birth or from old age and the farmers do not discover it for a while. By the time Carlo Carbonara gets the meat, it is long past fresh."

Papa nods. "That's right, Marco, and Carlo Carbonara is adding a mixture of beet juice to color it, garlic, vino, and any other pungent herbs to disguise the smell."

Octavio shakes his head. "He is claiming the meat is marinated in Signora Carbonara's ancient family recipe!"

"But this is terrible," exclaims Mama, abhorred. "You must warn his customers before they get sick."

"It's already begun," Filomena reports. "There is word at the market of fever and stomach ailments."

"And the frightening truth is his customers won't believe it is from his meat," Marco states in disbelief.

I make a silent note to steep a large batch of burdock, dandelion, and licorice for aching stomachs and another with cayenne and Echinacea for fevers.

"We have sent warnings through those we trust, but we have to be careful we're not seen as saboteurs of his business. "

"But the germs and the disease." Mama is shaken to her core.

"I know you smoke and cure meat with salts to keep it fresh like the Egyptians did. Why don't the Carbonaras?" I ask.

He smiles at me. "*Brava*, Arabella. You are attentive and wise. What a good businessman you would have made had you been born a son."

He pats my hand affectionately, but something odd has occurred— something so strange it must have drifted in on an unknown breeze. Previously, I would've thought this was a compliment, but now, I am insulted. I want to exclaim, *how dare you! I am not a son. I am me, Arabella, the girl who came into this family fourteen years ago! The one whose life you are giving away to create more successful businesses!*

It has become clear that gender does indeed matter in this family just as it does in all other families in Italy and most places in the world. Hard truth slams against my heart. *I am just a girl to be auctioned off to the most lucrative bidder.* I feel nauseous— seasick in undulating waves of realization that the Mandarinos are not modern. We're as old-fashioned as they come. I slide my hand away from Papa's and lift the crisp, linen napkin from my lap to my mouth. Apparently, I've paled. Of course, I have—the blood has been squeezed from my heart.

Mama is watching me.

"We've upset Arabella. I hope it's not your stomach, dear." Mama worries.

My stomach. My heart. My soul—all sick from a new reality. I have heard Gregorio claim that truth often hurts. It's in tale after tale, poem after poem, but I never understood it from the inside until now.

The conversation continues to swirl around the preservation of meats through brining, which dehydrates the meat and kills bacteria. I am only listening with one ear. The other ear is tuned in to the frequency of my heartbeat. Does a heart that is broken beat differently?

Octavio stands with a wine glass in hand. "I'd like to toast our new business venture."

"Another one?" I manage. There are so many changes happening much too fast.

My father stands. "Si," he nods his head. "The Mandarinos are the proud owners of a coffee plantation in Brazil. Here's to my sons and the fertile land of Brazil." He and Octavio look like the cat that caught the prized lizard, but Marco is still seated, eyes downward.

I look from brother to father to brother, stunned.

"Marco?" I inquire. "Brazil? Are you going to Brazil too?" He will not meet my eyes.

Octavio and Papa smile.

"Of course, my brother is joining me! It's *famiglia*! It's business! Raise your glasses, *salute*!"

Glasses chink a little too loudly for my ears.

"Why coffee? Why now?" I am not feeling celebratory.

Marco swallows. He seems relieved to be doing what he does best: telling a good story. "The coffee business began with a holy man. The story is far-fetched but interesting. Long ago, a Sufi mystic was traveling and teaching his way through Ethiopia when he took note of the unusual vitality of the goats in that country. Upon observation of their habits, he noted the berries they were consuming made them energetic—coffee berries. After consuming the berries, himself, he too had unusual vitality. That was the beginning of the thriving coffee business for the wealthy of Venice, Egypt, and Africa. And the Americans are wild for it too. "

"Brazilian soil will yield the best crop for exporting to America and even Venice! Now is the perfect time for expansion," adds Octavio.

"This is too much too close together," Filomena laments. "Octavio, Marco, and Gregorio will all be leaving Paola!"

"What?" I'm nearly hysterical. "Gregorio too?"

My mother tries to sound like all this is normal. "Gregorio has a once in a lifetime opportunity to study in Roma with master *professoro*, Novello. You of all people know how often he has applied to study with this scholar. He's been accepted."

Filomena is stoic but tearful. Marco's eyes are sadness personified. Papa and Octavio, merry. Mama, a façade of calm.

"Well," I huff. "He didn't tell me. It seems to me that men will come and go, but we . . ." I gesture grandly to Mama, Filomena, and me, "the women, will be right here where we have always been and apparently, always will be!"

It is clear that the life of a female is forever in the hands of her father, brothers, and then, her husband. *Non puoi cambiare, ci `o che `e. You cannot change what is.*

Or can you?

MAYBE WE SHOULDN'T KNOW IN advance how change will affect us, best to just deal with its aftermath. I bid goodbye to both my brothers, off to Brazil. Gregorio is here for just a while more, so I throw myself into my studies to keep my mind off the men's exodus—and my impending future as someone's wife. Still, I feel a bit off-balance until a most unexpected occurrence.

Signore Ruffino broke his leg, and now our *erborista*, Signora Ruffino, must be at her husband's side. She is counting on me to take most of Paola's sick!

She assures me I am ready, but I pour over my notebook full of plants and remedies all hours of the night. I check and recheck my tinctures, drying herbs, and medicinal garden. I try to convince myself that even if I cannot teach like Dr. Maria Montessori, alter history alongside the Suffragettes, or travel to Brazil to run a coffee plantation, I can heal people—at least I hope so.

I awoke this morning to find Pina sitting at the kitchen table holding the left side of her face. Pina, "*Cosa succede? What's the matter?*" I inquire.

She can barely speak (a rarity), so I know something's wrong. "Who knew something as small as a tooth could vex an entire body?" she whines.

Quickly, I riffle through the spices until I find some cloves. I mash them, releasing the pungent oil, and instruct her to rub them lightly around the tooth and gums. She moans at the relief. I set a small pan on the stove to warm some water. "In just a minute, I'll add some sea salt for you to gargle."

She nods and attempts a weak smile.

Filomena enters. "Aha," she teases. "So, you *do* know how to boil water!"

I roll my eyes.

"Seriously," she says, Papa is not feeling well."

Mama comes in. "He's feverish—and ornery!"

"I don't know about how to cure 'ornery' just yet, but I've made a new concoction for fevers," I excitedly report. "If he has nasal congestion, we need to steep some lemon balm or *Melissa officinalis* for him," I offer, pacing the room.

"No congestion," reports Filomena.

I detect a slight curve of her lips but she remains earnest. "Primarily fever then?" I inquire.

"With a slight cough," Mama adds.

"All right then. *Borago officinalis*, borage, is cool and refreshing. It tastes like cucumber. He shouldn't object to a tea of borage. It's a mild expectorant and fever reducer."

As I prepare that tea and give Pina the warm sea salt water to gargle, Antonio comes to the door. Apparently, Nonna Emelia is experiencing pain when she urinates. I nod and sit him down at the table next to Pina as I prepare a tea of chamomile, dandelion, juniper, and parsley, feeling much like the jugglers at *festas* adept at keeping several wooden pins in the air at once.

Mama rushes in and stubs her toe on the table leg. "*Managia!*" she shrieks.

I rush to her. For Mama to yell "*Damn,*" it must really hurt! I set the jars of herbs I used for Emelia's tea on the table and rub her foot. Papa growls for me to come to him. Standing too quickly, I knock the jars of herbs onto the floor, scatter tiny green leaves like grasshoppers in a field.

"*Managia!*" I yell without thinking.

"Arabella!" Mama admonishes.

I get busy picking up the fallen herbs as Filomena erupts in giggles, then Antonio, followed by Pina holding her face and, even Mama. Another knock on the door presents Signore Nessi needing more of my rosemary ointment for his wife's rheumatism.

My hair has fallen out of its ribbon into my eyes. Antonio kneels to tuck a strand behind my ear. His touch is soft, but it feels like a hot poker. I'm certain I am beet red. I quickly turn back to cleaning and instruct him to help Pina to the sink for more gargling.

The onslaught of patients is chaotic, but it feels like stepping into a perfectly made pair of shoes. More arrive, seeking my tinctures for everything from their upset bellies to headaches and diaper rash. They line up like silent ants in a row. I'm speechless by the number who have come for help.

Filomena calls me to the open door and nudges me. "Say something to them."

"What do I say?" I'm aghast.

"You have to assure them you will care for them."

"Can't you?" I beseech.

"No, you must." She pushes me forward a bit.

To say I feel awkward would not even begin to describe. "Um. *Ciao. Hello.* Um, I'm so sorry you are, um-

"Sick?" someone manages.

"Yes, sick."

"Can you help us?" another yells.

"I think so. I've been studying with Signora Ruffino for a while now and have tinctures and blends of my own."

"Has anyone tried them and lived?" someone quips.

Several laugh.

I take a deep breath. "I will do my best," I offer a bit testily. "If you want my services, I am ready. If not, feel free to go elsewhere."

"*Brava* Arabella," someone shouts.

No one leaves.

"Very well. Signore Puto, you are first in line. Come in and tell me of your troubles."

I feel the wind in my sails and instruct Antonio and Filomena to seat a couple at a time in our home. I attend them as quickly as I can.

That night, I could barely lift the soup spoon to my lips, but as I fell into bed, I felt something for the first time: fulfillment and purpose. Did San Francesco di Paola feel this way too?

"ARABELLA, THANK YOU FOR TAKING care of so many these past months while Mama was tending to my Papa," says Gregorio. "We're all so proud of you!"

"*Grazie.* I do feel part of something bigger than myself. "

"*Brava,* Arabella! Wisdom coupled with skill is a powerful combination."

"I may be developing my healing skills, but I am having difficulty with coping skills." I sigh.

"I know there are many changes for you, but all will be well."

"It's just that my brothers are gone and you are leaving soon! That's a lot to cope with at once."

"*Si.* I understand your feelings. But each person must find his own way." He pauses. "And when we love someone, we allow him that freedom."

"*Him* is correct," I reply. "Women don't have that freedom. We must accept whatever men decide. How is *that* freedom?"

"You possess the freedom to choose *how* you will view the people and events of your world—or galaxy, for that matter." He holds up some pictures of our Solar System.

"That's quite a segue, even for you." I smile.

"You see, the Solar System is a perfect example of how individuals work within a group."

"How?" I ask.

"Each individual planet knows when and how to rotate around the sun on its own path, its orbit. Different planets have different orbits. Just like family members."

"You're saying family is like the Solar System?"

"*Si!* There are planets as diverse as brothers and sisters traveling their own path, but the sun, with its gravitational pull, is like our love. It keeps us moving around it."

"So, people are like the star-filled galaxies?"

"What do you think of that explanation?" he prods.

I consider the people in my *famiglia.* "Well, it seems obvious to me that women are the Sun—the center. I think we have the kind of love that keeps the planets—or people—in orbit, aligns the stars, and keeps time with the cycles of the moon."

"*Brava*, Arabella. Poetically stated. Men love deeply, but you have captured the essence of women. We revolve around their love."

"Why are men and women so different?" I'm rolling through ideas in my mind. "Is it because women are mothers and descendants of Mary, the Mother of God?"

"That could be. What traits do you share with her?"

"Kindness? Compassion? Forgiveness?" Well, I'm hoping to develop those.

"What about your deep capacity to love?"

I think about Mary, Mother of God who had to make the ultimate sacrifice of watching her son die. It's going to take the love of all the women in my family to overcome my sense of loss, but at least they will all come back to me.

He reads the sadness in my eyes. "Arabella, you will be fine. You are strong and smart. Keep up your studies with your new tutor and my mama. Soon, I'll be home with enough knowledge to hopefully keep up with you!"

He continues his discourse on celestial bodies, gravitational pulls, and points to the drawing of one of the planets. But I remember reading that some planets move backward.

"PASS THE *PANNE* PLEASE," I ASK.

Filomena passes the basket to me without teasing that it's my third piece of *bread*. I miss my brothers. There are vacant spaces around our kitchen table like deep holes of uprooted trees after a storm. This table seems enormous with only three women and occasionally, Papa.

"Signore Tardino says you are not studying as you should be," Mama fills in the silence.

I wish I could say something biting like *"Why should I?"* But minding my tongue, I respond, "I'll do better, Mama."

She stands. "Girls, help me get this food into these baskets." She's at the counter with loaves of rosemary bread, plates of sausage, bowls of mostaccioli, and jars of olives. "Arabella, you are to deliver these to Padre at the sanctuary. He will get them to those in need."

"Yes, Mama."

Filomena helps Mama, trying to fill the emptiness by filling the bellies of others. Papa fills up the hours with work. He works long hours, leaving before we are awake. I do not think any of us could have imagined how deep a void would be left by the absence of the boys. If Papa knew this, would he have chosen to send them to Brazil? Of course. Business supersedes everything.

Pina explodes into the kitchen. She's holding up my stockings. "Arabella," she snips. "You are a young lady now! When are you going to learn to care for your precious belongings? When are you going to begin to appreciate your fine things?"

Without waiting for an answer, she stomps out of the room.

Normally, we would have used the opportunity for humor, but I only hear the clatter of bowls and jars being loaded into baskets.

As I head out the door with a basket on each arm Mama calls out, "No dawdling, Arabella. Padre is expecting those baskets *subito, now.*"

"Yes Mama," I respond.

But once I am on my *lungomare,* I cannot help but slow to a snail's pace, stop on the pebbled shore, remove my shoes and stockings (apologizing to Pina for not caring for them properly), and plunge my feet into the water. A sigh escapes. My eyes close. Ah, *Bello lungomare!* The calm I feel here is what I imagine heaven to be.

Suddenly, the hair on my arms and neck prickle to full attention. Someone is behind me, but I didn't hear anyone approach. Who's sneaking up on me? I quickly open my eyes and spin my head around. It's the oddest thing. There's that flash of light again like on my birthday. But now it's as if *someone or something* is there but, there is no one, nothing, there—like an outline of a person encased in light. I make the sign of the cross. Is this a departed soul? What does she want? Somehow, I discern *it is a she*. My heart beats double time. What do I know of ghosts but in tales like *The Ghost of the Black Friar* (who really wasn't a ghost at all) or *The Goblin of La Via del Corno* where the goblin and the master of the house lived companionably together? But these are children's stories.

I blink my eyes, and the apparition is gone. *Grazie Dio! Thank God!* That was a little frightening. Maybe I really didn't see anything at all. Am I hungry and lightheaded? No. Am I feeling guilty for dawdling? No. Did I make this up? No. Whatever the reason, I'm going to keep this encounter to myself. As I dust off my skirt and put my stockings and shoes back on, I'm reminded of an incident when I was about five years old. The adults were talking about going to confession.

"I don't have to go to confession," I declared.

"You will go when you are older," my father answered.

"Not me!" I held firm.

"Arabella. Shame on you. Padre Busardo hears our sins and talks to God on our behalf."

I shook my head from side to side. "My angel talks to me, and then she talks to God for me!"

"Your angel?" asked Mama.

"Yes, my angel. She visits me. She's my friend."

They dismissed this as a child's imagination, but who knows if the innocence of children offers more opportunity to meet angels. I must admit there is something familiar in what I saw. I perform the sign of the cross again for good measure, pick up the baskets, and head to church.

When I return home, Filomena is reading a letter from Gregorio. She seems happy and sad at the same time.

"What does Gregorio say of Rome?" I ask.

"His studies with the scholar Novello are most challenging," she answers in earnest.

"Even brilliant ones like Gregorio must work hard on their studies." I shake my head in disbelief. It must be extraordinarily grueling if Gregorio is struggling.

"He asks after you as well and how you are getting on with your new tutor."

"Do not remind me," I answer with a sneer.

Though I am dedicated to my herbal studies with Gregorio's mama, I have lost interest in any classical studies with Signore Tardino. Why should I care about any of that? What good will it serve me when I am but a wife and mother?

Disrespectfully, I respond, "Tell Gregorio I dislike this challenging man's yellowed, cracked teeth, jagged as a cliff's edge, his foul breath like an outhouse improperly tended, his sharp, clipped manner of speaking *'proper' Italiano*, and his apparent disdain at having the educational charge of a girl."

Filomena laughs. "Arabella, you cannot put that in writing."

"I know, *mia sorella*, but I can tell you!"

"*Si*, you can tell me anything."

I used to tell her everything, but I am too embarrassed by so much of late. I cannot tell her that Papa is wasting his money on my studies because I don't care anymore about anything but the healing arts. I don't tell her that I barely listen when Signore Tardino is lecturing; instead, I travel in my mind to the hillside to gather herbs or walk the *lungomare*, identifying fish. I have not told her about my apparition encounter either. What would I say? Your sister is seeing ghosts? I do not tell her that I do not want to be anyone's wife or mother- unless that included Antonio somehow.

"Filomena, what do you know of my betrothal?"

"I have nothing to share," she says, her eyes darting away from mine, "but please, *Sorella*, don't worry."

I should pay closer attention to people and the physical signs that betray their words, but I am too naïve. She goes back to her letter where Gregorio's love seems to lift from the page. I sidle up to her, wanting to try on their love as if slipping into a dress.

Her face lights up like the summer dawn. "He'll be home for good in eight months! And more good news, little sister," she beams. "Dust off your books about Rome because you are going to want to know everything there is for our *viaggio*!"

"What? A *trip* to Rome?" I'm incredulous.

"*Sì!* You, me, Mama, and Signora Ruffino are taking a train trip to Rome!"

I try to move my mouth, but it doesn't work. I try to eke out a response, happy if the frog or mouse thieves were back to speak for me, but there is no sound at all! Filomena's laughter rings out.

She wipes her eyes and professes, "This could be the first time ever you do not have a response—tongue-tied I think they call it."

We're both laughing and hugging and dancing around the room now, our hands locked in excitement. We spin and spin, and I find my voice in tandem with hers. We begin to chant, "*A Roma, to Rome! A Roma!*"

I add, "Piazza Novona, Bernini's fountains, the Temple of Venus, Sangallo's designs, the Pantheon!"

I take a deep breath to calm my thunderous heart as Filomena softly resumes the chant, "*Roma, a Roma.*"

Signore Tardino enters the room, takes one look at us, turns on his heels, and huffs out disgustedly.

We explode in a fit of laughter. *Le sorelle, the sisters,* are going to Rome.

BENEATH A BLANKET OF DARKNESS save for the pinwheels of starlight poking through the canvas of night, we move about in preparation. Mama has lit small candles instead of the bright candescence of the electric lights so as not to disturb Papa. Though Mama insisted I go to bed at sunset, I slept fitfully. How was I to drift off to the land of the sleeping when the excitement of my first journey to Roma was just hours away? My mind was the undulating sea: wave after wave of paintings, piazzas, architects, cathedrals, and our beloved Gregorio! I wonder if he will notice how I have changed during this year apart.

For the first time in my life, I will travel on *il treno* without the escort of a man! Of course, Papa has purchased our tickets and paid extra for the concierge to watch over us, and Gregorio will be at the *stazzione* when the train pulls into the *station* in Roma, but still, we will travel alone. Once there, we'll stay at Santa Pietro with our cousin, Rosa who is a nun there. However, the fact remains the same: I am going on my maiden voyage to Roma with the wonderful women in my life. The freedom and nervousness I feel must be what a fledgling encounters before its first flight.

Pina stuffs a basket full of food for the day: anise biscotti, mozzarella wrapped in fern leaves, *panne*, sun-dried apricots, and walnuts. When I enter the cucina dressed in a traveling blouse and skirt, Pina and Filomena stop abruptly, as if a foreign object has dropped down from the sky.

Filomena whistles. "And who is this beauty?" she teases.

I blush shades of red from tomato to cherry.

"Did Arabella just blush?" Pina asks in mock surprise.

I don't know quite what to say. When Mama laid out this traveling outfit for me, I was excited about the fitted skirt and tailored button-down blouse, that I might appear a proper young lady.

Mama enters the room, her traveling suit nearly sweeping the floor. Perhaps it is the view from my new young *donna, woman* eyes, but I am struck by her stately beauty. Is it the light of the candles or the glow of femininity that illuminates us today?

Now grouchy Papa enters the *cucina*, hair mussy, crumpled nightshirt. He is all business and bustle. "Hurry up this, don't do that, make sure to do this, watch out for that."

Mama smiles and nods attentively, patronizing him. Filomena acts serious, and I too play along. Good practice, for I am anything but adept at this kind of behavior.

Pina hands us our cloaks and winks as Papa endlessly instructs.

I SLEPT THE ALMOST-ELEVEN HOURS on the train, so I'm not in the least tired! While the nuns are at ablutions, we finish our cappuccino and biscotti. I've gobbled mine down, ready to dive into the treasures of Roma.

"Mama, *mi scusi*," I attempt interruption of adult conversation with the best of manners, but I am anxious to go out beyond the convent. "It's time to go, *si?*

The look she gives me would freeze most people in their tracks! Signora Ruffino gives me a half-smile, so I take advantage of that moment.

I continue with affective remorse, "*Mi dispiace*, I am sorry Signora Ruffino, I am a little anxious to see something of Rome."

She nods but continues talking to Mama.

I turn my back and roll my eyes. Gregorio enters the room, takes a quick look around, and assesses the situation perfectly. "*Pazienza*, Arabella." He gestures a slow movement with his sculpted hands. "We'll have ample opportunity to drink in the sites of Roma."

I mimic him. "*Sempre pazienza*." Adults can be so frustrating! "I do not feel *patient!*"

He throws back his head of coal-black hair and laughs.

Filomena enters the room. "*Ciao,*" she beams to all, but her eyes are glued to Gregorio in a way that makes me blush.

They head out of doors to the magnificent, verdant gardens of the convent. When I attempt to follow along, Gregorio smiles but shakes his head no.

I pace the room like a caged panther back and forth, forth and back. I am trying to train myself to become more patient, but I am failing miserably.

I am left to listen to the adult conversation of Signora Ruffino and Mama.

"How much longer can Italy remain neutral in this Great War?" Mama asks.

"And America too?" inquires Signora Ruffino.

Mama shakes her head. "I don't like to call it by its given name, 'Great War.' How can men call war 'great'?"

I know a rhetorical question when I hear it. I begin to slow my pacing and ask myself how I might consider such a question.

"Isn't it always about power? Perhaps that's why men think of it as *great,*" offers Signora Ruffino.

Or 'great' meaning its ravenous impact, I muse. And just like that, I am eager to hear their thoughts.

"*Si.*" Mama nods her head. "But what I don't understand about the minds of men is why they do not have forethought. How could the Serbs not realize that the Austrian-Hungarians would retaliate when they assassinated the heir to the throne?"

Bella Roma aside, this conversation with two intelligent women has me tingling with excitement. When I stop to consider it, to feel its texture and color, I realize what it is: the simple, yet powerful feeling of freedom. We traveled here without husbands, fathers, or chaperones, and now women are conversing openly, at their leisure, about politics and war.

"They picked a fight of grand proportions," offers Gregorio's mama. "*Grazie Dio* that Italy has not engaged."

"*Sì, vero, so true,*" offers Mama, "but I fear it won't be long before our men are called to secure our northern border with Austrio-Hungary."

Men called to war? No! If I were the head of the family, I'd insist my brothers stay in Brazil. And I'd hide Gregorio in the convent. And Antonio too! A growing sense of unease runs its tendrils over my heart. I peer out the convent windows to see Filomena and Gregorio in a timeless moment. They seem to reach for one another with their eyes. A stab of jealousy strikes as I try to accept the unlikelihood that I will ever experience such genuine, intimate love.

"Germany seeks its place in the limelight no matter the cost." Mama sighs.

I don't want to hear any more of this terrible war talk or even witness lovers in love. My impatience bobs to the surface again, but I mask it in what I hope is a clever charm.

"And Rome seeks those who will put *her* in the limelight," I proclaim.

Fortunately, the adults find me delightful. They rise from their chairs.

"*Brava,* Arabella." Signora Ruffino laughs.

Can a touch of cleverness or humor move people to action?

"THIS IS THE VERY SPOT OF THE *miracle of the snow,*" Gregorio explains. "According to the legend, the Blessed Virgin Mary appeared to Pope Liberius, a local patrician and his wife, in a dream on a summer day in August, 352. Mary spoke to them in the dream, instructing them to watch for a snowfall that would outline the church they would build in her honor. The miraculous snow fell down from the sky the following summer night and marked the place the church would be built."

We all perform the sign of the cross. What a miracle to be visited by Mary, I think (and wonder again who or what visited me on the *lungomare*).

I feel solid standing here on this sacred ground but also light as a wispy cloud. This Basilica di Santa Maria Maggiore, dedicated to the Blessed Virgin Mary, is large and imposing, like the love she had for her son, and her enduring love for us. This is the most powerful place of prayer in all of Roma, the largest of the twenty-six churches that honor the Mother of God. Its grandeur is fitting because without her, there would have been no Jesus.

Filomena and I reach for each other's hands as we pass through the magnificent entrance. There is something unspoken but very much alive within these walls. The colors seem to hum—crimson wine, plum, burnished gold, and white as innocence itself. Organic shapes from nature, coffered and domed, painted fresco stories, and tiled mosaic pictures add to its breathtaking beauty. I don't know where to look first: the coffered ceiling of Guilano da Sangallo, the Doric white marble columns standing like soldiers, the pictured tales of Abraham, Jacob, and Isaac on the left, and those of Moses and Joshua on the right? Standing here with my sister is like standing on a rock-hard promise.

We gingerly step onto the mosaic floor with its blooming geometric shapes. Above, the circular, cobalt-blue stained glass reminds me of the Mediterranean. We make our way around the great expansive cathedral through scenes of Christ's early life, to the illuminated painting of the Annunciation, past the triumphal arch and the gold-etched window frames. Beneath the dome of light of the apse, we drop hands to look up.

Suddenly, a beam of light like a lightning bolt strikes me in the middle of my forehead. I reel, then fall, seemingly pinned to the floor. The bell tower reverberates as golden light surrounds me, then fills me. The louder the peal of the bell tower, the broader the glow. I lie perfectly still, unable to move or rise, yet I am unafraid. The feeling is like drinking when you are thirsty: you part your lips, you fill your mouth, your throat, your chest. My body drinks the light, and I let go of everything but floating in this sea of peace. A familiar woman's voice calls my name, sweetly, tenderly.

Who are you? I call out with my mind.

I am a part of you, a part of love, a part of everything, she answers.

I'm trying to understand the enormity of that.

And then I hear, *Know this, and know this well. I am always with you to help you follow your honored path of healing. You will see me and hear me whenever you need guidance.*

The light fades. I am still for a few long breaths before I begin to move my fingers and toes. I blink, open my eyes. My family is staring aghast. I sit up slowly, but I am dizzy.

"*Grazie Dio!*" manages Filomena.

Mama wants to know what happened. Was I ill? Did I faint? Did someone push me? People have gathered around us. Gregorio says he's going for a doctor.

"*No*, please. I am fine. I was just overcome with, with . . ." I don't know how to describe it. Was it a miracle? A visit from Mary, Mother of God, an angel, or was I just overly excited? "*Non ti preoccupare, don't worry*, I am in good hands."

"But . . ." Mama insists.

Patting her shoulder, I assure her I am well. I rub the spot on my forehead where the beam of light struck me, silently reflecting on the experience. We file out of the cathedral arm in arm. Filomena keeps studying my face. I smile and nod to allay her fears.

We arrive back at the convent for evening prayers. I am sent to our room to rest. I lay on the cot, replaying the moment. Dare I consider I had my own miracle today? I don't think it was Mary, but it *was* a female, an angelic, glorious woman's voice that spoke my name as if it were heaven's song: *Arabella, answered prayer.* I truly felt like I was an answer to a prayer when I heard her say my name. What prayer I have no idea. And then to be told to pursue my healing, that she was part of me, and to always remember, well, it was all something quite extraordinary.

I drift off to sleep. Dreamtime comes to me in shades of raven-black hair topped with chamomile crowns, brushstrokes of *women's* faces chanting names of herbs, in frescoes of *women donne* singing, of wholeness and health, and scarves blowing freely in fragrant herbal breezes.

"TELL ME WHAT HAPPENED TO YOU at Santa Maria Maggiore," demands Filomena.

I want to tell her everything, but when I think of the apparition on the *lungomare,* the light, *and* the voice at the basilica, I am hesitant. Divulging these mysteries aloud will make them real (and make me *pazzo—crazy.*)

"I'm just not sure if I fainted from all the excitement of being in Rome or not having eaten much that morning," I offer weakly.

She doesn't believe me. "You and Antonio haven't . . ."

"What are you asking?"

"You would tell me if something was, well, um, not right?"

"Of course," I answer. "But there is nothing to worry about, *mia sorella.* "

"*Va bene,*" *very well,* she nods. "You better get back to your studies. I hear Professore Tyrant approaching."

I open a book of Shakespeare's sonnets and quickly begin reciting number 22 as Signore Tardino enters. He joins me, but our cadence does not match. It makes me think of how much I miss Marco and how we would recite these poems together. Signore frowns at me. I try not to frown back. I can hardly blame him for being displeased with my lackluster efforts and bad attitude these past months. We are both biding our time until Gregorio returns to Paola.

When Pina finally comes in to tell me to wash up for our meal, I arise so quickly I nearly tip the chair. I try a sort of bow mixed with a curtsy but nearly fall over my own feet. Pina laughs. I'm grateful for the bicycle bell ringing outside the kitchen door.

"*Buona sera*, Signore Pascale," I greet him.

"Ah, it is a *fine evening*, Arabella. *Come vai?*"

"I'm fine, thank you, just finishing my day's studies," I answer.

"And what has that brilliant mind learned about today?"

"I'm studying the sonnets of a poet, William Shakespeare."

"Mmm, no geography lesson today?"

"No, *signore*. Why do you ask?"

"Well, I have something here from a faraway place," he teases.

"Brazil? Something from my brothers?" I light up like a firefly. "A letter is like a visit from someone, isn't it, Signore Pascale?"

"Yes, I suppose so," he answers handing me a package. I want to tear it open immediately like a ravenous tiger ripping into its prey but it is addressed to the whole family.

After the blessing and the serving of the fresh fava bean soup *con spinache*, Mama's rosemary *panne*, Papa opens the parcel. Inside there are a couple of smaller wrapped packages and a letter. Papa lays the other packages aside and begins reading the letter.

My eyes scan the other packages, and I want to snatch the one with my name and run off to the *lungomare* to open it in private. *Pazienza*, I tell myself. *Patience*. But I am racked with impatience! And now Papa is reading too slowly!

"Papa, may I read the letter for you?"

"Grazie, *figlia*," he answers and hands me the letter.

Brazil, 1914

Cara Famiglia,

Café café café! We plant, grow, harvest, ship, sleep and consume the café of Brazil. The Americani demand it, the Europeans devour it, and we devote ourselves to it. Our laborers toil both in the fields and the mill from the early light to the setting sun so that we can provide the world of coffee lovers with their robust Brazilian drink.

We have discovered many fellow Italians here in this tropical paradise who are willing to work in the fields, able-bodied Italians who know the language of the land: soil preparation, coaxing a plant to grow and weeding, culling, and harvesting a crop of beans. These workers are the real reason for our success.

We marvel at some of the other wonderful but strange flora like the exotic Jaboticaba tree with its yellowy-white flowers that bloom on the trunk of the tree! The fruit begins to take shape bursting from the trunk like bunches of grapes- purplish-black in color. Eaten fresh is delicious but we've had jams and jellies, tarts, vino, and liquors made from the jaboticaba fruit. Arabella, you would be pleased to note that the skins of the fruit are dried for use in respiratory ailments.

Good news, famiglia. We are coming home! And we are bringing an addition to our famiglia! Octavio, being the eldest, has set a fine example of a good son. He has taken a wife, Sofia. We will bring our newest family member home with us in time for Easter.

Con Amore,
Marco e Octavio

There is a collective expression of joy. We jump up and hug one another, smiling and congratulating Mama and Papa. What a delightful surprise! Octavio will bring home a wife. A wife! A *sister-in-law*!

Mama immediately begins her discourse on what needs to get done before the arrival of her sons and new daughter-in-law. Their visit is many months away, leaving ample time for plans to be made, erased, and recreated again. Mama and Filomena begin planning the feast. Papa hands me my package, a beautiful red leather booklet of poems by South American, Olavo Bilac. Mama and Filomena open theirs and revel in the handcrafted *sabonete, fine soap.* I allow myself some dreamy reverie–South American romantic landscapes filled with exquisite, brown inhabitants conversing in an unusual language derived from Latin. I flip open the book to find a translated quote by Signore Bilac describing Portuguese as the last flower of Latium, the ancient city of Rome, wild and beautiful.

I ask to be excused as the elders drone on about the upcoming visit and festivities that will ensue and of grandchildren and future generations bearing the Mandarino name. I walk to the *lungomare,* book in hand, admiring the expansive sky at twilight. Sitting on the shore in the last light of day, I sense something over my shoulder. It's that light again, no longer a flash, just softly present, filling up an outline of a person. I shiver but recall the peace I felt in the cathedral and the sweetness of the message.

"Hello," I manage to whisper. The light seems to pulse (or is it my active imagination?)I take a deep breath, close my eyes. Perhaps the spirit is interested in the poems of Signore Bilac. As the sea plays her background melody, I open the book and read aloud the translated words of a man who possessed an insatiable appetite for stars and planets, heroes and love. I think of Gregorio's discourse on families and planets, women, and love. How I will come to understand the orbit of the galaxy and the people on this Earth is a mystery only God knows.

The spirit light is with me as darkness descends on the *lungoma*re. Walking toward home, I can almost hear her footsteps in rhythm with mine.

Italian celebrations begin in the kitchen. Mama, Pina, Signora Ruffino, and the soon-to-be Signora Gregorio Ruffino—Filomena—begin cooking for a special welcome home party for Gregorio. Filomena glows like the moon on its fourteenth day: the most luminous of its cycle. Does the love of a man and a woman illuminate the heart so strongly it can radiate out through the eyes? Gazing at Filomena, I believe it is so. She seems to know I am thinking of her, as if she can hear my thoughts, and she turns to me with her goddess smile. I wink at her and nod my head. She has waited for this happy occasion for a long, long time. Gregorio will be traveling some with Signore Novello to lecture in San Lucido, Naples, and La Scala, but for now, he is home.

I have laid out my drawings of plants to show Gregorio how much my knowledge has expanded. I have notes on the success of my Echinacea and dandelion tincture to mobilize the immune system, and comfrey with oregano to treat coughs. Under the tutelage of Gregorio's mama, I have come far in my study and practice this year. Even after Signore Ruffino healed, many villagers continued visiting me for consultation and treatment. My small medicinal garden has grown tenfold. Tending, coaxing, caring for plants that will heal people has become as important as the patients. What is that old-time saying about blooming where you are planted? If I am planted in Paola, I am determined to flourish here. It is my latest promise to our Virgin Mary, Mother of God that I will be happy and fruitful here in Paola. I take the small statue that my friend Antonio carved for me out of my pocket. I talk to her often, wondering if she and the spirit I encounter are the same.

Gregorio enters the room, and I am overexcited as I display my work and recite botanical names confidently. I attempt to read Olavo Bilac's poems both in Portuguese, Italian, and even a few words in English! I tell him I have added words and phrases to our language journals. Even though I mostly blunder, he is pleased.

"You are a breath of fresh air, Arabella," he tells me. "*Brava!* You have progressed well."

"*Grazie tanti, thank you very much*, Gregorio," I beam.

"I have a surprise for you!" he announces, pulling out a letter.

"Is it from my brothers?" My eyes are large.

"It is from Marco to me," he confides. "I haven't opened it, yet. I thought we could read it together."

I feel very mature to be a part of this communication.

Rio de Janeiro, 1914

Cara Gregorio,

Salute from Rio de Janero! Brazil is both a serene paradise and a center of chaos. Rainforests house exotic birds singing songs of the complexity of nature. They are as varied as the Brazilian people whose beautiful skin ranges from caramel to espresso brown. The classes of people here are much like Italia, though. There are the wealthy and the poor.

The need for change is urgent. Deplorable working and living conditions along with low wages weigh on the laborer- just like Italia! The rich get richer off the backs of the laborer. It seems the slaves of Brazil have been replaced by Italian immigrants. There are a tremendous number of Italians who are working on plantations. It is pitiful to realize that the Italians who left Italy for a new life in Brazil have found that they merely traded one soil for another, one master for another. If they would only unite like the stonecutters who staged a strike, they could negotiate better wages and conditions. But alas, the plantation workers live in constant worry of losing the little income they have. Fear holds them silent.

Gregorio, I know you understand the torment I feel witnessing our workers who are little more than slaves. Slavery was abolished in 1888, but over a quarter-century later, you'd never know it. I speak tirelessly to Octavio, calling to light our need for workers' reform. I remind him of Papa's business motto of fair treatment equaling increased productivity. But productivity and product prevail.

I have tried to make my plea more personal by relaying the story of Lorenzo, a native of Acri, Italia, who lives in a hut with his old, ailing mama. He requires a break in his workday to walk the two miles home to feed her broth and help her to the outhouse.

Dio Mio, do you know what my brother does? He docks Lorenzo's wages and treats him disdainfully if he returns late!

I appeal to my brother's heart, "What if that were our mama was needing that kind of attention? Think of that."

His response?

"Mama has Pina and the girls."

I am relentless, pointing out that Lorenzo has neither sorelli nor resources to hire someone like Pina. He tells me that Lorenzo probably drinks and squanders his money; that he should learn to save more.

Managia! It is as if we speak two different languages! The other day he declared, "Marco, you are not a businessman. Leave that to me."

"What am I?" I ask.

"You are a philosopher and a dreamer."

I have reflected on the truth of those words and, in fact, they compelled me to make an important change: I am leaving Mandarino Brothers Coffee business. What is it that was written over the gateway to the temple at Delphi? 'Know thyself,' or from Hamlet, 'This above all: to thine own self be true.'

I do know myself. I have found a home within the Anarchist Movement here. Their dedication to the greater good appeals to my philosophy. Anarchists possess the power to speak their minds, free from archaic ways of governing. The Movement encourages people to live outside traditional politics but supports citizenship and voter registration. In rallies, door to door, and street meetings, we point out the wayward degradation of drinking, tobacco, and soccer, and also expose the hypocrisy of the Church.

Gregorio, you alone are the brother who understands my

devotion to words and humanity. It is with great pride that I disclose my proudest achievement: I am writing for the newspaper Terra Livre! The great Russian anarchist, Peter Kropokin, has brought international attention to our newspaper by openly thanking us for our work! Still, with all my righteous fervor, I am reluctant to share this with Octavio, let alone Papa. I beg your confidence until I return in late spring to tell my family face to face.

Affectionately,
Marco

I feel like a toddler seeking independence yet simultaneously frightened enough to want everything to remain safely the same. Neither Gregorio nor I say anything for several minutes. I think he is as stunned as I am. The letter's pages are strewn across the tabletop like a disproportionate map of another world. We look at them and then at each other.

I break the silence. "If you knew the content of the letter before you read it, would you still have shared it with me?"

Gregorio sighs deeply. "I don't know, Arabella. But selfishly, I am glad to have someone to share both the burden and the excitement of this news." Sighing again, he smiles weakly and declares, "You are a deep thinker—a *kindred* intellectual like Marco and me."

It has been said that the three of us are *simpatico* because our hearts beat and our minds turn in the same rhythmic patterns, but anarchy, rebellion and outlawed publications have me quaking inside.

I sigh. "It's frightening, Gregorio. He pursues this at great risk, *si?*"

"I will not lie to you, Arabella. They are trying to overthrow a way of life many powerful people enjoy."

This information is a lot to bear. It doesn't surprise me that Marco would put himself in danger for the greater good, but that does not take away the weight of worry.

"Thank you for treating me as an adult, though I'll not lie to *you*; it is burdensome on the heart. I am glad he has the gift of you as a friend."

Gregorio smiles at me. "Speaking of gifts, I have something for you from a doctor friend in Rome." With a wide grin and a quick hand, he trades the letter for something in his briefcase. "Here is your new medical textbook, "he exclaims.

"Oh, Gregorio! I don't even know how to thank you!"

"No need, Arabella. I am so happy to pass this on to you. I'm sure you will have much to share with me when I return in a few days."

"What? You are leaving so soon?"

"Yes, just briefly. I'm accompanying Signore Novello on his lecture in La Scala. I will see you soon, precious one."

He plants a kiss on my forehead. I open the medical book and fall into the domain of the phenomenal human body.

NOT EVEN A LIBRARY FULL OF MEDICAL information could have prepared me for the terror that is upon Paola's doorstep. No expertise could allay the steady stream of fear that fills the space where peaceful security once reigned. Looking at the testimonial crutches and braces lining the walls of the sanctuary this morning, I feel like "Doubting Thomas," the disciple who did not believe Jesus could walk upon the water. But this crisis is not one of broken bones; it is death itself! The ravenous beast called cholera has set its sights on Paola, and one body at a time, it is sucking us bone dry. We don't know how it came to call on the inhabitants of Paola, but come it has, raising our death toll daily. Never have I shivered so fiercely in the heat of day considering the coldness of death. I am powerless one moment then propelled into mental gymnastics the next.

Padre is at the pulpit thundering on about sin and immorality. His message is clear: the cholera is due to our sins. Forgive me Jesus for my blasphemy, but that is as superstitious as the witch hunts of the 1600s when women were hung or burned for supposedly causing everything from weather storms to stillbirths! Just as there were practical, scientific reasons for ill weather and complicated childbirths, there are reasons the cholera is here—we just don't know what they are yet. I am determined to understand how the disease "behaves" in order to eliminate it.

"'1 John 1:9: If we confess our sins, He is faithful and just and will forgive us, purifying us from all unrighteousness', Padre Busardo booms. "Apparently, there is much to confess. I will stay until all confessions are heard."

Papa, Mama, and Filomena wait in the long, somber line for confession. I do not care for the dark confines of the confessional or the scratchy sound of the sliding screen before Padre asks the penetrating questions regarding one's sins. I sneak out to think in the evening's open air. Antonio is there.

"Antonio! My God, it's good to see you! How are you and your family?" I ask.

"We're all okay, yours?" He searches my face.

"Okay," I answer.

"Thank God! This cholera is horrible. What do you know about it? "

I tell him a doctor from San Lucido has been here and diagnosed the disease in the Gobilini family, Tomasellos, and the Coluccis, among others, and that the doctor gave the (ineffective, four vials of) medicine to the Padre, promising to return with more. I unburden my fear that we are on our own, that if I were a betting woman, I'd stake my *lire* that the doctor will not be returning to Paola. Once an outbreak begins, they don't return no matter how much *money* is offered. The cholera spreads dangerously fast.

He rakes his hands through his thick folds of wavy hair. "*Marone!* What are we going to do?"

I tell him I am studying the symptoms, diets, and circumstances of the Gobilinis and Farellos to chart the disease.

"How can I help?" he asks.

"I need to gather more information from others who are sick. Can you read me the names of the ill from the list on the wall over there?" I ask.

He reads me the names, families, and the part of the village they reside in. I am grateful for my God-given gift of easy memorization.

"Who makes this list, and who keeps it current?" he asks.

"I don't know. It doesn't say, and it is not dated." I sigh. "We need to keep it updated. The disease is taking over quickly, and we don't have the facts. It's as if the cholera is several steps ahead of us!"

"Then we will move faster; outrun it. We are young and healthy. We'll gather the information for you and Signora Ruffino to decipher."

I shake my head. "Signora sent word that her husband is not well. She didn't say it was the cholera, so I'm praying it's his leg again." I pause, perform the sign of the cross, choosing my words honestly. "Antonio, the reality is we're all alone on this sinking ship. I'm not sure I even have the right questions to ask or that I can make any sense of the answers." I sigh, completely overwhelmed by the enormity of what we are facing. "Who am I kidding? If a doctor doesn't know how to cure this disease, how can I?"

"You *can* because these are *your* people. You'll never give up on them! Arabella, there is no one else on Earth as intelligent or inquisitive as you." His eyes bore into mine. "And you, Arabella, you can never hide from a challenge. I believe in you."

I almost cry. It's his confidence in me. His admiration of me. His belief in me. His knowledge of who I am when I don't even know it. The emotion of everything combined drops me to my inner knees and lifts me to the clouds. It's an odd mix of juxtaposed emotions: assured yet frightened, empowered yet weak. I don't know what is true, only that I want him to hold me, comfort me, so I can throw my shoulders back and march down the streets of Paola delivering a proclamation to beat the cholera. All I can manage, however, is a quiet, solemn nod.

"I believe in you, and I will help you," his whispered vow.

If we weren't standing outside the church in this disastrous predicament, I think I would kiss him.

I clear my throat and mind. His safety comes to the forefront of my thoughts. "This is dangerous, Antonio; you put yourself and your family in harm's way."

"As are you. Arabella, we have no choice. You just said Signora Ruffino is taking care of her own. The doctor won't be back, and his medicine is ineffective, anyway. We may lose our lives to it, so let's try to *do* something!" He is emphatic. "I'll meet you in the *piazza* at sunrise."

We say goodbye as my family exits the church and climbs into the buggy. Papa guides the horses down toward the *lungomare* and home. Many of the villagers have drawn their curtains and locked the doors that would normally remain open. It feels eerily prophetic, a metaphor for the darkness upon us.

Along the dirt road that winds down toward the sea, Filomena asks Papa to stop by the Ruffino's to check on signore, to see when Gregorio will return home from La Scala or if he will stay until the cholera passes. Papa pulls the buggy up to the Ruffino home, and immediately, I sense something is terribly wrong. I feel it in my stomach and my thrumming heartbeat. It is too dark, too quiet, too still. All wrong for this home that is always full of light, noise, and bustle no matter the hour. Tonight, the windows and doors are shut tight as a frightened turtle in its shell. Adrenaline courses, unbidden. Filomena's eyes rapidly blink, a nervous reaction to her terror. We all feel it. It's the ominous looming fear of death. She takes my hand and squeezes it with the strength of Hercules but shakes like a fragile child.

Papa orders gently but firmly, "You will stay here." He passes the reins to Mama and approaches the house. The curtain is pushed aside, and an ashen face appears. Signora Ruffino shakes her head vigorously from side to side and wildly waves him away. We watch her holding our breath.

Papa calls through the windows, "Signora, *Cosa c'e che non va?*" *What's wrong?*

Signora Ruffino's erratic voice shatters the glass barrier. "My husband *lei e morto*," she sobs, "and now my Gregorio has the cholera too!" Her voice is the horror inside a nightmare.

Signore Ruffino *dead?* Gregorio ill?

Filomena stands in the buggy and screams, "No. Dear God, not my Gregorio."

She drops my hand and attempts to jump down off the buggy but Mama is quick as a Venus Fly Trap. She snatches Filomena, throws me the reigns, and draws Filomena in a shielding embrace. "*Povericina,*" *poor child,* she chants and rocks her grown daughter like a baby.

"Mama." Filomena straightens up and chokes out, "It can't be true! Gregorio is in La Scala. He is not here; he is not here." Beside herself, a bit like a madwoman, she rants, "Mama, it's not true; it's not true." She is pulling at Mama's skirt, her blouse, her voice the high-pitched screech of an eagle. Then she collapses into Mama's arms sobbing.

I am left with the charge of the irritable horses who are most uncomfortable with the antsy movement of the passengers and their primal sounds. I am left to protect my own heart from breaking into thousands of pieces too minute to recover. I take a deep breath and engage my mind- my best defense. Gregorio was in La Scala with Signore Novello. Did he contract the sickness there? Or was he already infected, thereby contaminating another village in *Mezzogiorno?* Mary, Mother of God help us! How can I stop this? I sense the light of my spirit messenger. She is near enough that my neck hair is standing straight up.

Making the sign of the cross I ask silently, *Can you help Gregorio? Can you save my village?* I close my eyes and breathe deeply, but my mind, the active pup chasing its own tail, sprouts a new fear: will Filomena become ill? I've seen them holding hands and I'm certain they kiss. If this disease spreads by touch, I will be stricken as well. Gregorio kissed me on the forehead before he left! I could become full of the germs that suck the fluids from my organs.

Arabella, I admonish. *How can you think of yourself at a time like this?* I won't. I won't think of myself. I will think of Gregorio and all the others who need my help. I will pray, yes, but I will find some answers.

The light descends on me, soft and soothing, almost like light rain on my skin. I drink in its gentleness but feel a charge of energy. Where did that idea that the disease could be spread by touch come from? It is a worthwhile premise to research.

When Papa returns to the buggy, the reigns in my hands scratch the air like electronic wave patterns. Mama and Filomena have already begun the beating lament, pounding their thighs, their arms, and their faces like the low beating of tom-tom drums. Papa takes the reigns and pats my hand. I look at my Papa, my strong Papa, sinking beneath the weight of defeat. I have to catch my breath, steadying myself on the sides of the buggy. Is it too late for all of us? Will cholera put us in the ground two by two or four by four? No! I cannot accept death for those I love.

Something fiery ignites in the depths of my belly. *I will put a stop to this sickness even it's the last thing I ever do.*

I SIT ALONE AT THE KITCHEN TABLE in the eerie silence of the night. Filomena and Mama finally fell asleep after a strong cup of lobelia, red clover, and passionflower with one measured drop of belladonna tea. I wasn't even nervous giving it to them, confident that one drop with the other herbs would coax them to much-needed slumber. Papa shut himself off in his study shortly after we arrived home.

I look at the pages strewn across the table. Some books are open to drawings, and others mark passages that may be useful. I have written notes in the margins and on separate pages trying to make sense of this disease. I read in the medical journal Gregorio's friend gifted to me, "The first outbreak of cholera in 1831 was thought to afflict only the immoral and the poor."

Nonsense, I think. Without science, people would be blinded by superstitions.

I read on. "It was further thought that the disease is not contagious because the attending doctor did not succumb to the symptoms."

Hmm, couldn't that be due to his particular body's resistance?

I read on to discover a theory that the drinking water in a certain town was infected with bodily fluids and feces of the sick, causing the spread of the disease. Oh, dear Mary, Mother of God—*La Fontana di Paola*! People have been washing, dipping vessels, and drinking the water from the *fountain*! That has got to be a large part of how we're becoming infected! A glow of spirit angel light fills the kitchen.

Good. I think I am on the right path! After I finish writing the names of the sick I memorized at the church, I begin to see another pattern that may or may not be related to the outbreak. I dash to Papa's study with my findings. Papa is asleep in his chair.

"Papa," I shake him. "Papa, wake up!"

"Arabella, *che c`e? What is it, figlia?*" he asks fretfully.

"Papa, I need to see your customer ledger."

He looks at me quizzically but opens a drawer and hands it to me. I compare it quickly to the list of the sick and the date they became ill.

"*Dio mio!* Papa, most of the sick are not your customers! They must be Carbonara's!" I pace the floor, rampaging a flurry of instructions. "Papa, we must act! You will tell people about his tainted meat. Next, we will cordon off the *Fontana di Paola*. I am certain the cholera germs are not only in the meat but also in the shared water. And the ill, Papa, the ill must be quarantined so the disease cannot spread to the healthy." I make the sign of the cross. "And the dead, Papa, we must bury the dead immediately!"

Papa is rubbing his head. "*Figlia*, how did you come to these conclusions?"

"I've been thinking and thinking, Papa. I made lists of people and symptoms and I've checked dates. I've been reading in the medical tome Gregorio brought me from Rome." It's hard to even say his name aloud.

He nods his head, pausing to absorb the scope and the implications of this knowledge. He stares at me for a moment, judging my conviction. I am resolute, firmly planted.

"Exposing Carbonara without real evidence is one thing, but I will find a way to inform people. But cordoning off the water supply? How will we survive?"

"We will all have to ration, Papa. We'll go to the mountain springs with every jug and barrel we can gather. Those who are healthy will ride up and fill containers to distribute to the village. We will organize a schedule, take turns. There is no doubt it will be a hardship to keep ourselves away from the fountain, but if we all dip from the same source, Papa, I am quite certain we will all die."

He nods. "But where will we put the sick?" He seems to be asking the air or some unseen angel. What would he think to know there is an angel in this very house?

"Yes, important question, Papa. Where can we house the sick?" I seem to be addressing the same air and unseen angel that Papa did. I pace the room with its array of book spines, narrow to wide, the gloss of the cherry wood, the glow from the round, green glass lamp. An idea emerges like flower petals opening. "What about using the barn in the back of the flour mill? We could move in bedding and tables for supplies; there's good light from the windows and fresh air as well."

"*Brava*, Arabella. You have thought of some excellent solutions. The village elders are meeting with Padre Busardo first thing in the morning. I will present your ideas." He opens the center drawer of his solid desk and hands me one of the new writing implements, a *fountain pen* with refillable ink pellets.

"For me Papa?" I thought I might have to wait for my next birthday, but maybe he thought we might not make it to our next birthdays.

"*Si, figlia, yes,* for you *daughter.*" He smiles faintly. "But let's put it aside for tomorrow. Now, it is time for sleep."

I kiss him on the cheek, prickly with the stubble of a long, tedious day. "*Grazie,* Papa, I will put the fountain pen to good use."

He lifts his eyebrow.

"Tomorrow, of course. *Buona notte. Good night,* Papa."

He walks toward his bedroom and I toward mine, but as soon as I hear his bedroom door shut, I head back to the kitchen table with my fountain pen at the ready, eager to make a recipe for cleaning germs from utensils, bedding, water, and clothing, and another to soothe the ache of infected bodies. I sneak out to collect water from the sea.

BEFORE DAYBREAK, I LEAVE THE HOUSE armed with a small bag of supplies and all the strength adrenaline offers. I walk briskly toward the *piazza* to meet Antonio. Even the *lungomare* appears agitated this fall morning. It seems to be reflecting my fears: how many are ill? How many more there will be? Is it too late to intercede? Who will I lose? Will I die? I fear heightened panic will ignite superstitions—another reason to keep the presence of my spirit angel—that's what I call her now—to myself. I could be blamed for the cholera.

My first stop is the Ruffino's. It's as eerily quiet as it was last night. I tap lightly on the door. Signora Ruffino comes to the window shaking her head, emphatically motioning for me to leave.

"Let me come in, please. I can help!" I beg.

"No, this is no place for you! Go home and stay there. This sickness is contagious."

"I know! I have been studying it. I've made a solution to wash your family's bedding and clothes. Look, *signora*." I take out a jar of a solution I have made of lime juice, sea water, and salt. "Here it is."

She cracks open the door. I push it open and enter the house.

Signore Ruffino is laid out on the dining table. The house reeks of decay. Bile rises in my throat. I was not prepared for this, but then, how could I be? Signora tells me I am disrespectful, that I shouldn't be there. I cringe a little at my beloved teacher's words, but I know she is overwrought. I cannot imagine the burden of her suffering.

Moaning drifts from another room. Gregorio! Without an inkling of what I'm about to see, I quickly move toward the sound. Signora Ruffino's emotions melt into an exhausted whimper, forbidding me to enter. One look at our dear Gregorio tells me he is more in the other world than this one, but I cannot accept it. I reach in my bag for my new tinctures and gently lift a vial to his lips. His skin feels like a branding iron. I urge him to take the liquid, but it is obvious he's unable to swallow. It dribbles down his chin.

"Try, Gregorio. You must try, "I plead, feeling the hot dread of futility.

Signora enters. "*Basta*, Arabella, it's too late." A sob escapes her lips. She wipes her eyes and looks straight at me. "Now, *figlia*, you trust me, *si?*"

I am reluctant to answer. She is strangely calm. "*Si, signora*. You are my teacher."

"*E vero. That is true.* And so, you must listen to me. Give me all the belladonna in your bag." She looks at Gregorio. "And leave here now."

It takes me a moment to recover from the unspeakable act she is considering. If I give her all the belladonna in my bag, it will kill him. "I didn't bring any, Signora," I lie.

"Arabella, I know you have it. I beg you, my son is in terrible pain, and I cannot bear it." The grief has rendered her irrational.

"No, *Signora*. I cannot."

"You love him, don't you?"

Now I cannot hold back the dam of sadness. "I love Gregorio like my own brother. That's why I've come to give him my medicine."

She screams at me now, completely undone. "Give me the belladonna so I can send him home to God!"

I make the sign of the cross. I cannot do that! That would be murder. "*Signora*, give him time and this tincture I have made. He will come around. He will."

"Arabella, you listen to me! It is too late, I tell you, too late for him! I watched my husband die." She falters then takes a paper from her dress pocket. "I documented the order of the disease from onset to death. Take this. Study it. You can do something to save others—it's too late for my son."

I just stand there, a frightened girl unable to fully comprehend what it is to save another by losing someone I love.

"Arabella, *dammi, give me* the belladonna."

I cannot move—not a finger or a toe. My body is frozen, but my mind is spinning. I never should have come here. What made me think I understand anything of sickness or healing or death? *Signora* is right. I should be safe at home. In a sudden flurry, she snatches my satchel, removes the belladonna jar, and throws the satchel back at me. She screeches for me to get out of her home. Unglued, I bolt like my clothes are on fire all the way to the *piazza*.

Antonio is waiting for me at *Fontana di Paola*. He asks me if I am unwell, but I cannot speak. I see him. I see the people dipping their vessels, linens, and hands into the water. I want to scream, *No. Do not use the fountain water*, but I am stuck somewhere between here and hell. Antonio is shaking me, calling my name. I don't know what he is saying. I stare into his eyes as the angel light glows behind him. Waking from my stupor, I hear a high-pitched voice yelling, "*Lascia l' acqua! Leave the water!*" It takes a few moments to realize the voice is mine.

They all stop. Signora Trombetta blusters a reply, "But Arabella, my son, Giuseppe, is burning with fever and thirst."

"And my Gemma is the same," Signora Abusco shares as her handkerchief dips beneath the surface.

"Can you help, Arabella? We hear *Il dottore* will not be here with more medicine for many days. "

"*Basta!*" *Stop!* I am in control of my voice now but out of control emotionally.

"Did the doctor say to stop?"

There is a dark, sarcastic voice in my head, *Il dottore? The doctor? He is worthless! stupido, and he doesn't care about us! We are left to die!*

A flicker of light bounces off my satchel. And I hear, *Arabella, answered prayer. Do not add to their burden. Rather, soothe their pain.*

I steady myself. "Please, I know we must not use this water. It's part of what is making people sick."

They take a step back as if from a predator. Some make the sign of the cross.

"We will go to the mountains and bring fresh water until this passes. The elders are working out a plan." I open the satchel and remove vials of potent peppermint, ginger, and black walnut. "For now, those of you with sick families, use these tinctures to ease stomach cramps and lower fevers."

They all look at one another and me.

"This is just for now," I calmly but firmly assure them. "The doctor will return and bring more medicine," I lie.

I give them the disinfecting solution, instructing them to wash all bedding and clothing immediately.

"Boil a tablespoon in a large pot of water to clean your utensils and dishes, two tablespoons for a bucket of clothes."

I wait for fall out, for endless rebuttals, but they simply nod their heads, take the tinctures and solutions, and disperse. I pour some of the solution into the fountain water, offer a prayer of hope for the living, and God help me, one for the dead—wondering if that includes Gregorio.

Antonio and I find some rope and create signs to alert the town the fountain is closed. I am not waiting for permission from the elders. We can't risk others being contaminated. I leave a note for Papa at the church pleading for the elder council to make the sign official by adding, "By order of the council."

Antonio and I walk the streets asking questions, taking notes. Should I tell him about Gregorio and *signora?* No, he will never look at me the same.

Concentrate Arabella, on words and science, study signora's notes, I admonish myself. But my mind strays, and my hands feel bound like the chains of a convicted murderer.

NOT EVEN THE WAVES CRASHING ON the desolate, wintry shore can drown out cholera's murderous battle cry. Constant as the waters falling down the mountain in spring, death's lament has filled the vessel of too many hearts. These two months, our days have been saturated by the burden of death, the endless to and fro of retrieving mountain water, the sleepless nights of brewing barrels of tonics to soothe the insides and clean the outside of things. And then there are the arguments over where to bury the massive number of dead. But most difficult for the living? How to carry on.

We did everything from quarantine to cleaning, but nothing worked. The teeth of the disease kept chewing us up. The names of the sick were added to the church wall, then crossed out, and moved to the deceased list. Some were moved to the building at the mill but only as a stop on their way underground. The doctor did return once with more medicine, but it proved as ineffective as my tonics. The healthy nearly sent themselves to the grave from the weight of worry and care, but Mama, Papa, Filomena, Pina, and I are all free of the disease, *grazie Dio*.

Sadness did descend as Papa's father, Babbo Piero fell to the disease, and Padre Busardo, after administering so many last rites, is also gone. There are many more, too many. Poor Signore Ruffino and his son, our dear Gregorio. How I wish the secret of my visit and the belladonna could be buried with the deceased along with my guilt and failure as a healer.

And though I remain wary of belladonna, I gathered more from the mountainside because nothing soothes Filomena's grief but a drop of it added to valerian every few days. Mostly, *mia sorella* lies in her bed sleeping the pain away. I look at her and ache for her loss that I may have caused. Though Signora's detailed notes on the disease put Gregorio's symptoms near the end of his life, I'll never know for certain. And, how could I forget: the belladonna came from *my* bag. Signora would not have had it if I had not gone there. Perhaps then, Filomena would not be without her fiancé.

This evening, as we gather to pray the Rosary, Mama is firm. "Filomena, you will join us tonight. "

I can almost hear her heaving herself from her bed to the study where we are already on our knees.

"I believe in God, the Father Almighty, creator of heaven and Earth."

I can't hear her voice, but I see her lips moving. I miss her voice. I miss her laugh. I miss the sister I joked with and danced with—the one who instructed me, advised me, teased me. I study her between the phrases, looking for signs of the beautiful, lively sister I once knew. She is barely there, a thin slip on bare skin.

After the rosary, she slides back into bed. Pina simmers a broth of beef, beef bones, cloves, garlic, parsley, and chives to stimulate the appetite. I prepare one of my many new concoctions for her depression: lemon balm, basil, and rose petals. But like my other failures, no remedy heals. Still, I note everything in my journal of herbal tonics and remedies—the appetite or lack of, the emotions, the heavy limbs, the sallow tones, the ineffectiveness to lift her spirits. I must learn from the mistakes to save my sister.

I bring the broth to Filomena. She allows me to spoon-feed her like a young bird in its nest. Setting the half-consumed bowl of *brodo di carne* down on the bedside table, I crawl into bed with her and hold her in my arms. I want to soothe her, but she is racked with spasmodic shivering and shallow breathing. I don't know how to help her! I take a deep breath. Feeling the light of my angel around us, I breathe in and out steadily. Maybe I can reteach her cells, lungs, and heart how to work properly.

"*Mia sorella*," I whisper. "Breathe with me." And then I count aloud, "One, two, three, four— take the sweetness of air." I push it into the cavern of my belly.

I've read mystic yogis practice this kind of controlled breathing to infuse healing. It makes me think of an ongoing conversation on religion and spirituality that Gregorio and I had throughout our friendship. I tense up with sadness—and guilt. My breathing reverts to its old, shallow habit, and I must begin the counting all over again. After a few minutes, Filomena's breathing matches mine. I pat her back like she has done countless times for me during my life.

"*Va bene, mia sorella, everything will be alright.*" I say this as if I have answers on how to slay the dragon of grief (and ease my own culpability).

Filomena grabs my sleeve, pulling her weak self-up. "Please forgive me, *mia sorella* but I cannot go on without him."

I take her gently but firmly by the shoulders. "I know you *think* you cannot go on, but you can! I'll help you find your way."

She whimpers and slowly shakes her heavy head from side to side.

"Remember," I continue, "remember you are the one who called me down from heaven. *Non ti ricordi? Remember?*" Tears are her only response. "Well, then, I will go too," I state testily, "because I cannot live without you."

Light flickers in her eyes. "No," she whimpers.

"Yes, and believe me, I know how," I add before my loose tongue can be reined in.

She looks at me questioningly before the waterfall of tears descend.

"Do not worry," I reassure her, smoothing her black hair from her forehead. "Together, we will get through this. Together."

BREATH BY BREATH, WEEK BY WEEK, and month by month, we make our way through the sorrow. The living either succumb and wither away toward death or will themselves to climb aboard the lifeboat. And after all we've been through, Italy is considering joining the world at war. More heartache, more disaster, more death.

Today, though, we enjoy a welcome diversion as we prepare for the feast that will greet my brothers, Marco and Octavio, and my new sister-in-law, Sofia. I form and reform, roll and reroll the meatballs. One is lopsided. Another looks like an ostrich egg, one like a child's play ball, and one like a pebble from the shore of the *lungomare* (where I long to be right now). Mama is patient as a saint. She gently throws the ill-formed meatballs back into the bowl and shows me yet again the over-under-roll and pat-perfect meatball.

I sigh deeply. "Mama?"

"*Si, figlia?*"

"Do you think Filomena will ever recover?"

"*Si, Arabella, pazienza.*"

"I am trying to be *patient.*"

Ssszzzsssszzzz. The hot oil pops in the skillet. Mama drops a small piece of meat to cook so she can test the flavorings.

"Eight months is a long time to be that sad," I say.

"You are most gentle with her."

"You know I'd do anything for *mia sorella!*"

"I know that. You sisters have the gift of heaven." She wipes her hands on her apron and then wipes her eyes. She looks at me with a most peculiar expression. "You must promise me you will never allow anything to come between you and your sister. "

"Of course, but that's not such a hard thing to promise."

"You are young, *figlia.* Life will be full of unforeseen challenges."

Like cholera and death? Before I can ask Mama what she means, the first of my well-formed meatballs sizzle in the skillet, *plip, plop.* She smiles at me, and a thousand rays of light shoot through my worries. My angel is standing next to her. Pina enters with fresh garden clippings of oregano, basil, and bay leaves—and a spirited discussion of the *pasta e fagiloi* recipe. There is the arranging of the onion, garlic, peppers, tomatoes, and carrots in one colorful array, the kidney and cannellini beans in bowls beside the vegetables, the chopped bacon next to it, and the generous glass of red wine waiting patiently for its invitation to the medley.

I fetch this and that but think about Mama's words. What could ever come between my sister and me? My insides *feel like dough before it is pasta—*flour and eggs—messy, uncomely, broken.

THERE IS ONLY NATURE'S VITALITY TODAY, a chapter from the book, *Heidi.* Brilliant grass, soft as layers of silk, gentle kisses of sunlight on our faces, golden chamomile flowers, and wild pansies of the mountaintop peeking their heads out of the earth. My sister, still gaining physical and mental health, leans on me a bit but breathes in the majesty. The spring zephyr presses Filomena's dress against her thin body, exposing a row of ribs like a child's raft of twigs. Her face is twice as thin as it once was, the healthy olive and rose tones washed away by the steady flood of grief. Even ravaged by grief, her beauty is striking.

"*Sorella*," she says, "thank you for all that you have done for me these many months."

"It was nothing." I squeeze her hand.

"You didn't give up on me, nor did you let me give up on myself. You kept Mama and Papa occupied, you nursed me back to health, and you took care of us all. "

But not Gregorio. "Filomena, may I ask you something?"

"*Si*, of course."

"Do you think you will ever love again?" And, of course, as soon as the words sail from the shore, I wish I could take them back. "*Mi dispiace. I'm sorry*," I offer.

She pauses, peers out at the dips of the mountain slopes, and sighs. "No, it's all right to ask. I am already twenty-four years old—an old maid."

"But Filomena," I protest, "you are more beautiful than the Medicis or Cleopatra!"

She gently laughs, a ghostly sound of happier times. "Cleopatra, eh? How do you know this, sister?"

"I have seen images in books."

"It's not so much how a woman looks on the outside as it is about her age. Do you realize that most women my age are not only married but have a few children? I waited for my Gregorio and do not regret it. I have loved once, and that is enough for me."

We continue to walk through spring's verdant awakening. Filomena seems to be coming alive with each step.

"Do you think I will ever love like you loved Gregorio?" I am thinking of Antonio Salerno and how I feel about him—and how my betrothal will be announced next year.

She kneels in front of me. "There are many kinds of love, Arabella. You will know love, *mia sorella*. Have no doubt; you will know love."

"But I know love now. There is your love and Mama's and Papa's, zios and our brothers. But will I know the kind of love you and Gregorio had?"

"May you be that blessed, sister." She smiles, but I detect sadness hiding in its curves.

We walk silently to the place where our feast will be. We pass *signorini* carrying thickly woven baskets filled with mozzarella wrapped in fern leaves. The clanging of goats' bells chimes their own mountain melody. This celebration is for Papa's successful businesses here in Paola with the Basillios and Spognas, the coffee business in Rio de Janeiro, my brothers' return after two years away, and our new family member, Sofia. Unspoken, yet invisibly wrapped in the linens is gratitude for our spared lives. The Basillio family (sans their oldest boy who fell to the disease) and the Spognas (who lost two family members) will join us too.

Mama hands me some linen napkins to fold and warns me, "Arabella, you are a hostess today. We all are."

"*Si*, Mama."

"Remember to be sweet, kind, and thoughtful."

"*Si*, Mama. I will do my best to be like you."

When the Basillios arrive, five-year-old Susanna Basillio jumps from the wagon to chase the goats across the meadow. The unmarried son, Felipe, closest to Filomena's age, tries his hand at urbanity, but Filomena follows the little girl. Aldo Basillio exits the buggy without a smile. He just stands there observing the scene. He looks oddly like a little old man in a boy's body. *Is he just going to stand there all day?*

Mama lifts her eyebrow at me. Right. I'm the hostess.

"*Ciao*, Aldo."

"*Ciao*."

How was the ride up?

"Long."

Does he speak any more than one word at a time?

Silence.

"Would you like some *acqua con gasosa* to quench your thirst?"

"No. The fizz of the water aggravates my stomach."

Perhaps he needs a dose of my gripe water.

"Oh, *mi dispiace.*"

More awkward silence.

"Well then, how about some cold mountain water with *limone? Lemon water* doesn't bother your stomach, does it?"

"That is fine."

I thank goodness for something to do other than trying to make conversation with Aldo Basillio. I glance over at the adults who seem so at ease with themselves. I think of Antonio and wonder why it is so easy to be with him. I carry the water over to Aldo, and he thanks me with a nod of his head.

"What a beautiful day for a celebration, don't you think?" I ask.

"We could be working."

"But isn't it good to give thanks with a feast?"

"Work is what makes us strong and puts food on the table."

"But it's such a pretty place for our *scampagna.*"

Silence. Squinted, narrowed eyes. "Fancy *picnics* don't suit me." He nods and strolls away.

I hear jubilant shouting and see my brothers pull up in their buggy. Forgetting my ladylike manners, I sprint over to them and exuberantly embrace them. Out of the corner of my eye, I see Aldo frowning. I am momentarily offended but realize he means little to me. Besides, I am more absorbed in the brotherly love that I have been craving. There is a lot of commotion, handshaking, and hugging. I barely notice the other man stepping down out of the carriage.

He is a roguish, handsome man of a stocky, muscular build. His confident manner displays a comfortable ease of being in his own rich, olive-toned skin. The healer in me notes the way he tries to hide the aggravated limp on his left side. His black hair, shiny as a polished onyx, are ocean waves, his eyes merry and mocking at the same time. His teeth, which he is showing through a wide, perfect smile, are the whitest I have ever seen, white as a dove's feather. When he turns his attention to me and boldly stares through my physical being into my very soul, I feel like the man has seen my insides. With a light upper flick of the eyebrow, he is both unsettling and charming.

I hear a whispered, inner voice. *Watch out for this one; he's dangerous.* A glow from my angel emerges, and I find the momentary courage to look him directly in the eye but immediately turn away, discombobulated as strewn shells on the seashore.

Octavio introduces him as Luigi Compretta, an Italian friend who works with them at Mandarino Coffee in Brazil. Luigi kisses my hand. I flinch, my stomach issuing a warning of unease. He laughs as he pulls my cheek, sing-songing, "Ah, *bella ragazza*," winking unabashedly.

I may be a beautiful young woman, and you may be an outwardly handsome man, but something tells me you are not beautiful on the inside. Just then, the most sophisticated woman I have ever laid eyes upon steps down from the carriage. It is Sofia, Octavio's wife. We are immediately enchanted by her sophistication and beauty. Marco inquiries about the whereabouts of Filomena.

As if on cue, Filomena comes from the meadow. She smiles at her brothers, sees Luigi, and blushes under the spell of his gaze. It brings a rosy hue to her pale skin that I haven't seen since before Gregorio passed away. Introductions are made. Luigi has not taken his eyes off Filomena.

"Oh, *papiagetti*. How *pleased I am to at last meet* the woman I have heard so much about—the alluring Filomena," he oozes.

My sister thanks him, still red-faced, not meeting his piercing gaze. She says she is pleased to meet his acquaintance.

He continues, "The pleasure is all mine; I assure you."

He makes the cordial response sound improper. Perhaps it's the smooth timbre of his voice or that hungry look in his coal-black eyes.

"You are too kind," she answers taking my hand and walking over to where the other women have begun laying out dishes of pasta with artichoke hearts, pecorino, and roasted red peppers, Asiago, fontina, mozzarella, slices of oranges, early melons, and Signora Basillio's thick, spongy breads.

We gather around the spread, and Papa leads us in saying grace. Zio's wine is poured, and Octavio lifts his glass. "To *famiglia*, friends, to health," and then he pauses and looks at Sofia. "To new life."

We chink the glasses like fairy bells and reply, "*Salute!*"

I glimpse a lingering glance between Luigi and Filomena before she turns away. I wonder how many women have fallen into the endless pools of his dark eyes. Filomena has been hiding her heart in the cave of sorrow these past months, so the attention of such a man might be inviting. Ah, there goes that imagination of mine! Luigi lives and works in Brazil. He is nothing like Gregorio. *Mia sorella* would never fall for a man like this.

"*Bravissima! Very, very good!* To the fabulous food and the spectacular *donne* who prepared it!" The *women* smile, taking in his compliment. Luigi turns his gaze unabashedly toward Filomena." With a foxlike grin on his animated face, he begins a colloquy of Brazilian fare, "In Brazil, we eat empanadas, little pies, stuffed with all manner of meats and vegetables—even pumpkin. Their bread is called *pao de queijo* or *cheese bread*, nothing as delicious as this," he claims. "And sometimes they fry small balls of fish, peas, and onions called *acaraje*."

"Sofia has tried to train our cook in the ways of Italian cooking," Octavio offers matter-of-factly, as her family is from Reggio di Calabria. She knows our *mezzogiorno* ways."

Sofia smiles. She is demure, lovely, the epitome of a lady. I sit up a little straighter, attempting to embody the traits of a proper woman. I may be able to imitate it for a while, but it would be more like an actress playing a role.

"Reggio di Calabria?" Mama smiles. "Why that is a lovely city, is it not?"

Sofia nods her head. "*Si, signora.*"

That is all. Two words with a smile. Is that what women should be?

More conversation ensues about Reggio di Calabria, about Paola and Brazil, but my mind is wandering through the fields of female possibilities. I vaguely hear Mama's voice drifting in and out of my reverie as she expertly draws the Basillios and the Spognas into the conversation. How does she know how to do that?

I snap back to attention when I hear Papa asking Marco about the coffee business. Octavio and Luigi exchange a furtive glance. Marco clears his throat. Too loud and too fast, I blurt out, "Please tell me about the music of the Brazilians."

There is a momentary pause. Marco winks at me and nods. "Of course! The Brazilians love music as much as the Italians," he begins. "The folk songs tell the story of their great loves and their great losses but mostly the sorrows of their poverty-stricken lives."

Now Luigi turns on the charm like the full moon in a starless sky. "Signora Basillio, I'd like to compose a song of your delicious *pasta!*"

"*Prego.*" She blushes. "It is *my pleasure.*"

"And your daughters' beauty? Obviously begotten from her mama."

Flattery and flirtation, marone! Disgusting! But everyone seems to be enjoying his praise, so I quiet the critic within me.

"And Giuseppe and Aldo," he continues, "strength and determination are sculpted into your face and muscles."

Giuseppe nods. Aldo frowns. *At least he is not falling for it. I will give Aldo that.*

Now Luigi turns to me. "What a fine husband Aldo will be for you, eh Arabella? A brilliant match indeed!"

There is a group intake of breath, quick, surprised, like a body's reaction to the frigid air. Luigi observes the stunned faces and bursts into deep-bellied laughter.

"Oh, *mi scusi,*" he apologizes but he seems to be enjoying this, as fodder for his pleasure. "*Excuse me!* I do believe I just let the marriage cat out of the bag!" He lifts his glass. "To Aldo and Arabella."

There is a faint chink of a glass or two, but it is not robust as such a toast should be. Filomena and Mama are boring holes into my face. I can feel it. I can see them, but I cannot move, let alone form words with sound. I look at the deadpan face of Aldo Basillio—he knows too! A heavy fog of betrayal descends upon my family. My eyes find my sister's. I can clearly see that she has known all along! Her guilty expression sends me over the edge. I hate her. I hate them all.

Disgust fuels my vocal cords. "Will you excuse me?" I ask, barely controlling my rage. I stand, letting the napkin drop at will. I hope it lands in the blood-red wine—that'd make a perfect metaphor for tainted innocence.

I walk toward the woodland then sprint as fast as I can, a thousand chaotic thoughts banging against each other like molecules in a test tube. Each family member claimed my future would be fine! *Ha! what a lie. How could they do this to me?* With a sneer, I answer myself. *Because you are a female, and your duty is to the family.* Forget that it's 1915! What is written on the pages of what has been will be written on the pages of what will be. A girl does this for her family. Period. But, *Dio mio*, Aldo Basillio? Could there be a more humorless boy?

Filomena is calling to me from the other side of the wood, and though I hear the pleading in her voice, I ignore her. The bile of deceit rises, foreign and bitter. I've waited for Filomena to be well again, and now that she is, I no longer wish to be in her presence.

Marco appears—a genie out of thin air. He opens his arms to me. I gladly enter the circle of his compassionate embrace. "*Povresina,*" he whispers as he strokes my hair. "*Mi dispiace.*"

"I am a *poor, sad thing* if I am made to marry that emotionless boy who acts like a *vecchio babbo*! No, I take that back. An *old grandpa* has more spunk than he does!"

"I am truly sorry."

I don't understand why I'm not angry with Marco. Have I already become accustomed to the fact that a man is not bound by the same emotional standards as a woman? Or is it that there is no doubt he empathizes with me?

Mama appears through the wood with an aggrieved Filomena at her side. Mama pulls me from Marco's safe harbor.

"Arabella," she begins, all business. "You are a young woman now, a year from our announcement of your wedding. Everything that happens is for *la famiglia*—everything. Decisions are made, and one abides by them—for the family's sake. I am sorry you learned of it this way, but you will not embarrass this family today or any day. Do you understand me, *capisce*?"

"No, *non-capito, I do not understand*! Not embarrass *you*?" I am incredulous. "What about how this family has embarrassed me?"

And then Mama does something she has never done before, nor ever done since. She releases her emotions as swiftly as a hummingbird in one stinging slap across my face. "You will watch your tongue! Compose yourself and return to our celebration with an attitude of decorum," she orders before abruptly turning and marching off, taking Marco with her.

I try to understand her reaction, but it's too much to sort out, like a complex mathematical equation I must break up into smaller pieces to comprehend.

Filomena kneels in front of me and tries to take my hands in hers. I pull away sharply. "Leave me alone." I spit the words at her venomously. "I don't want to talk to you now—maybe never!"

"Arabella, please, you don't mean that. You are angry and have every right . . ."

"I asked you. I begged you to tell me what you knew of my betrothal. You lied to me. *You, mia sorella*, you lied to me." I can barely breathe as the full weight of those words crushes me from the inside out.

"I know I should have told you everything, but Mama and Papa forbid me. I was torn as to what was right, but I swore an oath to them . . ."

"What was *right* was telling me the truth, but now I see you are incapable of it." I straighten my skirt, clear my throat, and imitating calm, I ask her to leave me alone. Then I simply walk away. It's all bravado, but apparently, my act is successful. She stays behind as I put one foot in front of the other, finding my way back to the feast. As I join the others, all eyes are on me. I continue my act, throwing my shoulders back, willing a smile to arise on my face. "*Mi scusi*," I say to Sofia as I wiggle in next to her. "*Per favore*, Papa, pass the *burra*."

I want him to look me in the eye as he passes me the *butter*. He does so momentarily and nods his head—my welcome to the world of adulthood. So, this is what I will be asked to do as an adult: stand at the cliff's edge . . . and jump.

I'VE CROSSED SOME VAGUE, invisible line between childhood and adulthood. I am trying to bear the weight of my familial obligation to marry Aldo Basillio. Therefore, I do not cry aloud, protest, or skip out on studies, the rosary, or filial duties. My silent grief is a wormhole, devouring any interest in the future, which will be devoid of the presence of my sister. I cannot forgive her; it is too much to reconcile her betrayal.

I think of the promise Mama asked me to make about never allowing anything to come between my sister and me. She must have known that something like this could break our bond. And as if all this pain was not enough to bear, Luigi Compretta has found every possible opportunity to be at Papa's side these past weeks. He has restructured things at the flour mill, and Papa is delighted. I think he is delighting Filomena as well. With a roll of my eyes, I consider what a perfectly deceitful pair they will make.

I seek out Marco in the study. "Brother, may I speak with you?"

"Of course, Arabella. I'm glad you've sought me out. I have noticed you are unusually quiet when we are all together."

I lift an eyebrow.

"I understand," he answers solemnly.

"Do you? I mean, how could you? You are a man."

"That's true, of course, but I think I can imagine how it is to be you."

"Mmm." I am not certain this is entirely possible, but at least he's compassionate.

"What do you want to discuss, Arabella?"

I sigh. "I'm having difficulty accepting the differences in the lives of men and women, especially in this time of change."

"Men are free, women are not?"

"Exactly! How can this be?"

"Sweeping social changes have not made their way to Paola quite yet."

"I'm certain of that!"

He adds, "I'm finding there are some injustices I can fight for, some I cannot. I realize I may spend my entire life in pursuit of change that may or may not occur."

I think of Marco's letter to Gregorio. "I suppose it all depends on the type of battle, *si?*"

"*Si.*"

Like his risk to write for *Terre Livre*.

"Marco, I know you're leaving Mandarino Brothers Coffee," I share.

"I see. How long have you known?"

"Gregorio read me your letter." I have to swallow twice to get his name out.

"I wish I could have told you myself, but since we've returned it is, well, unsettling. I didn't want to add to your burden."

"I'm more concerned about you. It seems a dangerous undertaking."

"Perhaps, but it is just what we are speaking of—social injustice, change."

"I admire you but worry for your safety." I let out a balloon full of air and slump my shoulders. "Marco, this brings me back to the confusion over why men can pursue their passions, but most females are trapped."

"There is no reasoning that makes sense. And not every man is free in his pursuits. But overall, men have set the rules for the way the world is run."

"And they don't want it to change because they like things the way they are. "

"Precisely."

"But people throughout history have joined together and forced change." I peer at the stories and poetry that embrace me in this room. "Look what the Suffragettes have achieved during their fight! Women's right to vote is spreading."

"*Brava*, Arabella. Those women have banded together for decades in this fight. Here, it's just the two of us fighting to overthrow the Mandarino regime!"

"Doesn't a movement always begin with one or two who hatch an idea?"

He nods.

Gold light flickers in my eyes. "Marco, I have an idea! I know what we can do." I'm so excited I think my skin will pop off my bones. "You can take me with you to Brazil."

He looks like a stunned fly swat by a linen towel. "No, no, Arabella. That is not a solution. Brazil is fraught with uncertainty; war is at hand. In fact, my writing could put you in harm's way."

"Marco, this *is* a good idea! We can make it work." I begin pacing, and the idea machine whirs to attention. "You could purchase a ticket for me on the boat but not tell anyone. Even if they found me aboard, I would be with you, so . . ."

"No, Arabella. I will be consumed with my work, with very little income to care even for myself and . . ."

I try to interrupt, but he holds up his hand.

"Let me finish, please. Rio is a monstrous city like Rome. You don't know the language or have a place to live. There is unrest and uncertainty—a combustible combination. Unless you'll stay with Octavio and Sofia on the plantation."

"Wouldn't that be a lot like living with another version of Mama and Papa?"

"I suppose," he concurs. "But you would be away from Paola and your betrothed."

"I can find work with the local healer and take a room with her. I just feel a certainty about it."

A light glow emanates just behind his left shoulder.

Marco fixes his eyes on mine. I don't dare flinch, breathe, blink.

I choose my words and tone carefully before delivering them with unrelenting conviction. "Marco, I am determined not to marry that humorless boy."

He examines my face carefully, nods, and leaves the room. I'm not sure what that means, but I make the determination to let it be, for now.

LATER, I HEAR MARCO AND PAPA conversing in the garden. I sneak behind the door of the larder to eavesdrop.

"Marco, I don't accept this line of thinking, and I am quite certain you have not given this proper thought."

"Believe me, Papa. Leaving Mandarino Brothers Coffee is something I have deliberated long and hard about."

"But *figlio*, think of the name itself: Mandarino *Brothers* . . ."

"Papa, you and I know a business name is just a name."

"'Just a name'?" Papa's voice rises. "It is *our family name*."

"Yes, Papa. I just meant the word *brothers* . . ."

"Brothers, mother, father, sisters—we *all* are part of that name."

"*Si*, Papa, I—"

"*Tutti, all* of us together create success."

"But success means making a difference in this unequal world."

"*Basta!* 'Unequal world'? We treat our workers well, offer a good product. Employing people is 'making a difference. You disrespect me by speaking otherwise."

"Please, Papa. I mean no disrespect. I just cannot be a part of it anymore. Please try to understand that I must live by my own accord."

I can feel the volcano's eruption before it spews from the center. This is where the heat of two opposing elements collides. I want to do something to stop it, but there are no tools in my arsenal that can prevent the explosion.

"Go then," a steel-voiced Papa responds. "Go to your own life, *vai.* Go. But know this: you go without my blessing, without our good name, and without the resources of this family."

I can feel Marco's ground shifting.

Then Papa offers the final punch. "And If you leave, *never* come back."

I don't know how my brother finds his voice. I am holding my breath, my throat, sawdust.

"Papa, *per favore, please.* I can understand you are angry and disappointed, but surely you don't mean to disown me."

The response is booming silence before my father's shoes slap the garden path.

I have never known my father enraged beyond forgiveness. I have no footing, like flailing in deep, churning waters. How could he be so unforgiving to his own blood? It's simply unthinkable! Only a man would react so unpardonably. But as soon as those words find form, something vibrates within me, a jangling of discordant chimes. When the noise fades, I hear an inner voice. *You recognize unforgiving words because you are guilty of the same crime of the heart. It is not limited to gender. Think about it . . ..*

And I do. In my bright, yellow bedroom, much too cheery for my mindset, I recall rejecting Filomena with anger that is as fierce and unforgiving as Papa's. *Mary, Mother of God, I am doing to Filomena what Papa is doing to Marco!* I'm plunged in the shock of a mountain stream in March, awakening every nerve ending that causes the ice around my heart to shiver and moan.

But not quite crack. These are complicated issues, layered with complexity I am unequipped for. But I try: it is obvious that I need to speak to Filomena, but I do not know *how* to do this—how to start, what to say. Time spent stewing in a state of wounded fury makes the distance back to my sister far. Do I ask for forgiveness? And for what? My words? Behavior? What about her? What if she isn't seeking atonement for her transgressions? What if she doesn't want to forgive me? Then what? Of this, I am certain, there'll be a deeper rut to house the pain. And what of the lingering echo of truth that clings like a barnacle to my heart? *My sister betrayed me.* How does one reconcile all this emotional damage? Just because you admit you have been unforgiving does not mean that you can forgive.

Gregorio taught me about how the meanings of words vary in different languages. The ancient Egyptians defined forgiveness as returning to the state of being *before* the giving of the injury, anger, or blame. Are people truly capable of this?

Restless, I leave my room. There are voices in the kitchen—Mama, Marco, Filomena.

Mama says, "*Qual `e il problema figlio?*"

Marco replies, "*The problem is your son* is going away Mama, back to Brazil and my life there."

"You mean you are returning to the Mandarino Brothers Coffee, *si?*"

" No, Mama. I am going to write for the anarchist newspaper in Rio."

Pregnant pause

"Please forgive me Mama, but Papa has forbidden me ever to return."

Filomena says, "Marco, he is just upset. Give him a day or two, and he will come around."

"I love you all," Marco says, "but there is no turning back now. I leave in the morning."

The door creaks, holds its breath, exhales, clicking shut.

The wailing, beating, flailing begins as Mama incants her son's name over and over.

I put my hands over my ears. I cannot bear this. Slipping out to the garden, I steal a surreptitious glance into the kitchen window. Mama and Filomena are slapping their chests and arms. My sister catches my eye, but I quickly turn away and scurry out the back gate and onto the *lungomare* path in search of Marco. He's not going to leave me here.

I DIDN'T EXPECT THE SWELLED wetness of wood, the salt embedded in grooves, and the dankness coated on the single window of this tiny cabin. I loathe the scratching of critters in the walls and under the hull, the sputtering snore emanating from the cabin next to mine, and the endless swaying that should feel like being rocked in a cradle but instead tosses your innards to and fro. I want to grab my limbs and organs in a stronghold, perhaps to steady the boat's tossing as well as comfort myself. I open my small valise clumsily packed for a hasty escape: a few precious books and my herbal notebooks, fountain pen, linen bundles filled with herbs, tincture vials and salves, a pair of boots, a skirt, blouse, sweater, Antonio's Madonna carving, and some paper for writing letters.

I owe Antonio and Signora Ruffino a letter. But my family? No. They received a goodbye note. No flowery phrases or profound explanations. I am certain they can figure the why of my departure and the repercussions of their actions for themselves.

A light rap on my door. "Arabella, are you awake?" a whispered inquiry.

"*Si.*" I open the door, a long groan from tired hinges.

"Arabella, how are you faring down here? "

"I'm well. *Grazie*."

"I apologize for this cabin so far away from mine, but it's all I could secure on such short notice. You are keeping this door locked, *si?*"

"Yes, of course. It's fine, Marco."

He sighs. "I do worry, Arabella. I am not convinced this was the best recourse."

"I assure you; it is." My voice is strong, convincing.

"Time will tell," he answers. "Oh, I almost forgot. I brought you something." He hands me some of Pina's *crispinis* and a chunk of Asiago.

"*Grazie!*"

"And this."

A petite book of tooled leather flowers abundantly filled with blank pages. I look at him inquisitively.

"I thought you might want to record your reflections and observations."

"It is beautiful, Marco. Thank you."

I hope he doesn't mistake my tears for sorrow. It is only gratitude for him and this opportunity that I feel.

THE BUGGY RIDE FROM THE SHIP down Avenida Central is a fairy tale of white stone buildings topped with spires, spirals, and crowns. The street is wide, an invitation for those traveling on foot and in horse-drawn carts to pass along tree-lined pathways. Elegant lampposts mark the walkway every few meters, and I long to view them in the evening hours when they will light up like captured moonlight. Aromas of garlic and onion, paprika, and cumin fill the air. Men in brimmed hats and starched white shirts move quickly from place to place. Women in fashionable dresses gaze longingly in shop windows at the faceted gemstone jewels. I look up at one of the Paris-inspired hotels just in time to see a stately woman on a magnificent balcony, her white scarf blowing behind her, her dress sweeping the air around her feet. I follow her gaze out over to Guanabara Bay, hugging the city like a nonna's embrace. Is she praying to the Christ Redeemer statue on top of Corcovado Hill?

Sofia and Octavio won't be back for a few days, so we will stay at the *fazenda* or *coffee plantation* where the staff still believe Marco lives. We'll apologize for the telegram that did not arrive alerting them of our arrival. Of course, there was no such document. We are cartographers of a new land called Deception. It is unsettling, but we must do whatever we have to subsist.

Once we've passed through the busy city, the landscape turns lush shades of the tropics: long, leafy greens from lime to olive hover like umbrellas, bushes boast sprays of orange, red, and lemon-yellow flowers, palm fronds tip their hats in greeting.

The driver is talking to Marco, but I can barely pick up a stray word or two. I open my poetry book to study, but the lull of the afternoon sun and the rhythm of the wheels make me drowsy. I fall into an uneven state somewhere between sleep and awake. When I feel the cart careen around a hilly bend, I startle alert. The horses must know they are close to home because they've picked up the pace considerably along this tunnel of mature banana trees that lead to the plantation's center. The workers dressed in white from their heads to their feet step out of the rows of bushy coffee shrubs. Men and women weathered by years in the burning sun incline their hats. Younger adults, closer to my age, in billowy sack-like dresses and baggy linen pants, bow their heads slightly in greeting and respect. They are a stunning blend of caramel and espresso, shiny night-hue hair, and penetrating eyes. They are beautiful, earthy, elegant in the way they hold their heads upon their shoulders. They merge back into the grove, as if dissolving into a sea of green.

Ahead, palm trees form two lines of elegant soldiers that lead up to the *fazenda*. The plantation home is a shade of reddish-pink that feels as cool as watermelon and fits so perfectly—like a giant fruit popped up from the gently sloping hills into this mini valley. There are three levels marked by gleaming rows of windows under a slanted, tiled roof. Flowering vines grip the walls, and flourishing flowerpots flank the entrance.

Marisa, the house manager, steps out and peers in our direction. When she sees Marco, a startled look crosses her face. She wipes her hands on her apron, scurries back into the house, and returns moments later with two others.

"*Signore*, we didn't know you were coming! Please forgive us, but we did not prepare for your arrival."

"Apparently, our telegram did not make it." He smiles. "But please, Marisa, there is no need for concern. We mostly need sleep and maybe a plate of cheese and mangos."

She nods and looks my way.

"Allow me to present my sister, Arabella Mandarino."

Her eyes widen, and a smile blooms on her face. "*Papiagetti,* "she offers.

Her enthusiasm is a charming welcome that oddly brings on a wave of homesickness.

"*O prazer meu,*" *The pleasure is mine,* "I respond in what I am hoping is passable Portuguese.

Her smile grows at my attempt to speak her language. Marisa introduces Salvo and Jarin, and they both nod in unison. Jarin takes the reigns of the horses, and Salvo reaches for our valises. Our driver walks around to the side of the house where I imagine the door to the kitchen is. We follow Marisa toward the front entrance.

Cheerful yellow-gold puff flowers greet us. Later, I learn they are Yellow Stifftia. My eyes follow an urgent, vibrating hum, and I am nearly swept off my feet by a blue sapphire hummingbird zeroing in on the flowers. I have never seen that color on a bird! Nature will offer many wonders here.

The front foyer is a gleaming array of marble columns and floor tiles from obsidian to dove gray and salmon to pale pink. Statues of women in graceful dance poses balance on pedestals, their palms reaching up to catch the dripping light from the crystal chandelier. Such opulence seems out of place in the jungle, but nonetheless, it's tastefully appointed. I am guessing the design is entirely Sofia's. It looks as sophisticated as she is. There'll be time to view the other furnishings and rooms later, but for now, I seek a bed, a pillow, and uninterrupted sleep.

Utterly exhausted, I settle into a room papered in pale rose and sky-blue hydrangeas. It's not just the physical strain of the journey—it's the emotional realization that I have successfully fled home—a fact that is a churning sea of contradictions of freedom, destiny, and commitment. Every limb, every muscle, every tissue begins to understand the repercussions of my actions, and suddenly, I can barely breathe beneath the weight of my actions. Panic squeezes my lungs, closing the door to breath.

What have I done? In my haste to escape, perhaps to punish, to gain control of my own destiny, I have abandoned what I know, *who* I know (breaking their hearts in the process), landing completely unprepared in a foreign land. My actions were not thoughtful or logical. I just ran. But staying would have been a choice too—one that I was not willing to accept. The gray shades of adulthood cover me like an itchy blanket. I add a drop of belladonna tea to a spoonful of my nerve tonic. *Sleep,* I beg, *tear me from the ravages of a confused mind.*

DAYS ROLL ONE INTO ONE ANOTHER as I gain lay of the land. A telegram from Paola arrives, frantic in its tone, imploring me to return home. Marco sends one back stating only that we have arrived safely and that I am at the *fazenda*. Nothing more.

I take long, languid strolls around the plantation with my journal, sketching plants and making notes of some I have seen in the medicinal dictionary in Sofia and Octavio's library. Marco is gone most hours of the days, putting the final touches on his life beyond the walls of the Mandarino Brothers Coffee business. He has made inquiries for me with a local herbalist, but no response has come yet.

"Marco, do you think there will be somewhere else for me to stay?"

His hands pass nervously through ebony waves of hair. "I don't know, Arabella. I am hopeful, but it might take some time. At least you have a place here." Quickly, he adds, "Just until another opportunity avails itself."

The last thing I want to do is burden him. "I will be fine here. "

"Thank you for saying that. I'm well aware it's not ideal." He sighs. "I leave in the morning to begin my work at *Terra Livre*." He pauses, his eyes meeting mine. "I will get word to you soon. You understand I cannot be here when Octavio returns, *si?*"

Of course, I do. He needs to be free and has taken the necessary steps to alter his life. Unlike me, he has planned this change, given it much thought and effort.

"Marco, of course, I understand! Don't worry about me." I smile my brightest smile and hope he doesn't hear the lie. "This change of scenery alone was worth it all. Thank you, brother."

Marco's departure the following day leaves me alone in a big house in the middle of the jungle with strangers. I was stoic and insistent that being here to study the language was the best course of action for me. I want him to trust my maturity and resolve. I made this decision to be here; the burden is not on him. I attempt to embrace the freedom of being a young woman on her own, but I am simultaneously terrorized by what is going to happen to me, a young woman on her own—sans resources. I fully understand I must secure work and housing. My hope is that I can live as an apprentice with the herbalist. Doubt floods me. Why would someone teach a foreigner his/her herbal knowledge? And, *Dio mio, my God* how will I communicate effectively?

Marisa finds me and pantomimes eating food and then slowly, loudly, as if I am deaf, speaks the accompanying words in Portuguese. I take a breath, realizing that life is full of risks both small and large. I clear my throat and state, "*Sim obrigado. Eu estou com fome. Yes, thank you. I am hungry.*"

She lifts her left eyebrow and responds, "*Brava*, Arabella. *Bom para voce. Good for you.*"

OCTAVIO IS APPARENTLY UNABLE TO engage in simple, polite conversation. He explodes. "Arabella, do you have any idea what you have put Mama and Papa through? Not to mention your sister? They are all sick with worry."

And guilt?

I say nothing. Sofia is parked in a white fan chair in the atrium. I sit in the one opposite her.

Octavio looms over me. "This is unacceptable behavior, even for you!"

That comment riles me (as intended), but I refuse to engage in a word war.

"You are going home!" he shouts.

"I am not." I look over at Sofia who is perfectly still, her back straight, her shoulders down. I copy her posture. "I have come here to learn from an herbalist . . ."

"Nonsense!" he spits. "You came here to avoid your familial duty. It is reprehensible behavior assisted by your irresponsible brother."

I lick my lips and attempt to steady my breathing, but adrenaline has taken hold. "This was entirely my decision," I state. I'm grateful to be sitting. If I were standing, my knees would buckle. "I will be working with the local herbalist," I lie.

"You will do no such thing. This is not Paola. These people are not the Ruffinos or other families we know."

"Then, we will get to know them."

His voice is tight as a stretched wire. "Arabella, you are a child who knows nothing."

"Then I will become a woman who knows everything."

"It is a wild, untamed place, Arabella. We hear talk of Brazil threatening to enter the war. Did you know that Italy has joined the Triple Entente? Italy is at war now." He pauses and looks at Sofia, "I do feel better knowing that Luigi will remain with my family in Paola."

That bit of news shocks me but somehow it makes sense. "I am not afraid. With the world at war, no place is safe, not even Paola. I am staying with or without your support." I am doubly flabbergasted. Italy has joined the war? I don't know what's worse: Luigi remaining in Paola or Italy in the war.

Sofia stands. "If you are committed to being here, I have contacts at the local hospital that could certainly use a volunteer." She lifts her chin to her husband, and her eyes implore him to call a truce.

"Come," she reaches for my hand. "I want to show you my special Brazilian garden."

I follow Sofia out through the atrium door, greeted by the whistle and gong of the many windchimes. The sound settles my nerves. Some are carved from the kapok tree, perhaps some from teak; long and medium-long tubes beckon the wind to sing. I have only been around the edge of this exclusive garden, which seems to demand a personal invitation. Now, wandering amid white fairy bells and eggplant purple cups, spotted and dotted clusters of star flowers, canary yellow orchids, upside down puffs of fuchsia balls, dripping fingers of coral, tapers of lavender and gold, unusual and organic shapes that resemble clumps of paint left on an artist's palette, it feels as if I'm inside a well-executed painting. I pause to inhale its beauty and its calm.

Sophia smiles. How wise she was to bring me here. Two gentlemen who are pruning bid Sofia good day, and she slightly bows her head to them, *cordialmente, cordially* but little more. She is the queen of this castle, not their friend.

She gestures to the deep lavender *cattleya labiata* or *corsage orchid*, stating that is the national flower of Brazil. She bends to inhale the scent of the triple pikake. It's reminiscent of a potent rose; in fact, she says it's used in perfumes and teas.

As we stroll, she takes my hand. "Arabella, it wasn't that long ago that I was young and spoken for, like you."

"Were you betrothed to someone other than my brother?"

"Yes, to a much older man my father met during his business trips to Brazil. The two families were to merge with our marriage."

Sounds familiar. "But you didn't marry him."

"No, there was an intervention of sorts."

"What do you mean?"

She performs the sign of the cross. "God rest his soul, Guilherme passed away on our wedding night."

My hand flies to my mouth. "Oh, I, uh-" What does one say in a situation like this?

"It was God's will. You see, Arabella, I know about familial duties."

"Yes, but you were, um, spared. And then you married Octavio; that is very different from my situation."

"Again, God's will." She pauses. "Arabella, you would benefit from praying the rosary and reading scripture. We will do it together, *si?* Surrendering is not always easy, but God is there to assist us if we do our part."

I have many ideas swirling about, but I do not want to alienate her. I need an ally.

"We will talk again later." She reaches into her dress sleeve and pulls out an envelope with my name on it. I recognize my sister's handwriting immediately. A flood of emotion storms in. "Arabella, the Bible reminds us, 'Be kind to one another, tenderhearted, forgiving one another as God in Christ forgave you. Ephesians 4:32.'" She looks deeply into my eyes—my very soul, it seems, before taking her leave.

I plop down on the bench tucked beneath a mango tree. *Forgiveness: it's a complicated concept.*

I open the envelope, preparing for a long lament, but there is but one page with very few sentences.

1915, Giugno

Cara Arabella,

> *I know that you feel betrayed by me, your sorella, and I ache for the pain I have caused you. I implore you to allow me to own my complicity in keeping the truth from you. It will be my eternal burden to carry the hurt I have caused you within my own heart for all my days here and in the afterlife.*

> *I do not dare ask your forgiveness, only to beg for mercy for Mama and Papa. Please send word to them. They suffer greatly from your absence. We all do. Italy has joined the war, and all the men and boys will soon be gone. Signora Ruffino has signed on to assist at the front. Nothing is the same, nor will it ever be.*

> *Whether it is the war or your absence, I feel it my duty to tell you that Antonio Salerno is now engaged to Talina Ubruzzo.*

Tua Sorella,
Filomena

Emotions mingle in a streaming river of sadness, regret, homesickness, love, pain, longing, confusion, and passion. I creep to my room to get my journal and fountain pen before making my way to the upper slope of the thick coffee trees to melt in the comfort of their limbs. How do I accept the idea of a world at war, a family broken, love lost, Antonio betrothed? No! I see us in the citrus grove and sitting idly on the *lungomare*. Antonio will no longer be my Antonio. Was he ever? We were childhood friends. This is a time of adulthood. Of insanity. Of war. What of my sister and my parents? Will they survive? *What am I doing here? What was I thinking?* I don't even attempt to wipe the flood of tears or my running nose as I sob for all that is wrong: unrequited love, injustice, inequality, fear, loss, impossibility. So much sorrow we wretched humans cause one another.

A rustling sound reveals an old woman no taller than a child of nine or ten. I try to regain my composure, but she seems uninterested in decorum. She points to my journal and says something I don't understand. I shrug my shoulders and shake my head. "*Eu nao entendo. I don't understand,*" I tell her.

She points again to my journal and lifts it with a nod. *Sim, yes,* I respond. With the fountain pen in hand and a blank page before her, she begins to sketch a plant, marking its leaves and stems, all the while, speaking in Portuguese. She seems to know I am a healer, and for the first time since I have been here, I both see and feel the light of my spirit angel around us both. This small woman closes her eyes and seems to be connecting with her too. After handing me back my journal and pen, she removes something from her dress pocket. It is the two different plants that she has sketched in my journal!

"*Obrigado, Thank you.*" I smile. The old woman rests her small, wrinkled hand on my arm and disappears into the coffee's green arms.

Like so many times in my life, I am saved again by nature and my insatiable appetite for learning. I head back to the *fazenda*'s study to find the books on Brazil's vegetation. My unexpected teacher has labeled one of them *achiote*, a bush with large, light red flowers used as a skin protectant.

She was patting my arm in greeting but also to show me *achiote* could be used for the skin. Brilliant! I recognize the other drawing as the mango tree. What I didn't know was the mango stem's resin is used to fight dysentery, and the bark, when cooked, is good for a baby's colic. Like days of old, I fall into the sheer power of new knowledge. I read and draw and imagine an array of new tinctures for my healing. Now, if there was one that could cure heartache and war, I'd fill the seas for all to drink.

DAYS BLEND INTO WEEKS. I write a letter to my family in Paola, a generic letter of sorts, as if I'm on holiday. I skirt emotional issues, promises, or apologies. When I write to Antonio, I don't bring up his engagement or my feelings about it. I want to send him off to war with tales of this faraway place, of the wild birds that screech in vivid, painted hues. He and the rest of the young men of Paola may already be called to war. *War*. My bones shiver at the word until my angel's light softly surrounds me. I wonder if there's a way to send her light to the battle front . . ..

Or to Marco who feels farther away than Cassiopeia. Octavio insists Marco has forsaken me (along with the rest of the family), but I do not believe that. Perhaps he just cannot get news to me, or perhaps someone has deceptively intercepted the communication? I'd like to get Marco a note, so I am observing Jarin and Salvo to see which of the two might surreptitiously deliver it to the *Terra Livre* headquarters for me.

In the meantime, I am stuck here under the watchful eyes of Sofia. Fortunately for me, her acquaintance at the hospital is out of the country. She has contacted someone else, but thankfully, they have not returned her communication. I want to learn from an herbalist.

Sofia and I have fallen into a routine of sorts: she calls me to pray the rosary each morning, and then we eat a light *"café de moua"* or breakfast of fresh papaya, mango, or avocado wedges and *pao de queijo*, small, baked cheese rolls. I am blissfully left on my own then, returning to the spot where my secret teacher baits my curiosity by leaving me a stem, flower, or drawing on bark. I take them back to the immense library and scour the books. Today, a breadfruit sits on a small, woven mat. It could be just a treat, but she is clever in sparking my appetite to investigate.

When Marisa sees the mat, she tells me it was made from the fibrous leaves of the breadfruit tree, recalling how her mother gave her breadfruit seeds to soothe stomach aches when she was a child. Later that day, a wooden bowl (perhaps carved from the breadfruit trunk) and filled with a paste waits for me. As I am writing in my journal, the old woman silently appears, carrying a small tool and a split breadfruit. Without so much as a greeting, she scoops the pulp of the fruit and whips it into a paste. Next, she takes my journal and draws an image of a body with boils and blisters. Breadfruit paste cures skin infections? *Eccellente, excellent!*

I'm just about to inquire in my best Portuguese who she is and where she lives when the scratch of wheels on the road sends her scampering into the trees. An elegant carriage pulls up to the house. Quickly, I scramble down the hill, sneaking in through the atrium door to eavesdrop. Men's voices emerge from Octavio's study down the hall.

"Good day, Octavio," a rich voice offers in Italian.

"Greetings, Riccardo. How are you faring?"

"I'm well, thank you. This war is good for business, my friend. The more they fight, the more they need my armaments. As long as my ships can traverse the waters, I am prospering."

"Good for you," Octavio responds.

"Grazie. Let's hope Germany will continue to respect the sea as neutral territory. "

"Let us hope so." There is a brief pause before Octavio continues. "And what brings you all the way out here today, Riccardo? Is there something I can help you with?"

"I am here in friendship to you."

Octavio is slow to respond. "It's my brother, isn't it?"

"Si. I am sorry, Octavio, but your brother's inflammatory writings are making powerful enemies."

Octavio sighs. "Please don't tell me he is interfering with your business."

"No, not yet. But he is playing with fire that cannot be extinguished. His writings accuse, name names, and report on activities that are none of his business."

"Dio mio. I have kept far away from that newspaper."

"I can understand that, my friend. As a courtesy to you, this will serve as his one and only warning to cease these writings."

I imagine Octavio straining to maintain his composure beneath the heaviness of embarrassment, anger, and fear.

His response is stoic, solid. "Thank you, Riccardo."

"I am sorry about this, but you know how important it is to protect the welfare of our businesses."

"Of course. Quite frankly, Riccardo, we are at a loss when it comes to Marco. I have warned him. My father has disowned him. He even brought my young sister here! Clearly, he is not thinking straight."

"I am sorry, Octavio. Truly, I am. Families can be a challenge."

"Indeed."

"How curious that he brought your sister here to Brazil."

"Si."

I hold my breath.

"I should be delighted to meet her."

"Of course. We shall send a dinner invitation soon. Thank you for the courtesy of your call, Riccardo."

I hear the rustling of fabric and feet, so I tiptoe out the way I came in. I peek from behind a vigorous, thick cascade of purple passionflower vines along the side of the house. Riccardo's driver places the temporary steps for Riccardo to climb aboard his sleek, black-roofed carriage.

"Arabella," I hear Octavio call to me.

I slowly count to ten before I round the corner to the front door. "Yes, brother?"

"Do you have a proper dress for dinner?"

"No, I don't. Why?"

He doesn't answer the question I already know the answer to. Instead, he announces, "Sofia will accompany you into the city to obtain some proper clothes." He dismisses me by walking away.

I returned from the city with an armload of lovely dresses but no news of my brother, Marco. I stole glances out the window of the opulent pink and gold salon on Avenida Rio Bianco in search of Marco. I searched for him as we promenaded along Avenida Central, but to my dismay, I did not see him. Newspaper vendors on these main streets either do not display or sell the *Terra Livre* openly. When a movement is shaking up what has always been, I suppose it must be done from back alleys and basements— an unnerving thought for Marco's safety.

Back at Sofia and Octavio's, it is entertainment time. I wear a scooped hem, an above-ankle gown of translucent purple layers from lavender to amethyst to violet. The low collar, short, billowy sleeves, and oversized pockets at my hip are outlined in soft ruffles. A cloth rose of pearl white is planted off-center, just below my collar bone. Beveled crystals circle it. In the evening's light, the total effect is that of a shimmery butterfly on a flower.

The clip-clop of horse hooves on the driveway announces Signore Riccardo's arrival. I am seated in the parlor, posed, poised, and prepared to be shown off like a doll. Because of my previous eavesdropping, I have some knowledge of this guest.

Signore Riccardo's face betrays his immediate admiration. I am reserved but cordial, indifferent to his charm. Sofia is anything but.

"Signore Riccardo, you must regale Arabella with your knowledge of Brazil's landscape."

"Would you like to hear about some of this country's wonders?"

"Si," I answer. Polite but unengaged.

For several minutes, he offers a vivid, verbal tour of the varied regions, highlands, waterways, and rainforests of Brazil. I listen because he is a good orator and this land sounds breathtaking, but I do not want anyone to mistake politeness for genuine interest.

"There is much to discover right in Rio de Janeiro," he adds. "For instance, you must allow me the pleasure of your company to Sugarloaf Mountain."

I don't respond but for a weak smile and incline of my head.

Sofia answers for me. "Oh, how delightful. Arabella, there is a cable car that takes you to the top to see Rio de Janeiro from a bird's eye view."

The evening follows a pattern of Sofia or Octavio parading my attributes before Signore Riccardo and the man responding attentively. What I'd really like to discuss is news of the war (and his part in it), but I am treading lightly, reigning in my tongue, lest it leads to a boat ride back to Paola.

Following the stuffed prosciutto, cannelloni di ricotta and spinach, and roasted lamb, the only Brazilian part of the meal, dessert, is served: passion fruit mousse and *quindim*, a yellow custard-like dessert of sweet coconut, butter, and sugar. Afterward, the men retire to the study for their cigars while Sofia and I wait in the atrium.

"He's incredibly handsome and accomplished," Sofia pitches.

"Yes."

"He's taken quite a liking to you."

Out of the boiling pot and into the fire. Does she not remember that I left Paola for precisely this reason? I will not be bartered to the highest bidder.

"Sofia, while a suitable husband is the dream of most women, it is not mine."

"But that is not your concern, Arabella. Your duty is to help your family grow in prosperity."

"Pardon me?" I manage, trying to keep calm. I thought she understood me because 'she too was once young like me.'

"No disrespect, my dear. You are lovely and intelligent with a good family name. If you do not want to marry into the Basillio family, you would serve everyone well by marrying an esteemed man such as Signore Riccardo."

"And my aspirations for healing?"

She nearly chuckles. "Oh, Arabella, once you are running a household, there is little time for such hobbies."

I stand, shaking from the inside out. "Please bid Signore Riccardo good night for me."

"Arabella, sit down," she hisses.

I hesitate for a moment but take my leave. The back of my dress chafes the smooth floor. I can still hear Sofia's seething breath as I pass the study. Disturbing words such as poison gas and grenades echo up the stairwell.

WEEKS HAVE TURNED TO MONTHS, but still, there is no word from Marco. My pleas to Octavio for news of our brother are answered with silence. I am worried sick. I can communicate fairly well in Portuguese now, and I ask Marisa if there has been any mail for me from Marco, but she looks away shaking her head no. I decide to use the only other resource I have. I draft a note to Signore Riccardo then slip it to Jarin who is going into the city for supplies. When I explain it is our secret, his eyes widen. I promise him payment soon (though, I am not certain how I will deliver).

Endless hours, I pace from the coffee learning slope, as I've named it, to the library to the gardens, and then I make the loop again. I cannot concentrate on anything. If Octavio finds out I've gone behind his back to contact Signore Riccardo, I will be immediately extricated. Everything rests on signore being so thoroughly enamored with me that he will not feed me to the giant. Finally, I hear the wagon pulling down the drive. I smooth my skirt and scurry to the outside kitchen door to meet up with Jarin. We are deep in conversation when Salvo notices us on his way to the stable. His eyes squint, but mine bore into his directly. *Don't you dare even think of speaking of this to anyone* I will them to express. Watching Sofia has been beneficial in several ways.

In my flowered room, I slip open the note:

Cara Arabella,

How lovely to receive your note. It will remain between us if you would do me the honor of accompanying me to Sugarloaf Mountain.

As for your brother, Marco, let it suffice to say he is well enough, for now. I will deliver a letter from him when we meet on Friday.

Best regards,
Riccardo

Blackmail! I must see Signore Riccardo on an outing to keep my inquiry a secret and receive word from Marco. With negotiations such as this, it's no wonder he's a successful businessman.

The next morning after breakfast and prayers, I prepare for my outing with signore. A knock on the door reveals a young man with not one, but two telegrams.

"Arabella, they are both for you," Marisa informs me, nearly as surprised as I am.

I open the first one. It is from Signora Ruffino imploring me to come home to care for the village, as she will be at the war's front. Paola has no one to rely on but me. The second one has my heart beating even faster than the first. It is from Mama. Papa has taken ill with painful bursitis and begs for only one person—Arabella. She beseeches me to return home, lest he should perish.

Papa sick? No! And the village stranded without anyone to carry them through wartime? I nearly buckle in the foyer. I'm looking rather shell-shocked when Sofia slowly removes the telegrams from my hand and reads them aloud. The effect is more devastating.

"Oh, my dear Arabella," she coos. "I am so sorry."

I break down, unleashing every stoic dam I have built over these months.

She holds me, and I let her envelop me.

The words tumble out, "I cannot bear it, Sofia. I will not have the blood of my village on my heart nor abandon Papa in his time of need."

"Then you must return to Paola," she answers.

My angel's light blinks.

SIGNORE RICCARDO COMES TO SAY goodbye and slides a note into my hand when no one is looking.

"*Grazie tanti*," I whisper.

As soon as I am alone, I rip open the envelope.

Cara Arabella,

Forgive me for not writing sooner, but I meet people secretly, day and night. I never know where I will be until I am there. Often, people are too frightened to show up, and we've driven many kilometers for nothing. But we are making progress, finding more evidence to expose the hypocrites and government thieves. It is thrilling work to put into words that which could alter lives.

Having said that, I need you to listen to me. Though I am fine and will be, there are many reasons that it is not safe for you in Brazil—even at the fazenda. I am sorry to disappoint you, but please, please, listen to me when I say that you must return to Paola immediately.

Please, Sorella, do as I ask.

Always,
Your brother,
Marco

It's settled. I'm going home.

WITH A WORLD AT WAR, it takes some time to secure a boat back to Italy. These are dangerous times of scarcity and terror but Octavio has made certain I am chaperoned and safe as possible. I have endless days to consider that my homecoming may be clouded by the circumstances of my return (and I suppose, the circumstances of my departure as well). The effects of war, boys and men absence from the village, Papa's inactivity and pain, the fact I will be my village's *erborista*, my arranged marriage to deliberate.

And what about my sister? Our war? We have chasms to cross before we can reconcile—or so I think.

Once I see her and she calls my name, I collapse in her arms without hesitation.

"I thought you'd never ever forgive me," she whispers in my ear. "And that would be so much harder to accept than even Gregorio's death."

That statement renders me a puddle of emotion on the floor. "It's not your fault," I manage. "I needed someone to blame, and maybe, somehow, I knew only you, of all people, would be able to forgive *me*. I'm thinking of marrying Aldo," I blurt, "but only if he can accept that first and foremost, I am an *erborista*. I will be a wife and mother, but there will be no interference in my commitment to healing. "

"I'm surprised, *Sorella*. Are you certain? What about Antonio?"

"Antonio Salerno is engaged to Talina Ubruzzo."

"But if he knew that you . . ."

"So be it, Filomena. He has made his choice."

"Let's pray for everyone to safely make it through this war." She hesitates, "Well, while we are speaking of betrothals, Luigi has asked Papa for my hand."

Love is a strange phenomenon. Who knows what it is that attracts us one to another? I can't fathom how the most perfect woman in all of southern Italy could want to be with Luigi Compretta, but it is not up to me, is it?

I hug her and wish her happiness. I'm certain my eyes have betrayed my true feelings, but it is the best I can do. It is strange to be here again in Paola with all the changes within me, the changes all around me, hearing only the voices of women and children, old men, and the infirm bouncing in the empty streets.

The beastly war has already snatched young men like Aldo and his brothers, Antonio and his brothers, the postman and his son, the men of the flour mill, and too many other villagers.

It seems a childhood ago in Roma that Mama and Signora Ruffino were speaking of the inevitability of Italy joining the war. In two years' ticking of the clock, the "Great War" picks up more countries in its stormy wake. Italy entered the war as an ally of Britain, France, and Russia, though just last year, Italy proclaimed Germany's war "aggressive" and announced her neutrality. But *Dio mio*, war flips everything upside down. Like women's stoic care of not just the young and the old but the fields and the crops, the machines and the mules, the broken and the bent.

In the *piazza*, after church, or at the market, we fill in the void with quiet conversation. Everything seems hushed as if in the quiet we could hear the voices of our beloved brothers, sons, and friends. Who knows, maybe Filomena and Luigi are right to seize an opportunity to love now. Who knows what tomorrow brings?

But today in the *piazza* I see the snake Luigi Compretta is. As I'm speaking with Signora Ruffino before she ships out to the war front, Luigi leans in a little too close to young Susanna Obello.

"Thank you for returning," Signora Ruffino says solemnly.

"I suppose it was preordained," I answer with a hint of a smile, peripherally watching Luigi.

She nods. "Arabella, you remain one of the greatest gifts of my life—and Paola's."

To be loved by a woman such as this is overwhelming yet soothing at the same time. How can she feel this way about me? It *was my belladonna that killed her son.*

"This war will reveal atrocities we presently know nothing about," she returns to the subject at hand. "Most likely, wounds will be hastily cleaned and sewn, temporary splints will hold breaks until you can attend to them here. Infection and exhaustion will be rampant. Spirits too will suffer greatly."

"*Si, signora.*"

"Your family is generous to offer the mill's barn as an infirmary again."

That makes me think of Gregorio. I'm filled with a deep determination to succeed as a healer—for his sake, for his mother's sake, for all those we lost in the cholera outbreak.

"I am here for all those who need me, *Signora*," I vow.

"You save us in many different ways, *Figlia*." My angel's glow reveals an idea I hadn't considered before: did surrendering the belladonna somehow save *her* from unbearable suffering?

I blink back a tear but acknowledge the compliment, "*Grazie, Signora.*" Out of the corner of my eye, I see Luigi now sidling up to Niccidi Olizza. Why can't that brute be shipped off to the front, limp, and all?

"I am anxious for you to share your healing knowledge from Brazil," my teacher says.

I bring my attention back to her. "My notebook and valise are full of stems, flowers, roots, and leaves I brought home. I'm going to brew my new tinctures and send them to the front." I think lovingly of my mystery teacher who seemed to emerge at the right time with the perfect information. I learned much from her.

"*Brava*, Arabella. I am so proud of you."

I tell her I will make notes for her to read on the train. She gives me a gentle embrace and takes her leave. I notice Luigi saunters off with Niccidi.

I throw my shoulders back. I have much to prepare for. I am in charge of Paola's health now. And, God help her, my sister is in charge of her own heart.

IN THE COMING MONTHS, Mama's kitchen is a laboratory of my boiling brews: cayenne, golden seal, and white oak birch to stanch hemorrhaging; red clover and passionflower from Brazil with lobelia for nerves; and my latest experiment of licorice root, kelp, dandelion, and cayenne for endurance and fatigue. (This one, admittedly, must have brandy to mask the taste). Stitches are practiced on scraps of fabric. I memorize bones tiny and large, from noses to toes to arms and knees, and tendons front and back. The medical book illustrations help me to visualize what I may need to set right. Filomena keeps me company while knitting.

"Was Brazil all you thought it would be?" she asks, completing another pair of wool socks for some lucky soldier.

"I had no preconceived ideas. It was a brash move to escape, and perhaps, to inflict a little pain."

"I can understand that."

"The tropical beauty and healing plants were of great interest, but it seems I traded one problem for another."

"What do you mean?"

"Well, I felt trapped here with the betrothal. There I felt trapped by enormity a foreign land and—"

"Our brother and sister-in-law?"

We chuckle. Oh, how I missed the bridge of our sisterhood.

"I learned a lot about standing on my own. Taking risks. And that, truly, no place or situation is perfect."

"Si, I agree, but with you home, this place feels a little closer to perfect again."

And what of the perfection of love? Or is it the imperfection of love? Each day Luigi leaves Papa's study at the precise moment Pina is carrying in the first dinner course. She doesn't even ask if he'll be eating with us anymore. He feigns surprise at the invite. I find his acting as tedious as his presence.

I look at him as we dine—handsome, clever, and obviously intelligent. Do I judge him too harshly? What does my opinion matter anyway? Papa seems quite taken with his efficacy and his manner, Mama blushes at his compliments, and Filomena hasn't been this vibrant since Gregorio, God rest his soul, was among us.

The discussion tonight revolves around the war. I've drifted a bit going over my latest tonic in my mind and missed the beginning of the conversation. I am jerked back by Luigi's statement.

"If only Queen Isabella of Spain had thrown out the Jews back in the 1600s, Europe wouldn't always have to be fighting."

My fork freezes in midair. I am waiting for Papa to set him straight, to challenge such ridiculousness, but *NO ONE* responds. They discuss the alarming lack of supplies and how Filomena's work of knitting gloves, socks, and hats comfort and warm our men, of my herbal contributions.

If they won't respond, I will. "Excuse me, Luigi," I begin. "What if someone of authority decided Italians are a disgraceful race of people to 'be thrown out of Europe'?"

Mama purses her lips, Papa squints, and Filomena gently shakes her head from side to side in a beseeching gesture.

Luigi laughs. "Arabella, how can you be so smart and yet so preposterous? That can never happen because Italians are nothing like the Jews."

"But your argument holds no merit. My hypothetical question is *what if* someone in power deemed Italians unworthy? What then, Luigi? *Your* opinion would be considered *preposterous*."

The room becomes quiet. Luigi's emanating anger fills the space like a blazing fire in the hearth. Can't they see what lurks beneath the surface of this charmer?

Filomena pours a cool stream of philosophy, "The past and the future are important to ponder, but right now, our beautiful countrymen are literally fighting for their lives—and for ours. The present must be our focus."

"Here, here, *salute*."

Glasses sing like the windchimes in Sofia's botanical garden—interpreted tones of one melody. I take a deep breath. I guess it all depends on the direction of the wind and what you're made of.

EVEN ALDO, WHO RETURNED to Paola a fortnight ago with a broken arm, has fallen under the spell of Luigi. The two have struck up an unlikely friendship, perhaps because they are betrothed to the Mandarino sisters. He's quite taken with Luigi and quite smitten with me—as woman and *erborista*. Often, he comes to the mill and watches me set bones, stitch wounds, and tend broken spirits.

One evening, Aldo and I stroll the *lungomare* at sunset, the sky awash in deep lavender and salmon lined with swallowtail yellow.

"Arabella, thank you for your care, I mean, you know, of all of us."

"*Certo*," *Of course.*

"You have helped a lot of people."

I am silent, lost in the glories of my *lungomare*.

Then, he reaches for my hand, and I let him take it.

"Tomorrow is your sister's wedding. It is a good match, *si?*"

"We shall see," I reply honestly.

"It's kind of funny, you being the maid of honor and me the best man."

"I suppose."

"I mean, well, because it will be our turn next."

"*Si.*"

It's the moment he chooses to kiss me for the first time. Our lips are puckered tight. And then, it's over. No fireworks. No butterflies. A foreshadowing of our intimacy—or lack of it.

IT IS A PERFECT DAY FOR A September wedding. A beautiful distraction from the vestiges of war. The rains have come to sweep away summer's heat from the water's edge, the *piazza*'s cobblestones, and the dankness of the church. Filomena has eaten just a half of a biscotti with her cappuccino this early morning, claiming butterflies have taken her stomach hostage. She is radiant, luminous.

"Now Filomena, keep your eyes open and alert as you walk to the church this morning," Mama warns as she fixes Filomena's lace veil.

"Yes, Mama, I know."

"But what you don't know is how nervous you will be as you walk with your husband beside you and the whole village looking on!"

"Yes, Mama."

"You just don't know all the tricks people have planned to see how you will react." She shakes her head. "I wish you would have let us plan this walk ahead of time so you know what will happen!"

Filomena sighs but smiles.

"You'll be all right, *mia sorella*," I announce. "I will be your eyes and your ears."

She squeezes my hand. We hear the boisterous voices of men approaching.

"*Buon giornio.*"

Luigi stands before my mother and kisses her on both cheeks. He does the same to me. Right behind him is Aldo.

Luigi, with the oscillating eyes of an owl, laughs, "Aldo, *che fai?* Arabella will soon be your wife. *Salutala de una bessa. Give* that little tigress *a kiss!* Mmm, if I were you, I wouldn't waste any time!"

Aldo turns cherry red. I busy my hands straightening Filomena's veil. Papa enters the hallway dressed in his finest suit, and I witness how quickly Luigi's air of flippancy dissipates. Where was Papa just a minute ago when Luigi was spouting off inappropriately? Papa nods, and the wedding walk to the church begins. Tradition dictates a host of pranks to test the couple's strengths and weaknesses.

Villagers are gathered at the water's edge, not far from our front door. A dove is released from its cage and takes flight over the sea. Filomena tugs at Luigi's sleeve, causing him to stop. She smiles and points to the bird, engrossed in its graceful flight.

"She has a sense of wonder, "someone calls out. "Important to notice the beauty in each day."

We continue, joining the chorus of "*la dolce vita, pui la dolce vita oggi,*" *the sweet life, more of the sweet life today.*

Next, a child is pushed before the couple. While Luigi noticeably steps back, Filomena stops and bends down toward the child's dirty face. What if the little scoundrel was instructed to touch her dress with his soiled hands? Filomena removes a lace hankie from the *busta* tied to her side (the pouch will hold gifts of money later). She wipes his face and hands. The little imp smiles.

"*Guarda,* look, she possesses patience and care. She will make a good mama."

I wonder why nothing is said about what the other parent will be like, the one who stepped away from the child.

Now a broom is thrown upon the path, meant as a jab that Filomena grew up with a helper like Pina. But quick-witted, Filomena feigns mock surprise, picks up the broom with exaggerated puzzlement, turns to Mama, and asks, "Mama, what is this for?" Laughter erupts.

"*Brava,* Filomena! Every marriage needs a healthy supply of humor."

The couple is nearing the *piazza.* Not once did Luigi step in to meet a challenge put before them. Is it a telltale sign that Filomena will be the one tending to each challenge in their marriage?

The church bells ping their song, piercing my reverie. The couple, along with the village in tow, arrives at the church. We all pass beneath the large bow tied at the threshold to remind all who enter that we are "tied into" and part of this marriage. I hope they are all up to the task of keeping this marriage from falling apart.

IN LESS THAN A YEAR, the union's foundation crumbles. The heavy air of August hangs like a weight on my sister, already pregnant with twins.

"Filomena, it's sweltering today, and you're in a long sleeve dress!"

"Oh, *si*, well, it's um, to protect my sensitive skin from the sun—and it's much more comfortable."

Hmm? I don't believe her, but I can see she is rattled. I tell her to sit down, pour some *acqua di limone*, and begin rubbing her shoulders. She winces.

Instinctively, I push aside the fabric. Purple bruises bloom across her shoulders and halfway down her back.

"Filomena? What happened to you? What is this from?"

She carefully repositions the fabric before looking at me with a sadness I have never seen, not even when Gregorio died. "It's nothing really, he didn't mean to. It was my fault . . ."

The dawning of a horrible thunderbolt of truth: Luigi has beaten his pregnant wife.

"I am sorry." I hug her.

This is not love! Love does not bear this burden! What can I say? What should I do?

I launch into action. "We'll pack a few things now and then come for the rest another day. Where is your valise?"

"*Basta, sorella. Stop.* I am not going anywhere."

"What? Of course, you are. You cannot stay with a man who beats his pregnant wife!"

She winces again, this time from the sting of my words.

She will repeat this response over the many decades of our lives. "I love him, Arabella. He is my husband. I will not ever leave him."

"But *Sorella*, he . . ."

She puts her hand over my mouth. "Say no more, little sister, not to me or Mama or Papa or anyone, *capishe?*"

It's my turn to flinch. I am to understand what? How to a silent witness, a bystander that does nothing but watch this abuse?

She doesn't wait for a reply. Cheerily she announces, "Now if you want to help your *sorella*, let's start the Mandarino Family Tonic!"

We both chime, "Minestrone!"

Her jaw is set as she moves to the mounds of diced vegetables from her garden—zucchini, green beans, carrots, onions, potatoes, tomatoes, and garlic. It's a miniature festival of colorful, costumed dancers at the feast of the Annunciation—earthy green, sunset orange, cloudlike white. But the *festa* is tainted by purple and blue! I invoke the help of my spirit angel so that I can play along with her marital charade. I move to the stove where the pan waits for perfectly hot, popping oil, and the garlic and onion. Once the aroma wafts, I douse the starter vegetables in marinara sauce. Efficiently, I move about the kitchen adding oregano, stirring in carrots, chopping basil. Filomena smiles and chides me as in days of old—before husbands and their bruises.

"Look at you. You act as if you know what to do in a *cucina* besides brew herbs!"

We laugh.

"Are you insinuating that I previously had no skills in the kitchen?"

"Are you admitting your lack of culinary mastery?"

"Certainly not! If I admitted it, then all of Paola might hear!"

After I add the water and set the lid on the pot to simmer, I bring out the fresh mozzarella wrapped in fern leaves and remove the lid of the fresh tomato salad with garlic, hot pepper, olive oil, and a splash of red vino vinegar, and Mama's bread.

"Ah, to make a *funa*." She sighs as we both dunk the bread in the rich juice at the bottom of the bowl. It's a funny expression derived from the verb, *funare, to drown*. I am drowning my bread, but internally, I'm drowning in confusion, not able to see what my place is here in this terrible arrangement.

Keep it lighthearted, Arabella. Do not add to her burden. The angel light pulses beside her.

Filomena tears another piece of Mama's bread and stacks it with a slice of fresh cheese, tomato, and a leaf of basil.

"Mmmm," she murmurs, lost in the burst of airy flavor. "Mama's bread is so perfect. I wonder if I will ever be able to make it like she does. *Allora*, I cannot make anything even close!"

"Well, it's your lucky day!" I burst, "Mama has sent you an extra loaf for tomorrow."

Panic flashes across her face. "No, no, Arabella, you must take this bread home with you when you go." She gets up nervously and begins fidgeting.

"What are you talking about? Mama made this just for you."

She sighs, realizing that I am not just going to do what I am told. "Luigi will not accept charity from our family."

"Charity? What are you talking about? We made this bread for you because it is your favorite, and we love you. This is what families do for one another."

"Si, *ho capito, Sorella, I understand*, but Luigi does not embrace our family's ways." She sits back down again, a jack in the box stuffed back into the box, shaking her doll-like head to and fro.

"Our 'ways'? He's been with our family for over a year. He knows our 'ways!' Are our 'ways' so different from his family's 'ways'?"

"Oh, his family was *bad*, so very *brutto*," she reveals.

Well now, there is something that makes sense. The apple does not fall too far from the tree, eh? *Brutto* begets *brutto.*

"In fact," she continues, "They used to beat him if he said the wrong thing or appeared out of line. He would do his best to help in the fields. He would take care of his five younger siblings, but nothing he ever did was right. They took out the frustrations of a hard life on him." She is nearly in tears. "Please, Arabella, no matter what you think, you do not know the whole story of this man. Wrap the bread up before Luigi gets home."

I think that many dark mysteries lay hidden beneath the façade of Luigi Compretto.

"*Ciao, esposa,*" the capricious charmer greets his wife and enters as if an actor on cue. Has he been listening to our conversation?

Filomena tries to gingerly lift herself up.

"Here, let me help you," he chimes.

How does she let him touch her? Is she afraid *she* is doing her best but will likely provoke a beating?

He pats her arm affectionately, but his black eyes spy the bread from Mama. A dismal preview of what could be released at any moment moves across his face.

He turns to me. "Arabella, aren't you the picture of beauty?" He oozes, sidling up to me.

I stare him down. *Take one more step, and you'll experience the picture of my power.* I am not afraid of him, but it's clear my sister is. She waddles over between us, smiling as she gently nudges me out of his path. Taking the cue, I lift my chin at him, kiss her puffy cheek, and bid her goodbye.

Luigi follows me to the door and catches me in an inappropriate embrace, releases a taunting laugh, and then he shoves Mama's bread in my arms. He stares for a lingering moment. I take a last look at Filomena breathing deeply, her nervous eyes bracing for what will inevitably come sooner than later.

THE SUN IS BEGINNING ITS descent as I head towards the *piazza*. Thoughts are spinning wheels of concern for my sister and her unborn. My head begins to throb as it does so often now since my return. I'll begin a regimen of honey mixed with lavender oil steeped in a hot bath before bed tonight. First, though, I'll stop at the church to say a prayer, just for good measure.

Entering the candlelit sanctuary quietly, I kneel in front of the Virgin Mary statue. "I don't presume to offer you any ideas, but could you please send Luigi away, somewhere, somehow? I'd be most grateful." I make the sign of the cross before scurrying out into the indigo twilight toward the *lungomare*.

My head is pounding so intensely now I must pause often. As I get closer to the sea, the salty charge of the air weakens the headache's hammer. I'm breathing a little easier. The rhythmic slapping of the water on the shore is a perfect waltz of calm. But just as suddenly as calm arrives, it is quickly pulled out to sea. If Aldo thinks I will tolerate such behavior, he will be in for a surprise! Why would anyone endure this treatment? Filomena is so much better than that.

I tell Mama and Papa why I was late, stopping by the church to pray on the way home. I dramatically unroll the loaf of bread from the linen embroidered with woodland flowers. I stand there with my hands on my hips.

"Why did you bring this home? It is for Filomena," states Mama, confused.

"Apparently you are not aware that Luigi will not accept 'charity' from our family." I raise an eyebrow.

Papa is sipping his bowl of broth with herbs and spinach. He looks up slightly, but I know he is listening closely.

I launch unabashedly into the whole sordid story of the bruises and the bread, asserting our need to intervene and rescue Filomena—*adesso! Now!*

Papa clears his throat. "Arabella, please do not meddle in your sister's marital affairs."

"It is not meddling, Papa. It is our duty to protect Filomena and her unborn children. It may require intervention."

"We are not privy to what goes on behind closed doors," offers my mother to assuage my fears. It only provokes me.

"What goes on behind closed doors is precisely what we should put a stop to!" I shout.

"Arabella, I know you think you understand, but you do not. And no matter where you have been or done, while you are under my roof, you are to abide by my rules. You will not interfere in your sister's marital affairs."

I look from one to the other before excusing myself. In my room, I peer out the yellow curtains at the moon, like a slice of half an avocado.

Mama enters. "Arabella," she soothes. "I know you are still readjusting to the many changes here. We're all adjusting to being at war. *Pazienza. Have patience.* Give it a little time."

"There have been many changes, Mama. But my sister being beaten by her husband is a change I will never accept. It is abuse."

"Abuse is a strong word, Arabella. What happens between husband and wife is . . ."

"Do not talk to me as if I am a child. I know what abuse is."

Gratefully, there is a loud knock on the door. Signore Pascale has come to inform me that his son and others have just arrived back and need my care. Mama remarks on the late hour and that I will meet them at the mill in the morning. I grab my medicine bag, walking right past Mama and through the door. Signore Pascale gives my hand a little squeeze, slipping a letter into it. I place it in my medicine bag. The light of the half-moon winks.

IT WASN'T UNTIL I WAS RESTOCKING my supply bag that I remembered the letter.

Novembre 1917

Cara Arabella,

You have returned home safe and sound to tend to our beloved villagers. Grazie tanti. I know it was a sacrifice for you. I was honored to receive your letter from Brazil. It's not the first time I felt inspired by your zest for life. Let's hope what we are doing here somehow leads to a better world for our countrymen and neighbors.

I have heard it said that Italy breeds lovers and Austria, Hungary, and Germany, soldiers. It's easy to believe. Those soldiers overtake us easily and often. Italian soldiers lack skill and weaponry while German battalions flex their extensive war muscles. Poison gases creep like toxic fog, machine guns spit holes in limbs and lungs at breakneck speeds, tanks and airplanes deliver swift doom. In a matter of minutes, gray rubble is all that might remain of an entire village. One doesn't get too close to others here as maybe tomorrow they will no longer be alive.

The surprise attack by the Germans at Caporetto left an estimated forty thousand dead, wounded, or taken prisoner. They took over three thousand precious pieces of our artillery. This one attack reduced our ranks by half. Now we use the phrase, "It was a Caporetto," to talk about anything from a bad meal to a lousy card hand. I suppose no one ever wants to forget.

I understand those who threw down their rifles yelling, "Andiamo a casa!" I don't blame them for abandoning their posts and going home. But some of us hold fast and stay the course, held here by responsibility, fear of tomorrow, some absurd sense of pride. Kind gestures such as your sister's gloves, hats, and socks, and sipping your herbal tonics have literally saved many of us.

I set the letter down. I try to fathom the sheer number who have fallen, the daily hell of destruction, decay, devastation. If only I had a concoction to open war makers' eyes to acceptance and abundance—to see there is room aplenty to fit all our forms and faces, our spectrum of colors, our broad scope of prophets. If I were a man, I would sit across the table from important rulers and share these truths. Perhaps the anarchists and the Suffragettes will usher in a time when all people can share their perspectives.

I pick up the letter and continue reading.

Of late, the Allies are deadlocked. Neither side can overtake the other, but neither will surrender. It's pazzo! Crazy! How can both sides suffer so but do nothing to make peace?

I pray you are well and Aldo has fully healed from his injuries.

Fondly,
Antonio Salerno

I cannot imagine how he endures these tragedies daily. Maybe it's Talina Ubruzzo who's keeping his heart warm and beating.

IT'S OFTEN REFERRED TO AS the circle of life. When one dies, another is born, but it will take many births to make up for all the losses of war. Today, Filomena is doing her part as she prepares to give birth.

Sweat, moan, thrash, cry out, repeat. She's been at it for several hours, looking more like a mythical creature than *mia sorella*—part twisting whale, part drowning lioness. Mama wipes Filomena's drenched face, lifting the errant, soaked curl from her forehead. I'm worried how birthing one child, let alone two, can be done by someone so visibly fatigued. Mama offers comforting sounds to Filomena, the kind of cooing that assures a nervous child that all is well.

The midwife, Signora Miscotto, lifts her head from between Filomena's legs and announces, "*Allora*, Filomena, the first one is coming, *spinge! Push!*"

Mama Filomena bears down, gritting and squealing as her firstborn son slides into the seasoned hands of Signora Miscotto. The newborn wails, flailing his reddened arms and legs. We usher him in with both laughter and tears—the language of women.

He is placed upon my sister's breast, birth blood, umbilical cord, and all. She runs her hands across his scrunched brow and counts his fingers and toes. She seems to step into another skin just then, another part of herself. She even looks different—not in the color or shape of her eyes or lips but rather an overall shift from maiden to mother. I make mental notes of the changes in Filomena and the quick assimilation of the child throughout the birthing experience for my journal. They are both fine, peaceful. We coo over the little newborn as the umbilical cord is cut and he's placed on Filomena's breast.

All is well for a short while until suddenly, everything changes. Filomena is agitated, throwing the blanket off. Mama quickly removes the child. The apprentice takes him from Mama. Filomena mutters then yells at someone or something we neither see nor understand. It escalates to hysteria.

"*Che cosa sta succedendo?*" *What is happening?* I demand.

Before anyone can answer, Filomena has gone silent but is writhing like a trapped snake in a bucket. The linens are soaked with enough new perspiration to fill a large pasta bowl. Mama touches Filomena's head and withdraws her hand quickly as she would from a burning pot.

"She's on fire!" she shouts at Signora Miscotto.

"*Calma*, Signora Mandarino, *calm*. This happens. The body induces a sudden fever to rid itself of what it *thinks* is a foreign substance—in this case, the second child. But we must work quickly." She turns her attention to *mia sorella*. Firmly, she instructs, "Filomena, I am going to count to ten, and you will breathe in and breathe out with me. When I reach the number ten, you will push with every ounce of strength you have."

The count begins and climbs to ten. She pushes, but the child does not budge.

"He is turned the wrong way—feet first," *signora* reports after examining Filomena again.

Panic spreads like wildfire within me. A breached child is a danger for both baby and mama. I search my memory of the birth canal pictures from the medical textbook. Something must be done to make that child turn. But what?

It goes from bad to worse in a heartbeat, but the midwife has an idea that if Filomena sits up, the pressure will move the child. We prop a barely conscious Filomena on pillows against the headboard. Her head bobs, loose on its guidepost. Her eyes roll around in their sockets like a child's ball in a rotating pan. Mama is talking to Filomena, loudly now, stern authority ripping through the veiled layers between us and wherever Filomena is. No response. Mama slaps Filomena across the face. But my sister only moans.

Signora takes Filomena's pulse. "We're going to lose her," she whispers.

Lose my sister? Absolutely not. I may not be a midwife, but I am a healer. One, admittedly who does not have birthing experience and who could cause more harm than good. But what is more harmful than death? What do we have to lose if the expert states we're going to lose her?

Think. Your sister needs you. Trust and remember.

Va bene, angel. I stuff everything messy and frightening down into the murky depths for examination another day. Right now, I zero in on my sister's face and on that little one stuck upside down inside of her. Mama is on the verge of shock.

I launch my inquiry to the midwife. "What course of action will we take?" I ask.

Signora Miscotto looks at me, sizing me up and down. She nods her head.

"*Allora,* she says. "Grab as many pillows as you can find. We'll use them to raise her hips above her heart. This may cause the child to flip."

It takes the midwife, her apprentice, Mama, Pina, and me to complete this task. We wait, but the child remains in breach.

"What other methods turn the child?" I implore.

She shakes her head. I can see her thoughts written in invisible ink across her face. She's done all she can. Death in childbirth happens all the time. You birth some; you lose some. *Come si, come sa.*

Surprising everyone in the room, I grab *signora* by the shoulders and shake her. "Think woman, there is something else. Think!"

Niceties can be served up on flowered platters another day.

Signora Miscotto shrugs her shoulders. I want to strangle her. You don't give up on people like this! With the fire of the dragon, I will scorch every obstacle. "Forsaking the unborn child and mother is not acceptable!" I sear.

The old midwife looks haggard. I think I see a tear spilling from the cracked edges of her weary eyes. I close my eyes to calm myself, douse the dragon, ask for help. Suddenly, an odd contraption appears in my mind's eye. I don't know where it came from. Maybe it's divine help from Mary, Mother of God herself, working with my spirit angel. However it appeared, it's all we've got. I explain the idea to *signora*.

Understanding dawns as she barks orders. *Get the ironing board, push the chair over near the bed, do this and that.* She tells Pina to clear an area of the floor and spread a few layers of clean linens there.

The ironing board is leaned against Papa's overstuffed reading chair. We need to get Filomena to it, but we can't budge her. It's like trying to move a barrel full of lead. Mama talks sweetly to her, but Filomena's eyes only flutter. Signora slaps her. Filomena barely mutters a protest, let alone attempts to take a step.

"*Basta. Stop.* Let me," I insist. I command everyone to leave the room so I can be with Filomena alone.

The midwife turns back warning, "Be quick. There's little time."

I nod. I understand the temerity of time.

I crawl onto the bed next to my sister, a sizzling tree trunk burning from the inside out. Tenderly, I push the hair away from her face, dip the cloth in cool chamomile water, and wipe her face and neck.

"Please help us," I whisper to the unseen world. *Tell me what to say. Inform me what to do.*

In an act of what can only be grace itself, words flow. Into my sister's ear, I describe her two healthy babies and the joy they are bringing to us all. I detail the ebony curl of the ringlets framing their hazel and blue eyes, their toothless smiles, their olive skin, and the song of their gurgling laughter like a brook in our *montanas*.

"Do you see them *mia sorella*? Now I chase them down the *lungomare*. See? *Lo visto?*"

A faint upturning of her mouth, albeit brief, yet an encouraging flash of consciousness.

"I know you can see them, and I know you can do this," I say with such conviction that my spirit angel infiltrates the hairs on my neck and arms.

"Mama, Pina, Signora Miscotto are all here. We're going to help you." Next, I put my mouth right next to her stomach and say, "Look here, little one, you can be as *testa dura, hard-headed* as you want, *after* you are born. But right now, you will turn and head-first enter this world. *Capishe?*"

I kiss her belly, stand upright, and call the other women back in. We scoot the chair and the contraption a little closer to the bed.

"Get up now Filomena," I command, considering how Jesus must have persuaded Lazarus to rise from the dead. Mama is supporting her back, the other women at her side.

I order, "One, two, three, up!"

Filomena uses her hand to prop herself up.

"*Buona, sorella.*" I smile.

She tries, bless her heart, sliding and dragging her feet. Supporting her under each arm now, we urge her onto the ironing board contraption on her stomach where we stabilize her head near the floor, hips high over her heart, all of her weight pushing on the baby. She whimpers, calling my mother, me, and the Virgin Mary interchangeably. I massage her back, reassuring her the baby is turning, that it won't be long. Then, her scream rattles the painting of the Virgin Mary hanging on the wall behind us.

"*Va bene, va bene,*" encourages Signora Miscotto, acting as limber and quick as a squirrel. To us, she says, "Hurry, let's get her off this and help her to squat."

Filomena is wobbly, but we literally and figuratively, hold her up. My thighs are screaming in opposition to the strain, my emotions a wiry electrical current.

She is more alert than she has been these past interminable minutes. The midwife has her hands inside of Filomena again. She announces, "The child has turned, but its head is too large to pass."

Expertly, she takes her knife and cuts Filomena between her vagina and perineum, stanching the bleeding with an herbal mixture of whipped egg whites, rose oil, and alcohol we prepared earlier. It will cauterize, soothe, and reduce inflammation. Filomena roars in protest, but now the midwife is telling her to bear down, to push. A ghostly wail envelops the room.

The midwife's hands are lost in the deep cavern of my sister. Her assistant holds the cloth with the staunching mixture.

"I've got it," she tells us. "Filomena, push!"

Several more attempts, and a gooey, angry little being emerges.

Filomena is softly weeping as we lower her onto the linens and pillows Pina has efficiently laid out onto the floor. She feeds Filomena another gulp of my lemon balm and fennel tea dosed with brandy, then hands me the needle and thread. I am to sew up Filomena, just like I've mended all those broken soldiers. It's trancelike, really. Just you, the injury, and the thread and needle—no determination of gender, emotion, attachment.

The angel light glows. My stitches are even and close together. Filomena will heal nicely because of that and my rose oil and lavender salve.

We all gather around the mother and sons, returned to the soft comfort of a bed. There is nothing more beautiful than the three of them acquainting. But here comes Luigi sauntering into the room with a lit cigar dangling from his stained lips, grandstanding, like he always does.

"*Poveracina*," he coos to Filomena, "*va bene.*" *Poor thing, all is well.* He blows a puff of malodorous smoke my way and winks. The smell of whiskey on his breath nearly sears my nose hairs. Filomena softly cries pointing out the first and second born.

"This one, our firstborn, will be Alessandro, the defender, the one who paved the way for the feisty Bernardo, our second."

Mama rounds up the birth attendants and ushers us from the room. I peek back over my shoulder at my sister. She's luminous. It's hard to believe she could transform so many times in just a few hours. I sprint back into the room kiss her and my nephews.

Luigi leans over to me as if I were going to offer him a *besso* too! I'd rather *kiss* a donkey.

"What's this, Arabella, no kiss for your brother-in-law, the father of your nephews?" He winks at me seductively and guffaws, startling the sleeping babies.

I'd like to put a spell on him.

AS THE TWO BOYS GAIN FOOTING in the world, we're still trying to cope with the staggering number of deaths in World War 1 that grew to eight and one-half million. Wounded, twenty-one million. All those papas, brothers, husbands, and sons. Gone. Maimed. We've banded together as a village to support the women, children, nonnas, and babbos left behind, with little more than their will to survive.

My beloved teacher, Signora Ruffino, died attending to a fallen soldier on the front lines. God rest her soul as she joins Gregorio and her husband. She takes our secret of the belladonna to the grave, leaving me with guilt to shoulder alone, leaving me with a village to tend as the official *erborista.*

Aldo's injury seems almost superficial compared to the loss of limbs, the loss of minds, the loss of lives. But I am thankful he healed with my salves, tea tree cleaning solutions, and strengthening exercises for his arm muscles. As I changed the bandages, we spoke of crops and weather, animals and seasons—nothing deep or reflective—a preview of our marriage.

MAMA IS STANDING OVER ME at the dressing table. As she wrestles with my unruly tresses she playfully exclaims, "This mane *will* behave on your wedding day!"

I meet her gaze in the mirror and attempt my best imitation of a smile.

Throughout the ages, women have endured arranged marriages. I will make it the business arrangement it is.

"Cara Arabella," she whispers, "*do not be worried, non ti preoccupare, figlia.* You will see that life as a wife and mother is rewarding."

"Of course, Mama." *I have my own ideas about being a wife and mother that I will keep to myself today.*

Filomena enters the room as Mama tucks a pile of my hair under the veil and pronounces me the most beautiful bride in all of Italy.

"Filomena, these rows of beaded flowers you crafted are the most exquisite I have ever seen! Thank you, again."

"You are welcome, *sorella*! I showed your dress to a girl in Cosenza, and she wants me to make one for her."

We congratulate her as the voices of the boisterous twins, Papa, Luigi, and Aldo echo in the front hall. Mama pats me on the back, prodding me out of the room. I am present but not. I see myself moving toward the door, a comely, nineteen-year-old bride on her wedding day, daydreaming that Antonio, not Aldo is my husband.

Reality yanks me back, for there is Aldo nodding, smiling, while Luigi rants about my beauty, and the twins' babble.

I tune everything out except my angel's voice encouraging, *Put one foot in front of the other.* It's as if *she* is in my feet, walking this nineteen-year-old body to the church, in my voice stating the vows, shaking hands in the receiving line when Antonio congratulates us.

"And congratulations to you on your engagement." Aldo shakes his hand.

"*Che?*" What engagement?" Antonio responds.

"To Talina. Well done, Antonio."

He looks from Aldo to me, puzzled, but he does not respond. It is most odd.

I think about his lack of response during the shattering of the large glass smashed beneath our shoes and the counting of those broken pieces predicting the number of happy years we will have together. I try to concentrate on the toast of *"Per cent'anni"* *for a hundred years* and enjoy the feast of roasted *bacchio, baby lamb,* and the pickled peppers, the calamari and the two pasta dishes; and during the tarantella wedding circle dance, the offering of candied almonds to our guests to symbolize the essence of marriage both bitter and sweet.

I excuse myself toward the end of the evening, stealing a moment outdoors. I make my way slowly, beneath the heavy fabric of the wedding dress to stand beneath a tree. I'm so happy to just stand there and breathe, thankful for the earthy strength of the tree's roots and firm base.

There is movement behind me.

"Arabella, do not be alarmed," a raspy male voice whispers.

"Who's there?" Most of Paola is at the reception. "Come out please." I admit I am a bit wary.

My brother emerges out of the evening shadows.

"Marco!" I go to him as quickly as I can under the weight of the gown, heeled shoes, and darkness. I get closer to him, and my heart nearly stops.

His head hangs slightly; his clothes are torn, his body, off-kilter.

"Marco?"

As his gaze meets mine, I gasp at the oozing sores, the patch over an eye, and the bloody gashes that mark his glorious face. What happens next can only be described like falling into a trance. I begin scanning his injuries: the patch over his left eye is dirty, dried with blood, and filled with discharge. What lurks behind that cloth is infected and requires my cleaning solution of goldenseal and calendula flowers, as well as those gashes, which will need a few stitches once the infections are reduced. After the initial assessment is done, I come back to the moment, nearly tripping on my dress, a reminder that I am a bride. But I am also Paola's *erborista,* and someone needs my healing.

Clear your mind of everything but Marco, Arabella, I hear. *Thank you, angel.* Yes. I will do what I do best—heal. In action mode, I devise a plan to get Mama, Filomena, and Pina to carry Marco home and to tell Aldo that I will

LA MIA SORELLA (MY SISTER)

not be spending our wedding night with him. I take a deep breath and gently, tenderly embrace my brother. He whimpers as he rests his head on my shoulder.

"*Va bene*," I whisper, the healer telling her patient all is well.

"Forgive me for arriving in this state on your wedding day," he whimpers.

"*Non ti preoccupare*." I touch him as gently as one would an injured bird. "*Aspete*," *wait here*, I instruct as I lean him against a tree.

Straightening my dress, I clear my throat, throw my shoulders back, and head back to the party.

"Arabella?"

Startled for the second time, I see Antonio standing in wait.

"Antonio. I . . ." I don't have a clue what to say. *I'm married now. You will be soon. My brother is maimed and I need to get my mother?*

"Arabella, forgive me but I just couldn't wait another moment to tell you that it's not true. I am not engaged to Talina. She made it all up. I'm sorry. I just didn't know, or I would have spoken of it sooner."

Dear Mary, Mother of God. This information, now? Focus on Marco, Arabella.

"Antonio. You are my best friend and confidante, and quite frankly, I need you now. Please get Mama and Papa's carriage. Mama will be out in a moment. Thank you."

"Of course, but . . ."

"I'll explain everything shortly."

Back at the reception, I smile and nod, passing the guests until I find the three women I need most.

"*Figlia*, you are scaring me," Mama says as she sees the expression on my face. "Are you ill? *Che fai?*"

"*Calma*, Mama. I need to tell you something that will not be easy to hear."

Filomena, a glass of wine or two in her, thinks I am joking. "Oooh, it must be about wedding night business?"

"No, Filomena. I am serious."

"Si, a wedding night is serious business, is it not?" adds Pina.

"It's Marco."

Mama grabs my hand and squeezes it with the strength of a boa constrictor. "What about Marco?" Mama's eyes search mine.

Filomena is calling the Virgin Mary, and Pina is making the sign of the cross. I see the light of my angel around all of us.

"He is here Mama, but he is badly hurt."

"Here? Hurt?" Mama's composure slips.

"He will be all right, Mama. But now Marco needs us focused and strong. *Capisce?*"

"*Si, ho capito. I understand.* But please, Arabella, prepare me."

Again, the healer takes over. "I was only with him for a few short minutes. His eye is patched but most likely, infected, his face, bruised black and blue and cut badly."

Everyone gasps.

"Most of all, he seems wounded from the inside out. "

Tears roll down Mama's face. "Take me to him."

I nod my head, and we walk out into the night where Marco slumps against the tree. Mama exudes both strength and tenderness. She helps him stand, gingerly touches his slashed face, and smiles a smile of miraculous light. Filomena and Pina greet him with restrained joy. Antonio arrives with the carriage and helps Marco, Mama, and Pina aboard. Filomena and I return to the hall. We tell Papa that Pina and Mama are going home. He's had quite a few whiskeys. Smiling, he nods and waves us away. Luigi does the same when Filomena whispers that she must go help Mama. I notice Clarissa Lupino demurely looking at Luigi. No wonder he let Filomena go so easily!

I stand with Aldo for a few minutes, smiling and gently touching his arm. At what I'm hoping is the right moment, I tell him it is time to go. There are good-natured shouts and comments about the wedding bed. Once outside, I steer the conversation.

"Aldo, you know you married the village *erborista*, *si*?"

"*Si*, what of it?"

"You know there are responsibilities I can do nothing about."

"Arabella, I know all this."

"Good because I must go attend someone now."

"Now? But it's our wedding night!"

"I know, *marito*, *husband*, but there is nothing to be done about it. You go on home, and I'll be there as soon as I am able."

His jaw hangs open. Hurriedly, I slip out of my wedding shoes toward the *piazza* where I'll catch up with the carriage.

Being an *erborista* will always take precedence over being a wife.

SOME THINGS YOU CANNOT take back, you cannot change. Like being married to someone. Like being marred, inside and outside.

Marco's eye was examined by two different "experts," but neither offered anything but temporary relief and a death sentence for his eye, which he will not hear of. He remains in a state of varying agony and depression, sharing very little of the atrocities that caused this injury. I ponder, read, and write about how much the physical part of healing is connected to the emotional.

Anna Maria, Filomena's third child, arrived a feisty ball of energy! And a few weeks ago, it was my turn to call on Signora Miscotto to assist in the birth of my son, Dominic. I felt completely taken care of during labor by my spirit angel and the other women. That part of becoming a mother was easy compared to the malaise I feel now. A peculiar, prevailing fog inhabits my mind during simple tasks, let alone complex ones. My patients find me unfocused. And I am certain my child finds me lacking the attentiveness he deserves. I adore my son, but I am just not good at mothering. Healing, yes. Mothering, no. I thank God every day that my sister has opened her arms and heart to my child, caring for Dominic because, quite honestly, I cannot. I am moody and worn at the edges like a scarf unraveling. And *marone*, I cannot sleep even when utterly exhausted!

I observe other mothers, natural mothers, like Filomena: though they may be tired or overworked, there is still a look of engagement in their eyes. The truth is I am a defective mother—seemingly one of a kind. There are no accounts of any women who had difficulty embracing motherhood in any medical texts. I haven't observed anyone else like me. But, then, would you admit to being such an abomination?

I look at my own mama this morning and see how the years are taking their toll. I note these changes in my healing journals. Her puffy eyes, slightly slumped shoulders, and poor coloring could be the beginning of her change of life. I pour Mama a cup of Mandarino Brothers coffee. Truth be told, there is nothing like a cup of cappuccino brewed with the Mandarino Brothers Espresso blend! I've already had three cups today, hoping the caffeine will clear my mental haze.

"Mama," I begin. "I am worried about you. You look tired."

"Ah, and so it begins: the child becomes the parent; the parent becomes the child." She pats my hand, "You have grown into an impressive woman I am proud of, Arabella. Paola's *erborista* and a mother!" She swallows, her emotions raw. She does not know of my motherly inadequacies or that my sister cares for my son most of every day.

Not wanting to disappoint her, I keep up the charade, "*Grazie*, Mama, but we are not discussing me; we're talking about you."

A laugh, the ringing of Christmas bells. "Arabella, you've always been single-minded!"

"Mama . . ." I lift my eyebrow.

She sighs. "The truth is I'm exhausted by the son/father seesaw! They simply refuse to agree on anything." She sighs. "I forced your papa to let Marco back into our home after he disowned him, and now, they argue about everything—whether the butter should be left out to soften or kept in the larder . . . how many stars are in the sky! They awaken, swords drawn, prepared for battle! I look forward to Marco going to oversee the mill for even an hour each day and your father going to work just so I can have some peace." She shakes her head. "I am torn apart: mother versus wife." Her tone rises considerably, a singer at the top of her range.

"Mama, I know you are at wit's end. I wish there was something I could do." The fog in my brain descends, and I push at it with all my might. It's so hard to think! I take a deep breath and feel my spirit angel's light around me when an idea dawns: Marco could live with Aldo and me!

LET'S SEE, I'VE GOT SOME OF Mama's crusty bread, the *sardines* the fish lady peddled this morning singing, "*Pesce, pesce di mare,*" that I'll fry together until golden brown, then add to my mostaccioli. What else could go into this special meal where the wife seeks a favor? I go to the pantry where our coveted Calabrian olives have been curing for several months. I pop the jar's lid, and whoosh, the undeniable aroma of lemon, bay leaves, and olives waft. I'll toss in a few of these delectable darlings to the mix! There are yellow, orange, and red banana peppers in another jar that will add to the colorful concoction. There is a school of thought that believes in the transformative power of colors. The Egyptians constructed color halls to sit in. They drank color waters to cure a host of ailments: red to stimulate the flow of blood and therefore, the flow of life through a lethargic soul, orange to infuse a sense of courage in the tentative or frightened, and yellow to promote both humor and intelligence. Perhaps these colorful foods will add life, humor, and courage to this meal. And I will try infusing water with foods of various colors to help my state of mind.

I chew on a red pepper as I think of how to convince Aldo of the benefits of Marco as a "tenant." How will it improve our lives? I pace, pumping renewed blood flow. What would Aldo want more of? *Soldi, money!* Marco works a bit at the mill, but he could also tutor! That would do his soul good *and* bring another income!

Very well. I've got a plan, but now I need to make Aldo think it is *his* idea. This year and a half of marriage has taught me to flip conversations on their proverbial ear, roll them about the table, floor, or bed until the idea becomes something Aldo believes *he* came up with! I set about chopping, boiling, and frying, feeling a bit like my old self.

After dinner, I freshen up with a touch of my rose petal-infused water and join Aldo on the porch. The evening air feels like silk caresses on my skin.

"Aldo?"

"*Si.*"

"Did you enjoy dinner?"

"*Si.*"

"It was the first meal with the olives we canned last year."

He nods.

I look at his chair. "I'd like to get you a new comfortable chair to rest in after such a hard day's work."

"It's not so bad."

"*Si,* but a wife likes to give her husband everything he desires . . ."

Now I've done it. I see what must be done. Slowly, he rises, and I follow him into our bedroom.

Our lovemaking is like the marriage—mostly business. He thrusts, slightly groans, and rolls over. I think back to the tingles that flip-flopped my stomach just being around Antonio. This is not that. This is primal procreation without joy or intimacy. I'm getting used to it.

As we lie in bed, I speak of Marco, Mama and Papa, throw in some computations about Marco's earnings, add a little white lie about a wealthy boy in Cosenza he will be tutoring (and the closer proximity of our house to Cosenza than Mama and Papa's), and how the small building at the back of our home is a perfect apartment, and before I know it, Aldo has come up with a plan for Marco to live here and pay us rent.

I slip from our bed to the kitchen where I drink a wild carrot seed blend to prevent another pregnancy.

THE BIRDSONG REJUVENATES, the earth pulses my garden today. Purpose and beauty color each plant and flower. Filomena and I tend a row of green beans. Marco and two of his pupils sit on a bench under the holm oak tree reciting poetry, and my son and his twin cousins chase the squawking chickens. It is a tender, familial scene. If an outsider looked on, they might not even know what a flawed mother I am. I remove dead vine leaves, wishing it were that easy to pluck my unforgiving characteristics.

Dominic has found a boy's living treasure: a squirmy worm loop-d-looping in his little toddler fingers.

"Worm." He holds it up to Filomena. He hands it to her, and eagerly, she accepts it, allowing it to wiggle about in her palm. He reaches for it again squealing with delight. She laughs with him and pats his round, padded behind. Suddenly, he turns to her and throws his arms around her in an unabashed display of adoration.

I watch, a bystander, pricked by the thorn of jealousy. *What do you expect?* I grumble to myself. *She is the one who is acting like his mother. Do you not think that even at two and a half, a child knows who truly loves and cares for it? You are smarter than that, Arabella!* That sobering thought makes me grateful for the millionth time in my life that I have a sister. If my son is going to know love, I cannot think of a better woman to deliver it.

But intellectual understanding and emotional acceptance are distinctly different continents. Just as suddenly as this insight bursts through dark thoughts, I am lit with lightning jealousy.

"Dominic," I scold. "Don't bother Zia with such pests!"

See what I mean? All wrong.

Dominic shrinks.

"Arabella, *che c'' e?* He is just excited by the wonder of all of this," Filomena exclaims with her arms spread out and her head thrown back, smiling into the sky, a goddess embracing her kingdom. Her cheeks are like the ripening tomatoes on the vines.

Dominic totters off to show his prize to his cousins. They are good to him, more tolerant than most four-year-olds would be. It is a testament to their adoring mama's love.

I return to my gardening and move to the orange-yellow squash blossoms. I close my eyes and inhale the pungent aromas of the surrounding herbs: basil, rosemary, oregano, thyme, lemon balm, sage, and tarragon, creating new tinctures of herbs combined with Egyptian color water therapies in my mind.

A cry erupts. My heart startles. It's Dominic! Filomena is already up on her feet and heading in his direction. Something happens, then. Though it would appear normal, for me, it is a timeless, precious moment—a profound event: Dominic pushes past Filomena making his way toward me, his arms outstretched, his eyes glued to mine, sniffling, "Mama, mama!" He reaches me and rolls his little body into mine, a joey in its mother's pouch. "Mama, mama," he repeats over and over grabbing my flesh as if holding onto life.

But it is I who hold onto him, not wanting to tame my wildly beating heart. We fold into one another, seismic upheaval followed by solid grounding. Dominic's azure eyes meet mine, and I begin to cry.

"No cry, Mama." He scrunches up his little face and pats my back. "*Si?*" And with that, he bounds off, returning with a part of an old calendula flower. "For you, Mama." He smiles holding the flower up proudly.

With the eyes of a mother's heart, I have awakened to the magnificence of my child. My spirit angel merges with a beam of sunlight directed straight at the middle of my forehead. Unlike the experience in Rome, I sit still and welcome it in.

For the first time since Dominic's birth, I am clear, whole—and utterly in love!

PART 2

1923-1939
Paola, Italy
Boston, America

"AMERICA?" MY TONE IS INCREDULOUS. The news from Antonio is challenging to hear, yet I couldn't be prouder of the bravery wedged between his broad shoulders.

"Sì. I'm going to work in America."

My stomach is a tumbling wave. Antonio leaving Paola? It's knocking me off-kilter. Did he feel like this when he learned I had left Paola for Brazil?

"Of everyone I have ever known, you, Antonio Salerno, deserve an opportunity to succeed."

One lingering gaze into one another's eyes before he launches into a soliloquy of American life, modern ships for travel, futuristic inventions. His enthusiasm is potent.

I ramble on about the adventure of traveling to a foreign land, but all the while, years of our friendship spin backward frame by frame: the barefoot days skipping pebbles along the *lungomare*, romps through the citrus and olive groves, the horrors of the cholera devastation, the atrocities of war to my marriage—the event which altered our friendship considerably. Still, I cannot imagine life in Paola without him.

You are being selfish, Arabella, I admonish myself. *This is about your friend Antonio Salerno's happiness! You have a husband, and a child, your healing, and a home. What does he have? Your unrequited love. If he stays here, he will continue to see only you, regardless that you are married.*

"What will you do in America?" I ask.

"You know Signore Sucero took his family to Boston a few years ago. He has a little *apartamento* building with a downstairs room I will stay in. I'll work for him in his shop until I have the savings to start my own business."

So confident, I think to myself. *Such courage*—appealing traits in a man.

"You will fare well in America. I can sense it here," I prophesize, pointing to my stomach.

"*Brava*, Arabella, now I know all will be well!"

"Do you know what kind of business you might want to create in America?"

"We'll just have to wait and see," he says with all the excitement of a child on his birthday. "I'll write to you," he promises, "and you can learn English along with me."

Anything along with him sounds lovely.

"Here," he says. "I almost forgot," handing me a basket. "Nonna Emelia and I baked your favorite butter cookies."

I pop a cookie into my mouth, indulging the goodness to float me down the river of ecstasy.

After we've said our goodbyes and I am walking toward home, I feel the movement of something else besides cookies sliding back and forth in the basket. I stop on the road and look in. It is a small treasure book of love poems from around the world, everything from Thomas Hardy's "The

Voice" to Robert Browning's "Life in a Love." I wonder if there is one about love unspoken.

FOUR SETS OF SHOES SHUFFLE ON the pebbled walkway outside my kitchen door. The boisterous twins, little Anna Maria, and their worn but smiling mama enter. Dominic hears his cousins and squeals with delight as he charges for the door.

"*Buon Giorgno, tutti!*" I say, holding the door open.

Filomena's arms are full of flour she has brought from the mill. The boys take off to the back of the house where their world will soon transform to knights and castles. We settle Anna Maria on the kitchen rug with some tin cups and wooden spoons.

"*Sorella, com 'e vai? How are you?*" I inquire studying her face.

"*Va bene, all is well,*" she lies.

I give her one of my raised-eyebrow, 'I-know-you-better-than-that looks.'

She sighs. "Things are not too good at the mill. Luigi is causing problems with the workers and, and," she sniffles, "there is talk of Luigi and Simona Vocce." Filomena is crying, full sorrow, taking me back to the pain of Gregorio's death.

And then the stuffed guilt plunges its pointed edge. I hold my sister as I concentrate on the gentle breeze rustling the leaves, the birds twittering, Anna Maria's gurgles, and the boys whooping in the other room.

When she lifts her head from my shoulder, I stand to get her a cup of Mandarino Brothers coffee and a linen to dry her face. Together, we mimic the slogan with our best actress voices, "A cup of Mandarino Brothers café adds endless joy to your day!" We laugh with comic relief.

"*Allora, mia sorella*, what am I to do?" she asks.

"What do you want to do?" I inquire.

"*Non lo so, I don't know*. What can I do?"

"Well, "I begin, treading lightly. "You could move back to Mama and Papa's house with the boys and . . ."

"No, no, "she wails. "I love him. I told you before; I will never leave him."

Now she begins the woman's lament, beating her thighs, her breasts, her face. It is a practice I never really took to because I believed it was about the powerlessness of a woman. But today I partake of this ritual with my sister and feel the true release of emotion. (If Luigi did this, would he not need to beat his wife?)

After an indeterminate time passes, the boys' play turns to jousting and knights, and we have had enough of lamenting. She looks at me and smiles. "You know who you look like?" she smirks.

"No, who?" I answer back.

"You look like the rabbit in the garden with its scrunched face and twitching nose!"

I make a rabbit's face, twitching nose, chewing mouth, and put my fingers up to my head as ears. She bursts into bell-toned laughter. I join her. The boys come charging into the kitchen, the sound of laughter drawing them to us.

"Greetings, knights," I intone in my best servant's voice, bowing down to them. "May we serve thou a hearty meal?"

The three boys charge to the table with pretend swords drawn. My sister and I scurry about the kitchen, tandem partners, pouring goat's milk, tossing spaghetti, buttering bread, and warming up the mildly spiced sausages. The boys dig in like they haven't eaten in days. We look on with simple pleasure.

ZZZrrring, zzzzrrrring, the bicycle bell of Signore Pasquale rounds the corner of the house. I step out to greet him, and he smiles at me. "Arabella, *come vai?* How are things with you?"

"Oh, fine, Signore Pasquale, and you?"

"*Va bene, all is well.* I have a letter for you all the way from America!" He hands it to me as one would a treasure. And that it is! Traversing the seas and roadways to make its way to me.

"*Grazie, signore,* I appreciate your delivery. Can I interest you in a cup of Mandarino Brothers café? "

"How I wish I could stay but I've got too many deliveries. *Ciao.*"

Filomena steps out into the sunshine in time to wave to Signore Pasquale. She shakes her head. "Did you see the way he looked at me? Everybody knows the gossip of Luigi and that girl!"

"Bah, not true, he just needed to deliver the mail. "I turn to the envelope, sleek and white with lines of blue and red around the edge. I gaze at the stamp marked March 1923, a little over a month ago.

"Read it aloud if you think there's nothing too personal in there," Filomena teases.

I carefully slip my finger under the triangular edge take out the pages, and begin reading,

Boston 1923

Cara Arabella,

> *Come vai? That's 'How are you' in English! I am happy to be on solid ground! We, in the steerage class of the boat, were little more than cheap cargo (though the ticket cost a small fortune). We were kept in the bowels of the great ship and served stew unfit for pigs! I will spare you the unpleasant details of third class, but the singing and stories sustained the soul during those eight days at sea. I have vowed that any further travel will be prima classe so that I may inhale the sights and smells of the sea from the upper deck!*
>
> *Oh, Arabella, you would thrive here in modern America! The "19ᵗʰ Amendment" was passed into law so that women may now*

cast their vote. Imagine that, Arabella, women equal in power and voice as men! And music pours out on street corners and through a broadcasting box called a radio! You would like jazz music with its layers of instruments and unusual melody lines. There are moving picture shows where filmed stories are acted out on a giant screen. I saw a movie called Toll of the Sea, the first one ever filmed in color.

Allora, even though World War I is long over, the Red Scare of Communistos is ever-present. They think because we are Italian, we automatically side with Mussolini (who is not honored here). Some Italians have bad reputations as "birds of passage"- those that send their earnings home to Italy with no intentions to make America their permanent home.

And there's the gangster Al Capone, an Italian bully. He defies American laws like the one forbidding alcohol, called Prohibition, by brewing and selling whiskey covertly! The Americans look at him and say, "Italians are lawless brutes!" Then, there's Nicolo Sacco and Bartolomeo Vanzetti, the dangerous Italian radicals who murder and thieve. When they were finally arrested, the newspapers presented all Italians as thugs.

I wish they knew me, an Italian who loves this country and plans on making it a permanent home. I go out to restaurants, the movie theatre, and markets, spending my dollars here.

All day I am in the shop. At 4 am, I knead bread dough and start the café brewing at the Sucero's store. I've been in touch with Octavio to begin buying and serving Mandarino Brothers coffee here. Just think, your family's coffee and my baking—a great match. At noontime, I have a twenty-minute break the Americans call, "lunch." I take a slice of ham and a slice of cheese and stack them on a piece of yesterday's bread with a pickle and some "potato chips" (little wafers of thinly fried potatoes that crunch when you bite into them).

There are no siestas here. We are open before dawn and close well after dusk. The days are long but rewarding. The Suceros treat me well, and the basement room below the shop is little like living in an underground cave, but I have made it my home. I have never lived alone. It can feel both empty and peaceful.

Enclosed is a little American for you! I told you we'd learn together.

I must go retrieve the batch of Nonna Emelia's butter cookies from the oven.

Always,
Antonio

I sit with the letter still in my hand and the little book of English phrases. For a moment, I daydream about practicing English alongside my partner, Antonio.

Filomena's voice shakes me from my reverie. "*Bravo, Antonio Salerno! He is faring well in America.* "

I try to reject a daydream of Antonio and me in America, but I will not lie; it's challenging. Wrangling in one's demon is like a cowboy trying to lasso an elusive bull. My rope slips off the back of the truth: I want to be there with him.

A knock on the door reveals one of the mill workers saying they need my help for hand injuries. I grab my bag, grateful to be of service, and removed from my reverie.

SIGNORE PALERMO AND SIGNORE VITO have split their hands wide open. I clean, stitch, and wrap their wounds as easily as I'd darn a sock. It's second nature now. Others need tending, mostly just someone to talk to, someone they think will understand them. I wish Marco felt that he could talk to me, that I would understand him. Perhaps, then a kind of inner healing could begin. What lurks behind the eye cloth is in a state of decay, of that I am certain. He will not even allow the *erborista*, me, to tend to it! I leave the bowls of the soothing calendula-infused solution, rose oil, lavender, willow bark oil for inflammation, and sterilized patches, and he administers himself.

At 3 am, I awaken with Marco still in my thoughts. I decide to get up and soak some lentils for dinner, then step out in the cold evening air to use the outhouse. I'm surprised to see a faint light burning at Marco's door.

"*Fratello?*" I whisper as I approach the door. "Are you awake?"

He comes to the door. His left eye is patchless. I try not to show my alarm at its condition: red, dark blue, and running like a narrow stream down his face. He has a handkerchief pressed to his left cheek.

"Arabella, *che fai? What are you doing?* Is it Dominic?"

"Mi *dispiace, I am sorry* to worry you. I came out to use the facilities and saw your light."

He nods his head, "*Va bene.*"

"What's not *good* is your eye, Brother. Please let me have a closer look."

"I am fine," a knife's edge in his voice.

I must tread lightly. The injured thinks he is successfully hiding his injury. I walk the line between gentle and assertive. My spirit angel has helped me learn to be still and wait for the best course of action that will come in words, feelings, or pictures. I sense straightforwardness is what is necessary.

"Let me have a look," I say firmly.

He acquiesces. It is bad; anyone can see that. Asking for guidance, I gaze at Marco's head. Images appear as if I "see" what is occurring from inside the eye. The discoloration throbs as the eye withers. It's dying a painfully, slow death.

"Marco, your eye is trying to clear what it considers debris." I pause. "Itself."

He looks like he wants to fold himself up like an old sweater and stow away in a long-forgotten drawer. Knowingness penetrates. I sense I am to cease direct reference to his eye for now.

"Will you consider resting your body today? I know you are to go to the mill, but just give me a list of mill tasks and I will attend to them." I issue a little white lie. "I planned on going to the mill anyway to check on Signore Palermo's hand."

His shoulders slump. "Please forgive me for the trouble I have caused you, Arabella."

I put my finger to his lips. "Shhh. That is nonsense. You risked much to take me to Brazil. You have done ten times for me what little I have done for you. "

"I doubt that is true, but every day I thank God for you, Arabella."

I'm so moved with emotion. It builds form in my throat and behind my eyes. I let go, allowing the tears to spill when this just tumbles out of my mouth.

"Marco, do you feel safe here?"

"Safe?" he looks at me quizzically.

"Yes, safe. Safe—physically. Safe—emotionally." I implore him with my tone and my eyes. Quite suddenly, I am convinced this is the time for him to finally reveal his story. It's as if I'm being directed by some other force. My angel's light pulses.

His hands tremble slightly. He looks at me and knows what I am summoning. "Arabella, this is not the time, please . . ."

I interrupt. Something I do not ever advocate, but here I am breaking my own rule.

"I will not say I understand how difficult this is for you, but I do know that if you are ever going to heal it must begin with the story of what happened."

I need some help here dear, angel. I breathe in, and I breathe out, calming myself and the very air we are breathing on the brisk morning.

"It's time. I am here with you."

And so is our angel.

The look on his face is panic. I take his hand. Minutes pass, seeming like hours. Nervous at first for what I know I do not want to hear, I just keep breathing in and out and wait, holding the quiet space for him to relive what I imagine are the most horrifying moments of his life.

"I was such a naïve fool." His head, a Brazilian Jangada fishing boat, tosses side to side. "I actually believed that once we shed light on who and what was corrupt and alternative ways to live, it would force real change."

I nod my head but remain silent.

"You witnessed it. You know how workers are little more than slaves, as if their sole purpose was to serve the plantation owners." He sighs, raking his right hand through his jet-black waves. "Who would give the downtrodden a voice?"

"You," I solemnly declare.

"Me." He laughs sardonically. "A lot of good that did. How could I think that my articles for *Terra Livre* would gain international attention, forcing the world would take notice? "

"Your writing is evocative, impactful. And it scared a lot of powerful people, didn't it?" I think of Signore Riccardo's warning to Octavio.

Suddenly he looks as if he is consumed with a quaking fever. "Arabella, I am glad you left when you did! I would not have been able to bear any manner of harm that would have come to you."

"*Calma, Fratello*, I came home with a fire in my belly you helped me ignite. I am stronger because that is what you do: show others how to find strength within themselves."

"But so many were wronged because of me! All I did was stir the sleeping monsters: the government agents and ruling members of the church. Octavio tried to warn me."

"Did he?"

A nod of his head.

"It was shortly after you left. He told me to go home to Italy, to cease my inflammatory writings. Out of respect for him as a businessman, he was informed I was on a list of troublemakers who would be shut down—no matter what it took."

So, he told him about Signore Riccardo's warning! It's as if I am there standing in the shoes of both of my brothers—one who stands for freedom, justice, and revolution and the other who is firmly planted in the status quo.

"I stood my righteous ground, spewing hate for him and the world he represented. I raged at him, unforgivable words of accusation and loathing—a culmination of uncontrollable anger for every injustice I ever heard, read, or encountered. It is something I deeply regret."

May you have the opportunity to make amends someday.

"Who knew this side of our brother?" he continues. "Kind, understanding, even. He tried to tell me that people on both sides of the dispute are dangerous because of their mutual desperation, and I just couldn't comprehend that concept—until it was too late."

"There's a certain comfort I feel in his wisdom."

"Yes. I just couldn't see it—no pun intended." He attempts a weak smile. "So, the desperate on the left and the desperate on the right got together, and I found myself in the center of their storm."

He looks right at me, his good eye full of pain and betrayal but also forgiveness.

"I cannot blame Signore Loscatto . . ."

I gasp. "Oh, the family with that precious little girl afflicted with malaria?"

As the story unfolds, my heartbeat gathers speed.

"He had no choice but to betray me."

My sharp intake of breath stops him. I nod, my hand on my heart.

"They offered him an ultimatum—to lure me to where they were or they would take his family away, rape his wife until she was dead, and sell his daughter to the highest bidder."

"*Dio mio*, such dangerous people," I whisper.

"*Desperate* people," he adds. "My writing only fueled my enemies' determination to keep things as they were. And so, Loscatto told me of a man who had not only a compelling story but physical evidence to indict a loathsome official. Loscatto revealed the location of the man who was waiting to meet me. How could I turn down that offer? I was seduced by greed."

"What do you mean?"

"I wanted that story more than anything, *anything*, Arabella. It was pure greed. And they knew I would be blindly driven to obtain the juicy details. I'm sure that is another reason they took my eye. A metaphor for annihilating blind passion."

He takes a deep, slow breath, his eyes closed, one of them, a seeping dark river.

"Three of them waited for me at the supposed meeting place. One more sinister than the other. Brass knuckles, bats, and boots ravaged my body. The biggest one snickered to the others about 'seeing the new world,' a reference to our movement's motto to stay the course. Then, he reared back, and with inner rage fueling his fist, he repeatedly pounded my eye with the brass knuckle. Somewhere after the fifth or sixth blow, I passed out. When I awoke, I was on a cargo ship back to Italy, nestled next to some sacks of Mandarino Coffee. My timely exit courtesy of the influence of our brother, Octavio."

I draw my arms around him, ever so gently, rocking him like I would a child.

"I was as pompous as they were," he whimpers, "to think my words would change hearts and open eyes. Instead, hearts were broken and eyes literally blinded."

151

My angel's arms enfold us both. The words come from her. "Sometimes, evidence of the work we do comes much, much later, but be assured, Marco, you have impacted many people's future."

"I doubt that, but I hope what you say is true," he responds.

"I know it's true because you have done that for me, and I will be forever grateful."

Pulling from my embrace he looks right into my eyes. "The eye is dead, isn't it?"

I nod. "*Sì*."

"Then it is time for it to be removed," he states, wiping a tear from his healthy eye.

"*Va bene, Fratello, all will be well, brother*. We will get you the best surgeon, even if we have to travel to Roma, Naples, or Milano. I'll be there to make sure someone is looking over their shoulders!"

"That poor doctor, "he teases. We both chuckle.

"Very funny! Until then, let me fix you some herbs and salve—and some breakfast. You get the list of things to be taken care of at the mill today. I'll be back shortly."

We embrace again before I take my leave to go prepare his calming tea with a drop of bella donna and numbing salve. I go to the shelf with my herbs and oil. I think I'd like a dose of it myself after the grueling tale and acceptance of eye surgery.

My grumbling stomach leads me to the larder for a hunk of asiago and a piece of yesterday's bread. I sit at my little kitchen table as the pot of water boils, and the coffee burbles on the stove, grateful but a bit shaken by what just transpired. Suddenly, the comingling aromas of everything cause nausea. *What in the world is going on here?* I was just hungry a minute ago, and now I am feeling sick to my stomach. It doesn't make sense . . ..

Unless, of course, one stops to calculate her last womanly cycle two months ago! My new tinctures of black cohosh, pennyroyal, rue, and myrrh did not prevent pregnancy! My careful concoction was ineffective. I will pour over my notes, measurements, and calculations later, but now I am trying to accept that I am with child! The undeniable truth is a vivid flower in summer's light, blossoming whether you are ready or not! I make it to the outhouse just in time for the morning sickness to take over. *Mother of God, pray for us sinners* (and that includes those of us who love their child but do not wish for another). *Amen.*

MARCO'S SURGERY IN NAPLES goes well. Mama and I accompany him, she the appreciative one, I, the irritating one with my hundred questions regarding every single part of the surgical process. To their credit, the surgeon and nurses at the hospital treated me with respect.

Now home, Marco's recovery and adjustment are arduous. Without peripheral vision, he cannot know when something or someone is standing right next to him; it is quite literally a blind spot. It is affecting his equilibrium—he teeters, stumbles, and sometimes, falls. Depression is becoming a common caller.

This morning I help his body adjust to the prosthetic glass eye. The dressings must be changed and the eye socket cleaned. He says it feels scratchy and he complains of penetrating, needle-like headaches. We keep sterile cloths in his possession to wipe any drainage. My valerian/belladonna tincture ensures that he rests most of the day. Mama comes daily to be with him, and Papa stops on his way to or from work, filling him in on the business and the gossip of the village. It warms my heart to see the bridge between them mending.

After dropping Dominic at Filomena's, I head to the mill with my medical bag and list to fulfill Marco's duties. Strolling up the winding road with my collection pouch, I gather dandelion and blessed thistle where the goats graze.

Golden chamomile blossoms glint like tiny balls of sunlight, stalky like wheat. Without wheat, we would be like the people of long ago who ate only tree nuts. Ceres, the goddess of agriculture and grain, was one of the only gods who saw fit to interact with the common person, teaching them to grow, preserve, harvest, and prepare grain. She was thought to be the god responsible for a land's fertile bounty as well as the love a mother bears for her child.

I need help bearing the weight of this child growing within. I remind myself how much I love Dominic. Still, it's been a long road from demanding infant to reckless toddler to independent 5-year-old! And now, I'll be starting all over again—tending the physical body and just as importantly, nurturing the spiritual and mental aspects of this child. I sigh deeply. A woman's life consists of the growing seasons of the heart.

At the mill, a version of the great inventor, Vitruvius's invention toils, busy workers transfer the grain to bins, stack barrels, feed the machine. Two of the workers approach me with a problem and another in need of wrapping for a sprain. Out of the corner of my eye, I notice Luigi standing too close to a young lady named Arianna. I wish I did not see that for myself.

I loathe that man and his wicked ways.

THAT WHICH WE DESIRE AND that which we do not seem to have a way of finding us. From babies that rule the body to leaders that rule the country.

"Have you read this quote by Mussolini?" Marco asks incredulously. "He states that 'Italy wants peace, quiet and calm. I will give these things with love if possible and with force, if necessary.'

I must admit I am not thrilled at the subject matter, but to witness Marco reading from a newspaper is heartwarming.

He continues, "Mussolini's Black Shirts, his *Fasci di Combattiment,* use all manner of force! Did you hear about the man over in Acri who made the mistake of talking about Mussolini in the village square?"

"No. I'm guessing it was not a favorable opinion. "

"They tied the miserable soul up to a tree and poured half a liter of castor oil down his throat before they added a lizard!"

Teetering on the edge of morning sickness, the image sends a wave of nausea. "My God." I have to sit down. "That amount of castor oil alone would purge the digestive system too quickly, causing excruciating cramping and emptying of the bowels. Followed by a live creature? Marone! The havoc on the way out of the bowels is unthinkable!"

"The Black Shirts have a motto spreading like the dandelion seeds of spring, 'Me ne frego.' Apparently, they indeed *don't give a damn about anything* except carrying out Mussolini's orders."

"But his newspaper *Il Popolo di Italia, The People of Italy,* states he will effect positive changes for our country."

"Propaganda is a powerful tool," Marco comments, perhaps remembering his experiences in Brazil, "and Mussolini is an expert, saying what the people want to hear. Do you know he's discarding the parliamentary system?"

I didn't.

"I'm not saying I agreed with all the tenets of our government, but he's thrown the entire system out the window. His dangerous new order gives him absolute power to rule. It is written that the people may not question the leader; he is above the law because he is the law. *Marone!*"

I search the rusty reels of my knowledge, rewinding history where people have suffered unthinkable agony at the hands of powerful rulers. Look at Jesus himself! He spoke his mind, pointed out injustice, shared an enlightened new way of being, and they nailed him to a cross for it!

I search the article. "What is this Acerbo Law?"

"Oh, that's a special one." Marco sneers. "It states if one party receives as little as twenty-five percent of the vote, they are awarded sixty-six percent of the seats in parliament."

"*Che? What?* That doesn't add up."

"No matter. It's law now. People I know report that Mussolini placed his henchmen prominently in the parliament chambers, pen and paper in hand to take note of who was voting against him."

"And in the face of such fear resolve crumbled?"

Marco nods then looks out the window lost in his own disturbing thoughts.

"Marco, I know your passion for injustice, but I hope you are treading lightly."

"Do not worry, sister. My days of political involvement are over. I will, however, remain informed."

"*Va bene.*"

We hear a voice coming up the walk singing the Farfallina song.

"*Buon Giorgno,*" Filomena beams. She approaches with a basket full of her exquisite lace flowers seemingly woven from the Milky Way.

Marco hugs her, and he and the twins inquire about Dominic.

"The little sleepy head is still in bed," I mock, complete with my hands on my hips.

"Don't worry," answers Bernardo earnestly. "We'll get him up, Zia." Alessandro bolts through the cucina door shouting authoritatively, Marco in tow.

"Another Mussolini, eh?" laughs Filomena.

"Oh, *Sorella,* that is not funny!" I almost fall apart.

"Arabella, I jest. *Che c'`e? What's wrong?*"

All at once, the ground I am standing on splinters like an ax through a log. I try to form cohesive sentences about all my worries including Marco's recovery and Mussolini's madness, but it all comes out in hiccup phrases.

"You snort like a pig," she teases.

"Yes, well, I am going to look like one in the next several months." I sigh.

She looks at me, taking in the words. "Arabella, are you finally with child? I wondered . . ."

All I can muster is a nod. What would I say, *Your sister is a sinner, purposely preventing pregnancy, but her latest batch didn't work?*

Filomena's face explodes with delight. "*Mia sorella*, so am I! So am I!"

She takes my hands and pulls me up from the chair at my table. Together, holding hands, we begin a slow circle dance as we did in our youth.

"Together, *mia sorella*, we are pregnant at the same time!" In full-blown ecstasy, she laughs and laughs, pumping my arms up and down. The angel light glows throughout the entire kitchen.

"Okay, wildcat." I pull my hands free and sit back down. "Take it easy on your little sister. I'm not faring so well with this one."

"Sit down then," she urges. "How far along are you?"

"9 or 10 weeks," I answer.

"Well, I am three or so months." She pulls her dress tight and I can see the tiniest melon of a child beginning to ripen.

"Do you really want to bring another child into a world where Benito Mussolini controls us like Punchinello puppets?"

"*Guarda, mia sorella. Watch yourself.* Please don't speak ill of Il Dulce. Do you know there are many Italians who find our leader promoting positive changes?"

"He says he is, but this man is a master at deception and manipulation."

"Some would argue he has helped the worker with the promise of an eight-hour workday."

"I'll give him that, but was it helping the Italian people when he allowed indecent war profits for the Industrialists?

She shrugs. "Because of Mussolini, Catholicism will be compulsory education, ensuring our faith is passed down properly. You see, there are positive contributions."

"But how we raise our children is for parents to decide."

"Arabella, Mussolini is trying to restore our country."

"Are you telling me you will stand behind a man who claims, 'A good beating never hurt anyone'?"

"There are always two sides to every issue. Are there not? And it cannot be denied that many of our people believe he is cleaning up corruption."

She is blinded by her need to see only good, a lovely trait, but there is more to it. Just like there is more to her husband's two sides: bad and worse.

IN THE CHILD'S GAME OF HIDE and seek, the seeker closes his eyes and counts to twenty while the hiders seek a place to hide beneath beds, behind coats in a closet, or wedged in a laundry barrel. The seeker calls out, "Here I come to find everyone!" and begins his search. Antonio and I played a version of it years ago in the grove. Luigi plays it with young *ragazza* of the village—*young women* like Arianna. It doesn't matter the type—blonde or brunette, short or tall, he chases after them with equal aplomb. And he's such an imbecile, he actually believes he's hiding the truth.

But everyone knows him. Tongues wag, revealing stories of his roving hands and roguish ways. And his temper tantrums? *Malenovamia!* Filomena's beautiful, pregnant body is too often marked by them. Though his children may be terrorized by his threatening words, he does not beat them—yet. Does he reserve his tender hands for the *ragazza?*

Arianna has been shouting from the rooftops that their intimate relations were not consensual. Papa had little choice but to intercede. When it comes to business, there is no room for impropriety. My long-awaited answered prayer came through Papa who has created a new position for Luigi—in Brazil! Octavio has agreed to take him back to manage a part of the Mandarino Brothers export business. To soothe the enormous ego of the beast, they have made it sound as if the business cannot survive without Luigi!

Filomena is beside herself with both sorrow and embarrassment, but slowly accepting this solution. She is in good spirits this morning as we women work like the string section of an orchestra, knowing exactly when to start, duck, pluck, or stir the ingredients for Luigi's farewell dinner. The pear-shaped eggplants are a glossy plum color. We debate the perfect size to slice them for *parmigiana di melanzane*.

"When you slice them on the thick side, they have the texture of meat," Pina declares.

"But then the insides never cook properly," I deliver.

"Thinly sliced uses less oil, "states Filomena.

"But they dry out if too thin," Pina responds.

Mama nods her head. "Ladies, let us split the difference, shall we?" And with authority and skill, she cuts a perfect centimeter slice. "Wha-la, as they say in gay Paree." She laughs.

We all begin an informal can-can line, kicking our legs in unison. It's a challenge for the pregnant sisters, but it's all about the fun. Laughter rains on the scene.

"Back to the *melenzane parmigiana, signorini*," Mama commands.

With precision, several eggplants are sliced in near-perfect centimeter rounds. She neither pauses nor deliberates. Pina cracks the eggs in the large ceramic yellow bowl that Mama has had for over forty-four years, whipping them with her fork like a tornado funnel.

"Ah, the heirloom bowl," teases Filomena. "You know Arabella, as the eldest daughter, this bowl will be passed on to me."

I feign a girlish pout, "Being the youngest in the family has its drawbacks." And in a whining child's voice, I remark, "Mama, why does she get everything?"

We all laugh as Mama hands the plate of eggplant to dip in the bowl of egg, cream, salt, pepper, and parsley.

"It is so good to have you girls home," she says. "The years have raced by too quickly."

My sister and I look at each other and smile with our eyes. Together we chant one of Mama's sayings, "The clock ticks whether you hear it or not." That elicits a warm chuckle.

"Mama, look at this family of yours," delivered perhaps a little too cheerfully. "You have your son Marco home in Paola again, and your daughters have three healthy sons between them, granddaughters and . . ."

"Two more grandchildren on the way!" chimes Filomena.

I continue, "And you and Papa are in good health, and the businesses are flourishing."

"Girls, you are right. Please forgive my self-pity."

Mama is in her early fifties. Along with the female cycle shifting and different systems diminishing within the body, the mind also experiences the end of an era, the realization that one will never again carry a child, the loss of a part of a woman's femininity. I make a mental note to mix her a tincture of primrose oil and a drop of black cohosh to take for just a few weeks to ease some of the symptoms. Too much black cohosh can put the liver at risk.

The heady aroma of hot olive oil is released into the kitchen, and we know the pan is ready. We ease into an assembly line of dipping eggplant slices, coating in flour and breadcrumbs, re-dipping, and coating again for a second time. The next step is placing the slices into pans of hot oil. The flavors are sealed quickly, the outside golden as the leaves on the mountains in October, the insides cooked but not soggy.

Filomena begins a song for us all to join in, "Fa la, fa la, to and fro and fro and back, tra-la, tra-la, spread the flour from the sack, fry them up and on the rack, fa la tra la na."

Mama's sauce bubbles in the pot, *plip, plip, plipping* to the rhythm of the song. The mozzarella, relieved of its fresh fern leaf wrapping, is sliced for the *parmigiana*. We continue singing as I oil the bottom of the large pans, readying them for the layering of the sauce, fried eggplant, mozzarella, parsley, and basil leaves, topped with parmesan.

Suddenly, I am doubled over in excruciating, stabbing pain. My belly is the crank of a machine heaving double time. I try to straighten up but am unable.

"*Mia sorella.*" Filomena perks up to soldier-like attentiveness. "What is wrong? *Parlarmi.*" *Speak to me.*

But I cannot speak, overwhelmed by the task to catch my breath. The depth and force of the pain overtake me, and panic breaks out in buckets of sweat, soaking my favorite bluebell print dress. Swallowing hard, I push back the bile, nausea spinning me around Mama's kitchen in undulating circles. I try to engage my *erborista* mind to read the symptoms: excruciating cramps, sweat, nausea—this fetus is in danger!

I try to show them I am lucid enough to know it is the baby. I clutch the bluebell fabric, but it's like I am squeezing the life out of those fabric flowers. The life within me is squeezing to be released four and half months too early.

The women are scurrying about, putting cold cloths on my neck and my forehead, holding me up, trying to get me to drink a sip of Papa's whiskey, but I am somewhere else outside of my body now, observing the scene. I gaze down at me, in the chair in Mama's kitchen. That's when I notice that the bluebell dress is steeped in the crimson of my blood. I fall into darkness.

I WONDER WHAT WE WOULD have called her? The new priest, Signore Viti, informed us that because my child was not baptized (therefore not free of Original Sin) she could neither receive a Catholic burial nor be buried in our cemetery. It is cruel to punish a mother like this after her loss. Signore claims she will exist in a place called Limbo—neither hell nor purgatory. What about God's mercy? I ask. He stares at the ground.

Once recovered from the church's rejection, I realize burying my daughter in the far east corner of our garden is the best thing that could have happened. She'll remain near to me. I will see her daily, albeit in a mound of earth. My emotions are still raw, and I find I am on a bit of a rocking boat of loss and guilt. Did I cause my child to miscarry? I took that new tincture for over three months. Perhaps it harmed my uterus, forbidding the child to hold on. Did my child hear with her tiny, but fully-developed ears that I didn't want another child?

Mama, Pina, Filomena, and the midwife tell me a hundred times that miscarrying a child is nature's way and has nothing to do with anything I did or didn't do. I would tell my patient some similar patronizing sentiment. But I know who I am and what I did. Shame plugs every pore. Imagine what these dear women would think of me if they knew what I've done to prevent pregnancies or my unmotherly thoughts.

My considerate sister wears one of Luigi's old shirts over her dress today to hide her healthy, growing child. Seeing her goodness amplifies the badness in me. I cry silently as she holds me like a child. This woman's capacity for love is as great as the Virgin Mary herself.

"*Mia sorella*." I sniffle. "You are so good."

"As are you."

"No," I whine. "I am a selfish woman and a horrible mother!"

"*Basta! Stop!* You are neither selfish nor horrible. Nature took its course. God and his angels were protecting you and the child."

It turns out I cannot bear the weight of this shame alone. "You don't understand," I croak. "I did this because the truth is . . . I didn't want another child." I cannot look at the face of my sister. She must be horrified to hear my ugly truth—well, not all of it. I kept out the part about my preventative tinctures.

But Filomena is the epitome of goodness, and just like the unconditional friend, mother, and sister she is, she shows me nothing but love's compassion. She rocks me, humming softly. As soothing as it is, it is almost worse. I wish she'd yell at me, call me names, tell me how disgraced she is by me.

The clip-clop of three sets of feet come marching into my room. Allesandro goes to his mom, but Bernardo comes right onto the bed with me, followed by his little shadow, Dominic.

"Zia Arabella, it's time for you to get up now," he says, tugging on my sleeve.

His mother tries to pull him off, but Bernardo has sunk his heels in. Same *testa dura* he was being birthed into this world!

"No, Mama." He shakes her hand. "Zia Arabella needs to get up."

Now Dominic is pulling on my other arm.

Filomena tries one more time to remove Bernardo, but he is adamant.

"I've got to show you something out in the garden."

I nod to Filomena. The child is right. It is time for me to get out of this bed. She helps me up, and Dominic takes one hand, Bernardo the other.

We walk through the kitchen door, a parade of family—three perfectly fit, happy, healthy boys, a little girl toddling, two sisters, one with child, one without. Bernardo is so excited his feet move double time. It takes all my strength to keep up with him and Dominic. Filomena tells him to slow down, but her motherly advice falls on deaf ears. This boy has a one-track mind.

We skirt around the edge of the harvested summer garden close to where we buried my child when Bernardo stops. We all put on our brakes like a train at the end of the line. His finger points animatedly.

"See, Zia? Do you see? It is blooming just for you." His round face explodes with pride—the explorer sharing his undisputable discovery.

Gingerly, I approach the lone, out-of-season poppy. My angel's light is glowing around it.

"Thank you for showing me this," I say to the boys as I embrace them. "I feel so much better! "And to Bernardo, I proclaim, "Bernardo, you were right to get me up and show me this miracle. Thank you."

He beams like the sun in the perfection of its own light.

"Who wants *latte di cioccolato?*" asks Filomena

"Me, me!" the boys shout.

We head inside to sit at the *cucina* table—my nephews and niece, my son and my sister—drinking our chocolate milk. I am nourished by the sweetness of small pleasures and immensely grateful for healing in all its forms.

FILOMENA HANDS ME AN AIRMAIL envelope from Boston, USA. If she is feeling jealous that I received a letter from a friend and she has yet to receive anything from her husband three months in Brazil, she doesn't show it. We received a telegram from Octavio in Rio de Janeiro that Luigi had arrived safe, but other than that, she has not heard directly from the brute. She sits down gingerly, her extended belly pushing to the edge of the table. I pour her a cup of coffee from the espresso pot on the stove and tell her we are in for a treat, Antonio Salerno style! I slide my small dicing knife under the flap and unfold the letter from Antonio.

Boston, 1926

Cara Arabella,

> *Salute from America where I am now manager, baker, and bookkeeper at Signore Sucaro's expanding shop. It has been the most exciting time for me. I wish you were here to share it! (Are you studying your English book?)*
>
> *I still awaken long before the dawn to begin the bread rising,*

biscotti batter, and a large batch of Nonna Emelia's butter cookies. Once all of that is going, I brew some perfect Mandarino Brothers coffee from Brazil for myself! We did it, Arabella. We are now doing business with your family's plantation, bringing it here to Boston where the Americans lap it up like thirsty kittens. They cannot get enough of it. Mandarino Brothers Coffee is superior to anything available here. And your brother, Octavio has asked me to become a distributor in Boston, and they will pay me for this work. (I would gladly do it as a service to you and your family). This business arrangement has helped me shape a dream: a business sharing my family's confectionary recipes! Loyal customers already come from all over the city in their vehicles and on the trolley cars. They have spread the word about my pastries. And this is only one city in one state. If one thinks big, the opportunities sweeping from Boston to San Francisco are endless. You know me, Arabella, I am not a man seduced by money, but money brings an attractive freedom of choice.

Please send salutations to your family and write me of your news soon. I will look forward to a visit with you in the form of a letter across the seas. Be sure to use some of your English words!

Fondly,
Your Friend,
Antonio

I am happy for my friend. He continues to heed the call to adventure, growth in the land of opportunity.

THE ENGLISH WORD FOR *BELLA* is beautiful! Filomena's second daughter, Natalia, is already striking. Her features, her skin, the shape of her face, eyes, and lips are indicators that she is going to be stunning! The birth went as smoothly as possible. I have a delightful memory of Alessandro, Bernardo, Anna Maria, and Dominic etched in my mind: after they heard Natalia's newborn cry, they cracked open the door, one head above the other, above the other, above the other, like a stacked block tower! Anna Maria was on the bottom then Dominic, Alessandro, and Bernardo. The sight was so endearing the women laughed, and the children beamed unaware of what a charming picture they made.

These are the times when being part of a family is *ogni cosa, everything*, everything that binds lives together. And in times when we're showered by fallen debris from the outside world, family can be a sheltering umbrella.

While the other women were busy tending Filomena and Natalia, I escorted the children into the birthing room. The seven-year-old twins walked toward Natalia, Alessandro holding the hand of four-year-old Anna Maria.

"You will all have to help me take care of our little one," she said.

They nodded their heads as quickly as a hummingbird flapping its wings.

"But Mama, are *you* okay?" asked Bernardo, the keen-eyed hawk.

"*Si, figlio, sta bene*," she reassuringly answered her son that she is well.

"But you look tired, Mama, so tired."

Filomena could not fool her Bernardo. "Well, you are right, Bernardo. I am tired. It's a lot of work to bring a baby into the world."

Alessandro took over. "Then you should rest, Mama. Nonna, can you take care of Natalia while Mama rests? We'll take Anna Maria."

"I am a big girl. I don't need you to take care of me," declared Anna Maria.

We all tried not to laugh.

"Very well," Mama acknowledged. "Everyone out."

They bid their mama goodbye. Bernardo kissed Filomena's hand, making my heart swell. Dominic came in timidly holding Marco's hand.

Marco whispered, "*Brava*, Filomena," meeting Natalia who was collapsed in the cocoon of her nonna's embrace. Dominic came to me, nearly hiding in the folds of my dress. I took his hand, and we crept out of the room and into the garden.

We sat together on the bench zio Benito made in honor of my little girl. Dominic was unusually quiet. Though my mind wanted to spitfire a thousand questions regarding his thoughts and wellbeing, I just waited silently.

Finally, after several minutes he lifted his head. "Mama?"

"*Si, figlio? What is it son?*"

"Didn't you have my sister growing inside you?"

"I did."

"But what happened to her?"

How do I begin to answer that? "I don't really know what happened, Dominic. Nobody but God knows what made her stop growing inside me."

But it was my fault.

"Will God let you grow another baby?"

"Let's hope so. "

He nods. That's it. All he needed was reassurance from his mama.

"For now, let's be happy for Natalia and Zia Filomena, Alessandro and Bernardo and Anna Maria, *si*?"

"Don't forget *Zio* Luigi too Mama."

If only we could.

WITH LUIGI IN BRAZIL AND MARCO tutoring more students, I have taken over Marco's duties at the mill. There was no contract or official passing of the baton; I just kept doing what I've been doing during Marco's recuperation. Mostly, it's just showing up, being observant, taking notes, and listening to people. My days are full but exciting. I am free. I create. I heal. I make decisions. I conduct business. And I am pregnant again. There were many facets to consider regarding this pregnancy: could I even get pregnant again or did the black cohosh tincture harm my reproductive organs; did I actually want to conceive; was I trying to revive the spirit of the child I had lost; was it guilt or obligation? In the end, I will tell you it was a kind of longing mixed with the calling of this child. I have decided to keep it secret until I'm showing.

At the mill, I take pride in my corn field—a first for Paola! The story of the corn venture thrills me. It began simply enough while I took a walk to clear my head of mill business one day. As I strolled behind the mill, I felt the easy presence of my spirit angel. Drifting into daydreaming, I softly gazed at the golden grasses, the cerulean sky, and the full, blossoming clouds, noting a vague image of the goddess, Ceres. Thinking admirably about her led to considering my ancestors and heroines like Signora Ruffino. I wondered about making something that would honor all the women who had come before me. Suddenly, the area behind the mill was lit with incandescent light. I moved toward it, but on closer inspection, the area was nothing but a burial place for broken spokes; old, twisted ropes; and empty burlap bags. Still, there was a feeling that the area could be coaxed to life.

What happened next was quite possibly the most unusual experience of my life thus far (save meeting my spirit angel, being touched by a beam of light, or giving birth to Dominic). As I contemplated putting a simple altar with a vase for fresh flowers, a voice intoned, "*The future is Robigo.*" And just like that, poof! It was gone. I didn't have a clue as to its meaning.

After observing the mill running smoothly and returning to the village to deliver my arnica blend for Signore Nugissi's sore back, I returned home to search my books. In the book of Roman mythology, I saw Robigo, goddess of *corn*! Perhaps the fallow field behind the mill could be planted with corn! Further reading referenced robigo, as a dreaded blight of red mildew that turns corn crops to dust. I knew without a doubt that I was to plant corn, so I designed a plan, presented it to Papa, and before I knew it, we planted a hectare of corn. It will come to bear fruit at the same time my child is born.

Today, after visiting patients and returning home from the mill, I hear the exuberant voices of children mixed with a somber, adult's voice. It's my sister. Between sniffles and deep breaths, she's explaining something to Mama. She falters, and I hear why. Luigi Compretta! *Che vada al diavaolo! Damn him!* Over 9,000 kilometers away and still he manages to hurt her! I have heard it said that we take ourselves with us wherever we go. If that's true, Luigi wasn't going to be different just because he went clear across the world.

Mama and Filomena sit forlornly at my kitchen table. The table is strewn with coffee cups and biscotti edged in the green of pistachio nuts. I greet them with a hug. My sister turns her head, staring down at the white-planked floor. I notice an envelope on the table postmarked Brazil.

"*C' e' ?*" I inquire. I want to know what is going on.

Filomena is sniveling. I take a deep breath. My stomach flip-flops, and it is *not* due to morning sickness!

Mama says, "There is trouble in Brazil."

"Trouble?" I inquire, tip-toeing lightly through the prickly field of emotions.

Filomena finds her voice. "The trouble is a young Brazilian *ragazza, capisce?*"

"*Ho capito.*" *I understand*, yes, that time and again Luigi does one thing well—he disappoints. For my sister's sake, I stuff my rage at the man who continually finds ways to bruise her.

I sit beside her, taking her hand. As I do, I swear to you, I can both *see and feel* the angst of her heart. It's as if I am inside her body, devoid of air. I'd like to knock the wind out of Luigi Compretta, but my angel nudges me to ease my sister's sorrow.

"*Sorella*, a person can have a kind of sickness . . ." I pause, searching for the right words, "of the mind. In some cases, there is no control over *urges*." I sound a bit like a doctor and a priest rolled into one. "We all know Luigi loves you and wants to make you happy. He doesn't *intend* to hurt you! You know that, don't you?"

She nods her head. She is glued to my every word. I feel a slight glow and know my spirit angel is providing these words.

"I've read in a health journal that men like him do not even realize there are consequences to their actions. They just act on their impulses."

I do recall reading about some mentally ill minds who do not have the capacity to control sexual urges. Even though my opinion of him is lower than a sludge rat, Filomena deserves peace.

Filomena hugs me, stands, and begins to pace the floor. Mama mouths a thank you to me.

There is more to the story.

"What?" I ask. "What else?"

"Luigi has left Brazil."

"For Italia?"

"No."

"No?"

My sister takes a deep breath. "Luigi is on his way to America," she announces.

"America?" I look from Mama to Filomena back and forth as if my head is a saloon door swinging.

"The children and I are to join him there."

"There? Where?"

"America!" Filomena blurts out and quietly mews like a lost kitten.

I put my hand over my mouth to keep it from spewing expletives about the man I just defended. I feel faint. It could be pregnancy hormones and emotions mixed. The room sways slightly, and my hearing is far away from my ears. It has gone to some inner chamber a hundred kilometers within. Though my body remains there in that room, I am traversing the hollow roads of the near future without my sister. I hear the echo of loneliness pervading every pebble, stair, limb, bowl, and cloud.

I become aware of the room again, reattaching myself to sinew and bone, to blood and eyes and hands. Now it is *my* heart splintering into a thousand pieces. Silently, I repeat over and over, *I need help.* Mama is softly beating her thighs and face and rocking back and forth. Filomena is frozen, watching my every move.

I swallow, syncing with the pulse of my angel. "I cannot imagine a life in Italia without you, (*slight pause for intake of air*) but you must do what is best for you and your family." My insides are a rumbling river of torment. The arms of the angel vibrate, steady me. "Your family should be together."

I cannot believe those words came from my mouth. What I want to scream is, "Be done with that bastard! Let him go to America and cheer for the good fortune that takes him out of your life!" But I say none of these things.

Mama, Filomena, and I come together—arms around arms. In our embrace, we are the sphere of the sun rising boldly over the horizon of the Mediterranean, the fullness of the moon holding back the empty darkness of night. We are the wholeness and the unity of women.

Lifting my head, I see that other-worldly one weaving streams of brilliant light around us in a wide arching circle.

BECAUSE OF ALL THE PREPARATIONS for Filomena's departure, we must carry on like a cart on a downward slope. There are the *must haves*, the *I-think-you'll-need this*, and the *what-if-I-don't*. The *who am I kidding I cannot do this* and the *I wish you were coming*. The seemingly endless conversations teeter on the brink of excitement then plunge to sadness. We fill trunks of house wares and *pantolones*, dresses, shoes, and precious books.

Antonio Salerno has succeeded in opening a bakery of his own in Boston's North End, aptly named *Salerno's*. Salerno's became one of Luigi's accounts, and that is how this employment opportunity came to be. Though I am grateful that reliable Antonio is part of this plan, I am also irked that he hired Luigi, thereby taking my sister away.

"Filomena, let's practice your English," I prompt. "Greet me and tell me you are pleased to meet me."

"Ahloh," she timidly starts. "Will I know you?"

After I correct her and we practice that line, I ask her to tell me where the train station is.

"How to go to train?" she tries.

Not bad. The English language is chopped and carved out of seemingly nonsensical grammatical rules, but once she's there, she'll catch on. We'll keep practicing with some of the materials that Antonio has sent. Still, I worry. How will she adjust to an American lifestyle? Who will be there to cook with her, laugh with her, accompany her to the market for zucchini or parmesan? (Do they even have parmesan in America?) If I allow myself to think beyond the practical preparations for Filomena, the twins, Anna Maria, and Natalia getting to America, I'd crumble like one of Antonio's butter cookies. I focus back on the long list of what needs to be packed. I put one item from the list into the trunk and check it off the list.

As I labor, I hum the *Farfillina* song:

Butterfly, beautiful and white, flying, flying, never gets tired, circling here, and circling there, resting on a flower. Again, again, turning on a white rose, circling here, circling there.

If I were a butterfly I'd follow my sister across the seas, flying, flying, never getting tired, circling the ship and circling the sky, resting on my sister's soft shoulder. Then, we'd always be together.

And in America, I could be with Antonio Salerno.

THE KITCHEN BUSTLES WITH PANS of caramelized onions popping, wooden spoons whooshing in velvety cream sauce, corks bursting from wide-bottomed green bottles, Pina's knife crashing through clumps of oregano and thyme, clinking glasses, silverware, and plates. *Allora*, when all else fails, Italians throw a party! The women cook and bake, sauté and boil, layer and arrange platters of delicious fare—from vegetable lasagna to smoked pork, from *fettuccini alfredo* to sautéed spinach con artichokes and *cannellini* salad. If the heart is hurting, the body is aching, the mind is troubled, *se mangia*! You eat!

I'm going to need more than food today! Alcohol has never been an appealing vice, but today I am completely unnerved. Time and again. I poured a small shot of vino in the pot of tomato sauce and then poured some in a glass for me. The jewel-toned liquid felt soothing.

The relatives and neighbors, the workers from the mill, the girls from Filomena's knitting group, the priest, marketplace vendors, and nearly the whole village have come to bid farewell to their beloved Filomena. I am not out there talking of Filomena's adventure for fear I will fall apart in front of everyone. How many years I have taken her presence, her friendship, her mothering for granted. Keeping myself busy throughout these weeks has kept the emotion at bay. Today, in Mama's *cucina*, stirring, folding, and pouring, I direct helpers to stuff the zucchini with kalamata, mozzarella, and yesterday's bread chunks, arrange the tray of antipasto with salami, prosciutto, and provolone, place the loaves of *panne* con sundried tomatoes in the oven, and baste the rack of lamb rubbed in mint and basil pesto. Better to occupy my mind with the flavor of nature's bounty rather than the bitterness of sorrow.

Pina comes back into the kitchen, directs the helpers then, tells me my presence is requested at the party.

"I better stay here to make sure the lamb . . ."

"Arabella, come now. This is for me to do. Your family is missing you at the party."

I straighten my dress, run my hand through my hair, and walk out just as Mama is coming in to get me. She narrows her eyes to study me. "Arabella, your face is all blotchy," she admonishes in a hushed tone. "How many glasses of vino have you had?"

"Oh, just a glass," I lie as I sashay past her.

"Mmmhmm," I hear her disbelieving answer behind me.

I go to check on Dominic who is tucked into my old bed with his cousins. He doesn't understand the magnitude of the change to come. He and I will learn how to cope together. I kiss his smooth little olive-skinned forehead, and he mumbles something about a horse. Ah, the pleasant dreams of the young.

I try and join several small groups of people who are in the throes of conversation. The subjects range from Mussolini to America to the deliciousness of the Portobello mushrooms stuffed with asiago and anchovies. I don't feel a part of any of this, but I paste a hopefully convincing smile and roam from group to group. I hear my sister's ringing laughter and cross the room to her.

Aldo, his brother, and some other friends are with her. They all look my way as I approach. Filomena hides a smile. She sees my compromised condition. Aldo raises an eyebrow declaring, "Arabella, you're *ubrioco!*" I don't think he realizes just how loud he was. It must be the shock of seeing me *inebriated!*

Others stop their conversations to gawk at me. My face turns redder still, and I try to shush him, but even my shushing is slurred, and there is a chuckle or two. Filomena rescues me by telling a story of the first time Octavio and Marco got into zio Carlos' winemaking grapes. The attention is shifted from me to my brothers with such eloquence. It's like a genie from a fairy tale waving her wand with words.

Papa makes a toast. "To my daughter and her family. May you be filled with love and prosperity in America."

Glasses sing as voices cheer, "To Filomena! A thousand blessings."

Marco walks over to her and opens a small leather journal like the one he gave me years ago. He reads his poem,

All roads lead us back to the heart,

back to the longing

that is Love.

Narrow or broad,

hard or soft,

what we leave behind,

ushers us forward,

carrying the sweetness of everything we have ever known,

back to the heart

back to the longing

of Love.

It feels a little like a wedding celebration. Filomena will be the first Paolian female to venture to the land of opportunity! There is much respect for her in that alone, but since Filomena is the kindest, most beautiful of our village, there is the extra salutation.

Marco comes to my side and says softly, "Arabella, come walk with me for just a minute." When he realizes my wobbly state, he gently takes my arm. I am grateful for someone stable to lean on—literally and figuratively. We walk toward the *lungomare* in silence.

"Your poem was eloquent and moving, I say.

175

"*Grazie.*"

"I know Filomena was grateful."

"Arabella, I want to talk about Filomena. You know as well as I do that passage on a ship across the sea with a newborn, a toddler, and those two rambunctious boys will be a great challenge."

"Why didn't her husband come for them?" I spit disgustedly.

Marco gives me a look of understanding.

"I know that wasn't helpful." I sigh. "But what can we do about Filomena and the children?" I inquire.

"Someone should make the voyage with her." He pauses. "I wish I could, but I don't think a one-eyed brother is the one for such a task."

I try to protest, but he puts his hand up.

"It's not just that. I don't have the stomach for such a trip. I feel like the weakest of men admitting this, but the truth is the truth no matter how it sounds. Besides," he beams, "Arabella, my students are just beginning to come together in their learning group. I think I'd lose them if I left. Is that terribly selfish?"

"Marco, I am so happy for you–and that your students have such a passionate instructor."

"*Grazie*, Arabella. That is a great compliment coming from you."

"I know you've thought this out, Marco. What plan do you have for Filomena and the children?"

"You could go with her!"

"Me?" The surprise sobers me considerably.

"I am certain it should be you, Arabella. You are the strongest of us all—inside and out. I will care for the mill in your absence—that's the least I can do. And it will be good for Dominic to stay with his grandparents for a healthy dose of spoiling after our daily lessons. He'll need to adjust to the absence of his cousins and aunt. Aldo and I will have our meals together. I am sure Mama and Pina would hover around us to make certain we are properly doted on!"

"I don't know how to respond, Marco. My equilibrium is off."

"Is that due to the wine or the subject?" He smirks.

"Very funny, brother. No, I have my wits about me, but who else will agree with this plan?"

"You and I will launch a campaign to make it so. I'll convince Mama and Papa. You, Aldo."

We talk further about some selling points including the most important fact: I have experience traveling on a ship.

"Best get back to the *festa*, eh? "he says.

"Give me a day to work on my part of the campaign, and we will speak again of this soon," I answer.

He nods his head, and we stroll a little quicker back to Mama and Papa's house.

I stay out of sight until the celebration winds down. People hug Filomena goodbye and thank my parents for their hospitality. Helpers carry, stack, sort through the food and the empty bottles. Platters that held the angel-wing cookies have little on them but piles of powdered sugar, miniature snow drifts, like remnants of winter in the mountains.

"PAPA, THERE ARE NUMEROUS challenges aboard a ship. Simply managing the seasickness can be a nightmare! And with children in tow? What happens when Filomena is incapacitated and one of the children wanders from the cabin? How will they be fed and put to bed? Then there are the people moving about the cabins, dining rooms, and decks. Some could be dangerous."

Marco continues painting his picture.

"Even as a man, I found at times I was completely overwhelmed by the endlessness of the sea. It can be a lonely experience, even when others surround you. Arabella knows all of the ins and outs aboard the ship because she has experienced it firsthand."

Papa flinches slightly. We don't ever speak of my escape or return from Brazil.

I interject, "Calming nerves, securing healthy meals, and managing seasickness may not sound like much, but when one is dealing with all the other elements of sea travel, this means peace of mind and security." *Even from a pregnant woman who will keep this secret to herself until her return.*

Now Marco speaks to Aldo. "I contacted my acquaintance, Roberto Umbro at the Naples ship office to discuss various cabin options for Filomena and the children. During our conversation, he mentioned the ship doctor's assistant had resigned. Remembering that Arabella is an *erborista*, he inquired if she would be available to assist him on this journey. He offered her own cabin and a thousand *lire* as part of the arrangement." He pauses.

Aldo perks up a bit when he hears of the income. "I see. So, the doctor would be supervising the women then. Hmmm. That is quite different." He nods solemnly.

Mama adds, "I will be more at ease with Arabella to care for everyone and for the sisters to be together on this voyage."

"I would not ask this of any of you, including Arabella if I thought I could cope alone. Please Papa, Aldo, Mama. I will be forever in your debt." Filomena chokes back a tear while imploring each of them with her eyes.

That did it. Very few can refuse a request from the captivating Filomena.

I WAS GRATEFUL TO HAVE A MONTH of preparation to study "modern" medicine's use of insulin, the side effects of vaccines for tuberculosis and tetanus, and more of the English language before we all boarded the Saturnia for America. *Do I know where the laboratory is? Do **you** know where the lavatory is?* Such a language! Pouring over the English notebook Gregorio and I created so many years ago was bittersweet. As was reading the book of phrases Antonio gave me.

Antonio. If I had time for contemplation while aboard this ship, I am certain I'd be an emotional mess thinking of him. All day, every day, I'm needed in second class and steerage while Dottore Dormatto attends to the demanding first-class passengers. Since we pulled out from the harbor at Naples four days ago, I have set a broken foot (running on a ship's deck), reduced fevers (always frightening as it could be something horrible like the Spanish flu—thankfully, it wasn't), soothed a rash from a tetanus shot, and of course, tended to increasing numbers of seasickness—including Filomena and the boys. I am glad to have my bag filled with tinctures of uva ursi, calendula salves, and my latest blend of red raspberry, ginger, and catnip for the seasickness. And *grazie Dio* I have met a young *ragazza* who cares for Anna Maria and carries Natalia back and forth on the open-air deck cooing and humming as she walks. Most of the time I am so exhausted after attending to the other passengers, Filomena and the boys, I fall into my bed, fully clothed with my shoes on.

But I wouldn't trade this experience for anything—not even an *eleganza* first-class room! Dottore Dormatto and I have breakfast in one of the ornate dining rooms with purple velvet chairs and silver coffee urns to go over the day's agenda. Dottore likes to share a little gossip over a strawberry and crème filled pastry, regaling me with stories of the linens, carved mahogany beds, and formal sitting rooms of the first class. He says there is American royalty onboard, a "flapper" star named Louise Brooks.

"I thought flappers were considered indecent," I comment.

"*Si* and no. They've made a name for themselves with their strong political views and their fashions. "

"I've seen images of their short dresses and bobbed hairstyles. And they were smoking cigars! Shocking but alluring," I add.

"Once women gained the right to vote a few years ago, everything changed." He raises one expressive eyebrow.

I pause for a moment before I answer. "Such as freedom for a woman to make her own decisions?"

"*Absolutamente!*" He smiles before sharing another animated story about a jazz performance and flapper showcase, but I am drinking in the feeling of my own freedom. I could get used to that freedom.

Boston 1927

SOON, I UNDERSTAND THE MORAL weight of such freedom.

In America, Filomena, the children, and Luigi need time to settle into their quaint apartment in Boston's North End. Luigi and I barely acknowledge one another, which suits me fine. He makes some inappropriate remark about how he'd be there if I got too lonely in the small, borrowed apartment downstairs. But I hardly see them at all.

Antonio Salerno keeps me busy exploring the magnificence of Boston's 1926 sprawling streets of bricks, its towers, and its history, the first public botanical garden in America with a pond of swans and a swan boat to see them up close all in the middle of the busy downtown district! At the Parker House, I sample "scrod"– delicious young whitefish. We stroll across the Freedom Trail where the American Revolution began. After dining on plates of oysters and consuming a large glass of wine at Ye Olde Union Oyster House, I almost kiss Antonio goodnight (now I believe what they say about oysters as aphrodisiacs).

Day by day, I could easily sink right into his embrace—and his American life. Pregnant Arabella! But I tell you, the entirety of it is intoxicating—the easy way we fall into conversation, the matched rhythm of our stride, our enthusiasm for life.

One day as we walked past the grand Orpheum Theatre, I had the nerve to ask him, "Antonio, do you have a lady in your life?"

His eyes said it all as they gazed into mine: *none other than you.* It was the stuff of fairy tales. And I wanted the fairy godmother to shed the skin of my marriage and poof! I'd emerge as a modern woman, willing and able to accept his love.

"I am very busy with my business." He waved his hand and looked away, "I just don't have the time to properly court a woman."

It was a lie.

There were so many paths I could have taken at that moment—lead him to a hotel, his hand in mine, kiss him passionately right there in the middle of the passersby on Boylston Street, or, what was right—set him free of the burden of our impossible love.

Freedom's weight is an anvil around your heart, but when you love someone as I love him, I found I had no choice.

"Antonio, look at me." I take his hands tenderly. "I want you to promise me something."

"*Si?*"

"Please promise me you'll find someone to share your life with."

He looks at me again—eyes I could simply fall into forever.

"Arabella, I . . ."

"Promise me," I insist.

A reckoning, "*Lo prometto. I promise.*"

"*Va bene, very well,*" I lie, my heart swelling and shriveling simultaneously. Clearing my throat, I say," Now then, tell me more about Salerno's Confections.

He speaks of his plans that include a small warehouse near the wharf for mixing and baking and a storefront in the North End to sell his Italian pastries and cookies. I think of Luigi working for him, and the worry shows on my face.

"What is it?" he asks.

Are you aware Luigi is not only unreliable, but he's also abusive, volatile, and a snake?

"May I be candid?"

He chuckles. "Arabella, aren't you always?"

"It's just, well, I'm concerned, I . . ." I stutter a mixture of anxieties in no cohesive order.

"Arabella, please do not worry about your sister and her family."

"But I . . ."

"Non ti preoccupare," he assures me.

I want to believe I have *nothing to worry about.* I really do.

FILOMENA AND I ARE REARRANGING the furniture for the tenth time today. We get the giggles about the time we tried to fool Mama but got caught. She doubles over laughing, but before I know it, she is crying.

"You leave in three days," she wails. "I cannot be here without you!"

"I wish I could stay with you, *sorella*," I barely squeak.

"Then stay! Be with Antonio Salerno and be near to me."

"Filomena! I have a child in Italy. And Mama and Papa and Marco."

"I notice you didn't mention your husband."

My feathers are ruffled, "Well, you didn't give me a chance."

She realizes her error, "*Mi dispiace*, sister. I am out of sorts with the new place in a strange land, an infant, a toddler, the boys, and Luigi."

"I understand."

But I don't understand how she is going to make it here, why she's giving Luigi another chance, or what will happen when Luigi abuses her again—or what it will be like in Italy without her, Antonio's devotion, or the newfound feeling of total freedom.

WITH A HEAVY HEART, I say goodbye to my sister, to her children, to Antonio. I board the ship and return home much in the same way I came across the sea. This time, I longed for heartache medicine or something that could lighten this heavy feeling of loss. I existed on cups of milk thistle for my morning sickness and sucked on pickled raw grapes with salt and pepper.

But now in my fifth month of pregnancy, and the first month without my sister, I'm determined to spend more time with my family, oversee the workings at the mill, meet with the women caretakers of the corn field, and give extra tender loving care to my patients. That ought to keep the daydreamer lost in America at bay. Dr. Dormatto insisted we keep in contact. He told me I'd make a fine *dottore* and that I should consider going to medical school. The compliment alone lifted my spirits. Studying medicine? Something else to add to the American daydream.

At Mama and Papa's house, we fall into a familial familiarity. We are to each other the soothing balm of heartache. We don't speak of the gigantic pit of emptiness left by Filomena and her children's absence. But, wonder of wonders, we have a newly adopted member of the family: Pina's niece, a young herbalist named Rafaella came for a visit but decided to stay in Paola—in my old room, in fact. She and I spend time tending Mama's garden, and I find her personality delightful, her knowledge extensive, her intellect sharp. I notice that Marco is visiting Mama and Papa more often than usual, and this brings me great joy.

Mama is doting on me today with her fresh batch of *"Brutti Ma Buoni"* cookies aptly named *Ugly but Good* due to their unshapely, discombobulated appearance. But the mix of cinnamon, almonds, hazelnuts, and egg whites are full of healthy goodness.

"People are like cookies, eh Mama? There are the *bella e buoni* and *brutti ma buoni*." The *beautiful and good, the ugly but good.*

She smiles.

"You, Filomena, Antonio, Marco, zio, Rafaella would be a *"bella e buoni* cookie!"

"And what about you?"

"I'm more *bella e brutti*."

"Arabella, that's not true."

It's the secrets that I keep, I want to tell her, *that make me bad. It's the way I feel less than capable as a mother and how I take tinctures to prevent conception. It's the way I barged into the Ruffino house and supplied the bella donna that killed Gregorio. It's the fact that I would leave this life behind to be with Antonio Salerno.*

"Arabella, you are honest and forthright."

"*Grazie,* Mama, but people can be entranced, si?"

"What do you mean?"

"Like in Giambattista Basile's, *"Sol, Luna e Talia,"* "Sun, Moon and Talia," where the curious Talia gets a piece of magic flax beneath her fingernail and falls into a deep, hexed sleep. When she awakens, the wicked queen's creamy words deceive her, and Talia falls prey to the queen's nefarious plan. It reminds me of Luigi and Filomena. "

"I don't know about that, Arabella. But I do know that love is both feet, both hands, and the whole heart invested in its success. And it always seeks the good— especially when you can't see it."

"*Si,* Mama. `*E vero.*" *It's true.*

Rafaella comes into the room with a paper in her hands. She is lit like the sun's sheen on a rose petal. "Arabella," she beams, "I'm so happy you are here! I have some ideas about rotating the herb crop and expanding the medicinal garden."

I feel a kinship with her. Of course, she is an herbalist and a sweet person, but it's something more. I think it's that she says my name in a tone reminiscent of my sister. She rambles on excitedly and I think, so *this is how it is*. To survive—no, to thrive—women find one another, connective threads weaving another square in their safety net. Sisters may move away, be taken, or be married off, but we are sent another—not to take the place of, but to add to the quilt of sisterhood.

Rafaella is still chattering away. I smile, acknowledging how our spirits are truly cared for—she is much more than a girl who just happens to be an herbalist, who just happened to come to Paola when my sister left. I close my eyes for a moment taking in the gift of her. My spirit angel is right beside me, glowing. I can feel her hand on mine as I close my eyes. When I open them, I see that it is Rafaella who has taken my hand in hers.

"You are overwrought, Arabella. The growing child requires so much of you," she soothes. "I'll fix you a cup of chamomile."

Mama begins putting a mountain of cooled *brutti ma buoni* cookies on a plate.

Being pregnant tosses one about in a current of emotional undertones, but as Mama and Rafaella tend to the tea kettle and the cookies, I offer gratitude for the company and the connection of women—for their kindness, their kinship, and their knowingness of what it is to walk, breathe, love, and live in the skin of a woman.

I KNOW IT IS PAPA COMING up the path to my little house. I hear the alternating chugging and sputtering of his latest acquisition—a motorcar! It's an older model—not one of those new sporty models that wealthy, fearless souls are spinning around in Rome, but it's the first of its kind in Paola. When word spread that Papa had purchased a motorcar, the line of curious seekers at their home was a human snake ebbing its way from the *lungomare* to the *piazza*!

Papa took the villagers on short rides in this machine with its carriage that rests on four large, inflated wheels. Papa commands it with a steering wheel, a clutch that sets the vehicle in motion, a pedal that propels, and another that brakes. A long seat runs the width of the car in the front area, and there's another seat in the rear. Mama, Pina, and Marco won't ride in it, but my little Dominic is completely enamored by it.

After I heave myself into Papa's motorcar, we meander the roads of Paola. Papa is in no hurry and is relishing every moment in his rumbling toy. I look over at him and see the twinkle in his eye. He has always been a straightforward, ambitious man with a big heart, but I've rarely observed him so relaxed. Some of the villagers wave and call out greetings, and Papa gladly toots the low bellowing horn to honk a response. He appears giddy.

"Papa, I haven't seen you look this relaxed in, well, I don't know if I *ever* recall you this way."

He pats my hand. "You always did say just what was on your mind, Arabella. Looking back, I see I was always thinking of the businesses and making our future better. I did not always take time to enjoy these simple, pleasurable moments."

We roll bumpily on in silence for a moment, each of us absorbed in thought. My child shifts its position in my expansive belly before settling right on top of my bladder! One of its little feet continues to kick my side to the beat of the chugging motorcar.

"These feats of ingenuity are so exciting! And, may I add, you are most dapper behind the wheel!"

He laughs, and I see a glimpse of him as a younger man responsible for a family. His pride, his pluckiness, his planning, as clear as the shallow waters of a creek. It is when the child becomes a parent, she learns to accept her own parents as people—just people, with flaws and issues like anyone else who traverses life's roads.

"Well, if you think this is special, the next surprise will astound you." He beams.

I begin guessing, feeling like a child on one of our excursions up the mountain. "Did you get Mama one of those new electric dryers for her hair?"

He chortles, "No."

"Hmmm. A radio so we can listen to programs and news?"

"I have ordered one of those, but that is not the big surprise."

We round the bend, and the full blast of sea air fills my lungs. I sigh a little, and Papa winks and smiles.

We putter to a stop. An animated Mama comes out to greet us. She reaches her arms out to me, and I gladly go to her. Little tears hover on the outer corners of her caramel eyes.

"What is going on here?" I ask, a bit nervous and excited at the same time.

Mama grabs my hand and pulls me in as Papa, well, Papa smirks!

We go inside and sit in the drawing room. I don't notice anything different. Mama tells me to sit down as Pina drifts into the room with a hug and a cup of chamomile and mint tea.

"Arabella," she coos. "You look so healthy. *Brava*, Arabella."

Mama nods to her, and Pina leaves the room surreptitiously. I look from Mama to Papa, and there is an odd exchange. Mama sends a stream of questions my way regarding my eating and sleeping habits. Inherent in each query is the underlying warning of taking extra care so I won't lose this baby too. I understand her concern, but I know that this child will come into the world healthy and whole.

"Why are you acting strange *and* evasive?" I ask.

They both laugh.

"I don't understand your laughter!" I'm instantly irritated. "What is going on here?"

He leans towards Mama and in a stage whisper says, "She always was impatient, eh?"

Mama, coy as a young *ragazza*, giggles behind her hand.

I roll my eyes just as I hear a loud ringing noise from the kitchen. Then Pina yells, "Pronto?"

"What in the world?" I inquire.

Now Mama pushes me toward the *cucina*, a stream of delight cutting a path behind her.

Mounted on the wall is a rectangular wooden box. At its center is a protruding cone, on one side a crank handle, and a long, tubular cord attached to another small cone on the other side of the box. Pina is shouting in the cone at the center of the box while holding the smaller cone to her ear. It is a *telefono*, considered the next generation of the telegraph where people's voices are sent through the lines from thousands of kilometers away!

Pina is nodding with fervor as she motions me to it. There is a slight crackling like the faint trail of lightning, and then I hear, "*Sorella?* Are you there?"

I am nearly speechless! "Filomena!" I'm yelling now. "*Ma va! No way!*"

She is laughing and yelling, "*Sì*. I'm here!"

We talk about the 9-year-old twins, Alessandro and Bernardo, and toddler, Anna Maria and 8-month-old Natalia, my Dominic, and the health of this pregnancy; I inquire after her study of the English language, and she impresses me with some Americana phrases, but mostly between the squiggled lines of sound is our love. It fills and empties the huge, gaping crater of loneliness I have avoided since I left her in America. It is like the ebb and flow of the sea, releasing and pulling, filling and pouring. She thanks me for my letters that she claims are like "bits of you and my beloved Paola."

My turn to sample the wonders of the Industrial Age is over, and I plop down at the kitchen table. Mama and Papa speak to her. When the earpiece is set back on its cradle, we sit in silent awe of being able to speak to Filomena in her little Americana *cucina*. And then, the reverie bursts, and all at once, we are talking about the marvels of this modern world. The inventions of the 1920s—from Band-aids to televisions and toasters—all changing the way people live!

Rafaella comes in from the garden, and she and Pina bustle about setting out olives, prosciutto, Romano cheese, and Mama's bread. We all sit around the table talking about some of the smaller, mechanical inventions we can look forward to helping us at the mill. Now, if they could just find a way for me to get to my sister for a face-to-face visit and then get me home in time for breakfast. Didn't Leonardo di Vinci's sketchbooks reveal flying apparatus?

THE WINGS THAT FLEW ACROSS Paola were nothing like Da Vinci's flying machine. They weren't from exotic birds or butterflies. These seemed sent from the devil himself.

"They covered the face of the whole Earth so that the land was darkened; and they did eat every herb of the land, and all the fruit of the trees: and there remained not any green thing in the trees, or in the herbs of the field." -Exodus 10:15

The invasion of the estimated fifty million locusts called *"cavoletta"* for their horse-like heads that appear to be charging into battle devoured every living plant and leaf in Paola. There was no road, no field, no garden impassable to them. Every squash, eggplant, every grape, and olive, every ear of corn and stalk of wheat, every verdant blade of grass was consumed; nothing but stubs of plants looking much like a man's unshaven face remained. The picture is straight out of a nightmare or a Surrealistic painting. With their airborne hooves and mustard-colored wings, the millions of locusts painted an eerie yellow tint in the sky like Georgio de

Chirico's *metaphysical "pittura metafisica."* I understand this strange art form now as Paola looks like a painting of the absurdly unexpected juxtaposed with what's real.

Adding insult to injury, the now barren landscape is strewn with millions of rotting locust corpses. They line the shore of the *lungomare*, float belly up in the *Fontana di Paola*, zig-zag the masticated fields, and lay like unwelcome guests just inside homes and markets. Many of them were at the end of their eight-week life cycle and after gorging themselves and mating, they laid down and died. The stench is as unimaginable as the destruction. Imagine odorous cheese such as Limburger combined with rotten fish and an untended outhouse and you'll get a sense of the redolence of these vile creatures. Our villagers come in droves to Rafaella and me for our blends of heady marjoram, geranium, lavender, and peppermint to ease the overloaded olfactory glands.

"*Grazie tanti*," says Signora Palli. "We cannot be outside without your scented oils on our handkerchiefs!"

Signora Dueno told us she placed rags with the blends in the pens for the nervous animals.

There are too many frightening questions to ask about our future so we busy ourselves sweeping, cleaning, and burying the small beasts. As Rafaella and I work with our jars of herbs and tinctures, my mind keeps coming back to the basic question of survival. Our food sources are quite definitively gone. What we have stocked in our larders is all that there is. Winter is coming—without fall's harvest.

My spirit angel's light is right next to me, and I can hear the words. *Think beyond the fear of famine; reach beyond despair.* But despair is all I see in my mother's anguished eyes, my father's furrowed brow, my husband's despondency.

Think, Arabella, think. Life is full of those who overcame insurmountable odds—from the Suffragettes, Mary, Mother of God, WWI refugees and widows, those maimed and broken by suffering of all kinds.

But what could I possibly do that would make a difference? Making herbal tinctures is one thing; saving us from starvation, quite another. The small offerings by the government won't last more than a few weeks, if that. With America in the depths of the Great Depression, there will be little help from there. Supplies from Octavio and his comrades in Brazil will be a long time in arriving and will not be enough for a whole village to sustain itself.

We're going to have to save ourselves. Somehow. Some way. I sense there are answers, but I don't have the eyes to see them. I am too blinded by the severity of our situation in this moment. However, I will not underestimate the power of the will to survive. I'll fight for my daughter who grows inside me, for myself, my son, and my village. With the combined help of others, we can succeed. And the angel's light tells me it is so.

Just begin, the voice of optimism whispers. But where *is* the beginning? This is about my fellow villagers. People . . . .

"Rafaella, can you help me compile a list of villagers?" I don't know why I ask this exactly, but I know it's the right place to start."

"Of course," she quickly responds. Names only?"

"Names and ages."

"*Ho capito*," she answers. "To calculate how much food we need to survive?"

"*Essattamente! Exactly.*" Once we begin to talk, the plan unfolds. "I'll get with Papa and Aldo, and we'll estimate the number of animals and how much feed we'll need for them. Marco can get some of his friends to inventory what is in jars of storehouses and on kitchen shelves. Mama and her friends can organize. Papa and the elders can meet with Padre Giamo. The young priest is adept at calling people to action."

The kitchen is aglow. I feel alert, alive, in tune with something bigger than us, bigger than the problem.

We assemble the members of our family for a discussion. We note Paola's tradesmen and craftsmen who could barter their services for food in other villages. We list the skills of men and women alike. Maybe Papa's and Marco's friends in Naples can help with a work/trade program. A hopeful plan of action burbles up. Rafaella leaves to begin her tasks.

As I tuck Dominic into bed, I make a new vow of protection for his welfare. I notice the spirit angel sitting on the edge of his bed. *Thank you for watching over him,* I pray. *I'm grateful that you are watching over all of us.*

Passing our bedroom on the way to the kitchen for warm milk and honey, a muffled cry startles me. It's Aldo. The locust annihilation affected Aldo's livestock. No grain, no food, hungry animals, starving people. The whole scenario is a huge chain reaction of interconnected doom. I should go to him and hold him, comfort him.

I crack open the door. "Aldo?"

"Leave me be," he hisses.

I close the door. Vulnerability is not easy for some of us to show.

Marco peaks his head in the door. "Arabella?"

"*Si, Fratello.* Come in. I am glad for your company. I don't know about you but one moment I am filled with hope, the next utter despair. It's like being on a treacherous path: one false move and down I'll go."

He nods his head. "*Ho capito.* Tutoring the young ones keeps my focus on something other than dread. Speaking of focus, do you recall me describing the crossing of the suspension bridge in Brazil's Atlantica forest?"

"Oh *si*, it was terribly high, wasn't it?"

"Seventy meters or so."

"Ayaiyai!"

He laughs. "The guide gave explicit instructions to keep our eyes straight ahead, focusing on the end of the bridge only."

"Right and never to look down at your feet or below."

"Yes, because that's when terror sets in."

"Causing one to sway and falter."

As I pour us each a cup of warm milk with skullcap and valerian, I sway a bit from side to side.

"Thank you for the reminder to keep my eyes on the end of this bridge rather than the treacherous depths beneath me," I say.

"Let's make that our vow," he declares.

PAPA HAS CONTACTED HIS FRIEND in Napoli who has the ear of Mussolini's right-hand man. Through the ranks of his command, Mussolini has given Papa the nod to coordinate relief efforts (but of course, Mussolini will take all the credit).

Papa and I have traveled in his chug-chugging motorcar to San Lucido, Cosenza, and Castrovolari. I never knew that seemingly extravagant vehicle would be of such great service. We've traveled to twelve different villages so as not to tax any one area with our needs. People have been kind. It may be due to the direct orders of Mussolini, but in the end, *the denizens of Paola will survive.* When we share our story and show the official government documents that support our efforts, we gain allies. We have traded I.O.U. documents with vendors and farmers and nonnas and pappas, goat herders, and those who raise chickens.

Upon the final harvest of all tomatoes, zucchini, eggplant, Lima beans, grains, melons, and peas, we will receive rations for our families. Chickens, roosters, and hogs will come at the end of winter once our supply of meat has been depleted. In exchange, our villagers will travel to our neighbors' villages to perform all manner of work from canning in someone else's *cucina* or sewing a quilt to road maintenance, tree pruning, roof patching, trench digging, or wood chopping. Some workers will travel on government train vouchers to the appointed places and are excited to travel outside of Paola for the first time in their lives. Our mill workers will travel in borrowed carts or on donkeys to surrounding areas throughout the harvest season and into the winter months.

Not everyone is thrilled by this plan, but it is a testament to their character they've agreed to follow it. The tasks before us will be wrought with challenge. Inventory and distribution of food must be fair. There can be no impropriety. The fear of not having enough food can ignite unsavory behavior. We're hoping to eliminate that fear by organizing deliveries *before* the larders are empty.

It turns out that in fact, this disaster may have been a blessing in disguise for us. Establishing close relationships with our neighboring villages has opened us to learning new things. In the inland village of Acri, I met a most fascinating family of herbalists and gardeners who have experimented with various materials that act as a perfect summerlike growing environment for plants *all winter long!* Can you imagine coaxing tomatoes to grow in December or having an unending supply of fresh garlic whenever you need it? These folks piece together scraps of glass into wood frames to fashion "glass house" growing environments that trick plants into thinking it's their natural growing season!

Signore Gofullo gave me a history lesson about the Roman emperor Tiberius and his appetite for fresh cucumbers. Being emperor afforded him brilliant thinkers who created the first glass growing houses: *specularium*. They embedded sheets of mica into glass walls to absorb the sunlight, thereby providing a warm growing environment for the plants. Later, the design was improved and renamed *giardini botanici* because it also housed exotic plants brought from foreign lands. In France, "orangeries" were built to protect precious oranges from freezing weather and to produce fresh oranges throughout the year. Pineapples, too, became a delicacy, and "pineries" were built to perfect the consistent production of year-round pineapples.

I furiously took notes and sketched as Signore Gofullo shared his passion for glasshouses. An Italian interested in herbs and medicine named Charles Lucien Bonaparte designed the most modern "greenhouse" like the Gofullo's. Using my notes and drawings, Marco and his friends are constructing a greenhouse in Paola for medicinal herbs and food. (It could be due to Rafaella's participation. Marco would do anything for her!) The Gofullos gave me seeds of cucumbers, tomatoes, and squashes for starting our greenhouse garden.

My husband does not share our enthusiasm. I assumed that like a jolt of electricity in a power line, he would catch the excitement of our endeavors, but he slumbers in bed most days complaining of aches and pains but refuses my treatment. He drags himself to the table for dinners but pushes the food around the plate. I try to keep our home atmosphere lighthearted for Dominic's sake. I am concerned about Aldo, of course, but my days overflow with meetings, riding with Papa (though the scope and weight of this pregnancy are becoming quite cumbersome) and tending to both my patients and our son. Marco has kept up the routine of study and practice to maintain a sense of normalcy in Dominic's life. With the focus of his days being study, side by side with Marco's other students, there is camaraderie and purpose.

This morning, Papa and I are finishing a report for Mussolini as well as planning a route to San Mango. The papers are spread out on the table in Mama and Papa's house. We are looking over the extensive list of what has been pledged and what is needed still. Mama brings me some biscotti and a cup of Rafaella's latest herbal tea blend. It is bursting with lemon and some other flavor I do not immediately recognize. Papa and I are chattering away, heads bent over papers so that I barely notice Mama there glaring at us with her hands on her hips.

"What?" I ask defensively.

"You even have to ask?"

Absentmindedly, I dip the biscotti into the tea and nibble a piece. *Ah, hibiscus flowers; that's the mystery ingredient!* "It's so delicious." I moan.

"Your flattery is ineffective, Arabella."

Apparently, I am in for a lecture. Never mind I am a grown woman, married and a mother, myself. Once a daughter, always a daughter, eh?

"Mama, *che fai?*"

"Arabella, you are, what, eight months pregnant? It's improper for you to be gallivanting around all of Italy in such a state—even if you are escorted by your father." She gives him a look, and he clears his throat and looks the other way. "And your husband? How is he? You are caring for all of Paola, but your husband needs your attention!" Her voice is rising, and the red in her cheeks resembles a hibiscus flower in full bloom.

"Please, Mama, not now. Papa and I must go to . . ."

"You and your father aren't going anywhere today. Someone in this family must think straight, and apparently, that duty falls on me!"

In her voice, I hear the world tugging on her exhausted heart. Papa unruffles her feathers quietly, nods to me, and assures her he will take me home. I detect a subtle twinkle in his eye as we sit in the vehicle headed for my home. But where Papa should have turned south, he instead turned the machine north, towards San Mango.

"Papa." I feign surprise. "You are not following the direct orders of the 'only one in this family thinking straight'?"

He laughs, and I join him. We are comfortable in our role as ambassadors for Paola. I think back to our early rides in the cart when I was but a child badgering him about the future and who I could be and who I wanted to be, filled with the angst of youth. I couldn't have known then that my ill feelings and disappointments would dissipate with the years. I did not realize then that life simply finds a way of transforming us. I couldn't have imagined that being in Paola would find me head over heels in love with my son, encourage the healer in me to grow, and allow me to work with an angel, or help salvage our village's future.

Papa is going over our strategy for the day, the names of the people we will speak to and his anticipations before rumbling on in comfortable silence. I drift off to sleep in the ambling rhythm of the automobile and wake up with the feeling of cool spring water on my skin. It is there, refreshing and restorative, and then it is gone. Papa is talking about what he is expecting today when suddenly, the seat underneath me is completely soaked with water. Dio mio, my child's arrival is not what *I* was expecting today.

But here I am, thrust into the event of childbirth, where suddenly, all my stuffed fears surface like a whale out of the sea. Even though I'm convinced that all will be well, the powerful undertow of fear pulls me down. The loss of my other daughter claws at my sanity: my shoulders tense, sweat covers this massive body in a slippery layer of sheen, and adrenaline pumps a demanding, albeit, shallow breath.

"Papa?" It is the squeaky mouse voice of the child, Arabella.

"Arabella, your voice is strange? What is it?"

"Papa, I . . ." How am I going to tell him that his daughter's labor has begun in his motorcar, on a dusty road in the middle of nowhere with no obvious help in sight? How do I tell him that he may be delivering his grandchild?

He pulls the automobile to the side of the road.

"*Figlia*, are you ill? Can I get you some . . . ?" It is then that he sees the water on the seat and my soaked dress. "The baby is coming? "His voice rises on the tide of terror. "But you have weeks before it is due." And he goes on repeating that fact, which now strikingly resembles fiction. He is talking to himself really, not to me at all. It is the sign of someone in shock.

"I will take that drink of water, Papa." Giving him something to do with his hands will help him focus and buy me a moment or two for strategic thought.

He pours a cup of water from the bottle in the backseat and offers it to me with trembling hands.

I muster a thank you and a slight twitch of a smile. With one hand touching the cross at the base of my throat and the other lifting the water to my lips, I drink slowly, willing the water to drown the beast of fear. I peer out the window. Trees and more trees, a feeling of being hopelessly lost in the woods. I blink back tears, squeezing my eyes shut. As I open them, there's a flash of movement through the trees. A closer look reveals my spirit angel, her light like a comet tail revealing a narrow, high road.

We're supposed to go there. I sigh, relieved, just as the first contraction squeezes what little breath I had from me! *Don't fight it,* I hear. The pain or the feeling of what I am supposed to do? *Both!* Am I really going to follow a spirit, a feeling? Am I *pazzo*? *Crazy*? I pause to consider if there is another option, but there is nothing. If going to the high, narrow road turns out to be nothing but a road, well, I'll have to deliver this baby there.

Oh, why didn't I listen to my mother? Mama must have had a sixth sense about me today. I didn't even stop to consider her prescience. I try to clear my mind, breathing in, breathing out. My angel will not steer me wrong. And I am not hallucinating or crazy! No matter what it looks like to someone else, I am being guided. This boost of assurance momentarily tames the beast of panic.

I'm ready to speak to Papa, direct but calm. "Papa, the baby is coming, but I know that we will be all right. I know without a shadow of a doubt." Now I'm patting his hand, smiling a soothing smile—his child acting as the comforting parent!

He looks beseechingly in my eyes.

I hold his frightened gaze before declaring, "I know where to go, Papa." Pointing in the direction of the road my angel was on I continue, "through that expanse of trees, there is a narrow road. At the top of the road, there is a little house with people who'll help us."(I didn't know this until it came out of my mouth of its own accord). "Can you drive Papa?"

"Yes, but . . ." Confusion has been thrown into the stew along with dread, shock, and fear.

"It is okay, Papa. *Andiamo, let's go.*" Another contraction delivers a jagged stab to my belly, a dull pounding to my back. I grip the door handle, riding the wave of pain in the ebb and flow of tug and release.

We maneuver up the nearly hidden road where a tiny house appears, resting in a grove of parasol pines. An old woman with a kindly face emerges from the doorway as if she is expecting us. It feels like a vision. Then, another woman joins her. I sense they are *sorelle, sisters.* One of them speaks to Papa with a voice that shimmers like heavenly chimes. My breathing relaxes. We're ushered into the cozy casa. Papa's poured a glass of something caramel-colored. He nods his gratitude, still holding his hat in his other

hand. I am thinking I'd like a decanter or two of that liquid myself! The
sorella offers him a plate of something to eat (which he refuses) and sits him
in a chair.

They lead me to the bedroom that is separated from the main room by
a white lace-backed curtain. The room is tidy and simply appointed with a
sturdy, rough-hewn bed and a small round side table inlaid with a three-
toned fleur de lis. A candle is lit, and there are a few linens on the table. My
angel is here. Gentle, golden glowing light reminiscent of the entrance of
Santa Maria di Maggiore leads me to thoughts of my sister. A pang of fright
hits me along with another contraction. After it passes, I try to explain who
we are and where we are from, but they shush me sweetly, then coo and
smile and repeat in a dozen different ways that all is well.

The next few hours I am in and out of consciousness, releasing and
letting go in more ways than a person can believe is humanly possible.
Everything—from bodily systems and organs to mental focus is solely about
safely delivering the child to the world. With each ripping, torturous grip, I
conjure the Mediterranean Sea to ride its rhythmic waves until I'm holding
my daughter in my arms. It's easy to forget every exhausting push, every
ounce of sweat, every excruciating ache. A wave of absolute love and grace
enfolds me and my daughter, Luciana, my "light" who beckoned the sun to
wait as she took her first breath of life before the sun set. What a relief to
count ten little fingers and all ten toes. And that shock of black, wavy hair,
that blissful, cherub face fills me with abundant joy.

The *sorella* informs me that Papa left for Paola to pick up Mama and bring
her to me. They said he was quite torn about leaving me, but they convinced
him it was the best course of action. *Povero! Poor man!* He is brave to have
ventured home with the shocking information that their daughter had their
grandchild in a stranger's forest home! Mama is going to be mad as a coiled
snake! She told us not to go on our mission, and we went against her explicit
order. On the other hand, I am sure Papa was happy to be out of the stranger's
tiny house where his daughter labored just a few feet away behind a curtain.

I marvel at these women who are like my angel sisters! They are both widows with grown children who live within walking distance of one another. Aquilina, whose house we are in now, had plans to visit her son this morning but awoke with an overwhelming urgency to scrub her little home from the "rafters to floor." She dismissed the feeling as she wanted to see her son and grandchildren, but when she walked out the door with a small basket of jams and other homemade treats, one of the jars lost its lid spilling over her and onto the floor. Never in her decades of making jam had a lid ever come off a jar with its generous covering of pectin and wax. How could it have escaped? Aquilina was forced to return to the house to clean herself. She wiped her dress free of fig jam as best she could, but when she turned around suddenly (she said she felt someone in the room with her), she knocked over the basket and spilled the fruit juice all over the floor! She decided to heed the signs to stay home and scrub her house. She laughed as she said she knew better than to try to ignore "a divine message."

The other sister, Brigida, begins animatedly relaying her story of encountering an angel in a dream. She was told to go to her sister's house at a determined hour. She knew the dream was a "message sent from above," so she followed the directive and set out for her sister's home at the appointed time. Both the sisters winked at each other and smiled. So many thoughts were ricocheting through my mind! I wondered if *I* was dreaming! I knew it was my spirit angel who led us all to be here in this place for my daughter's birth, but they have absolutely no problem talking about it!

Brigida inquires, "You know of this angel messenger, *si*?"

I nod my head.

Aquilina chuckles and pats my hand. "It is okay, my dear. You are safe with us! You see, you are in the company of the '*Strega Sorelle*.'" They both laugh.

"The *Witch Sisters*?" I ask tentatively.

"*Si*. We are known in these parts as the witch sisters."

Brigida and Aquilina begin a fascinating story of their childhood when they were first visited by those who had passed away and wished for them to deliver messages to their loved ones. Brigida and Aquilina confided in one another and were comforted to know they were both experiencing these other-world encounters.

It was easy to be in the circle of their sisterhood. They spoke freely of their early experiences and their innocence. They thought by bringing these messages to the grieving, they would be doing a great service. But all too quickly they learned how cruel people can be when they are driven by fear. These pure-hearted sisters were shunned, labeled as devil witches, and the family was quickly ostracized from the folds of the village. They were not invited to any celebrations, be it births, weddings, or feast-day gatherings. At best, they were simply ignored, as if they were ghosts or spirits themselves.

How difficult it must have been! They did not ask for the visits from the departed souls! Often, the sisters would have to surprise a person on their way to church or the cemetery to deliver the message. Some people sought the sisters out in secret but would vehemently deny it. But the sisters speak of the joys rather than sorrows; a touching aria, richly narrative. They were loved by brothers who came to the village quite by accident but never left. They had children. They know love, they offer love, they deliver healthy babies, and listen to messages from other spiritual realms.

They can see that I am fatigued and leave to fix me something to eat. They give me some time alone with my thoughts, my angel, and my daughter. I fall asleep with the comforting light of my spirit angel encompassing the room.

ONCE THE DRAMATIC STORY OF Luciana's birth hits the streets of Paola, all manner of visitors come knocking on our door. There are sweet gifts of booties and lace bonnets, a tiny gold chain, some linen diapers, a quilted blanket, a carved crucifix for her crib. There is an outpouring of tenderness for Luciana, for new life. It's as if Luciana represents hope for the future.

Her father, though, is more despondent than ever. In another *telefono* conversation, I told Filomena of my great joy, Luciana, and of my concern for her depressed father. She spoke of the tremendous growth of Antonio Salerno's biscotti business (called "cookies" in the United States). Maybe Aldo should think of coming to America, she offered. He could live with them and work for Antonio.

The disturbing idea took hold of me. It seems there is nothing here in Paola that can bring Aldo out of his depression, his eyes unable to see promise. Maybe a change of scene and focus would help him come back to himself. I have thought of all the pros and cons regarding this Americana opportunity. But a future where I would leave Paola to join my husband there? I shove the notion behind the boxes of old memories of Antonio in the darkest corner of my mind, away from any possibility of finding the light. For now, we will regard Aldo in America as a way to patch a bruised lifeline that only Antonio Salerno can offer.

JUST AS A CHILD TRANSFORMS FROM sleeper to observer, so too can a man change from depressed to enthusiastic. For Aldo, the shift occurred after an invite from Antonio to join Salerno's Confections in Boston. And just like that, poof! He is gone. Was his decision made easier by my focus on the survival of the whole village? Did I overlook him? Didn't I try to inspire him to get out and help us? It doesn't matter now. He is in the land of the free, home of the brave.

But Paola is brave too! We saved ourselves, reached for solutions previously unheard of. And I am brave to live without a father to our children. It's not that I am going to miss being a wife, but I have grown used to Aldo. After 10 years of marriage, two people and their children build a home, a family life. But now, I am left in charge of maintaining a stable family unit while the papa is off working in a faraway land. Papa, Mama, and Marco remain a big part of our family life.

I go to the crib where Luciana sleeps peacefully. Every mother thinks her child is beautiful, but my olive-skinned, rosy-cheeked Luciana has an inner light. Even if you cannot see it, you can feel it. Everyone who has come to meet her has proclaimed the same sentiment in varying ways. Even Dominic sits next to her talking or just watching her. Her presence seems to calm us all.

I hear the chugging of Papa's automobile coming up the road and smile as I open the door. Neither Mama nor Papa has been able to stay away from their new grandchild. Marco and Dominic come out of their lessons, and we all greet one another with familial ease. There is much of life that has elapsed, images that once stood out of focus, now clear: Dominic, a young, handsome boy of nine years learning the language of ancient scholars, Mama, a content nonna, Papa and Marco standing on common, stable ground, Rafaella, a sister of my heart, now betrothed to Marco.

Mama asks how long Luciana has been asleep. Papa and Marco and Dominic head inside, and Rafaella lifts a sack of something from the backseat.

"We have a surprise for you," she says to me as she conspiratorially winks at Mama.

"Well, I love a good surprise." I laugh. "If it does not contain varmints or pickled pig's feet."

Raffaella looks dejected. "Oh, you spoiled the surprise, naughty Arabella."

"We all know how much you've been eying those jars of pig's feet in the larder, so we decided to share them with you," mocks Mama.

"Ha. Now stop this teasing and tell me what is in there!"

"Oh, no, that would be much too easy. Let's play a little guessing game, shall we?"

"Oh, brother!" I complain. But secretly, I love this!

"No, this is your new *sister*," sasses Mama.

We all laugh.

"Okay, here are your clues," says Rafaella.

"What requires a fingerprint but does not involve a visit to the police station?"

"And what, besides emotions does an Italian boil?"

"What never crawled or flew or slithered but had eyes just the same?"

"And is to be smashed like the bugs beneath your father's wheels?"

"Hmm. Well, of course, this is about food, so let us begin there. Fingerprints. Could be Mama's thumbprint cookies filled with jam, but there is no boiling something with eyes . . . with eyes that weren't a bug or creature and requires smashing. Something one boils . . . eyes . . . Aha! Potatoes can have 'eyes,' and one boils them and smashes them with . . . fingerprints, fingerprints oh, I've got it. *Gnocchi di patate*! You have all the ingredients to make one of my favorites, *potato gnocchi*!"

Everyone claps. The joy in life is indeed sharing pleasures with others. They excitedly explain how they found the unexpected treasure of potatoes in Marco's storage bin (we'd put them there without his knowledge) when Rafaella was organizing.

"I'd never been so happy to see a tub of potatoes!" Rafaella laughs.

"And then the Delmonico family up in the mountains of Sila brought down some fresh eggs from their chickens and some of their Capino goat cheese for our sauce as a gift for helping their nieces after the locusts left!"

"What are we waiting for? Let's get started!"

Papa reaches easily and effortlessly for Luciana, and he, Marco, and Dominic leave. I think about how time does seem to heal. Who would have thought that Marco and Papa would be so comfortable in one another's company? Who would have thought that Papa would sweep my child up in his arms like a sack of precious potatoes?

Bowls clatter, pots clank, and spoons clink as the song of a kitchen comes to life. We cook the potatoes in their skins in a pot of boiling, salted water. We dust our work area on the table with some of our last bit of flour, reserving most of the container to mix with eggs and the cooked, mashed potatoes after we've removed their skins. All the while, we are a noisy orchestra of Stravinsky's *Fireworks* symphony. The clanging of lids and cabinets, chairs scraping floors, voices lifted in harmonious banter make for the kind of melody my home and my heart have missed.

As if on cue, I can hear someone coming up the path. The scratching of a bicycle tire on the tiny rocks and the ding ring of a bicycle bell alerts me to a visit from Signore Pascale. I invite our postman in for a cup of coffee, and he accepts all the while chattering on about the occurrences in and around Paola. So and so is going to have another child, so and so is rebuilding a fence in preparation for pigs from Acri, so and so's daughter is betrothed to so and so's son. He is happy and engaged as our town crier.

"I almost forgot, Arabella. I came to bring you this." He hands me a letter and bids us farewell. I can tell immediately by the writing that it is a letter from my sister. I am not one bit upset that it is not a letter from my husband!

Carefully placing my knife beneath the sealed envelope, I rip through it to remove three pages from the American life of my sister.

Boston, 1932

Cara La Mia Sorella,

> *Come vai? How are you faring? Has anything begun to sprout in that glasshouse of yours? How about in your heart? What is growing there, little sorella? Is it a vine of love that wraps from your heart and out to all of Paola? You are a fiery jewel of possibility, Arabella, one who never accepts the debilitating word "no," one who would never accept defeat. You are Paola's savior and protector. It is no surprise that you were born*

on the same day of San Francesco di Paola's ascension! I am so proud to be your sister. I sing your praises to my children, my husband, and your husband, to Antonio Salerno and the old men playing bocce ball in the park, to my upstairs neighbor, and the postman. Before you even come here to America, you are a bit of a legend.

Your husband is well. He stepped right into the busy life of America. He is a master mixer at the cookie factory already, a dedicated employee who works the whole night through. During the day he sleeps, then wakes for dinner, a stroll through the neighborhood before his night shift. He is a man of few words, yet I am beginning to read his moods. He does miss you; I know for a fact. Sometimes, he just stares out the window. When he and Luigi play the card game, Pinochle, bidding and tricking, passing and adding, I hear him speak your name. It always sounds like the whooshing waters of the lungomare, sweet and delicious.

Have you thought of when you will be coming back here to stay? The Depression is on here, maybe too much like Paola right now, but do not worry. We are fine. With employment at Salerno's and our little garden to sustain us, we are blessed.

How long will it take to pack up Mama, Papa, the children, Marco, Rafaella, and Pina? You know you can leave the rebuilding of Paola in the capable hands of others, si? You have done enough! I can see your scrunched-up forehead, dear sister. Do not worry about how it will come to be. It will! Anna Maria and Natalia who speak in two tongues- Italian and English. We'll learn the new national anthem together, "The Star-Spangled Banner!"

For now, I must go, but I wait to hear of your arrival each day.

Con Amore,
La tua Sorella,
Filomena

I get up to retrieve the potatoes from the pot of water. I spoon them out to dry on an old lace linen of my grandmother's. Thank goodness, I have something to do to occupy my hands as my mind whirls. I begin peeling back the browned, cooked skin of the first potato while standing at the sink. No one says anything for a long time.

I have peeled a couple of potatoes before Mama asks in a strange whisper, "Arabella, did you know of these plans for us to go to America? Has this been discussed without me?"

"No," I answer thoughtfully. "Filomena has mentioned me joining Aldo someday, but it was just words. Aldo will be coming back to Paola." Though I can see now he has no plans to do so anytime soon.

Rafaella speaks, "I will not leave Italy. And Marco has said nothing of this plan! Could I be marrying a man who has such plans?"

"Now wait a minute," I respond. "We do not know anything except that Filomena is missing her family terribly and wishes we can all be together. Let's not jump to conclusions."

"Well, I think it is all rubbish," states Mama. "Filomena and the children, Luigi, and Aldo will be coming home to Paola soon, not *us* going there. That will never happen. Our home is here, in our beloved Paola. I will live out my days here."

"Here, here," says Rafaella and they both join me at the sink and begin discussing the gnocchi.

The flour, eggs, and potatoes are mixed smooth. Mama rolls out perfect sausage-shaped rolls, cuts them in bullet speed. Side by side, they run forks across the shape to make miniature avenues for sauce. They see-saw beneath thumb and forefinger. These women create more than food; it's the delicious memories keeping the heart of family alive, preserving it for future generations. It makes me long for the day that Luciana will join the circle of women.

Another line of *gnocchi di patate* is cut into knuckle-size pieces, rolled into ovals with grooved fork tines to catch the sauce for perfect gnocchi. We lay the pieces out on Mama's linen towel that is marked with memories of dinners past. It holds a hint of Zio Benito's red vino, a pinkish stain of Mama's sauce, a slight outline of a serving dish in brown. Our meals leave indelible imprints on both the linen and the memory. Will these family memories sustain us if we find we are seas apart?

RAFAELLA IS SO EXCITED ABOUT the new glasshouse that Marco designed using the information from our friends in Acri and the library in Napoli. Our millworkers have completed everything but the finishing touches. She begs me to go with her to the mill to see its progress. How could I possibly put a damper on such infectious enthusiasm? I accept, and we invite Mama and Pina to join us. They decline, citing their need to tend to the food and the baby. We all pack into Papa's vehicle, Dominic riding what is called, "shotgun" in the front seat, Marco and Rafaella snuggled in a wool throw in the back.

How beautiful it is to witness true love. Marco and Rafaella would tell you that they are the most unlikely couple to have found love. Neither was seeking love. In fact, both were a bit hardened to even the idea of it. But the truth is that love can melt the stubbornest of ice floes in a human heart; love can crush the hardened mortar and rock walls with just one look. I think of Antonio Salerno. Here is a man with such love for me and our family that he has taken my husband in as one of his prized workers.

The villagers we pass wave enthusiastically to us as Papa lets Dominic toot the horn. Some touch their hearts and nod their heads as we pass. There are, indeed, all kinds of love to experience in this life, eh?

Rafaella insists I close my eyes as we enter the glasshouse. She tells me to take a deep breath. The wet, rich dirt surrounds my senses with the aroma of life. And, I smell something sweet, something familiar, but it's as if I don't want to believe it. Could it be they already have something growing in here? Cucumbers?

"Cucumbers!" I shout and throw open my eyes as if they were a hinged window. The others laugh and clap.

"We thought to honor Tiberius with cucumber seeds. Come see them! They even have flowers on them, Arabella. They're covered in flowers! We'll be making cucumber salads in the cold of winter! And we didn't stop there as far as honoring our ancestors. We know the Romans used all manner of beans at their festivals, so Marco, after much horse-trading, secured the important beans of long ago: Fabius fava beans of the Fabius family, lentil Lentulus' family, peas of the Pisos, and chickpeas of the Ciceros." She gestures wildly. "Come over here! See the furry sprouts of tomatoes and the shoots of zucchini tops pushing through!"

I am overwhelmed by the goodness that surrounds me. We could be facing a time of starvation and despair, but instead, we are growing vegetables indoors in a building constructed of glass and wood in late autumn in a village ravaged by destructive beasts less than a year ago. Instead of isolated doom, we have met new friends and neighbors who have expanded our learning and our ways.

The workers, my brother, Dominic, Papa, and Rafaella are all staring at me. It is a tender moment of realization that this is their way of giving back to me. Up until this moment of reflection, I have been single-minded in my efforts to ensure that life in Paola continues to thrive—not just survive. I see that others have taken note of this.

I take a breath and swallow the lump in my throat, "Well, with all this abundance, I suppose the Christmas feast will be at our home this year, *si*? But may I ask, who'll bring the *vino*?"

THERE IS A FLOW TO LIFE here in *mezzogiorno* that rolls in and out like the sea itself. These years have restored much of Paola's verdant shades of green. It's important to take note of all we planted, tended, and harvested— all that we borrowed from neighbors and restored with our young goats, rabbits, pigs, and chickens, the bins of wheat and corn— enough to fill bellies and bins; the newly improved glasshouses built at the mill with their better light and heat-producing walls, and the growth of independent, fifteen- year- old, Dominic, and the dynamic three-year-old, Luciana, following her every curiosity.

I remember the quiet marriage of Marco and Rafaella and the visit by our brother Octavio, his wife and son, and the mending of the brothers symbolized in the exotic gifts of fruit acai and jaca, the furry skinned chuchu vegetable, and the manioc—all which now are cultivated in our glasshouses. Following their wedding last year, Marco and Rafaella moved in with Mama and Papa, their presence filling holes of the emptiness of people gone away. My sister. And my husband. Though I do miss him, it's not in the way I think one is *supposed* to miss a husband. It's more that the children have only one parent now. And an out of sight papa is an out of mind papa. Dominic's memories fade. Luciana has none. When I think of Aldo, my mind aimlessly wanders like cloud formations on a windy day, leading me to America—and thoughts of Antonio Salerno.

What would my life be like if I had pursued that love? I'd be in America, for one, away from my beloved Paola and parents, Marco and Rafaella, and those others I have come to love. Or maybe Antonio would have stayed in Italy and pursued his business in *Cosenza, Napoli, Roma, or Firenze*. Who knows One thing I do know, this line of thinking is a runaway train without brakes.

I hear the distinct bicycle bell of Signore Pascale coming up the path. He and I share a cup of Mandarino Brothers coffee and one of Pina's amaretti before he hands me a letter from my sister and one from Antonio. I am anxious to read the news from America.

The first page of Filomena's letter is meant to be an inspiration to all of us about the power of the human spirit and recovery. The recovery from the great stock market crash that devastated so many Americans and the ripple effect beginning with the elite who lost their money, trickling down to the family no longer working because factories have closed. Or those who carried, lifted, and towed the lines on the now-empty docks. There is no money to pay for the supplies for all manner of businesses let alone to pay workers. Even if the butcher on the corner can still offer meat, most have no money to buy it. I know what it is like to be fearful your basic survival needs will not be met. I know what it is like to lose nearly everything you worked your life to secure.

This detailed letter from the hand of Filomena goes on and on describing the climate of hope that surrounds her. Aldo must have relived the devastation of the locust destruction. I shake the terrible memories and replace them with gratitude that throughout the Great Depression Salerno's Confection Company remained a thriving business. Antonio was so wise to diversify his products all across America.

They are all coming home! My sister, my husband, and Antonio are all returning to Paola for a few weeks! The Salerno factory will close for equipment updates *and* so that Antonio can go on a proper honeymoon with his new bride. *Antonio has a wife.* That will take some getting used to. Ever the gentleman, Antonio's letter tells me about his bride, Stephanie, born in America to a Polack father and an Italian mother, about her thoughtfulness and dedication to him and his business ventures, how she looks forward to meeting all of us, that Filomena has been most kind to her. Of course, she has. She is the magnanimous Filomena. And she is coming home. Thank you, Mary, Mother of God, my *sorella* will be here in Paola. I'll have to endure that husband of hers, but that's the price I must pay.

I bustle about in circles like the wheel of Papa's automobile turning and turning. Three years is a very long stretch of time to be apart. How have I changed? On the outside, my hips are wider and my middle meatier. I even have a few streaks of gray. Will these people who have known me still find me winsome?

And how will the children respond to their father? Aldo left when Luciana was an infant, so it will be like meeting her papa for the first time! And Dominic is growing into his adolescence. They will have several weeks to become acquainted. And *Dio mio*, I will have several weeks of bed business! The man has been away for so long, he will be like a pawing puppy dog. I will be trying out my new tinctures, for the last thing I need is to conceive, carry, and raise another child while my husband is in America. Motherhood is a gift I have come to respect, but I will be the one to decide when that gift will be given. Having the herbal wherewithal to control conception is my secret of choice.

WE'RE WORKING IN MAMA'S KITCHEN, preparing for the homecoming. I marinate a large pork loin in seasonal juniper berries, bay leaves, Benito's vino bianca, and olive oil. It is Aldo's favorite meat wrapped in strips of bacon and tied with our glasshouse fennel before roasting. Mama and Pina are making some fresh linguine: mixing, rolling, then cutting thick, perfect narrow strips. Mmm, the smell of Mama's sauce makes me feel that I am truly home. Here, every muscle irons itself out like a *ragazza's* youthful skin.

Marco is transporting everyone from the train station in Papa's automobile. Perhaps he wants to be seen as a progressive man living in a modern country, but here, many hope for things to remain the same as they were for their great grandmother, grandmother, and mother. And though I do understand the safety net of sameness, the world evolves constantly. Education broadened me. Stimulating discourse with Gregorio, Marco, and even Signore Tardino opened me to a broad spectrum of enlightening ideas, people, systems. From the classics of Socrates to the emergence of *metafisica*, *metaphysics*, old versus new crossed boundaries. And on the other side of those borders is the knowledge that there is more than one way to live, to think, to be.

Sometimes, I wonder where I came from, and then I remember: it was my sister who called me down from heaven, beams of light that lit my mind, angels who spoke in my ear, and herbs that called me to know them.

FILOMENA AND I FALL BACK INTO our pattern of laughing and crying, cooking, and creating. Together, we are balanced cogs on a wheel, smooth and moving. I relish the present and, in our daughters, Anna Maria, Natalia, and Luciana, the future.

It's not quite so easy with Aldo. The changes in me are as obvious as a bull in a China shop. When I say something that he views as inappropriate for a woman, his face is full of disapproval. And oddly enough, living in America has made Aldo more unyielding. It appears I am more like the progressive Americans, and he is old and rigid. Luciana stays clear of him. He yells at her constantly, declaring I am too lenient. But he and Dominic spend time together and seem like two peas in a pod. Aldo came home with quite a stash of money (just like a "bird of passage"). He's speaking to our fellow villagers about purchasing property. He is doing this without my input (though I've managed to sneak it into conversations wherever possible: why not invest in the further expansion of the family business—like the mill and the glasshouses or Mandarino Brothers coffee sales in Chicago, New York, and Philadelphia?) But, bah, a woman could not, would not, possess any business sense (even one that is conducting business right now; even one who put her business sense to work to expand her village's chances for survival). A proper Italian wife and mother follows her husband's lead, stays quiet about finances and business, takes care of the babies, makes sure she cooks and cleans and spreads her legs whenever the husband has an itch. *Malenovamia! Woe is me!* I've tried another angle, asking Papa to talk to him about investing in businesses, but Papa says that a father-in-law should not tell a son-in-law what to do—that it's not dignified.

"What about a daughter's dignity?" I want to know. "What about her respect?" I receive a blank look as a response. "Can't you simply bring it up in conversation?" I cannot, will not give up until I've said all I need to say. I continue, "Can't you come up with a way to plant a business idea he can take credit for sprouting?"

"Arabella." He sighs as he pulls his eyes away from me. "You must stop now."

Yes, I must stop because the unquestionable fact is this: as a man, my husband is considered the superior head of this family. Period. My business acumen and knowledge cannot exceed his. The male ego and superiority must remain intact. I'll tread lightly for now. My husband lives in America, and even when he is here, I still have my patients and the mill. I've plowed a rare road of freedom.

I let him do what he will with his American dollars. I have my own Italian *lire*, and through the help of Signore Losso at the bank, I have secretly invested in my own property near the mill. Who knew quietly helping Signore's wife through depression would allow me my own business investments?

PAPA AND I ARE GOING OVER THE books and business at his home. Luciana pitters about Mama and Pina clanking around the kitchen. Suddenly, I hear a distinct three-knock pattern on the door. A surprising rush of excitement courses through me. Papa calls for Pina to see who it is. I know who it is! I put my hand over his.

"Papa, I've got to go now."

"But we've just started," he answers.

"Yes, I know. I'll return shortly, but I've got to take care of something. Mama, can you watch Luciana for a little while?" I ask hurriedly.

"Certainly but where are you go . . . ?"

I'm already heading out the door.

Mama's tone is one of exasperation. She tells Pina that it is true that a zebra never changes its stripes.

It *is* true. There is much about me that is the same: my *bull-headed testa dura* determination; my strong desire to live a fulfilling life. I begin my walking- jog down the *lungomare* and up to the grove of citrus and olive. My muscles are aching from the pace, but I feel like an unhindered child—no worries of finances, patients, sustenance, husbands—just the deliciousness of fresh air, fun, and my childhood friend. The dew on my flushed cheeks is a wonder balm turning back time. I feel thirteen again, that is, until I must stop and catch my breath! With all this panting, Antonio will be able to hear me coming a kilometer away.

I look around this grove that refused locust annihilation. It may have lost the initial battle, but the laurels of victory belong to it. Nature's survival, against all odds, is evident in the strength and size of the trunks and the limbs, the depth of roots, and the prolific growth of fruit. The narrow streams of sunlight through the trees are like comet tails on the earth's floor. I breathe it all in, listening to the voice of the gentle wind encouraging me to fill my lungs, my chest, my very soul with the freshness of the *mezzogiorno*. Why does it take Antonio Salerno coming back to Paola to get me to appreciate it?

Antonio Salerno! Where is that rascal? I close my eyes and listen. Some birds are sharing a song, leaves swish and sway, and a soft wind murmurs to the sky. And then I hear the slightest brush of fabric against bark and turn in that direction. The slightest movement behind an olive's twisted trunk catches my eye.

"Tsk, tsk, Antonio, you know better than to move your position once the keen-eyed Arabella is in the grove!" I sashay toward the tree where he is hiding, and he pops out.

"Well, this frame doesn't seem to fit behind these trees anymore. Too many biscotti di Emelia, eh?" He laughs good-humoredly.

I pat my stomach. "I couldn't agree more."

"Arabella, stop. You are more beautiful than ever." He continues easily, in a friendly tone. "The years have filled you with vitality. Motherhood has made you even more radiant."

What a lovely compliment.

"Motherhood keeps one young at heart to be sure! Are you and Stephanie planning a family?"

He blushes.

"Oh, Antonio, forgive me. You know me, Signora Blunt! I didn't mean to pry on such a personal subject."

"Stephanie should not bear children due to her weak kidneys. God forgive me, but I am glad she has not conceived. It could be fatal." He takes a deep breath and looks directly into my eyes. "Arabella, I implore you. Please help me."

"Of course, but what can I do?" And heaven help me, I want to say, *conceive a child with you and then give it to you and Stephanie to raise?* I must be feeling light-headed from all the activity.

"You know so much of herbs and remedies, that I was wondering, well, um, is there nothing she can take to, you know, prevent conception?"

I look at the face of my long-ago friend—rugged, handsome, refined by success. His tailored suit is made of expensive fabric. All that success is wonderful, but if someone you love is at risk, what does that matter?

"*Mi dispiace*, Antonio. *I am so sorry* to hear about Stephanie. I do have knowledge of herbs and such, but what you ask . . ."

"Please forgive me. I'm just beside myself with worry. I would not want to put you in any jeopardy." His fear is twitching along the edge of his nervous, shuffling body. "An organization called Planned Parenthood would be able to help us, but she is too private a person to go to such a public place."

I would like to know more about this fascinating organization, but this conversation is not about that. "Have you discussed this with Stephanie?"

He looks up at me with hope in his eyes. "Not really. It is too emotional for her, but she respects you and your knowledge."

I answer slowly, unable to deny him. Look at what he has done for our family. "Antonio, the herbs you are inquiring about are powerful, and the regimen must be followed exactly."

"*Ho capito.*"

"And this must be our secret, *si*. No one, no one must ever know. *Capisce?*"

So much is at risk here, but if it saves a woman—namely, Antonio's wife, I'll do it, sending my formula across the seas. Then he tells me they'll soon be adopting a child.

"Right now, there are too many children on the streets of America begging, shoeless and destitute. We're going through the process to adopt."

"What a noble undertaking," I offer, "to save a child."

"No, it is the child who will be rescuing us," he responds.

"*Bravo*, Antonio." I pause, rescuing makes me think of someone I worry about. "Antonio, may I speak to you about Filomena?"

"Of course."

"How is she faring? I worry so," I sputter. And before I can swipe it away, a tear tumbles down my cheek.

He lifts my chin and wipes the tear with a gentle touch. I have no choice but to look him in the eye.

"Oh, Arabella. There is no one else on God's earth like you. Wit, intelligence, beauty, and the heart of an angel."

I think I have stopped breathing.

"Do not doubt my love for Stephanie. It's just that standing here as a man in our secret grove, I cannot help but wonder if I met you at this time in our lives if we could have been together. Do you?"

"Yes," I breathlessly whisper. "How could I not?" The desire to melt into him like chocolate in a warm pot is overwhelming. It is he, the gentleman, who takes a step back.

"But life had other plans for us, *si*?" He clears his throat, and just like that, our encounter is over. "Arabella, we watch over Filomena as much as we can without being intrusive. Be assured, we all care for her. I made sure that they accompanied us home to Paola, didn't I?" He winks.

"Thank you," I manage.

It seems Luigi is the same swine he has always been and will always be.

And I am still in love with Antonio Salerno.

A zebra cannot change its stripes—indeed.

THIS MORNING, DOMINIC ENTERED the *cucina*, posturing like a peacock.

"Mama. You and Luciana need to know that I am the head of the family in Papa's absence."

Looking at my fifteen-year-old son in command of his voice and stature is no easy task, I tell you. I search his face for the sweet boy who looked to his mama for love and assurance, but he's buried in bravado. It's as if this creature had consumed the tender child I once knew.

"What is all this about?" I inquire in as even a tone of voice as possible.

"It is about this family," he quips.

"What about 'this family'?" I ask.

"Papa told me I am to make decisions from now on."

While part of me wants to laugh, I am quite certain this new commission came straight from Aldo.

"Dominic, what did your father tell you?"

"It's obvious, isn't it? In his absence, there needs to be a man in charge of this family."

"But Marco lives here, and zio and Babbo Mandarino are all a part of our family."

"Marco is your brother, zio your uncle, and Babbo, your father. I am the eldest son of Aldo Basillio and will be the man of the house while he is away."

Aldo enters seemingly on cue.

"Aldo," I begin calmly. "Dominic was just telling me about his role as leader of our family."

"Si." Same ol' Aldo. A man of few words and fewer emotions.

"I see. May I speak to you privately?" I sugar coat every syllable as I hold my temper. How could he just strut back into our lives, issue commands, make decisions, and then just like that, leave again? How indeed. He is a man.

We leave Dominic looking quite smug in the kitchen and go to our room.

"Aldo, what is the meaning of all of this?"

He shakes his head disgustedly. I'm sure he's thinking, *Just like a woman, too stupid to understand the ways of the world.*

"While I am working my fingers to the bone in the mixing room of America, my son will be in charge of this family."

And what I am doing? Playing pattycakes all day? Attempting to keep an even tone, I ask, "And what may I ask prompted this decision?"

He looks at me disgustedly. "Do you know what I heard in the piazza yesterday, Arabella?"

I shake my head no.

He nearly spits the words, "They were talking about how you act like a man. It's time someone pulls the reins in on you."

"Oh, Aldo, people have been saying that for years! Since I was a little girl and I . . ."

"*Basta! Enough!*" he yells loud enough for my son, Marco's students, and, I am certain, the fish in the sea to hear him.

"Please watch your tongue, Aldo. I am not a child."

"You act like one. A spoiled child! And someone's got to take control of you."

"And you think the person for that job is *my son?*" I almost snicker.

"*Our* son," he answers and storms out of the room.

It is customary for the eldest son to take the place of an absent father, but this is meant to be punitive. There is a new dynamic between father and son that I don't like one bit. Moments later, my son knocks on my bedroom door, and in his first command as the young General Basillio, he demands *pranzo, lunch* to be on the table at precisely 2pm.

I am enraged, but it is not my son's fault. If Aldo thinks he can come back into our lives and take control, he's in for a shock himself.

The boat back to America can't leave soon enough.

"ARABELLA, *FIGLIA*, I KNOW YOU ARE SAD."

Mama appears worried. She has no idea!

"Your husband living far away is a hardship."

Not really. I like him better there. "I miss my sister." The only honest response I can muster. "I am an Italian through and through, but so much of me is in America!"

So much of me–in the heartbeat of my sister, in the dreams of Antonio Salerno, more medical knowledge, and that part which is bound by duty to Aldo Basillio. There's the unfounded part as well: the woman *I could* be if I lived in America. From the time I learned of Maria Montessori to the awakening moment I learned of the Suffragettes, to caring for my patients, taking over the mill, and establishing relationships with other villages. If this is who I am becoming in this land, imagine who I could be in the land of opportunity!

"*Rendeti utile*," I admonish myself. "*Make yourself useful.* Go care for the aging Signora Distefano's inflamed joints." Thinking about her makes me think more about the human body. In particular, *my* body. My *pregnant* body. It's hard to even admit! Wouldn't Mussolini be proud of me, I sneer, increasing Italy's population just like he's ordered? In fact, I could file the paperwork and get *lire* for being pregnant!

Though Aldo had issues with my decorum, his appetite for my body was insatiable! Maybe I should have increased the dosage of the preventive remedies in one of the endless sessions of bed business upon bed business. Did I conceive the night he awakened me erect as a fence post, grunting and aggressive? Or the morning when Luciana was fussy wanting only the attention of her mama? He was so jealous of her, he had to have me several times that one day. *Allora*, no matter the when of it, *I am pregnant*. Again. My husband and sister are across the world in a place called America. My eldest grows into obstinate manhood. My sweet, intelligent daughter is a sponge for knowledge.

I drag myself to the shelves of dried herbs and oils. I mix a salve of rose oil, lavender, and willow bark for Signora DeStefano's aches. She will be here any time now.

And so will this child.

IT IS FAR TOO SIMPLISTIC TO merely state, "I did not want this child," nor would I ever admit it to anyone. My fellow Italians believe that it is God's will when we conceive, and that may very well be true, for look at my record! I possess knowledge of herbs and the human body—including a woman's cycle of fertile days, and I still conceived Dominic, my lost girl, Luciana, and now, Vincenzo. There is no guidebook to prescribe the number of preventatives versus the steady stream of sperm during my fertile cycle. Does that mean that God had a part in it?

It's dangerous to think like I do (and to put in practice what I do with my preventatives). It's against the law of our Mother Church in Rome and contrary to what our leader wishes for our country. Women having children is what we do, what we were made for, si? Our purpose in life. I submit (secretly) that it is not. Maybe it is best I have conceived three children so as not to arise suspicion.

My third child, Vincenzo, demanded every part of me as he prepared to enter the world. My belly grew enormous on the outside as I turned increasingly inward. Maybe I slept so many hours of the days away because it was far easier than dealing with the burdensome weight, weariness, swollen ankles, and vertigo. My thirty-six-year-old body was not prepared for the absolute dependency of the fetus.

Mama, Pina, and Rafaella became my daily fairy godmothers. They cooked *piatti*, *dishes* of layered lasagnas, bowls of herbed cannolini, and anchovies *ensalata*, cleaned, and took care of the laundry. Marco oversaw activities at the mill when I was unable. Rafaella tended to my patients, and after word spread of her bedside manner and skills, she was accepted with open arms. Papa intervened when Dominic wanted to join Mussolini's Pontine Marshes program to reinstall pumps and dikes all over Italy. Papa reminded Dominic that he was acting leader of the family and could not be that far away from home.

"I want to do something useful," he shouted in his cracking, adolescent voice.

"Being here with us is useful," I answered.

"With a little girl and a pregnant lady? No!"

Marco tried as well. "I could use help running the mill and . . ."

"That is not useful man's work! My *mother* does that job."

His disdain was painful, but I tried not to take it to heart.

When our demanding, vocal Vincenzo did arrive, I could see he was intended to be part of our family. Is this how Filomena felt when she "called me down from heaven?" As if I was a missing limb on the body of the Mandarinos? Maybe I called Vincenzo down to us but didn't realize it. Perhaps there is a connection between deep psychology and what happens in our life.

I did some reading of both Dr. Sigmund Freud and Dr. Carl Jung during the pregnancy because my dreams were intoxicating. Awake, my body felt heavy and swollen like Mama's bread dough rising. But while I was sleeping, I walked long, moist, mysterious passageways, tasted juices dripping seductively from fleshy peaches, and observed myself with unknown male forms. I existed in a realm of unbridled sensual explorations that I have not experienced with Aldo. Some of this can be attributed to the hormones that coursed through my pregnant body, but according to Dr. Freud, there is more to the story. Our dreams, he claims, represent our unconscious desires and repressed emotions. All those tunnels and landscapes apparently symbolize my female genitalia, breasts, and men's penises—everything having a specific significant meaning. It's disturbing yet tantalizing. I just do not think of myself as a sexual being like Dr. Freud states. I am a woman, yes, a wife, yes, but sexuality, pleasure, and desires have not been a part of my life save the few brief romantic fantasies regarding Antonio.

I also read the work of psychoanalyst Carl Jung, which did bisect Freud's in certain ways. Jung speaks of examining dream places, objects, people, and animals in terms of what they mean to the individual rather than preset, assigned interpretations. Instead, I might look for a connection to everything I dream with everything I want to be—and everything the "collective soul" of this world is hoping I will become. I tend to fall on the side of Jung's analysis as it makes me think of all the ambition I have carried within me like a fetus waiting to be born.

TODAY, ON THE FEAST DAY OF San Francesco di Paola, 1937, I turn another page of living—37-years-old. *Dio Mio*, how the time races on (and I can hear the voice of Mama stating with precise diction, "The clock ticks whether we hear it or not"). And what have I heard? The lull of the sea, deep-throated, belly laughter, mournful grieving, the binding vows of marriage, the cries of challenging childbirth, the deafening wings of locusts, and the cawing of Brazil's parrots, the spitting fire of ingenious inventions; the shuffling of babies' steps, the expectant song of healing, the clang of war, the timbre of a boy's voice growing into manhood.

After chatting with some of the workers at the mill and visiting with Padre who has a bad case of bursitis in his left shoulder, I stroll through the *piazza's* festivities toward the *lungomare*. I smile, recalling a time when I thought I could encase myself in a cloak of invisibility going from the *piazza* to the *lungomare*. *Como, no?* I ask myself. Why not give it a try again?

I am pleased to see someone I know on the path down to the *lungomare*. It is Zio Benito on a bench away from the boisterous festa.

"Zio, *come vai?*" I ask.

"Arabella. *Buon giorno* and *buon compleanos!*" He pats the space on the bench next to him, and I gladly sit.

"Grazie, uncle."

"Ah, there is nothing on this earth like the *aria fresca* of *mezzogiorno*.

Niente! Nothing." He takes in a deep breath, and I cannot help but do the same.

"*Si. The air* is *perfetto,*" I respond.

"If we left the world to God, it would remain this beautiful, this lovely," he says wistfully, "but then we humans have our issues."

"What are you speaking of?"

He picks up the newspaper from the other side of the bench and hands it to me. "Wartime approaches again," he states matter-of-factly, as if he is reciting the average rainfall for the year or the kilos of sardines caught this month.

I lift the journal from the bench and read.

Giornale di Italia Spring 1937
Mussolini Visits Hitler to Sign the Anti-Comintern Act
One million jam Berlin's Olympic Stadium to hear "Il Duce" and
Hitler speak.

"Mussolini's dragging Italy into another war," my voice slow, hard.

"It's an agreement between Nazi Germany and Japan," answers Zio Benito. He takes the paper from me and reads aloud, "The aim of the Communist International, known as the Comintern, is to disintegrate and subdue existing States by all the means at its command; convinced that the toleration of interference by the Communist International in the internal affairs of the nations not only endangers their internal peace and social wellbeing but is also a menace to the peace of the world desirous of cooperating in the defense against Communist subversive activities."

"And Italy's part in this is what exactly?"

"Mussolini is going to make Italy better. He's teaming up with Germany."

I hear the words, but they are the wheels of war roaring in my ears, deafening all celebratory music and voices from the *piazza,* all birdsong from the trees. *Where have you been?* I ask myself. Apparently, these many months of motherhood, I've had my head buried in the proverbial sands.

"Arabella, aren't you proud of Dominic?"

"Well, most of the time. But of late he's been a brash adolescent boy with an attitude."

There's something in his eyes that unsettles my equilibrium, but I feel the presence of my angel calming me. Just knowing she is here brings comfort and strength.

"Well, he is joining the *Avan Guardista, si?*" he asks.

"Avan who?" I question.

"Mussolini's military group for adolescent boys. Just this morning, I saw him at a drill outside of town. He looked quite the fine picture of a soldier!"

The weight of worry descends like a thousand bricks upon my head, anvils on my shoulders, a tsunami in my stomach. My hands become the hands of my mother who, when faced with overwhelming helplessness, use the emotional release of beating my thighs. The need to unleash these emotions is so powerful I am not even aware of my actions until a burning fire erupts on my skin.

Zio continues, so used to the emotional pounding of women. "That Il Duce is a master! Imagine the genius of the *Avan Guardista* where boys experience the thrill of being uniformed soldiers? They are preparing to fight alongside Germany and Japan. I am so proud of Dominic!"

I simply do not have the capacity to speak. If I could, I would offer quite a different stand, a mother's view of this duty that has young boys brainwashed into thinking that going to war is romantic bravado! I know it is the duty and calling of young men to serve their country. I know this. But not my son. Not this war (which I sense will be even more insane than the last one). Instinctively, I reach for the gold cross resting on the base of my throat. *Dear God*, I pray, *help me find a way to keep my son from this tragic madness.*

"Come," he says. "Let's stroll down to the beautiful *lungomare* and celebrate this day that God gave us, Arabella."

I manage to put one foot in front of the other down the hill and the steps toward Mama and Papa's haven. When the sweet aroma of Mama's cooking hits us, I wonder if we couldn't save the world one scrumptious, heavenly meal at a time. What if we sent the leaders of Japan, Germany, Russia, and America platters of Mama's *lasagna di forno* to fill them with the deliciousness of kindness, abundance, and joy instead of the insatiable appetite for power? If the world were left to women, would we come up with methods such as these to heal the inconsistencies of man?

ALL THROUGH THE EXQUISITE meal of all my favorite dishes, I longed to speak to my sister, to hear her council, to be comforted by her voice. It came the following day in the form of a letter—perfect in its timing and message. I gaze out on the calm, sapphire jewel of the Mediterranean Sea as if I can trace the very path of this letter.

Signore Pascal hands me the envelope, shifting nervously from foot to foot, anxious to hear news of Aldo and Luigi, and to learn more of Americani factory life, of how much *lire* an Italiano earns in America. He is eager to lap up news of Presidente Franklin D. Roosevelt's views on Hitler and Mussolini and to hear a continuation of the last letter's list of strange inventions of beer in a can, and a moving picture box called a television, but I'm not in a sharing mood today. I tell him we will catch up soon, and he departs on his sturdy bicycle. I'll savor this moment, inhaling my sister's presence like the first fragrant spoonful of basil, garlic, cannolini, and vegetables lifted from a simmering minestrone pot.

In the sea of turmoil and confusion over the impending war, my son's involvement in the youth troop, a demanding toddler, and a daughter growing so quickly she barely fits in her own skin; it is my sister who I wish to connect with more than anyone. I'll follow the thread of her words, inch by inch across seas, time zones, and skyscrapers, fist over fist. I turn the letter over and over, conjuring her spirit like a seasoned *strega,* deep into her *witch*'s trance, so that when I read her words, I will hear her mellifluous voice. I slip my fingers under the tucked edges of the envelope, remove the pages, and unfold my sister's presence.

It doesn't surprise me that my introspective nature today is matched by the same tone and emotion that my sister had when she wrote this letter.

Boston, 1938

Cara Arabella,

Ciao e salute from America. Alessandro and Bernardo are young men who are finding their way on the streets of adulthood. Anna Maria has too many young men circling. Natalia has learned to print words on paper using a machine called a typewriter. Aldo and Luigi manage Salerno's mixing room for nine hours each day! I am in the cucina all day trying to keep up with insatiable appetites!

Forgive me in advance of these words, dear sister, but I have played at the charade of being just fine living apart from you! My God, I do not know how I have made it here without you! When I look at the world with my eyes, I notice only the zoomed-in details of the world: the pesky bugs on my peppers, the dirt on my floors. But yours are the eyes that take in the curious panorama of life: the vastness of cerulean skies, the scalloped edges of montanas, the totality of the circle of family. I know that it is increasingly hard for you there in Italia managing your three children, your patients, the glasshouses, the mill, and watching over Mama and Papa. But now there is the impending doom of war and your Dominic to consider.

I hear the words of Aldo often, how he'll be returning to Italy for good with his fortune "someday." At dinner following Sunday mass I asked him about his return to Italy, how maybe you and the kids should come here while he's making his money. His gruff answer is always some version of this. "Filomena, you are not to speak of America with Arabella."

"Oh, si, Aldo, of course," I respond. Bah, men are such fools when it comes to women! Does he think just because he says so, I will stop talking to my sister? Your sons need their father, and your daughter would have opportunities here you cannot even fathom. Remember all your dreams of becoming a professora, or dottore and how you wanted to join the Suffragettes? Well, in America, a woman can teach, write, heal, and vote! Imagine that for your Luciana.

You are my mirror, Arabella, reflecting my strength, my beauty, my happiness. Please excuse the poetic drama of this letter, but I've kept it inside for too long. It is how I feel, and my hand and heart have minds of their own this morning as I sit down with a cup of Mandarino Brothers cafe and think of you.

I know I have written other letters beseeching you to come to America, but times are different now. Marco and Rafaella are there to be with Mama and Papa. Marco can again run the mill, and Rafaella can take care of your patients. Their child will fill all their hearts and days with love. But you sister, you need to come to America. It is time.

Con Amore,
Tua Sorella,
Filomena

I clutch the letter, a rope to lift me from the bottom of a thousand foot well. Maybe my angel put those words in the heart and hand of Filomena just for me.

The pan of *polpetta melenzane* sputters, spitting olive oil onto my arm, snapping me from my reverie.

"*Managia*," I yell, jumping up to turn the meatballs mixed with eggplant from the mill glasshouse garden, yesterday's bread, and ground pork. They are Dominic's favorite. Maybe the promise of them and the aroma will bring my son home for dinner. Marco, Papa, and even our neighbor, Signore Puto oversee the willful Dominic, but he sneaks money from my purse, then tiptoes out of the house all hours of the night. Will he even come home tonight?

Another spatter of oil burns my arm, and I cry out again.

"*Mama?*" questions the raven-haired Luciana.

"*Non tipreoccupare*," I respond as nonplussed as possible, but Luciana is so sharp, she can almost see through walls and most certainly through human facades.

"Mama, I can help. Let me."

I hand her my apron and the spoon while I contemplate all the help I have been offered. But who is helping Luciana grow into her full potential? I keep replaying Filomena's words about what she could accomplish given the opportunities in America. And *Dio mio*, little Vincenzo is quite frankly, a wild, fearless terror too much for me to handle alone.

Suddenly, I hear the familiar yelp of my youngest son's warrior cry! He's heading toward the imaginary battlefields just outside our front door. Signore Puto is standing outside his tiny *groceria* across the street, wagging his gnarled finger and shouting, "Vincenzo, you are a bad boy! You get back upstairs, *adesso*, immediately. You hear me?"

I hustle down the stairs in time to recognize that scrunched-up look of determination on my son's face. He picks up a handful of rocks and hurls them at his Goliath with the tenacity of David. I watch in stunned embarrassment as the small weapons sail past Signore Puto's hairy ear and land with a CRACK on his shop window. An elderly villager dressed in black walks past, lifts her chin, and clucks her tongue in disapproval. Dominic rounds the bend to witness the embarrassing scene.

"Mama, again?" he queries. "Again? Vincenzo cracked Signore Puto's window *again*? He needs a beating! He needs to be punished! Are you going to do it, or am I?"

"And who will beat you for stealing from my purse and running off into the night?"

Now Luciana comes running down the stairs and tries to scoot Vincenzo back into the house before their older brother gets to him. All the while Dominic yells that he is in charge of this family. Signore Puto continues his rant of children, broken windows, and the cost of doing business. I assure him we will replace the window (again) and redirect Dominic to clean up the mess.

The pungent smell of burned eggplant meatballs pours into the hallway. My brain's circuitry feels burned as well, fueling the bonfire of reasons to leave Italy for America.

But God help me, I will put off the inevitable as long as I am able.

I AM BARELY ABLE TO KEEP my head above the current. Marco is reading me the official government papers addressed to Dominic.

"Dominic Basillio, It is your time to prepare for our great country's imperial expansion."

The words are screeching wheels on the train track of fear, metallic words grinding. I come reeling back to my kitchen table, but my feet, my apron, my heart reeks of the burn.

"'*Imperial expansion?*' My God, Marco, they make it sound as if war is a spiritual calling!"

My *simpatico* brother shakes his head. "Arabella, this is no good. I have known firsthand how righteous men fight for justice and end up torn to pieces. In the great tomes of history, one can witness greed for power and religious domination. Being involved in the Spanish Civil War is one thing but getting in bed with Hitler is quite a different story. What big men of war do not see is the aftermath. Broken bones and broken spirits, destitute widows, fatherless children. The hammers of war smash everything in their path scattering slivers of irretrievable souls to distant shores."

"What am I to do? Tell me, Marco," I implore.

"What do you want to do, Arabella?"

I sigh deeply, trying to expel the frog in my throat. "I want to save my son from the terror of war—and keep my family together."

"Then there is your answer."

"What do you mean? That's a desire, not a solution!" I bark.

He takes my hand. *How can he remain so calm?* It makes my behavior more egregious.

"Please forgive me, Marco. My mind and emotions are spinning so wildly out of control that I can't see the forest for the trees!"

"Arabella, listen to yourself. Not only do you care for the health of the people, you're responsible for the mill and the glasshouses, overseeing our parents' health, but also raising your three children *alone* during an uncertain political time. You just stated, 'save my son Dominic and keep my family together.' The only way you are going to successfully achieve that is to get out of the country. Your husband and our sister are in America. There is your answer, for now."

"It is too far from home."

"It's a drastic solution for desperate times," he answers.

"But how would we get Dominic out of the country?"

He looks out the window at some memory I cannot see. "A generous number of lire can convince many an official to lose Dominic's papers."

"Of course," I acknowledge. "Politicians have been paid off since the days of Jesus and Caesar! Why not for the safety and welfare of my son?"

"This is one time I am grateful that Papa knows people who can accomplish this sort of work."

"Yes, and that we have the funds to do whatever is necessary to leave Italy."

"*Sì.*" Marco is solemn.

"My motherly heart aches for all those who do not have the resources."

"So, then, you've made up your mind?"

"Well, more like Mussolini and Hitler made up my mind for me. "

I am going to America.

I AM IN THE KITCHEN OF MY childhood a few months since we decided to go to America. We were advised to allow Dominic to attend military training camp so as not to draw any attention until the right people are paid off and proper paperwork is obtained. This decision also serves to appease an enthusiastic Dominic who does not know of our plans. It has given me time to adjust to the idea of leaving.

Today though, memories rush in to circle my heart. There, in the corner next to the window, is the wood oven where I learned to bake Mama's crusted bread. And here, in the middle of the room whose walls are painted with history, is the table handcrafted by one of my *famiglia.* How many meals did my siblings and I share here without an inkling of future separation?

And there is the stove Mama is at now preparing escarole and *pesce.* I open and close my eyes once, twice, three times clicking the shutter of the memory's camera. Will I ever see her here in her kitchen again? Will I ever stand at her sink and gaze out at velvet-sloped *montanas*? I admonish myself. *Arabella, this is a temporary arrangement. You are protecting your son. Once the war is over you will all return.*

My father's hands shake as he reads the telegram from Aldo, and I realize how this decision is like rows of dominoes. One family domino falls, and the entire line of dominoes topples. First, there was Octavio and Marco, then Filomena and the children, and now I'm leaving too. I'll come back like Marco, I vow, for the moving away and returning affects everyone.

Papa sets the telegram on the table and I too tremble as I pick it up and read:

Western Union

Booked passage for you, Dominic, Luciana, and

Vincenzo on Conte di Savoia,

August 1939 (stop)

Will meet you in New York (stop)

Aldo

Could my father command me to stay? Could the war not come to claim Dominic? Could our family story still have a happy ending here in Italy? Sadly, simply, the answer is the same: no, no, and no. Hitler has invaded Poland and is on the march for world dominance. Together, he and Mussolini will use every last man to achieve it.

"Oh, Papa, how am I going to do this?" I ask.

He takes a deep breath. "*Figlia*, we do what we have to do. You have done this throughout your adulthood. This is no different." His words fall apart. He is forced to look away, swallowing hard.

I nod nervously, butterflies catapulting from my stomach to my mind. *We do what we must do.* I always have, *si*? Yes, it is true. Squeezing my eyes shut, I muster the strength from some newly-tapped well of courage, managing a smile for my papa. I feel like the Gold Rushers of early California I read about who spoke of "hitting the mother lode." Discovering courage you didn't have a minute ago is like that. And it takes courage to protect my child, no matter the cost.

Papa and I speak of the logistics of getting us out of Italy, how to sedate

Dominic for the voyage, the details of duties at the mill and glasshouses, getting the last of my patients comfortable with Rafaella and vice versa, and the requirements of ship travel. Once I have transferred my attention from emotions to business, Arabella Mandarino Basillio moves to action.

ROOTED HERBS FROM ARTEMISIA and basil to mayweed, primrose, and valerian, dried bags of host herbs, notebooks of herbal knowledge and tinctures labeled in both Italian and my new language, English; family photographs, Antonio's carved Madonna and book of love poems, Pina's handwoven flowered wool rug, seeds of cucumbers, beans, tomatoes, two aprons, sketches of glasshouses, Mario's carved salad tongs, one-two coveted books from each of my bookshelves, mountain baskets, paring and dicing knives, two good dresses, Filomena's handwoven lace curtains, espresso pot, three sets of white sheets, feather hat, minestrone pot, slips and stockings, three sets of clothes for each of us, two pair of shoes.

Mama is here with me, sorting through a lifetime of belongings.

"Arabella, have you pulled every single item out of every drawer, cabinet, and shelf?"

"Si. I thought I'd make piles of everything from spoons to socks, towels to tongs, pans to panties."

She nods. Do I tell her that by removing each and every item from its known place, I remove a part of me that has belonged here? Item by item I disinter my past.

Mama's voice is overly cheerful. "More memories are waiting to be created, *figlia*. You will see! And just think, you and Filomena will be together again living in the same house!"

It's my turn for optimism and a little humor. "It's called a "*duplex*, Mama. It's two houses in one building. Filomena, Luigi, and the kids live downstairs in a separate house, and we will live upstairs. This is how it's done in America," I state this fact as if I am an expert.

"Well, whatever it's called, it does not matter. All I know is that my girls and their families will be together."

This thought of being with my sister and my son's safety keeps my hands moving like a factory machine belt, setting some objects to the "no" pile but placing others into the trunks.

I close my eyes and picture Filomena, and then I see Mama. I see Aldo, then an image of Papa. I see the place in the garden where my unborn daughter lies. My heart breaks a little more.

"*Cara Arabella*," Mama whispers. "*Non ti preoccupare.*"

I open my eyes. Her arms await me. I fall into her embrace. When we separate, she hands me a rather recent photograph of her and Papa.

"We wanted to surprise you with a recent photograph of us so you will remember who awaits you," she states. As if I need a reminder where a large portion of my heart will remain.

I wrap it in my grandmother's lace tablecloth and tenderly lower it into the trunk.

PART 3

America

1939-1950

New York Harbor, 1939

WE WAIT, IMPATIENT BUT EXHAUSTED, nervous but excited.
The waves of change pitch and pound against our unsettled sea legs.
One can sense the fast rhythms of America in the vibrations of the
ground. There's a hurriedness in the cacophony of orders, the steamer
trunks and wheels scraping stone-cold floors, the shuffling of
thousands of worn, leather soles and the tap of clicking heels; words
shoot out of the men's mouths like forceful bullets—some clipped,
others courteous.

We have every piece of paper in order. Papa secured valid visas
from the proper authorities at the embassy in Roma. I did not ask any
questions about how these coveted items came to be during this time

of limited number of immigrants allowed in the United States. However it was done, I am grateful to be away from the grip of war.

Finally, we are through the inspection station, and there, just ahead is Aldo, Anna Maria, Natalia, Luigi, and my *sorella*! Like a circus performer, I catapult into Filomena's arms. We hold each other as if we are glued together. Vincenzo, the Tasmanian devil, grips me like a barnacle on a rock. Fortunately, the men attend to our trunks, leaving us to bask in the reunion.

The Mandarino *sorelle* caravan heads for the train that will take us to our new home in Boston.

IT IS DIFFERENT TO VISIT A place than to live there. Where I found Boston to be a charming mix of history and modernism when I came here with Filomena and the children, as a home, it feels sprawling and cold. There is no Mama, no Papa, no expansive healing herbal garden (though Filomena has a matchbox patch of soil), no familiar faces to meet upon the street. I don't know how my sister made this adjustment with only her husband and children to comfort her. And what kind of comfort could he possibly have been?

I noticed another of his bruise marks on her this morning. She gives me a look of nonchalance then shrugs her shoulder. I suppose this has become as common as making a pot of sauce. *Nasty, foul man!*

One commonality in our Little Italy neighborhood is *sauce*! Those from *Calabria, Sicilia, Roma, Napoli*, all share the comfort and sound of home in their pots of sauce: garlic popping, marinara bubbling a hint of red wine mixed with the ebb and flow of the Italian language. Occasionally, I hear the comforting voice of an old friend—Antonio

Salerno. Along with his lovely wife, Stephanie, and their darling adopted girl, Bella, we blend tales of our old life with new hope for our future life. Stephanie and Bella are beautiful inside and out. They feel like an extension of family. Stephanie and I build on the bond created around our preventative tincture secret.

Grazie Dio, Dominic adjusted to his new American life better than we hoped. I am sure his father had something to do with that as well as the group of young men he has befriended. They helped him get a job with a pharmaceutical company that makes new kinds of medicines for the infirm, from arthritis to the common cold. I can tell he feels his work is important and that he is part of something big. This too has helped him to acclimatize.

Luciana is getting to know children her age. She is a good girl—the same as she was in Italia, but here she is exuberant about her studies. At first, she was in the schoolroom with six-year-olds until the school acknowledged her understanding of English—and her intelligence. Now, she is in classes with other nine-year-olds. Evenings, we study her lessons together so that I too am learning grammar and structure. I converse in complex English phrases—not that you need English in Little Italy! I see why Aldo, Luigi, and Filomena continue to speak mostly Italian. The streets, the shops, the people appear to be a replica of Italy, but ladies and gentlemen, you are definitely not in Italy anymore! Where are the mountains? The *lungomare*? My Mama and Papa? Perhaps all the facsimiles are just mind-play to keep homesickness at bay.

My own daughter is playing Americana games! She has changed her name! No longer is she *Luciana*; now she is *Lucy*. Aldo and I had difficulty with this switch, not wanting her to forget her heritage, but she was persuasive. We acquiesced. Then she began a campaign for Vincenzo! She calls him Vinny. If I must have an American name for him, it will be Vincent.

That is the way it goes with people, eh? We give some, and we take some, and sometimes we're forced to walk towards a middle ground. *Allora*, some of us, like Aldo, glue our feet in whatever cemented place we wish to remain. This is true of the subject of Vincenzo.

"Aldo, Vincenzo is a child. And children cannot be made to change overnight."

"Bah." He responds eloquently. "Rubbish."

I try another tactic. "Aldo, can you call to mind what it was like to be a frightened child?"

"No."

I persist. "Please give him time to adjust. He has been ripped from all that is familiar. His routine is disrupted . . ."

"See, this is what is wrong with women: always excuses for unacceptable behavior."

"Aldo. Whatever you think of women is one thing, but we are speaking of a child. On this subject, you need to heed my word, *capisce?*" My tone is sharp as a lioness's claws.

He's fuming with anger, but I hold my ground. I will protect my son.

"Every night of our child's life, he has slept beside me. This is what he is used to."

"I am his papa. He will obey me and sleep in his American bed," he rails on.

"He *will* obey you, and he *will* sleep in his new bed—give him time."

He is shouting now, "*Basta! Enough!* I will not tolerate a child in the marriage bed, Arabella."

Of course, what was I thinking? It all comes down to bed business.

And though I try every trick in my mama book from relaxing teas at bedtime to stories like *Mike Mulligan and the Steam Shovel*, to snuggling with him in his 'American bed,' I cannot convince Vincenzo to stay put. Night after night, he crawls into bed beside his mama. Night after night he is spanked, yanked out of our bed, and thrown into his own by the unfeeling stranger called "Papa." This cycle repeats, as sure as a moon's rising.

I did not foresee this problem or the glaring discontent of being under the rule of Americano Aldo! Though, I have been the one in charge of this family day in and day out while he was in America. *Cretino! Nitwit!* I realize with stinging reality that without the strong presence of the Mandarinos, without my status as healer or manager of the mill, I am on slippery footing as *solamente, only* the wife of Aldo Basillio. My eyes were only focused on Dominic's safety. No wonder I easily forgot the pieces of my own life.

IT TOOK AN INNER STRENGTH and perseverance to acquire some new coping skills where the Italian me intersected at the corner of the American me. Mostly, it was accepting the roles of wife and mother and little else.

"Your favorite ladle from your *cucina* in Paola is holding up well all these years later."

"*Si!* It's holding its shine better than I am."

Filomena laughs. It's so easy being with my sister. We know each other so well, we actually anticipate one another's moves. Someone watching would see a kind of cooking minuet. I stir the chopped onions, carrots, leeks, and celery in Filomena's heavy skillet while she cleans the chicken livers we bought at the butcher this morning. I reach for the salt and pepper while she maneuvers around the back side of me for her favorite ceramic bowl. She sees me wrinkling my nose at the smell of the chicken livers that are not as fresh as what I was used to.

"There are some things we've had to accept here," she offers.

"Mmmhmm," I mutter.

"The water is funny," she begins to rattle off the list I have heard spoken numerous times before. "It smells like metal; pasta does not cook the same. I use more *vino* instead of water in my sauce!"

"Tsk, tsk, an obvious excuse to drink more *vino!*" I tease.

"Well, everything affects everything! Luigi and Aldo complain that their wine is not the same due to the water! They complain it's watery, not rich, full."

"I have a feeling that nothing made here could ever compare to the perfection of Italia, no?"

"Quite true!" she says. "Until you get to Italia, and then everything there wouldn't be like it is here."

"Ah, *si*. What is that popular saying here? 'The grass is always greener on the other side.'"

"Yes. Except there is hardly any grass here in the North End."

"I know. It is still a shock to the system, much like jumping into the *lungomare* waters in December."

We are both quiet for a moment thinking of the place we love and the people we carry in our hearts. Before I know it, I am missing Mama and Papa and Pina and Marco and Rafaella and Zio Benito and the *piazza* and our home, my patients, the mill, olive groves, and the sea so profoundly I simply fall apart like a pastry improperly baked.

Filomena holds me, and though I desperately try to stop it, the faucet of emotion streams. From a place outside of my body, I can hear the strangeness of my own stifled cry, and now, it suddenly seems funny. I bend over to free the bubble escaping my innards, laughing through tears.

"Oh, Arabella, you are a strange one," she admonishes just as she did decades ago.

"Yes, *si*," I agree, strange indeed. She knows that about me. All at once, I unload decades of concealed secrets.

She has already added the chicken livers, red wine, and tomato sauce to the pan. The aromas and the gentle sizzling sound are smooth trails for disclosure. I bare all—every detail of the powerful light at the cathedral in Rome, the spirit angel's appearances and guidance that even led me to the *sorelle* who delivered Luciana in the middle of nowhere.

When I have finished my lengthy story, I feel like a ragdoll, devoid of bones to hold me up. Filomena has pulled her chair across from mine and is stroking my hand.

"*Poverina*," she coos. "You have shouldered so much on your own: visitation from spirits, the weight of our family, your marriage, your patients, most of Paola, not to mention, love with a man that can never be."

I look up at her.

"I wish it could have been different for you both, but it was not to be. I think God sent you an angel to guide and comfort you—when I could not, when Mama could not, when Antonio could not, when your husband could not. "

It's an interesting perspective. And she knows me so well that a buried question surfaces. "*Sorella*, do you think I am *pazzo*? Isn't it only the *insane* who see the non-living?"

"Do you consider Mary, Jacob, and Joan of Arc *pazzo*?"

"No, but those were holy, chosen people. I am an average girl from Paola."

"Arabella, there is nothing 'average' about you. If you could see yourself through the eyes of others, you would see how extraordinary you are."

I take a deep breath. "I don't think you'll feel that way when I tell you the truth about Gregorio."

She bristles at his name.

"I killed him!" I blurt.

She performs the sign of the cross. "Arabella, why would you say such a thing?"

I tell her the whole story about sneaking to their home that terrible morning to deliver medicine and sterilizing solution and how Signora Ruffino took the belladonna.

"But you were just a child. It wasn't your fault! Signora took the medicine from you."

"Can you ever forgive me?"

"There is nothing to forgive. I cannot imagine how you carried this in your heart all these years. You are so brave."

"And *pazzo*?"

"Maybe a teeny bit," she teases.

"Can you imagine if the men heard this conversation?"

Filomena dons her best Aldo stance and furrows her brow. "Arabella," she bellows in an exaggeratedly low voice. "What has gotten into you? Are you feverish or just insane?"

She is a good impersonator. We giggle uncontrollably.

When we're quiet again she adds, "God delivers help in many forms. I have never seen angels or visions, but I am not you. You stay close to innocence. Perhaps it's easier for God's messengers to reach you."

"Me? Now you're talking like a crazy woman! You are the one who is sweet, kind, and pure. It is you who are the holier one."

She laughs, wind chimes gently playing notes. "It is not as easy for me to open to such things as you." She smiles and makes the sign of the cross. "I don't have any answers, but let's keep this our little secret, eh?"

"Si! Thank you for letting me spill my troubles. I feel at least four kilos lighter."

"Hmm, let me look at you," she mocks walking around me, studying me. "Yes, indeed, at least. In fact, I think you should try on this dress I've been making you!" She goes to the bedroom and returns with a simply beautiful shirt dress nearly complete. The fabric is printed with butterflies. "My little *farfallina*." She smiles. "You will always be."

I slip on the perfect fit as she prattles on about the butcher and the price of parmesan and the neighbor's dog. I am lost in a field of chamomile in the meadows above Paola, head thrown back, twirling, and twirling about as I hum the *farfallina* lullaby.

WE STOP BY OUR LITTLE GARDEN on the way home from mass to cut some peonies, zinnias, and Queen Anne's lace to bring to the Salernos today. I arrange them in a plain glass vase wrapped with one of Filomena's small lace flowers on a violet ribbon. It is not a beveled cut vase from Europe, but it is a striking presentation, nonetheless. Dominic is working today, but Luciana and Vincenzo are with us.

The parade of Basillios rides the trolley to the glamorous neighborhood of Chestnut Hill. Old elm trees and maples line either side of the streets and the sloping lawns lead to winding beds of sprouted color from lilac to crimson. Colonial Revival and Italianate mansions stretch their sprawling boundaries on giant plots of land. Four large families could live comfortably in one of those houses! The neighborhood is an elegant, peaceful respite from the city's brick and mortar.

"Mama, the Salernos are *ricco, si?*" a wide-eyed Luciana asks.

"Of course," answers Vincenzo. "You don't get to live here unless you are *rich.*"

I marvel at how our lives have turned upside down. In Italy, our family was considered well-to-do and Antonio's, the working class. But here in America, we are the workers, and he is the flourishing business owner. Though we receive a generous stipend from the sales of the Mandarino Coffee Salerno distributes, Aldo, the bird of passage, sends it back to Italy to buy more land. As it is, with our duplex mortgage, school, music lessons for Vincent—and basic living expenses, we make a modest living.

A short lady in a starched black and white uniform opens the door. She takes our hats and gloves and ushers us into a foyer of sunlight, marble, and rainbows bouncing off chandelier crystals at our feet. Grecian columns stand like soldiers guarding the Cubist art on the walls. It is like a museum! The Salernos emerge from a room off the foyer with smiles and friendly embraces. Lovely Bella greets and beckons our children to something called a "game room."

As we sip sherry from petite crystal goblets in the library, the conversation flows from seasons in our children's development to seasons of a world at war. Italy, siding with Germany and Japan in the perpetual struggle for more land and power, now faces America and the Allies. It appears that our beloved homeland is in over its military head—again.

"*IL Duce* is not considered the '*sweet one*' anymore," Antonio reported as if on the frontlines. He cited both newspaper articles and the community's opinions. "There are more disgruntled Italians than ever. People are sick of Mussolini's broken promises, war debts, and lack of leadership. Our inadequately skilled countrymen are the butt of jokes. And I loathe stories of Mussolini's henchmen like Rudolfo Graziani 'the butcher.'"

"He's annihilating whole villages and towns without recourse," states Stephanie.

"And the Japanese bombing of Pearl Harbor was despicable," I say.

"War is war," my husband, the rigid philosopher states.

"What do you mean?" I ask.

"What is unacceptable during times of peace is acceptable during wartime."

"Hmm, no wonder men support war," I quip and receive a frown from my husband. "Under the guise of war, men can commit so many atrocities."

"I agree," offers Antonio. "And now, Americans are worried about us." He sighs. "Just this week, I was visited by the Office of Strategic Services."

"Who are they?" I ask.

"The ones surveilling Italian-Americans without citizenship papers—*the enemy aliens.*"

"But you are a US citizen!"

"I'm afraid being a US citizen is not enough during these frightening times. I am a successful Italian-American businessman in a country at war with Italy—that alone makes me suspect."

Stephanie adds, "They took our radio as a 'precaution,' as if we were using it to contact the Italian military!"

"Wartime hysteria against the Japanese, Germans, and Italians is growing. We must all be on high alert," admits Antonio.

"We can be on our best behavior, but men with excessive power like to pick fights," I add.

"America is gunning for their enemies," Stephanie suggests.

"But Antonio is a proper businessman who has lived here for twenty-two years. Is he seen as a threat?"

"No one is exempt," Stephanie replies.

"However, the large numbers of Italian-Americans who have enlisted to defend America have impressed President Roosevelt," Antonio states. "Otherwise, like the Japanese, many more Italians would be sent to internment camps."

Stephanie sighs. "I cannot imagine the indignity of those who must wear a yellow star, dragged from their homes and sent to the horrific German internment camps. Those places are said to be inhuman."

"It's war," states Aldo.

"But innocent people are being starved, tortured, and killed because of their religion and their success." Stephanie wipes a tear from her eye.

Her husband reaches into his jacket pocket and removes his monogrammed handkerchief for her. She offers him a faint smile. He smiles back. I nearly melt like butter on an August day. I cannot imagine being loved like that. Or can I?

"Forgive me," she whispers. "I cannot bear even the thought of such barbarism."

"My dear, without tender souls like you, this world would be too harsh. A *salute*," he cheers as our crystal glasses chime.

Stephanie asks me to join her in her glasshouse full of new species of orchids, white as snowcapped mountains with splashes of violet watercolor.

"*Che mozzafiatto!*" I exclaim, *breathtaking!*

She smiles. "Such exquisite purity in nature, eh?"

I smile, beguiled by the flowers.

"If only people sought these qualities in one another." She sighs.

"Are you speaking of anyone in particular?" I inquire.

"This war has too many innocent victims. Besides the Italian-Americans, Japanese, and Germans, the German Jews of Boston are being harassed, condemned, and targeted!"

"That doesn't make sense."

"Indeed! But too many people are pointing fingers at them because they came from Germany."

"*Dio mio!* How *ignorante!*"

"Arabella, it's horrible. Too many have lost their jobs, and many of their lucrative businesses are suffering. There is widespread squalor where there was once comfort."

"But that is terribly unjust!"

"*Vero. True.* I have been wanting to discuss this with you. I visit these neighborhoods with all manner of supplies from oatmeal and soap to socks. But they need the care of the body and spirit, and I know someone like you can provide that. Will you help, Arabella?"

I hesitate for reasons ranging from inadequacy to fear.

Stephanie fills in the void. "I know it is asking a lot. I know that you would be putting yourself at risk, but sometimes we are called to action by something bigger than us."

Immediately, I am transported to the Basilica di Santa Maria Maggiore where my angel told me to follow my sacred path as a healer, and to the cholera outbreak and the locust devastation.

I know what Stephanie is referring to, but still, I respond, "Give me some time to think it over."

WE RETURN TO OUR APARTMENT, and Dominic is sitting in the

paisley, overstuffed chair. Something is amiss, but I see the light of my angel in this room, and instead of calming me, I am unsettled.

"*Che succede?*" *What's going on?* I ask.

Dominic stands, picks up something from the chair, and puts it on.

My eyes can barely focus. Here is my son—the one I came to America to protect, dressed in the olive-green coat and hat of an American military man!

"Dominic?" I inquire, as if I don't recognize my own son.

"*Si*, Mama. *Mi dispiace. I am sorry.* I know how you feel about war, but it's my duty now to fight with my American brothers. I ship out tomorrow."

Aldo hesitates for a moment before shaking Dominic's hand. "Be safe son," he states unemotionally and exits the room.

My heart is plummeting. "Dominic, I don't think you've considered everything. I can appreciate you want to represent the best in men—whether Italian, American, or Italian-American, but not this way, please."

"It's done, Mama. You've seen how others look at us, as if Italian-Americans are the enemy scum of the Earth! We're going to show them who we really are."

"Who is 'we'? Please don't tell me your cousins are joining too!"

"*Allora*, they tried, but they are both flat-footed and cannot be inducted into service."

"*Grazie Dio*! Why couldn't you have flat feet?"

"Mama," he admonishes.

"But the sacrifices we made to keep you away from the horrors of war."

"This is not time to think of one person, Mama; it's time to think of the many."

So many emotions overwhelm me: pride, fear, disbelief, defeat. I consider the eyes of my son and see there is no turning back. I embrace him, surrounding him with a bubble of protective love only a mother can conjure—and an angel sustain.

That sleepless night, I wore a path on the little Americana cucina floor thinking of my son and his bravery. I consider what duty I have as an *erborista.* And I hear that voice again, the one that said I would know what to do as my angel's light pulses around me.

AS MY SON SERVES WITH THE US Army, I launch my own plan of service. Stephanie Salerno and I will work side by side at the homes of the infirm Germans and Jews living in Brookline, Somerville, and Charleston neighborhoods. There is much frenzy and misinformation—just as the Italian Americans are surveilled with suspicion, so too are the Germans *and* the Jews. Many have lost their jobs or their businesses, causing squalor in these once flourishing neighborhoods. Unwilling to draw unsavory attention, many doctors and nurses will not attend to the sick. Though I understand fears, I cannot abide by the abandonment of oaths—and more importantly, innocent people: I've been called to action.

It has been a while since I've packed my bag of remedies. Not long after I arrived here, Stephanie introduced me to an apothecary on Tremont Street to procure the necessary herbs for our preventative blends. But for this new endeavor, I'm not certain what to expect, so I've stewed tonics of cayenne, Hawthorne, alfalfa, dandelion, and kelp in a honey base for general fatigue and energy boost. For fevers, I've discovered myrrh, poke root with Echinacea, and golden seal. My headache blend of chamomile, catnip, fenugreek, ginger, and lobelia now has a new ingredient: the leaves of wood betony. I feel a kind of adrenaline thrill to be using my knowledge once again.

I'm not exactly surreptitious, but I don't tell anyone except Filomena that I am volunteering with Stephanie. There's no need for my husband or children to know. Like days of old, sweet Filomena is preparing enough food for both families to share. I just need to be home when Luciana and Vincenzo arrive at 4pm.

I meet Stephanie at the trolley stop at Coolidge Corner, Beacon, and Harvard Street. She embraces me like a sister. I feel a kinship similar to Rafaella. She chatters on about how noble it is that I join her and thanks me profusely for coming.

"It is you I should thank," I say. "I have time and skills that should have been put to good use ages ago."

At the first brownstone, we encounter the stench of backed-up sewage. I place a couple of drops of lavender-mint oil below my nostrils, offering some to Stephanie. We meet the Feinstein family comprised of three children under ten and their parents. Stephanie goes to the galley kitchen to prepare some oatmeal and cut fresh oranges. I slide easily into *erborista* mode, barely noticing the pathetic lack of furniture or belongings I'm deducing they were forced to sell.

The family's emaciation demands my attention.

"Please describe how you are feeling," I ask the mama.

"I am too tired to even hold my head up," she answers. "We all are—including most of our neighbors in this building."

That could be from the general sense of malaise.

"What else?" I turn to all of them to inquire.

"My tummy hurts all the time," the youngest offers.

That could be from the pangs of hunger or something more.

I keep them talking to establish a rapport. I haven't physically examined them yet, just using my acute senses to observe. I want them to feel comfortable with me. My spirit angel light infuses the room. It is so comforting to have her here with me. I continue even stronger now.

"Do any of you have a headache?"

They all nod their heads in the affirmative.

"My nose bleeds a lot," the papa reports.

Then, the middle child, about nine or so, pulls up his shirt. His torso is covered in a red-dotted rash!

Inner bells are gonging. His temperature reads 102.5 degrees. After sterilizing the thermometer in the alcohol solution from the apothecary, I take everyone's temperature. Three have high fevers; two do not.

I give each of them my cayenne-Echinacea blend, excuse myself, and ask Stephanie if I could see her out outside. I need a bit of air and some privacy.

"Stephanie, the fevers are high. I'm going to go to the phonebooth and call Mr. Hogan at the apothecary."

"All right. What should I do?"

"I think you should consider not going back in there. If it's viral, it's highly contagious. Bacterial could . . ."

"I will not abandon them," she interrupts.

"But if . . ."

"My mind is made up," she replies.

"I've given them something to help reduce the fever, but that is not a cure. Everyone must wash their hands with hot water and soap—immediately and often." I instruct her to boil pans of drinking water.

Back inside, I tell the family that Mrs. Stephanie will be with them until I return. I encourage cold sponge baths to ease the fever's heat.

With pen and notebook in hand, I speak with Mr. Hogan from the phone booth telephone. I take notes and share my observations. He reminds me he is not a doctor but I encourage him to give me his professional opinion I have come to trust and respect. He tells me the fever could be typhoid fever, highly contagious, requiring hospitalization and specialized medicines to kill the culprit bacteria. He informs me that there is a vaccine.

"But these people do not have access to a hospital or the money for treatment. What are they to do? What can I do?"

He talks to me of quinine, sterilization of utensils and bedding, of letting the disease run its course. I know of these treatments from the cholera. He also instructs that I should leave the premises immediately and procure vaccination.

But I cannot leave. I failed as a healer during the cholera outbreak, and I will not fail this time! Back in the apartment, I attend to each patient—some with soothing salves of lavender and arnica, some with teas of peppermint, licorice, and anise. In each apartment, the story is identical: fevers and lethargy, hunger and despair; red spots, stomach aches, and loose bowels. By the time Stephanie and I leave, we are wrung out like washcloths after a bath. But I have a while until I need to be home, so I bid Stephanie goodbye and head to Coolidge Corner Library.

I scour the latest medical journals and search through older articles on typhoid fever. Salmonella, coliform, and other bacteria are major causes. Contaminated food and drinking water carry the disease that is so easily transmitted. An article from 1928 by Sir Alexander Fleming introduces Penicillium for bacterial infection. He discovered it quite by surprise as he observed certain bacteria was not growing close to certain types of fungus. He wrote, "One sometimes finds what one is not looking for." Further reading leads me to the highly functioning ancient Egyptians who treated infections and wounds with a similar poultice of sprouted, moldy bread. These findings have evolved into modern medicine's anti-infective therapy, penicillin.

In the meantime, with Filomena's culinary and household help, Stephanie and I go two to three times a week to minister to the downtrodden. It's exhausting and exhilarating at the same time. There is nothing like being of service to others, using my skills to heal and extend hope.

Today, though Filomena and I are side by side. My spirit angel glows around us.

"Arabella, *ho bisogno pui parmigiano. I need more parmesan cheese*," she instructs.

As we dip and fry breaded chicken cutlets with cheese, flat parsley, garlic, and oregano, she asks what Dominic revealed in his last letter.

"He maintains a cheerful demeanor, describing the tropics of Hawaii, but not much else. I suppose their letters are censored." I sigh.

She tries to cheer me up. "Have you heard the latest news from Paola? They finally married off cousin Adella, the little contessa!"

"Really?"

"I beg you to guess how many goats, chickens, and acres of our uncle's mountain it took to find someone to marry her?"

It's naughty, so unlike Filomena, but she does it for me.

"*Tutto? All of it?*"

Natalia, Lucy, and Vincent are in the next room. We don't want to disturb their concentration so I cover my mouth to stifle a wave of laughter. Filomena puts the spatula in front of her mouth as if that could stop the eruption. It's no good. We let loose the dam of sweet release. War, problems, sadness suspend in a timeless cocoon.

Alessandro and Bernardo enter to tell us they are off to work at the meat market. Filomena gives both an embrace and a kiss on their cheeks. They roll their eyes, but I know how much they love their mama. We've sobered up for a moment, but the childlike banter begins again.

"Want to guess who the lucky groom is?" Filomena asks lifting her eyebrows seductively.

"Someone from America who doesn't know of the spoiled, indulged Adella?"

This thread of family leads to stories of relatives in our beloved homeland. We layer the fried cutlets of chicken breasts with sauce and mozzarella. We sprinkle the top with parmesan then place the pans in the oven.

"It makes me ache for home."

"This is my home now, Arabella. Though, of course, I long for our family there— and the mountains and sea."

"I miss it all," I blurt. "But my children are flourishing here. The education and opportunities seem endless."

"Not to mention *your* education! How many times a week do you take the T to Copley Square?"

I laugh. "I know! The Boston Public Library has been one of the greatest gifts! Not only are there medical textbooks, but the number of journals and articles is staggering. I have so much knowledge at my fingertips!"

"*Brava*, Arabella."

"And Stephanie introduced me to Mr. Hogan at the apothecary some time ago. When I am able, I visit simply for robust discussion."

"I bet you miss your large medicinal garden."

"I do, though I'm grateful to have our little garden patch here. But to have a place with a yard for chickens and a large, medicinal garden would be wonderful. And really, sister, it is not out of the question. Do you realize that with the profits made from Salerno's sales of the Mandarino Brothers Coffee we could be living in a suburban neighborhood with so much more land?"

"I suppose, but to be together in this upstairs-downstairs apartment is like living together. I love that our children are close to one another. And speaking of children, Arabella, you are a wonderful mother."

"I don't know about that. I can't believe Dominic ended up in this war despite all our efforts to keep him out."

"Pearl Harbor's bombing was horrible. It is noble that he enlisted. I know, easy for me to say since my sons are here."

"They say once the Americans take over Italy, the war will end."

"I hope our village will be safe—and my son returned to me whole!"

She does it again, steering me with humor. "Speaking of *hole*, are you finding Aldo's socks more hole-y than usual?"

"Holy moly! Or holy *moldly*! Maybe we could scrape some of it for our own brand of penicillin!"

"They reek that bad?"

"*Sì!*"

"Have you tried clothespins?"

"Clothespins, to clean socks?"

"No, silly, to clamp over your nose!"

And with that, we are off to the realm of laughter again, erasing any melancholy.

"Aldo's underclothes couldn't be as bad as Luigi's," Filomena offers. "There must be seismic explosions occurring every hour on the hour!"

And we're bent over laughing again.

Nearly the exact moment we both say, "The chicken parmesan!" heading to the oven to check it. That's how it is with us and our inner, synced-up mechanisms. As we lift the casserole pans from the oven, Filomena looks pensive.

"What is it?" I ask.

"You and Stephanie have been spending a lot of time together. How is that for you?"

"Filomena, I love using my healing skills and having a purpose outside of children, cooking, cleaning. And Stephanie is *simpatico*. It makes it easier to be happy for Antonio."

"*Va bene*, but I do worry about you and Stephanie exposing yourself to all that sickness."

"We're taking all precautions."

"Promise me you'll be extra careful?"

"*Lo prometto, I promise*," I answer.

Lucy comes into the kitchen, "Papa and Zio Luigi are coming up the street now."

Filomena and I shuffle about putting the salad in the bowls, the bread on the cutting board, pouring tureens of pastina and spinach, and wrapping the casserole dishes for our respective tables. I feel a little tipsy, like I've had two or three glasses of *vino*—maybe it was all that laughter. Filomena gives me a hug and a wink, then she, Anna Maria, and Natalia hustle downstairs to make certain dinner is on the table when Luigi walks through the door. I'm so terribly thirsty I drink two large glasses of water in a row.

ALDO DEMANDS SILENCE AT THE DINNER TABLE.

"*Mangiamo e non parliamo. We eat don't talk,*" but Vincent insists on breaking this cardinal rule.

"Mama, you would've loved Biology class today! We looked at animal fur through a microscope," Vincent chimes.

Aldo shoots him a warning look as he slurps his soup, but Vincent isn't bothered one bit.

"Lucy, pass the *panne, per favore,*" my attempt at distraction.

But fearless Vincent continues. "It was so exciting!" he says, ignoring his father's flashing eyes. "Everything small, tiny, then POOF! under the microscope, it's GROSSO, *BIG!*"

"*Silenzio,*" Aldo sputters, green entrails of the spinach attaching to the outside of his lip.

"Aldo, Signora Ogden, Vincenzo's *professora* insists that children speak aloud of their daily lessons." I wink at the kids.

He grunts.

"Lucy, what did you learn in French cl–"

Suddenly, downstairs, there is a flurry of horrifying activity: chairs overturn, glass shatters, a male voice booms, a strap cutting a road across tender skin, a woman pleads, and a door slams.

Lucy's eyes grow simultaneously frightened and emboldened. "Mama," she begins incredulously. "Zio Luigi is at it *again!* We've got to do something!"

Aldo shoots me a "stay out of it" look, but here is my almost thirteen-year-old daughter standing up for my sister and her family.

"Mama," Lucy implores, standing. I stand up too.

Aldo pushes his chair back from the table and rises like a grizzly bear on its hind legs, poised to attack. "Luciana," he growls. "*Sietate, sit down! And* use your mouth to eat, nothing more. *Mangia, solamente, mangia!*"

"Aldo, no need to . . ."

He pushes me down. I fall into my chair, shocked. He has never manhandled me like that.

"Papa!" Lucy screams at him. "Papa, what are you doing?"

He stops, stares straight ahead, perhaps shocked by his behavior. Meanwhile, downstairs, there's shouting, hitting, whimpering.

Aldo finds his voice, "What happens in that family downstairs is not our business. *Capisce?* We," and he spreads his Caesar-like arm to gesture, "Basillios stick together. We mind our *own* family business, *solamente*. We say nothing; we do nothing to interfere with that family downstairs!"

"'*That family downstairs*' is OUR family!" Lucy blurts.

"*BASTA! ENOUGH!* I will hear no more of this talk in my house," he thunders ominously, his hand at the ready to strike Lucy's face.

Lucy slumps in her chair, bruised from his verbal beating. When she finds her voice, she excuses herself and brings her plate to the kitchen. Vincent follows suit. I stand up abruptly to join them, but I lose my balance. I am hot all over, a burning ember, consumed by flames. And then, as in one of those funny Saturday morning cartoons, I fall face-first onto the floor.

I AWAKEN TO STARK, WHITE WALLS, white uniforms, white lights, white shoes, and white bed linens. Antonio and Stephanie are beside me wearing white masks over their mouths.

"You collapsed, and Lucy called us," Stephanie says. "We were so worried we called an ambulance."

"Stephanie has filled me and the doctor in on your work," Antonio says with a nod of his head.

"The kids? Aldo?" I manage.

"They are out in the waiting room. No one knows anything except you are ill and need medicine."

I'm relieved.

"They're giving you penicillin!" Stephanie smiles. Is it me or does she look pale?

I manage a faint smile but I can't keep my eyes open. Days pass. I dream the dreams of the delirious. Mama and Papa are in the rumbling auto driving in circles around North End trying to find us; a lone boat drifts out to sea near our home in Paola.

Gregorio is calling my name. I can see him, book in hand, waving from the boat. The mountainside is thick with belladonna. I pick leaf after leaf, steeping them in my teacup that I sip with Signora Ruffino.

One morning, as I reach consciousness, I can hear the doctor speaking.

"You have all received the typhoid vaccine, correct?"

"Yes, all of us," answers Antonio.

"The adults and the children," adds Stephanie.

"Good. But I must tell you honestly, Mrs. Basillio is not responding to the medication."

There is moaning and beating of flesh. It is Filomena.

"I don't understand," says Aldo.

"I'm sorry, but it seems the bacteria is multiplying faster than the medicine can kill it."

"But there is something else can you do," Antonio implores.

"We might have to remove the site of the infection, the gallbladder. It seems to be regenerating the bacteria."

Filomena moans louder, and the beating increases.

"Doctor, whatever she needs, I want you to assure me you will do whatever it is, no matter the cost." Antonio is adamant.

"Of course."

"Promise me!" Antonio demands.

"I promise. Now, I know her children are waiting to see her. Let's give them a moment with their mother."

Lucy is crying, a muffled, mewing. I want to reach out and tell her I'll be fine, that everything will be all right, but I cannot speak. I will my eyes to lift, but their weight is five kilos of wet cement. Vincent is calling to me, but the veil between where I am and where they are is too heavy to lift. Darkness descends, devouring me.

I AM A LOST, LITTLE GIRL IN THE dense forest on a moonless night. Wherever I step, I fall, blinded by nothingness. I stand only to be pulled in the undertow of fear. I have never been so alone. I cry out, but the silence is deafening. Where am I and where is God, Mary, or my angel? *Hello*, I try again. *Hello, it is Arabella. Are you there?*

Slowly, a soft light blossoms. I breathe a deep breath. Tranquility fills the space entirely, and unease falls away like a cloak slipping off my shoulders. I am weightless, free of worry. My spirit angel appears within the ethereal light. I can see her whole, as a person—not just spirit light. She is spectacularly beautiful—not just in her form, but in the love she is emanating. I have never felt such love. It is so intense that at first, I hold my breath. I hear my own voice, *to really experience this, open your heart more fully.* Yearning for more, I eke the door of my heart open a little wider. I am met by undulating waves of wellness and a sense that everything is *absolutamente perfetto, absolutely perfect* just as it is and always has been. I am washed clean of apprehension and doubt because, in this moment, I somehow understand that *I am loved by Love Itself.* I have always been and will be taken care of in every way. I drink the sweetness of this knowledge like golden nectar. Peace surrounds me.

My angel speaks. "Arabella, do not be concerned about your health or your future. In fact, there is never any reason to worry: for you are loved and adored by so many here and on Earth. You are healed. No matter how it appears, everything is as it should be. Continue your work. Follow the voice within that is us guiding you. Go now, Arabella. Return."

I feel the density of flesh and bones resting on the bed. I wiggle my fingers and toes, feeling the *physicality* of me, Arabella Mandarino Basillio. At the same time, that spirit part of me is present, here in this room.

In the dim morning light, I see my sister asleep in the chair in the corner. She looks like she's been here for days, her face taut, strands of hair coming out of her clip, dress wrinkled, stockings amiss (the fashionista will be appalled if she looks in the mirror). It takes me a couple tries, but I manage to find enough voice to call her name.

Her eyes fly open, and she rushes to me. "Arabella, you're back!" she yells.

"How did you know I went anywhere?"

"I am your *sorella*! I could see you were one foot in this world and one in the next." She performs the sign of the cross.

She calls Aldo and my children into the room. Lucy and Vincent flock to me, and Aldo takes my hand.

"Mama, you're going to be okay," more a statement from my daughter than a question.

"I am."

Vincent sighs. "Thank goodness! Lucy needs some help with her homework!" Then he nervously smiles.

The doctor comes in with a nurse and shoos everyone out.

I use my best mama voice to tell the children to do well in school today. I tell Aldo and Filomena I will see them later.

The stern, pale doctor with pinched features looks at me disdainfully". I'm not going to lie to you, Mrs. Basillio. It was touch and go there for a while. You will not require surgery." He pauses, furrows his eyebrows, shakes his head. "At any rate, it was most foolish of you to put yourself in harm's way."

I just nod my head. This man does not know of angels, of my kind of healing. He does not approve of me helping the forlorn. I don't tell him that I'd do it all over again. I don't tell him that I am a healer who soothes the pain of others. This American doctor doesn't care to understand the girl from Paola who collected chamomile and wild parsley from the mountainside, helped her village through an epidemic; mixes tinctures for ailments, for peace of mind, for preventative birth control. I hear a voice saying, *Do not be concerned. He has no capacity to understand just now.* The nurse gives me more penicillin, and the doctor writes on my chart before they both leave me to rest.

I am thanking my angel and God and Mary for all the love that's been showered on me. I have been to the dark side and to heaven and have returned more resolute than ever.

"Arabella, you're awake!" Antonio's voice is wild as he scurries into the room.

Why is his eye twitching?

"*Si.* Yes, I am. Thank you for . . ."

"Arabella, oh my God. Arabella, I, oh my God, I . . ." he babbles.

"Antonio, *calma.* Everything's okay."

"No, it's not! That's what I'm trying to tell you! Stephanie's temperature is 104 degrees since last night! They cannot get it down."

"*Dio mio!* "

"Help her, Arabella. Help her."

He is not thinking straight. I can barely sit up! "She is in good hands," I reassure him. "The penicillin is a miracle worker."

He's so nervous he nearly trips over his own feet as he paces the room, hat in hand. "She has to beat this, she has to!"

"'The doctors here are capable."

But I know this fever can be fatal. And Stephanie's kidney issues could weaken her immune system considerably.

"Can you take me to her?" I ask.

I am too weak to walk, so Antonio pushes me down the hallway and into the elevator in a wheelchair.

My angel is outside the door of Stephanie's room, like she's waiting for me. My heart thumps faster. I try to calm myself. Antonio asks one of the nurses about Stephanie's condition when suddenly, machines beep and squawk and more nurses come running in, nearly pushing us aside. I roll my wheelchair out of the way. Stephanie's hands are wringing, her torso flailing, her mouth foaming as her whole body convulses in a terrible seizure. Antonio tries to go to her, but a doctor rushes in, and we're rushed out. My angel is in there with them now—and another spirit light too.

Antonio literally falls to the floor with his head in his hands. He keeps repeating over and over, "No, no, don't go, please don't go."

It seems like we're suspended in a bubble of timelessness, but I know she is gone. I know it even before I hear the flatline of the heart monitor or the "clear" from the doctor, and "The time of death, 10:23 am" announced.

"I am sorry, Mr. Salerno. We did everything we could, but her heart gave out unexpectedly," the doctor tells him. "Someone will be along shortly to help you with arrangements."

Antonio doesn't lift his head. He is the male version of Pieta, the statue of sorrow, frozen in this moment of shock and loss. I try to reach out to him, but he pushes my hand away. I try to push away the guilt of being the one that survived. I try to speak to him, but he is so lost in his grief, he doesn't even know I am there. A nurse exits Stephanie's room, assures me she will attend to him, then wheels me down the pea-green hallway and back to my room.

THERE IS ENDING, THERE IS BEGINNING, and the years in between.

The war ended. We buried our friend, Stephanie Salerno, my son returned, in good health, but for a bullet wound that grazed his leg. Antonio and his daughter, Bella, moved to Italy. My children continued to grow and change.

To ease my guilt of being spared I've continued the work Stephanie and I began. It is in Stephanie's name and in her spirit that I ride the Orange Line to the Veteran's Affairs Hospital in Jamaica Plains. Mostly, I sit with the men who are alone and lonely, change bandages, read to them, and scribe their letters. One of the doctors, Doctor Griffy, has encouraged me to begin taking courses toward a college degree, the first step before any kind of medical training. I realized that combining herbal knowledge and new medicine offers more powerful, diverse healing options. He helped me secure a scholarship so I would not have to worry about anything but my studies. My children do not need me like they used to. Aldo works nonstop at the Salerno factory. The timing couldn't be more perfect.

Dominic, Vincent, Lucy, and I sit around the table one evening.

"Mama, we hardly see Papa anymore," Lucy states matter-of-factly.

"Your papa has taken on much more responsibility at the factory so Antonio could return to Paola."

Everyone is quiet for a moment thinking of the Salernos.

Vincent, roguishly handsome, gives us one of his crooked smiles and beams, "Well, I've got some good news."

I wonder if I should share my news of college, but this is Vincent's moment.

"What?" We're all eager to hear.

"I am one of two students selected to take lessons from a man who performs with a jazz band. He's even been on a record!"

Lucy and I are talking at once, congratulating him and asking twenty questions.

Vincent laughs. "He's not as famous as Harry James or Woody Herman, but it is a great opportunity to learn from a professional."

"Oh, I bet someday you'll be on a record like *Candy* by Johnny Mercer and the Pied Pipers!" a proud sister chimes.

Dominic is sour-faced. "Music is not a career, Vincenzo. I hope you are not thinking that it's anything more than a hobby."

I intercede, "Let's just enjoy the moment."

"But Mama, he needs to know . . ."

"Get your instrument, and play something for us," I encourage Vincent.

Vincent goes for his accordion and Lucy for the *torta di mele, apple tart,* for dessert.

"Dominic, please allow your brother to savor this achievement."

An older version of the little commander I saw in Italy warns, "Mama, please do not *encourage* him."

"*Perch`e no? Why not?*"

"Papa and I think it is a bad idea for him to be part of that kind of life."

"Hmm, you and Papa decided this?"

"Yes."

He stands, and my God, I see how he is as rigid as his father.

I smile. "We'll see," I say evenly, but the fierce lioness is growling within.

Paola, 1949

Cara La Mia Sorella,

> *Come vai? How are you faring, dear Arabella? I trust you are busy as you have always been, caring for others, reaching for the moon, filling your mind with knowledge.*

Rafaella, and my son, Giovanni, and I live a simple life. Between my students, the mill, and Mama and Papa, days slide into weeks and weeks into months. Years after that blasted war, we are finally returning to our mezzogiorno way of life, of work and rest and family-and of course, mangiamo!

Won't it be wonderful to be together for Octavio's 60th birthday in Rio next year? I was hesitant to even consider it at first, but Octavio assures me that most that I knew are gone from the area or gone from the Earth, God rest their souls; that my name has nothing ill attached to it. He must have done some serious cleaning up after his little brother, eh? The nerve and verve of youth. I am happy we reconciled. Some brothers would not have come back from that place of divide and hurt.

Speaking of hurt, I see poor Antonio often, strolling the lungomare aimlessly. We've invited him over to share a meal numerous times and once, he did join us. The poor man pushed the food about his plate, his sad eyes barely able to meet ours. All he did was apologize for his morose behavior. It was terribly uncomfortable for everyone. I am glad that some of his family remains here in Paola, in one of his new, modern buildings. He really has done well for himself. Perhaps once through his grief, he will be able to enjoy the fruits of his labor.

Mama and Papa are aging, but well. We keep them as busy as we can with our son and our visits. You will see for yourself soon! Pina is slowing down with too many aches and pains to name. Rafaella cares for her with the love of a daughter.

I will see you soon,
Your fratello,
Marco

OMMPAPA, OOMPAPA, DEE DO, *oompapa, oompapa-* Vincent and his obsidian polished accordion provide the music for Filomena and me to promenade around my kitchen with girl-like gaiety. Vincent is the youngest person to ever be invited to sit in with several "big bands," and we have been to the swanky clubs to hear him perform. He is movie-star handsome, I must admit, and his talent is obvious. I am so proud and happy for him.

I put my arm around Filomena's shoulders to sidestep like the Parisian *cancan* dancers. She flinches, and without thinking, I peel the collar away from her neck to reveal Luigi's fingerprints imprinted in black and blue. Why did I expose her bruises? I'll tell you why: when you love someone, your instincts are to correct what is wrong.

But, let's face the facts here, Arabella, there are no tools in your arsenal to fix Luigi's abuse—or her acceptance of it.

Vincent stops playing and looks from me to her and back to me again. I attempt to look nonplussed and shake my head. He looks awkwardly at his aunt.

She retorts, "It's nothing, honey. He cannot help himself." And with that, she waltzes closer to Vincent. "*Bello, ragazzo, handsome boy.*" She smiles into his face. "And such talent! You just concentrate on your music. We're so excited you get to play on a live record!"

"What? You didn't tell me," I chide.

"He told the twins just this morning, and they told me," Filomena beams.

Dominic enters right on cue. "He's making his *first* and *last* record, *si?*"

Vincent stands still as a fence post.

"You can tell them why you won't have time for those daydreams anymore. Go on, tell them! "

But Vincent remains silent.

Dominic barrels on, "Well, I'll tell you. We are going to open an Italian restaurant! Perfect, *si*? Vincent will finish school and work nights and weekends. I'm even considering asking Bernardo and Allesandro to join us in the business."

Vincent is oddly silent, but Filomena is effusive.

"Oh, *grazie Dio*, thank God. *Perfetto! Perfect!* Our boys in business together!"

She and I beam a sun ray or two from within. Our boys in business together? The American Dream indeed!

"*Va bene*. We're looking at locations all around the wharf and here, in the North End. It will be elegant—no pizzeria for us."

"*Bravo*," Filomena offers.

"Speaking of food, Zia, isn't it time you went home to make dinner?" Dictator Dominic delivers.

"Of course, you're right," she agrees, gathering up her belongings.

I give him a look of disdain. How dare he speak to his elder like this? But of course, women are to be treated like children by all-powerful men. Still, I'm just about to put him in his place when Lucy comes through the door cheerfully, sees Filomena, and looking down mutters, "Oh, excuse me, Zia, Mama. I have a lot of homework to do."

She leaves, and Vincent follows her out of the room.

Filomena gives me a quick hug goodbye. I do not understand this scene taking place in my home. My home! I do not know why my daughter behaves like this, and I am not certain what is happening with my son Vincent and his music. However, I know all about my son Dominic, the commandant junior, for he is his father's son! I go to Vincent's room first. He sits sullenly on the floor. It is easy to read someone who wears his heart on his sleeve. I sit down next to him.

"Your ol' mama is getting too old for this floor sitting, *figlio*."

"Mama, don't say that; you are not old."

"Try to convince my bones of that!"

We sit in silence.

"What is this about giving up music?"

"I can't fight Papa and Dominic on this."

Where is the feisty boy who always did what he wanted, not what someone else told him to do?

"So, my talented, brave son is allowing himself to be bullied?"

"You don't understand."

"Help me understand."

"It's not pretty."

"Okay, give me the ugly then."

"Dominic knows people, Mama, some not-very-nice people, if you know what I mean. And he has made it known if that if the bands allow me to play with them, they will never get another gig."

"Come now; you don't believe that, do you?"

Heavy shoulders slump. His posture tells all. When I say his name with a slight tremor in my voice, he looks up at me and nods. "I am sorry Mama, but it's true and I do."

I manage a lame offering, "I'll speak with your brother and father."

"Save yourself the trouble," he answers.

A mother is supposed to be a champion for her children. I'll not give up.

"Don't you worry," I say pushing myself up to standing position, "like the saying goes, 'It's not over til the singing lady gets fat.'"

He throws back his handsome head, rolls his eyes, and smiles. "The expression is, '*It ain't over til the fat lady sings.*'"

"Oh, well, it means the same thing, no?"

"No, it doesn't!" He smirks.

I don't know what I'm going to do on behalf of Vincent, but you can be assured if this plump lady was a singer, it darn sure wouldn't be over! But now I've got to see what is going on with Lucy. And here I thought my children didn't need me.

269

"LUCY," I CALL.

"I'm in my room."

"What made you behave like that with Zia Filomena?"

"I cannot tell you!" she yelps.

I sit on her bed, affecting calm. "It's ok, *parlami, talk to me.*"

Her voice steps out, falters, picks itself back up. "It's that imbecile Luigi," she blurts out. "I hate him!" Her face flashes, a lightning bolt of anger.

"Lucy, hate is a strong word."

"It fits a man who terrorizes my cousins, forcing them to take refuge in closets—a man who beats up on sweet Zia Filomena until she is the color of eggplant!"

How can I respond? Her observation stands out like a zebra in a field of horses.

"I know. I know how troubling it is . . ."

"Then why don't you *do* something about it?"

How do I tell my daughter I have no answers, that relationships are complicated, that each person walks the road they choose for themselves? This is a pivotal moment that demands an honest, adult answer rather than the soothing promises meant for a child.

"*Figlia,* relationships are complicated. People love and commit for different reasons. What seems impossible to one person seems perfectly suitable to another."

"Mama, violence is never suitable! Infidelity, wrong. It is written in the Bible."

Ah, yes, but tell that to those who incite world wars in the name of God and men with mistresses all over the world.

"You are absolutely correct, but it is also written that love is patient and kind, not easily angered, and keeps no record of wrongs. You see, when Filomena looks at Luigi, love is what she sees—not the marks he has left on her body or her heart."

"Inflicting harm on another person *is not love*. And what he does with others who aren't his wife is not love. Doesn't that verse in Corinthians also say that love does not dishonor another?"

I sigh. "The truth is that it doesn't matter what you or I or even the Bible says. It is what Filomena believes that matters. And please understand this; when it comes to her relationship with Luigi, no one can convince her to believe differently." I pause. "Don't you think I have tried to get her to see with clearer eyes all these years? It is futile."

"What then? We turn a blind eye, allow people to behave abhorrently, and . . ." She pauses. "*This* is what happens?"

My heart flutters errantly. I look at my beautiful eighteen-year-old daughter full of budding womanhood, recalling how she could not look at Filomena and her disgust of Luigi. I ask her again to tell me what happened.

"What 'happened' was that I came home, and he was in *our* home." Her eyes blaze, and my heart leaves the tropical world of butterfly wings for the frozen tundra of fear.

"Who?" I ask, my voice as far away as Venus.

"Luigi! In *our* home when no one else was here." Her voice falters. "He knew you and Zia were at the market, Papa and Dominic working, and Vincent rehearsing. He came to see *me*! *Me*! He told me so as he stood close enough to touch my hair, my face, my—"

"Oh, *Mary Mother of God*, no!"

My daughter takes a deep breath, fanning the flames of her fury. I remain still, no chance of turning stone to dust.

"Don't worry, Mama. I may be emotional right now, but I did not display one iota of fear! I told him he had better leave immediately and stay away from me or—"

"Or what?"

"Or I was going to tell my father!"

"My God, Lucy. Your father would kill him."

"Precisely," she answers.

For years I have stood by and let him act however he chose, but he crossed the line with my daughter.

AFTER SOME CONNIVING, I got Filomena to run an errand for me when he was home alone.

"*Buona sera.*" The snake charmer smiles as he answers the door.

"I don't think you'll be wishing me '*good evening*' when I get through with you."

"Oooh, that sounds thrilling." He raises his eyebrows seductively.

Keeping my composure is challenging. He's hoping to throw me off-kilter.

I take a step into their home and stare into his face. "Luigi, I have always known what a vile creature you are. I have tolerated you only because I love my sister. But I swear to you before God that if you *ever* take a step near my daughter again or ever come into my home uninvited, you will pay, and let me assure you—you will pay dearly."

He laughs. "Arabella, you've always been so feisty. It's an enchanting trait!"

"Take heed." My voice is hard, unforgiving steel. "I might *enchant* you, but it will be with a very special concoction I have dreamed up only for you." I pretend to be concocting it right then and there. "Oooh, and I will revel at slipping it secretly into your coffee cup one unsuspecting morning." I pretend I am pondering, but I have rehearsed this speech many a time. "Or perhaps it will land in your soup bowl one night, or in your lunch box thermos." I am very quiet as he turns white as flour. "Then, ooh, then I will sit back and watch as it destroys you slowly, excruciatingly. Hmmm." I pause, ever so dramatically. "Come to think of it, I may even concoct a little something that incapacitates that little thing of yours—once and for all!" I raise my eyes and look disdainfully at his private parts.

He looks at me with absolute shock, then fear. Mary, Mother of God forgive me, but I enjoy this immensely, the proverbial table finally flipped. It helps me gather even more confidence.

"You know I have the wherewithal to do this, and believe me, I will not hesitate to hurt you, and hurt you bad." I pause, letting the images of his own imagination swelter. "All that you are thinking now? Trust me, it will be much, much worse than any of that." I stare him down. "I don't know why I haven't thought of this sooner. It would be so much fun and fix so many problems, eh Luigi?"

He is a frozen snowman.

"Are you understanding me?"

He just stands there.

"I need an answer, Luigi. I need to know you have heard me loud and clear."

He gulps several times and nods his head.

"I want to hear your voice acknowledging you understand."

"Si," his high-pitched squeak.

As he clears his throat a few times, I simply stand there and stare him down, conjuring every trait of a witch I can. He shuffles from foot to foot.

"Very well then. And one more thing."

"Si?"

"We will keep this little heart to heart between you and me."

There's no snickering or taunting now. He's turned a whiter shade of pale.

Before I slam the door, I look over my shoulder at him and hiss, "Take heed; you've been warned."

From then on, Luigi barely looked in my direction and more importantly, my daughter's. We attended family functions as one happy, united group, but rest assured, he stayed clear of the *Strega* Arabella! It wasn't long after that that my Lucy met a brilliant young man at Boston College, aspiring to be a professor. They wed in the charming historic Martha-Mary Chapel in a beautiful town called Sudbury, amidst weeping willows, a lily pond, and spacious, tranquil grounds. One year later, they are expecting their first child! I'm to be a *grandmother*, a *nonna*!

My daughter studied Communication, and I, across the Charles River near Chinatown at Tufts University, studied to earn a Physician's Assistant degree. 25 months of classes ranging from Diagnostics to Clinical Anatomy, supervised clinical experiences, a written examination, and a 3.85 GPA helped me secure the piece of paper with PA next to my name, Arabella Mandarino Basillio, Physician's Assistant.

Imagine, all these years later, to blend my knowledge of herbs with the wonders of modern medicine. Only in America. In Italy, I use the money I tucked away in the bank to invest in a small business with Rafaella. *Medicina Sorelle* now bottles up our tinctures of herbal remedies to be sold in pharmacies and small markets throughout the country.

PART 4

Boston and Paola
1950-1965

Boston, 1950

Dear Antonio,

    Over the years of our friendship, you have remained my staunch supporter. You saw in me what I could not see with my own eyes. Tanti grazie! A thousand thanks, my friend.

    As I stood on the platform in a cap and gown, a 49-year-old middle-aged lady amongst young ragazzi, I could barely fathom having a medical certificate. Of course, my study of herbs and being an erborista in Paola is an undeniable honor but being in America has encouraged me to blend the old ways with modern knowledge. The moment the dean called my name and I crossed the stage, bedlam broke out in the audience! Filomena and my children, half of the North End residents, and anyone I ever attended to erupted with whoops and hollers, making quite a scene! For a split second, I thought they would be thrown out of the auditorium, but then even the dean and the rest of the audience joined in the moment laughing and applauding. My fellow classmates gave me a standing ovation. It was so humbling I thought I would break down emotionally, but somehow, I kept myself standing. I did take a little bow before exiting the stage. The scene is etched in my memory forever: the sound and sight of pride and success.

I think of you often, Antonio. I miss you. I miss your beautiful Stephanie who was a dear simpatico friend. Be well in the arms of our beloved Paola: the aria fresca, the sea, the history, the magnificence of the mountains.

Your friend forever,
Arabella

"What do you think of this?" Filomena grins as she pulls out a fuchsia flowered chintz dress from a Marshall Field's bag. Its neckline plunges dramatically and ascends in a "sweetheart" style above her ample breasts. The waist houses a thin belt of shiny plastic (patent leather it's called) with a silver rectangular buckle. The skirt flares out full and wide like a knee-length ballerina's tutu.

She prances about the kitchen swirling her dress in front of her as if it were a dance partner as I whip sugar for our cappuccino into a frenzy. "Filomena, you are going to be the envy of every woman! You could be the next movie star, like Carmen Miranda!"

"Grazie sorella! I bet she wears dresses that feel like this. It's how I imagine a sunbeam to feel."

"I know the sun would be pleased to have you wear one of its beams." We both laugh.

"How about something new for you, Arabella? Let's go to the store and buy you some pretty new things for our trip."

"No. What I have is fine. I don't need anything else."

"Come on, Sister. Spend some of that money of Aldo's before he sends it off to Italy to buy more land!"

I sigh. "All these years sending money back to Italy to buy more land, but how can we ever go back there? Our children would not come; they are Americans now. I don't think I could live away from them." I sigh. I'm lost in disturbing thoughts. "Filomena, do you think Mama and Papa forgive us for leaving them?"

"Mama and Papa know that their children's lives were not theirs to live. Look at Octavio. Papa sent him out of the country to build the Mandarino Brothers Coffee business years before we left."

"Will Vincent forgive me if I'm unable to convince his father and brother to let him continue his musical pursuits?"

"Vincenzo will excel at whatever he does. He can always keep music as a hobby. And think of all our sons in business together, *Sorella!*"

It reminds me of Sofia saying that my healing aspirations were a child's daydream.

FILOMENA IS SO EXCITED, her voice breaks. "I read the descriptions in the travel brochures of the '*Cidade Maravilhosa*,' *The Wonderful City*, but none of it captured Rio de Janeiro's magnificence!"

"It is one of the jewels of South America." I smile. We're looking down from the giant airplane's window below. Wedged between the sea and cliffs of green that jut from the water like oversized sandcastles are monoliths of protruding rock. The 72-kilometers of shorelines remind me of Paola's *lungomare*, though here, tenement upon tenement wind along the shoreline like rows of dominoes.

As Mama, Papa, Marco, Filomena, and I luxuriate in a stretch limousine cruising through the city to the Copacabana Palace Hotel, all are mesmerized by the beauty of this tropical wonderland. There're the gardens, the people, the aromas, the architectural genius of old Europe as well as the new, modern buildings. They marvel at the vendors driving their horse and buggy carts stacked with bananas, rice, black beans, and fried manioc root (like potato chips). Papa and Marco's eyes bug out of their faces at the sumptuous strutting women. It's a feast for the senses!

Arriving at the Copacabana Palace, eager attendants treat us like the famous that often stay here. Our bags are taken, and we're whisked off to the elevator opening to suites with sprawling beds, marble baths, and balconies overlooking Copacabana beach. Mama, Filomena, and I received velvet boxes wrapped in ribbons on our beds. Filomena's held an elegant set of tourmaline earrings for warding off mishaps. Mama's topaz earrings with the healing powers to soothe and promote truth and forgiveness.

It's too late, of course, but I wish I was suited up in that topaz during the months of arguments over Vincent's pursuit of a music career. But we all knew the outcome of those conversations, *si?* The restaurant is being built, and Vincent will be a part of it. Period. Vincent has assured me he is glad to be part of this stable business plan. But does he really believe that? Do I?

My gemstone gift is a pair of blue sapphire drops with a note about using this stone to access the angelic realm. Does my family sense that I am in touch with a spirit angel? That she has become as much a part of me as breathing; able to assist me medically and emotionally, helping me see that even with staggering issues such as Vincent pursuing music, I must let go. If indeed I do believe in angels and God and Mary's presence in our lives, then my actions must demonstrate those beliefs. Right now, I must stop thinking of the men's decisions so I can fully embrace this experience with Mama and Papa, Marco, Filomena, and Octavio. It's rare in this time of change, of families living across the world from one another to revel in our shared history. Family camaraderie is rejuvenating medicine, and I'll drink a large glass of it, thank you very much. I rest my head on my family's shoulder, traveling back through the winding roads of my life, all the way back to my childhood to appreciate where I am now.

Tonight, at the *fazenda*, everyone is dressed in their finest, and the house is ablaze in golden light, crystal, and China. (I did notice proper Sofia looking disdainfully at Filomenabrigida's décolletage!) Everyone is lighthearted and happy as Octavio's birthday feast begins: churrasco, polenta, and salted anchovy, the stew, feijoada, with pork and beef tripe, black beans, and greens served on elegant China rimmed in cobalt blue and gold. Fancy scrolled "M" is etched on every gleaming piece of silverware. We savor crimson wine in crystal etched stemware. It's a lively evening of food, stories, and music. From the ambiance to the delicacies, it is a perfect evening.

Back at the hotel, we joke about Sofia's disapproval of Filomena's dress. Several times she looked on with near horror as Filomena's generous bosom rose and fell with each deep-throated laugh.

"I don't think our pious sister-in-law appreciated your risqué dress," I tease.

"How long does it take our brother to unfasten the hundred buttons that reach her chin?" She laughs. "Lord, the way she dresses you'd think it was 1901!"

Mama knocks on our door, and the three of us talk and reminisce into the wee hours of the night. We make plans to explore Rio as the men tend to Mandarino Brothers Coffee business. Filomena has a list as long as Rapunzel's hair of things she wishes to see and do in Rio.

And so, throughout the week we exhaust ourselves trying to keep up with my sister! She seemed infused with an insatiable appetite for the "real Rio." In the shops and cafes, Filomena feasts on all the offerings of Rio— *tutto, everything!* And she does so with whoever's there. Every stranger becomes her friend. She samples fresh *abacate* breakfast drinks in the mornings made of avocado, sugar and milk, *balidas,* with passion fruit, coconut, and strawberry, *garapa* sugar juice with lime or pineapple.

"Filomena, per *favore, guarda, please be more cautious,*" I warn her. "We don't know if the fruit is properly washed or if the milk is fresh. There are parasites and . . ."

"Oh, come on, Arabella! Live a little! Taste the culture!"

Several times she begs me to share the *chimarrao* with her and a group of strangers. The specialty tea is a social event where each person takes a sip of the tea from the metal cup before passing it on to another. I decline. Mama as well. But Filomena relishes in these customs. One of my papers in school was on public health issues in America compared to South America and Europe.

"Filomena, please," I whisper as I pull her to the side of the café. "I have seen too much sickness spread from person to person like this, and my studies have revealed the dangers."

"But no one is sick here, *sorella.* Lighten up!"

Even Mama warns her, but Filomena is having the time of her life.

"Grand Opening! August 5, 1952"
Celestina Restaurant -A gourmet Italian restaurant
that'll take you to heaven and back!

LUCY, ANNA MARIA, AND NATALIA insist on taking Filomena and me to Filene's for new dresses. Silk-flowered, straight skirts, belted, turquoise-striped, checkered, plaid, solid pink, buttoned, pull-overs, pleated. *Dio mio,* how many dresses did we try to squeeze our bumps, bulges, and folds into? Filomena Loren decides on a purple taffeta cross-front dress with a jeweled broach on the lapel and a matching hat that dramatically tilts to the side. I choose a long-sleeve navy and white patterned dress with a three-tiered flouncy skirt. The white patent leather belt is made for a smaller waistline, but I feel sophisticated. I'll wear my sapphire earrings from Brazil.

A month later, we are in the huge interior of the gold and red-carpeted interior of the Celestina Family Restaurant, elegant, yet comfortable, with a menu featuring our own Mandarino family recipes. There is Lucy's professore husband lending a hand setting up the tables and Dominic's brother-in-law in the kitchen. Lucy is gathering extra piles of the crimson red linen napkins. But wait, where are Filomena's daughters? Where are her sons? My stomach lurches a warning roll. *Calma,* I advise myself. Everyone is probably just busy in the kitchen or getting ready for the ribbon-cutting ceremony.

The bell chimes calling us to the front of the restaurant. Excitement permeates everything. People are packed on the sidewalk near the entry: from the local newspaperman talking to politicians and local royalty to the fascinated denizens of the neighborhood. But where are Allesandro and Bernardo? Shouldn't we wait for them? My sons step up to the ribbon, pose for the photographer, and snip, it's over. Applause explodes.

Filomena charges over to me and hisses in my ear, "Do you know where my sons are? They're stacking meat in the freezer, their new suits now caked in frost! Your sons have them hidden away."

A tear rolls down my cheek. This is anything but an auspicious beginning.

Someone in the crowd notices me and coos, "How sweet! Even the mama is crying with joy."

How could she know these tears come from the well of worry?

THE MANDARINO SISTERS LIVE on a fault line. Beneath the surface that appears sturdy enough to carry out the successful dreams of our sons lies roiling disagreement. It will sooner than later send the needles of the Richter scale quivering until the seams of solid ground irrevocably split. I wish I could dip a darning needle in a healing potion to repair the tear. The biting truth is that my sons have reneged on their promises. Bernardo and Allesandro are not partners at all. They are my sons' backroom boys.

While my sister and I struggle, Aldo and Luigi deal their hands of Pinochle as if nothing is out of place between our families. I can still hear Aldo screaming at young Lucy about famiglia sticking together *no matter what*. Aldo and Luigi respect that law. How can they continue to pretend all is well as they toss their cards and bid at our kitchen table? I'm reading a New England Journal of Medicine article on the effects of factory water pollutants on the human body.

"I bid 250," Aldo begins.

Luigi chuckles, "Too bad, my friend. I bid 270."

On they go, following Luigi's trump suit, hoping for the jack of diamonds and the queen of spades or a marriage: a king and queen of the same suit. I wish they'd talk about the marriage of our sons' business, how they failed to make a written contract between them, choosing to seal the deal with a handshake and a shot of whiskey. But a promise is a promise, no matter its form. When it is made, its tendrils wriggle out into the sunlight to become part of the air itself. And these vows, powerful as the winds that funnel and tunnel, can whip and wear and tear down familial bonds.

If I were the one dealing the cards of this family, I'd stack the deck if I had to, rig the games, assure a favorable outcome. I'd do what it takes to adhere to the agreements to give Alessandro and Bernardo their rightful cut in the successful Celestina Family Restaurants. Yes, a second restaurant has opened in the affluent neighborhood of Newton, with another one planned for Boston's famous wharf district.

"It's so easy," I would assert, "*Guarda. Watch.* Pick up the pen. Spell out Alessandro's name on one bank check, Bernardo's on another. Next, fill in the amount with a nice, generous number and then sign your names on the bottom right line." *Allora! Tutto bene! All is well,* just like that! Then my sister and I can live in harmony instead of *sempre, always,* on this broken subject of her sons being cheated by my sons.

I set the journal down. I understand too well the concept of pollutants sinking into pristine places.

"MAMA, COME ON, WHADDAYA DOING?" Bernardo drawls impatiently. "*Per favore, please,* don't do this."

"Bernardo," my sister explains. "Zia Arabella is here to listen so she can help."

"Mama, Zia, *no mancanza di rispetto, no disrespect,* but neither of you can do anything to help this situation between us, Dominic and Vincent," sensitive Allesandro states.

I silently agree with him, though I wish with all my might we could.

"*Talk, talk, parli, tell her,*" Filomena insists.

Realizing his mother's claws will remain firmly gripped until he explains himself, Bernardo acquiesces. "Zia Arabella, here it is: your sons offered us partnership in Celestina restaurants through our contribution of labor— hours on the job, extra duties, training of the staff, security, maintenance.

We did it all, seven days a week, 365 days for three years. Your sons were going to begin sharing profits after two years."

"And it's been three years," Allesandro chimes a sorrowful note.

"Boys," I begin, nervous as a young actor with stage fright. "I . . . I . . . I just don't know what to say, I . . ."

"Don't *say* anything. *Do* something," Filomena explodes.

She has never used this feral tone with me before. Who is this woman and what has she done with my dear, beloved sister?

She continues, "You are their mother. Do something, dammit!"

And she's never sworn at me before either.

I unravel, just like that. A tight ball of tempered frustration and gut-wrenching exasperation spews from my mouth. "What do you want me to do?" I screech. "Do you tell the men in your life—namely your husband—how to behave? Would he listen?"

"Well, something this important, at least I'd try." She raises her voice to hysterical levels.

"How dare you imply that I haven't tried to intervene," I nearly scream, vibrating with uncontrollable rage. "Why don't you *do* '*something important*'? How about something like telling that brute of a husband to stop fooling around with other women? Oh, wait, no, I've got a better idea! Why don't you order him to stop beating you, eh? Is that 'important' enough?"

The arrow has struck its mark. Bull's-eye! Everyone is paralyzed. I feel victorious for half a second until I hear my sister gasp with a look that is both the fierce, protective mother lion and its wounded prey. The boys walk out of the room, shaking their heads. I am filled with remorse, aching to take back those atrocious, damaging words, but I'm also still angry. "Filomena, please, let's try to . . ."

But she turns her back and walks out of the room. Even my spirit angel vanishes.

Can what's been done, be undone?

I HAVE WORKED WITH A DOCTOR in Somerville who needed a physician's assistant while his regular assistant was out of the country. Five days a week for one month, I traveled on the subway from Haymarket Square to Sullivan Square to tend to the waves of patients who needed attention for everything from the flu to sprains and their yearly physicals. In those weeks, my sister and I did not speak, the time moving along like a perpetual factory conveyor belt unaware of our rift.

And the men? They all continue to work together, putting one foot in front of the other to get the new restaurants opened and the success rate flowing. I heard my sons and husband speak of Bernardo and Allesandro being too deep in the business to go anywhere else. Stuck in the muck I'd say.

After a month of non-stop work and subway travel, I finally have a day all to myself today.

The phone rings. "Hello?"

"Mama, it's Vincent. Can you please help us out today at the North End Celestina? Both our cooks are sick."

So much for quiet aloneness! "Of course, *figlio*. I will get ready now."

"*Grazie!* And Mama, can you call Zia Filomena and get her to come too? We have a big private party today, very important people. We need you both."

Apparently, our sons are not paying attention to the row between us. Business is business; you simply carry on in the name of commerce.

But as I begin to think of the unlikeliness of the restaurant needing both of us on the same day at the same time, I acknowledge it as a summoning, a sweet summoning by love itself. I sense it in my spirit angel's light.

I hang up with my son and dial my sister's number.

"*Mia sorella.*" I dive in immediately. "We are needed at the restaurant today in the North End. The cooks are sick and there's a big, important party."

The pause feels like a very long, dark hallway.

"I will be there as soon as I get ready." The line goes dead.

So much for the sweetness of a summoning.

CELESTINA IS A FLURRY OF silverware clanging, glasses, and China chinking, waiters and waitresses scampering about like squirrels with treasured acorns. I make my way to the kitchen where my son, Dominic, thanks me for coming and hands me a red apron with the fancy gold printed *Celestina,* on the front. He refers me to Allesandro who hands me the party's menu for today—all from our family recipes. At least that much about today is easy.

Filomena comes through the back door telling the young worker that the numerous boxes by the door are hazardous. She cares greatly for this place, this business, of that there is no doubt. She orders him to move them as soon as possible. He nods but rolls his eyes.

Allesandro kisses his mother's cheeks, momentarily softening any hurt in her heart, before launching into the necessities of the day. When he leaves, we are left standing side by side.

"Filomena," I start. "*Come vai?*"

"I'm fine. Let's get to this menu." Her voice is hard cement.

"Very well," I bristle. "I just wanted to know if . . ."

She calls the two assistants over to begin a batch of Mama's now-famous marinara sauce in a giant vat large enough for a child to hide in! The garlic, parsley, basil, crushed chilies, red wine, and whipped anchovy fillets pop in the olive oil straight from Cosenza.

As Filomena directs the pastry assistant on Mama's rosemary panne dough, I begin today's soup: *stracciatella*, chosen for today's meal because the clients are clothing designers and *stracciatella* looks like shreds of fabric. I boil the whole chickens with onion, celery, and carrot to make the base broth for the soup. As I'm working, I think about the metaphor of this soup: what if Filomena and I can tear up or shred *our problems* to melt away in the warmth of family? If only it were that simple.

I whisk the eggs, flour, parmesan, Romano, pepper, and nutmeg together until blended. We'll strain the chicken broth before serving, pour the egg mixture into the broth, stir and simmer again. Once the egg batter is cooked (looking very much like torn fabric pieces) we'll top it off with a drizzle of olive oil and a dash of red pepper.

We are so busy in the spacious kitchen with an array of helpers dicing, scrubbing, setting up, and prepping, that Filomena and I hardly glance at one another. It's a fast-paced, grand-scale operation, but I can still feel the harmony of two sisters preparing a meal—this one just happens to be for 48 people!

Lamb chops are dredged through the semolina flour sprinkled with sage, thyme, rosemary, and marjoram then placed in roasting pans with pools of melted butter. Day-old bread is put into a large vrooming grinder by a young man. He hands me the fresh breadcrumbs to sprinkle on top of the lambchops. I drizzle more butter on top of the chops. The angel hair pasta rests on a plate ready for the boiling pot. A meal at Celestina is not complete without pasta topped with Mama's sauce.

The antipasti are arranged on ceramic platters of indigo blue and sunflower yellow: prosciutto, pepperoni, banana peppers, provolone, salami, and dressing mixed with fresh herbs, balsamic vinegar, olive oil, oregano, and basil. Bread is sliced and placed in gold star-shaped baskets, butter squares stamped with the Celestina logo. It's a beautiful symphony of flavor and fanfare! Though it's a little stressful to coordinate all the parts of the cooking and serving, the staff is able and good-natured, and save for a couple of spills and a lamb chop undercooked, we pull off the party with aplomb. The wait staff is thrilled by the large tip from Vestida Clothing.

"Ladies, thank you for saving us today! It was superb!" Peppi, the manager gushes.

"*Prego*," we answer in unison.

"Are you ready to leave now?"

"We still have some work to do." *The inner kind.*

"Very well. I trust you won't mind leaving from the back entrance then? I need to lock the front door as well as the kitchen door from the dining room side. And I know you have keys to both the back door and the outside metal door."

"Yes, we do, thanks. But what is this new door between the kitchen and dining room?" asks Filomena.

"The metal garage door out back is secure, but the front door is more vulnerable. Signore Basillio found this new impenetrable door that protects the expensive kitchen apparatus in case someone breaks in the front door."

"Hmmph," Filomena answers.

When Peppi's gone, I turn to Filomena. "What a day! That meal was some feat, eh?"

"All I know is that *my feet* are screaming bloody murder."

Ah, there's my sister!

We both laugh but then there is an awkward silence.

"*Sorella*, I . . ."

Her voice is nearly a whisper, "Please, Arabella, I don't want to argue."

I'm offended. "But I wasn't going to argue. That is not fair!"

"There you go again." She shakes her head.

"Oh, *Dio mio*, and there's the finger of blame again." I thrust the words at her like a sword.

There is a snicker from the back room, "Ha! The great Mandarino family, right?" sneers the youngster Filomena reprimanded earlier in the

288

day. He takes a drag from his cigarette and waves sarcastically before we hear the door slam. Fortunately, he was the last of the staff to hear us sparring down Argument Lane.

"Your sons buy an expensive kitchen door but are too stingy to give my sons a piece of the business they deserve."

"Filomena, my God, we've been over and over this!"

"*Sì!* And nothing is resolved."

"But haven't you noticed that our boys continue to work together and . . ."

"Of course, my sons are still working for your sons! Where would they go with no proper capital to start their own business!"

"Well, first of all . . ." Suddenly, I smell something acrid. "Filomena, do you smell that?"

"What? Rotten promises?"

"Filomena, I think it's smoke!"

We quickly scan the kitchen. Light tendrils of smoke are coming from under the back-room door.

"That kid was smoking back there!"

I remember her telling that kid to move all those boxes, that they were a hazard. It's like *she knew!* I search the kitchen for a fire extinguisher, but they must be in the back room that's now enflamed. *Call for help,* I tell myself. But it dawns on me that the phone is in the dining room on the *other side* of the new, fancy, (locked) kitchen door!

Filomena hurries over to me. "Arabella, my God, what are we going to do?" She looks like a child lost in the woods.

I shake my head. We're trapped, locked in a kitchen that will soon burst into a raging inferno! But there's always something, I tell myself (though myself is being overtaken by absolute fear). *Remember, Arabella, you are a problem solver. You possess a strong will, and you have a divine helper!* But all I see is impending doom and a terrified sister. *No! There's got to be a way out. I won't accept defeat.*

Filomena is crying, calling out to God and Jesus and Mary. It unnerves me.

Think, Arabella, tune everything else out but a solution. The first thing I see is cool waters trickling down from the mountain streams. Water!

I grab a stack of kitchen towels, instructing Filomena to soak them in the big porcelain sink. I wring them out then grab the onion-cutting goggles to protect our eyes. Next, I give her the giant vat we made the sauce in earlier and large spoons.

"Filomena, start banging on these pots as hard as you can. We've got to let people know we're in here." She puts the pot between her legs like a drum, one hand thrumming the pot with a large ladle, the other holding the wet towel over her mouth and nose.

A wave of nausea hits as the smoke spreads its greedy arms toward us. I step a little closer to the back door, hoping we could get it open and make a dash. But it's too late for that. The emanating heat feels as if I am standing on the sun.

Please help us, I whisper. It's one thing to think of covering our noses with wet towels and protecting our eyes with the goggles, but the truth is we are trapped in a fire that will soon devour us. Can I accept that I am going to die today with my sister at my side? No, it is too much to bear. I squeeze my eyes shut behind these silly-looking onion goggles. I open them and see, just beyond the haze of smoke, a glowing light slinking *up* the kitchen door. At first, I think it's the fire or a hallucination because, well, it seems *alive.* I blink again, but it's still there.

Oh, dear Mary, Mother of God, it's my angel! I follow her movement. Between the top of the door and the ceiling is a narrow, rectangular window I would never have noticed had it not been for my angel!

I move the wet cloth from my nose and mouth, "Filomena!" I nearly scream pointing to the window. "*Guarda! Look!*"

Her eyes lift to the window, but she shakes her head. "How can that narrow window way up there help two old ladies down here?"

Good question. Well, at least we could break it open and get fresh air from the dining room. It's a start, and it's better than just standing here dying helplessly.

"I don't know, but it's something! Let's get up there and break it open."

I try to remove the towel, but the smoke is too thick. We work together, me, with my left hand, Filomena using her right. Together, we make one set of hands gathering crates and giant vats around the kitchen to build a makeshift stepladder. Once it's high enough, we gingerly climb up together. Filomena hands me a large rolling pin, and I smash the glass out. Shards fly haphazardly, some sticking in my arm, large pieces on the floor of the dining room, some onto Filomena.

In a wild minute of unleashed passion for life, I've obliterated the window. Filomena is right, squeezing through it doesn't seem feasible, but the air from the dining room is like a mountain breeze! As I breathe in a long breath, I get an image of the large meat cleaver.

"Filomena, get some fresh air. I've got another idea!" I nearly fall off the contraption. She stays and I climb down.

Quickly, I locate a cleaver that could cut a cow in half while she gulps the dining room air. I sidle up to where she is, she moves down a bit. With all my strength and the strength of angels, I mutilate the wood around the window's frame. I've got to get that opening wider. Adrenaline is coursing through my muscles as I hack viciously. I know this is our last shot before the insatiable fire overtakes us.

Just then, Filomena screams. The fire bursts through the back-room wall and beats a dangerous trail forward as if it knows the vats of cooking oil will feed its belly.

"Hurry." Her jagged voice is a desperate plea.

Mary, Mother of God, help me. How am I going to squeeze this body through there? Heaving myself up to the opening, I admonish myself for eating all those extra pieces of bread, Salerno's butter cookies, and my American favorite, Oreos! But I push and push again. Oh God, how I push. It's a lot like childbirth. You know you can't give up, though your body is begging you to. I wriggle and squirm, ripping my skin as if it were nothing thicker than a thin cotton dress. My hands are sliced by pieces of glass left in the casing and splintered with rough, serrated edges of the wood. It seems an eternity, and I want to quit several times, but soon I've heaved myself through the space, thumping hard onto the dining room's red carpet. Of course, I try the new kitchen door, but it is stubbornly locked. I think of calling 911, but by the time they get here, Filomena will be burned alive.

As quickly as I can stand (I think I've sprained my hip and right foot), I drag a four-top table to the wall and yell for Filomena to come climb through.

"*Non posso farlo.*" She gags.

"You *can* do it and you *will*," I yell.

"*I can't do it.* Tell my children . . ."

"Tell them yourself! *Capisce?* Now, put your hands on the edge, and I'm going to pull you through!"

"I'm too tired. Just let me go, Arabella. Let me go."

"No! That is not an option."

She tries to get through the opening, God bless her, but she cannot lift her body even halfway through. I should have pushed her through to safety first! My body protests in pain while I reach up to her on tip toes with the table as my base. I grab her wrists to hoist her through with all my strength. She barely budges! The fire is overtaking the kitchen—and my sister's life, one flame at a time.

"My shoes are melting!" she sobs between coughs. The reality of burning alive dawns.

The velvet curtains in the dining room radiate.

"Filomena, I'll be right back! See if you can pull your knees up away from the flames."

Wincing, I step down from the table as quickly as I can, I yank a thick, velvet curtain down from the rod and drag it with me back up to the opening. "Filomena, wrap this around your waist, then brace your hands at the opening and push with all your might! I will pull you through."

When she's got it around her, I step down again, a piece of the curtain wrapped around my wrists and glass-slashed hands. With the sheer might of heaven, I begin hoisting my sister through the window.

At that moment, sirens blare, and firemen with their axes burst through the front door of the restaurant, and the world goes dark.

WHEN I WAKE, the first word out of my mouth is, "Filomena!"

"*Si?*" comes a voice in the bed next to me.

We're in the same hospital room, crammed with people all talking at the same time. There're our daughters, our sons, our husbands, restaurant workers, even a fireman or two. The nurse enters and brusquely runs everyone off, saying visiting hours are over. Almost all of them remain just outside the window, waving and smiling.

"What a group!"

"Bunch of squirrels !"

"Poor hospital staff!"

There's a lot of commotion, and then they are gone. It's quiet in our room, and I take the opportunity to observe the brilliant profusion of lilies everywhere! Tables, counters, the floor, and windowsills bloom a host of Stargazers, Madonnas, Tiger lilies, and more.

"My God, all these flowers! You'd think this was our funeral."

"They are *all* from Antonio! There's a telegram hiding somewhere in those blooms."

"I don't know what to say." *So, he does still think of me.*

"My sister, tongue-tied? That's a first."

"Ha, ha. *Sorella*, tell me about your injuries."

"They give me oxygen treatments several times a day for smoke inhalation. They say it's a miracle that my feet have only second-degree burns! They are blistered and burned but you rescued me just in time."

"I don't remember. The firemen came through the door . . ."

"You'd already gotten me out of the burning kitchen!"

My angel. Did she bring some of her friends?

My hip is wrapped in a tight brace. There's a sharp twinge as I attempt to get out of bed. My right foot, wrapped as well, doesn't quite hold me. Falling back on the bed I examine my hands covered in small stitches.

"Okay. I guess I won't be running the Boston Marathon this year."

"What you did to save me was epic enough for one lifetime."

"I wasn't going to lose you."

"Arabella, you will always be my answered prayer."

I scoot on my bandaged hands and knees in search of the telegram from Antonio. Once I've found it, I make it over to her bed. We're laughing through our tears as I crawl in with her. My spirit angel is already there along with the healing words of Antonio Salerno.

"MAMA, I'M COMING OVER to give you a driving lesson," Lucy declares.

"No, *figlia*, driving an automobile is of no interest."

"But Mama, we live in Natick, Zia Filomena in Sherborn, and you and Papa are in Weston with Dominic's family! We're too far apart."

"America 1961 is a speeding highway, *figlia*. Everyone is on their way to somewhere else—in a hurry."

"I know it seems that, but we want what's best for our children—good schools, a backyard to play in."

"*Sì*. I understand."

"But Mama, if you drove a car, you could visit whenever you want."

"Like the days of old when we lived upstairs-downstairs," I reminisce.

Lucy pauses, wondering if she should bring up the subject of my sister. "It did the heart good to see you and Zia Filomena together during those months you were healing."

"Surviving that fire was a miracle, *grazie Dio*, as was the chance for us to reconnect." I sigh. "But we know nothing stays the same."

"Do you think Papa and Luigi sold the duplex because of the impending lawsuit? I am sorry to bring it up, Mama, but don't you think we should all be talking more?"

"I just don't know. Talk tossed my sister and me into unsavory waters. As far as the building sale, I am fairly certain they're selling what they can to move their assets to Italy."

"Do you really think Allesandro and Bernardo will actually file that lawsuit?"

I take a deep breath. "I hope not, figlia." Visions of an angry sister, hostile cousins, and our family business paraded before the public makes me shiver.

Lucy returns to her campaign, "Mama, please consider sitting behind the wheel of a car just to see how it feels."

"Lucy, I like to walk and use public transportation, like I did in Boston. Did you know Planned Parenthood is just a fifteen-minute walk from Dominic's?"

She sighs. "Hmm. Speaking of that, I hear some fanatics are protesting the services of Planned Parenthood. I may not agree with everything you are doing, Mama, but . . ."

"Every woman should have access to birth control, Lucy. I will not hear anything against that fundamental right."

"I know what the Pope thinks of that stand, but what do Papa and Dominic say?"

"Your brother, sister-in-law, and papa are so busy at the restaurants, no one pays attention to what I do. I am here when your cousin, Rosa gets home at 5, and dinner's at 7; as long as that happens, I am left on my own."

"Well, that's not right either, Mama. You're taking care of Dominic's daughter, their home, and I worry about you being alone too much."

"Alone?" I chuckle. "One neighbor told another who told another, and now, I am the lady doctor who makes house calls. I tell them, no, I am not a doctor, but they insist on calling me that. I give the diabetic across the street her daily injections of insulin, and sometimes I stitch a youngster's cut or wrap a sprain, or steep a tea for a cough, cold, or fever. It feels good to care for others in my community."

I feel a pang of longing for Paola, for Mama and Papa who need me as they grow older, for Marco's son I don't know; for Antonio, who chose to remain in Paola after selling his company.

"That's so sweet, Mama. I'm happy you are using your skills."

"*Grazie. Thank you* for the call, but I've got to go now."

I need time to breathe in the books at the public library on my way to my job at Planned Parenthood, and to borrow F. Scott Fitzgerald's *The Last Tycoon*. I wonder why a story of doomed love set in glamorous Hollywood can somehow soothe the soul. Reading remains one of my greatest joys—sparked by dear Gregorio. Ah, Gregorio, what would life have been like if the cholera had not taken him? What if Antonio and I had stayed in Paola together?

After work that day, Vincent waiting for me. He has sad news from Paola that Pina has passed away.

"And I'm sorry to deliver more bad news Mama, but tomorrow's newspaper's headlines will announce the lawsuit. This is going to be ugly, Mama, really ugly."

Boston Globe, July 25, 1956

Celestina Family Restaurant-Not so heavenly!

The Mandarino brothers, Dominic and Vincent, of the highly-acclaimed Celestina Restaurant chain are being sued by their cousins, Alex and Bernard Compretta for breach of contract. Apparently, relations within the family are not so heavenly after all. Following the fire that ravaged their North End restaurant, trapping and nearly killing their mothers, the cousins ignited some issues of their own regarding shares in the successful company.

THE STORY BROKE, AND SO DID THE TRUST I had in family. No one speaks face to face nor answers phone calls (the lawyers forbid it). As this family drama plays out in front of the whole country, the irritability levels rise between husband and wife, brother and brother, mother and son. And my sister and I? We have not spoken. Those imbecile men will eventually have to give up some money and power, no doubt. But what of the sisters? Haven't we given up too much of our hearts already? Big, important, immigrant family fighting over the spoils of success makes exciting headlines. Photographers and journalists stalk us—even my grandchildren, too young to understand the issues. I can't walk anywhere alone. Even leaving the house is like being at the Vatican's St. Peter's square during Easter mass. *Molto gente! Too many people!* I can't breathe with their bullet questions suffocating me, their cameras aimed at my tormented face.

The phone rings, and I wonder if it's just another damn reporter wanting a comment, but something tells me to pick it up.

"*Sorella?* It's Marco."

"Marco! I just heard of Pina's passing. I will write to her, but please convey my sympathies to Rafaella."

"*Grazie, sorella.*"

"Your voice is like balm on a wound, Marco! Have you learned of the lawsuit?"

"Si. `*E triste, it's sad.*"

"I don't expect you to take sides. The whole situation is terrible and wrong and will be the death of this family."

"Arabella, I am so very sorry." He pauses. "I'm afraid I have worse news."

I hold my breath and wait.

"*Sorella?*"

"*Si,* I am here. *Dimmelo, ti prego, Please tell me.*" I brace myself for the worst, an angel light beside me.

"Mama, *sta morendo.* Mama *is dying.*" He's crying now, barely able to get out the details about how she wasn't getting over the stomach flu, and finally, Rafaella took her to the hospital in Cosenza, and there, it was determined she has cancer.

"I'll be on the first airplane," I promise.

AT LEAST FILOMENA AND I WERE together at the end of our mother's life. I know Mama found solace in that. Filomena and I made a pact to not speak of the lawsuit. In truth, I don't think either one of us had the energy for it—especially Filomena.

Dear God, it didn't take an expert to understand just how sickly Filomena was! There was the pale-yellow tint of her skin, her hollow eyes, the extreme weight loss. When Marco asked after her health, she claimed it was from the stress of the lawsuit. Rafaella and I knew better.

"Arabella, your sister is not well. Her coloring would suggest something with her liver."

I hide my head in my hands for a moment. "It's all too much, Rafaella, Mama on her deathbed, and Filomena in dire condition. I see that you are right about the jaundice of her liver, but truthfully, we haven't spoken in several weeks. Can you imagine, the Mandarino sisters do not even speak to one another?"

She holds me, just like days of old, knowing, caring, compassionate. "You will find a way to mend, Arabella. She is your sister and *noi siamo qui, we are here*," she coos.

Having other family members bear a burden lifts a few ounces of pain. I'm grateful to also have some joy with Rafaella. On our walk to the mill and the glasshouses one afternoon, she animatedly gushes.

"Arabella, because of your generous investment in our tincture business, *Medicina Sorelle,* we have customers as far away as London, England! I'm using all our recipes, and people are lapping them up. *Grazie tanti, sorella.*"

Being thanked by someone as dear and wholesome as Rafaella is like a shot in the arm of vitality. And our tinctures are helping people! Too bad we don't have a tincture to revive Mama.

Day by day, she slipped in and out of consciousness. We prayed the rosary, held her birdlike, chilly hands, recanted *famiglia* stories as my angel (and I sensed, many others) held the vigil of love with us. One morning 8 days after we arrived, I watched Mama's breathing weaken considerably. I awakened Filomena, Papa, Marco, and Rafaella. Just as the sun dressed the morning in pastel shades of pink, Mama peacefully took her last breath.

Papa was so wrought with grief I worried that he was going to have a stroke. We gave him sedatives. The man who never took so much as an aspirin never even asked what the pills were. I held him, rocked him, and thought about how true it is that the children become the parents. Maybe we can convince him to come back to America for a while (or maybe I will just stay here and care for him).

Filomena and I prepared Mama's body for burial. Performing this final act of love was bittersweet. It's one thing to work on cadavers in school, quite another to clean your own Mama's mouth out with vinegar and wash her still body. Under her chin and around her head, we placed a kerchief to keep her mouth closed, and we dressed her in the black wool dress we sent her from America with her fine black leather pumps. To keep her eyes shut, we placed coins from the year she was born. Her favorite amethyst rosary from Brazil was positioned in her hands.

We made the long, funeral trek to her final resting place in the cemetery on the hill near San Francesco di Paola's sanctuary. Papa hired the professional wailing mourners who I swear could've been heard in Naples. We set the house in order to welcome those who came to pay their respects.

If only it were that simple to put my inner house in order. It has been struck by a tidal wave, everything strewn about, scattered by the winds of grief for the passing of my mother—and fear for the life of my sister.

"ARABELLA, HOW ARE YOU FARING?" asks Antonio.

How could he still be so handsome after all these years? That shock of silver hair and the lines at his eyes draw me to him even more than when we were *ragazzi!* And his compassion lights him up from the inside out.

"*Cosi, cosa,*" I answer, flipping my hand over and under. "I still can't believe my mama's gone."

Just like our youth, he quietly holds the space between us until I am ready to speak.

I take a deep breath. "We're prepared for living, but not dying." I sigh. "Come to think of it, I don't even know if we are truly prepared for living!"

"Well, you certainly are! Wherever you are, *dottore* Arabella, good happens."

I try to dodge the compliments, but he won't hear of it, and honestly, I drink them in, tonic for the soul. Before we know it, we are in the groves of flourishing citrus, seemingly without any memory of locusts. We converse about our daughters and grandchildren, steering clear of brothers and lawsuits. Fresh air and shared history wind around us with easy flow. He tells me how content he is in Paola's peacefulness, how surprised he is to not miss the hustle-bustle of the U.S.A. *Or a woman at your side?*

When I return home, Papa is sitting outside in the garden.

"Papa," I begin stoically at first, then fall to my knees, crying.

He brushes his gnarled hand across my cropped crown of curls. There are no words that make sense, so we just sit together for a while watching the dragonflies and butterflies maneuver the air. When I peek inside, I observe Filomena napping peacefully, but her gaunt, sickly appearance is startling. I ask Mary, Mother of God, my angel, and San Francesco di Paola to heal my sister and save our family. I squeeze my eyes shut to block out the fear that they are both too far gone—even for miracles.

SNOWFLAKE *PIZZELLE PASTRIES* FRIED and sugared for the Christmas celebration and almond moon cookies baked for the Easter feast kept us side by side in the kitchens of our daughters. Most of the women advocated for a truce with their brothers and their fathers, but in the end, words were fruitless. The sisters and cousins became shining examples of love to demonstrate that nothing—not even a well-publicized lawsuit dragging on and on- would get in the way of their relationships. I know it wasn't easy, but they took turns helping each other through the emotions of betrayal and hurt, and disappointment. They took turns showing us all that we can find ways through the sludge to the shore of who we are first and foremost: a *famiglia* born of love. We fed one another's bellies, but also, our souls because we are women, the caretakers of the heart of the family.

My Lucy told me about going to her father to plead in the name of peace, to settle the lawsuit out of court. She informed Aldo that her brothers should pay Allesandro and Bernardo what was owed to them. His response? He shouted at her—the pride of his heart—to shut up!

But did that stop the pride of *my* heart?

"Papa," she scolded. "This lawsuit is ruining our family. It's torn my mother and her sister apart. That is a crime in and of itself. Now, stop it by doing what is right once and for all!"

"'What is right' is the Basillios stick together as a family, no matter what! *Capisce?*"

"'No, I don't *understand* 'sticking together' when you and my brothers are wrong."

Revved up like an overheated engine, he blew. He raised his trembling hand to her face, and through gritted teeth, he spat, "If you weren't married, I'd slap your face."

"And if you weren't my father, I'd hate you!"

This rift between Filomena's and my sons will make the lawyers rich when that money could have easily been used to strike a compromise. *Marone! Damn!* Is there no machine in this new world of inventions that could take us back to the early years of promises? Maybe then we could take out pen and paper and put everything in black and white. Maybe then my sister and I could bask in a family united. Maybe she would regain her health. I'd return Vincent to his youth and make sure he followed his music dream. I'd make sure my nephews got their due—perhaps each of them their own Celestina Restaurant!

How can I grasp the concept that one of the culprits is success itself? Too much success equals too much money, equals too much pride, equals too much greed. I often wonder, *What if the caretakers of the heart were the ones running businesses?* All bad, spoiled boys would go to bed without their spaghetti! We'd take away their toys—their boats and their Cadillacs, their land and their buildings—we'd level the playing field under the firm hand of love that gives and receives the truth. In time, they would see that there is indeed *enough, more than enough,* for *everyone* to succeed. We'd hug and congratulate one another for our hard work, but more so for honoring the best in one another. I bet JFK, our visionary president, would agree with me.

I think of Mama often. How would she advise me during our family unrest? She'd proclaim, "Arabella, the most powerful tool you possess is love." She mastered walking the single file path of men sweeping up the mess of their decisions. I think of one of her favorite sayings. *Ragazzi piccolo, problemi piccolo. Ragazzi grande, problemi grande. Small children, small problems, big children, big problems.* And a mama can do nothing to fix the big ones.

One of those *big ones* is Filomena's declining health. How many times was she warned to be wary of what she ate on the streets of Brazil, not to share tea or utensils with strangers, not to risk her well-being? She had the time of her life there, carefree, her magnetic smile charming all of Rio. How many times did she chide me, the one with knowledge both medical and discerning? "Arabella, you look like the statue of Pieta, sadness herself! Stop worrying!" But I did worry when she helped that poor, bleeding woman and her baby, when she shared not only her food but her utensils.

Now that 'fun' is eating her liver. It's called hepatitis. Even the miracle pill, penicillin, cannot cure her. Must I accept that the cycle of life is ending for her? Mama's gone, and who knows how long Papa has—any of us for that matter.

My children, though . . . always my children, are grown with lives and children of their own. And so it goes. It is hard to believe I am a "nonna" with ten grandchildren. If only Mama had been able to meet her great-grandchildren, to sit them on her padded lap and sing the lullaby that soothes the child to sleep, "*Canta, canta, bella figlia mia, vai, vai dormire, contento fantasia.*" Sing, sing, beautiful child of mine, go, go to sleep, happy dreams."

What I would give to have witnessed that. Any or all of the American luxuries, I would gladly offer to God in exchange for another day with Mama, to turn back time. I would have demanded Filomena make better choices. But there is no such machine that turns back time or makes someone behave differently.

Small kids, small problems; big kids, big problems.

"EVERYTHING IS IN ORDER FOR US TO GO HOME."

"But Aldo, *home* is where our children and grandchildren are."

And my dying sister is. Where her sons and my sons quarrel in front of the whole world.

"You knew this day was coming."

"We've built a nice life in America, Aldo."

"*Si*, but I want to go home."

"I don't want to leave my children and grandchildren, my patients, and my work."

"The kids will come to visit. You can help people in Paola again."

"It's not so black and white, Aldo. My life here is complex . . ."

"Precisely why we need a life that's simple, easy." Excitedly, he announces, "Arabella, it will be different now because of all the land we own! We're *ricco*."

"Why do people living a simple, easy life need to be *rich*?"

He gives me a look of disdain signaling the end of the discussion. "We leave in one month."

I may, or I may not. I could stay to care for my sister, to be a vital part of my grandchildren's lives, to continue my work at Planned Parenthood, to volunteer with the Women's League of Voters. I could live alone in an apartment or a small home all my own. At the library, I make long lists of pros and cons, perplexing options that have the same number of votes *si* and no. I don't talk to anyone about these considerations—only myself and my angel. I know it is possible and barring my sons' probable indignancy and my husband's shock, many others would understand and appreciate my decision to remain in America. Unlike Brazil, I am now a woman with a degree and income of her own.

My percentage of *Medicina Sorelle* profits would be enough for me to live on. I study the classified for rentals in places I have passed on foot a thousand times to and from Planned Parenthood. I make appointments to see them. Standing alone in those galley kitchens gives me a sense of loneliness and loss, but also freedom and adventure. I imagine a bed where only I sleep (or a grandchild snuggled up next to me). I could make it a reality. I am at a standstill, so I ask for guidance. I pray. I wait. I plunge my hands into the dirt of my little garden for grounding.

And then, about two weeks before we are to leave, the long invisible lines of communication reach across the seas. Marco informs me that Papa has fallen, broken his hip, and all he does is call for me. 93-years-old and he's asking for his daughter. And I know right then and there that I will go. I will go to Papa. I will go home to Italy because I know that if I want to return to America, I can and will. I am a woman with options and opportunities.

If it wasn't for the disruptive extra heartbeat of being apart from my sister, I would be at peace with my decision to return to Italy.

June 10, 1962
Alitalia Airlines Flight 1229
Boston, Ma. to Rome, Italy
Mr. and Mrs. Aldo Basillio

All twenty-nine members of la famiglia show up to see us off. Brothers, sisters, in-laws, children, grandchildren, and cousins take up most of the area at Logan's Gate 20E. We hug, we smile, and we wipe away tears. Filomena's sons and my sons avoid one another like planets orbiting different galaxies. The new generation of young cousins, however, gravitate to one another like magnets to iron. That warms the cold ache of discord. And of course, there is food! Someone has brought sfagglatalia, another, biscotti, and angel cookies (we could use a few more angels today).

The workers at Boston's Logan airport look on this family scene with envy.

"What a beautiful thing! All these people showed up to see the mom and dad off to Italy!"

"I wish my family cared about each other like that," another exclaims in awe.

Apparently, these folks don't know we've made headlines for being anything but caring.

I go to my sister. I think how much like hostages we are in this business catastrophe, quite aware of what it is to be pawns, used, broken. We're both tired of it, aren't we? And we know if it were up to us just how to repair it. By the look of her and geographic barriers, we better start patching up as best we can, *rapido, fast*.

"Flight 1229 Alitalia to Rome boarding at Gate 20E."

Hurriedly, chaotically, Aldo and I are pulled into embraces with every niece, nephew, in-law, grandchild, and child.

Filomena is the last one to bid me farewell. We hold each other for an extra heartbeat. Our love's been beaten up and frayed, but it's still there. We are the *Mandarino sorelle*; we are *sisters*. We cry for time lost to anger and disappointment, for precious words unspoken. Maybe our hearts used that extra heartbeat to convey our commitment to one another.

Aldo comes to my side. He puts his arm through mine. "Time to go home." He coughs, deep, rattling sounds. He waited so long to take my borage tea expectorant or go to the doctor for medicine that he's wracked with spasms. He rights himself and repeats, "*Andiamo a casa di Italia.*"

But I have come to understand that home is not a physical place, an address with numbers, or a street name. Home is where we feel love.

I'll find that love in the presence of my *simpatico* brother Marco and dear sister-in-law, Rafaella, and in the sweet scoop of friendship with the person who has always spoken the language of my heart: Antonio Salerno.

Up ahead in the aisle of the airplane, I see a familiar shape. My spirit angel beckons me forward. As I sit in the calm radiance of her light, I conjure my sister, I ponder that extra heartbeat. The power of communication does not always speak with audible words.

"ARABELLA, WELCOME HOME," Rafaella beams.

It feels so good to hug her and my handsome, simpatico brother, Marco. "You two are a sight for sore eyes!"

Marco and Aldo shake hands and bustle about with the luggage. Rafaella puts her arm through mine. "I can hardly believe you are here, *sorella*. We have missed you! And your papa too, and did I mention all the people of Paola? When they heard you were returning after getting an American doctor's education, they were almost making up problems so you can attend to them!"

We laugh, and I ask her if she reminded them that I am not a doctor, but rather, a PA, Physician's Assistant.

"Bah." She laughs. "Here, you are Dottore Arabella."

"And Dottore Arabella, your papa needs your healing touch. He is old, yes, but I think his heart is lonely for your mama, Carmella, and for his girls."

I swallow a couple of times. "*Grazie tanti*, for all you have done to love and care for our family, Rafaella."

Papa still looks good for 90 plus years! Yes, he's shrunken, lined, and thin, but when he took me in his arms, he had the strength of Hercules. Love's restoration, eh? I help him get comfortable sitting up in his bed, and though we're talking about the journey on the airplane, I am assessing his health. His voice is strong, though tinged with some indication of pain, his breathing fairly even.

"So, my Arabella has come home to me."

"*Si*, Papa. I am so happy to be with you."

"But not anyone else?" He lifts an eyebrow humorously.

"Well, a girl's papa is always her number one love," I remark.

He is silent. I wait.

"I only wish you had been free to pursue your true love. Is it too late, *figlia*? He's here in . . ."

I put my finger to his lips. "No, Papa, regret is for those who believe they've made mistakes. I don't feel that way." Do I? No, everything unfolded in Antonio's and my life as fate dictated. His successful business, Stephanie, his daughter . . ..

I change the subject to news of his great-grandchildren until I notice he's slowing down between responses.

"*Allora*, I need to see to my belongings. Who knows where they'll end up?" I kiss him on the forehead.

He takes my hand. "Arabella, my answered prayer."

Beyond a doubt, I know I was meant to be here now.

I AM MORE COMFORTABLE HERE, alone on the stretch of heaven I call the *lungomare* than I am with Aldo's newfound associates in my family's home. They're boastful, smoking their cigars, slapping themselves on the back. Aldo is happy in his new role as village *Sunto, esteemed elder*, though almost immediately upon setting foot in Italy, his cough escalated to bronchitis.

We took him to a doctor in Rome, but he threw away the medication saying he didn't like the way it made him feel. Reducing the inflammation of tube linings that carry air to the lungs is key, but he is not responding to my comfrey, oregano, and thyme tonics or cough medicine we buy at the *farmacia, pharmacy*. He dismissed the severity of the illness from the onset. He does not wish to see that he has a responsibility to his body. Even when I described the long-term damage of not being able to breathe on his own, he shrugged his shoulders and walked away. Another day I showed him drawings from a medical book complete with descriptions of failing lungs and infected mucus. *I'll be fine* is his standard answer.

So, I concentrate on Papa: reading to him, exercising, and stretching his muscles, making sure he's eating well, and telling stories of Mama. Day in and day out, we listen to Aldo coughing his way through his land deals from Papa's study. I refuse to clean ashtrays of cigars and cigarettes he should not be inhaling! And I will not serve rounds of anisette in stout glasses. I told them all one day, "Drink all you want but you are drinking with a sick man." That went over very well, I assure you.

When Papa is napping, I slip out to the *lungomare*. Today, on my timeless, *bello lungomare*, strewn memories are etched on the shore. There I am as a fourteen-year-old escaping the noisy piazza, as a young lady pondering my fate, the wide-eyed girl meeting her spirit angel, flying a kite with Antonio, Mama calling me home for dinner, Filomena announcing my birth. Fast forward to the trance of here and now, aware only of the wind kissing my face, the salty exhale of the ocean, the hum of a changing *Mezzogiorno*.

I glance up at the hill no longer a haven for chamomile, mayweed, and wild daisies. Hotel Basillio, a modern eight-story glass box is a sign of changing times. It's already booked for the summer, I hear. Apparently, a famous German stumbled upon Paola, and now it is on the European seaside resort map. It seems the Basillio men had perfect business timing.

Aldo and my brothers also invested and lease out one and two-story houses that now pepper the fields next to the mill. But Rafaella and I have preserved the mill and glasshouses for our *Medicina Sorelle*. My own land sits adjacent to it. I am so proud of that and have a sudden urge to visit the mill and glasshouses. I begin the trek from the water to the *piazza* to the mill. The stairs up to the piazza make me feel nostalgic, but as I climb the stairs today, my heart beats erratically. I am so winded I must stop every other stair. This is not just a sign of an aging body. Something is amiss. Have I just sloughed off symptoms like one of my dismissive patients? Like my husband and his bronchitis? I pause to assess myself in the refreshing mist of *The Fontana di Paola*: shortness of breath, fatigue, weakness. Is it any surprise my heart is at risk?

Someone taps me on the shoulder, and I nearly jump (which would be a feat for this body).

"Antonio," I nearly squeal. He smiles and hugs me with such affection I stifle a moan.

"Arabella, how wonderful to see you! Are you well?"

Has he noticed something slightly off with me?

"I'm fine, just fine," I lie, "though Aldo has developed a terrible case of bronchitis."

"I am so sorry, but lucky for him, he gets the best care from Paola's best *dottore*."

"Stop, Antonio. You don't know what you're talking about."

"Hmm, maybe you're right," he teases.

It's easy to lose myself in the effortlessness of our friendship. He has been such a good friend to me and my whole family—from employing Luigi and Aldo to watching over Filomena, the partnership of Salerno's and Mandarino Brothers Coffee. We promise to meet again soon.

I'm too exhausted to walk *to Medicine Sorelle*, but the newly renovated *piazza* church with its domed ceiling, white marble altar, and opulent chandeliers is just around the corner. It's not the same womblike feel, but in the deeply grooved pews, the flames of candles like soldiers of light, the incense, the widowers in black, the statue of Mary and Jesus under the glass dome, the ageless embrace of faith, I find gratitude for all my blessings: my dear brother and sister-in-law who keep the family fire burning, for my friend who seems to show up at just the right moment, for my one and only sister that God so generously shared with me all these years. I kneel before the altar, part of me wanting to beg God to save her, to heal Aldo, my Papa, to mend the relationship of my sons and their cousins, but He already knows my fervent requests.

Hello, God, it's me, Arabella Rosa Mandarino Basillio, thanking you for my life.

WE'RE EXPERIENCING A BIT OF the fabulous olden days here in Paola because *all* phone lines are disengaged due to impending improvements. No one knows how long this will take (and the joke is, does it take more time to grease an official's palm than it does a frying pan?)Delightfully, everything has slowed down to where if you need to talk to someone, you must do it face to face. For communication across the seas, we're sending and receiving letters. Lucy told me that Filomena is weakening day by day. I cannot stop thinking of her so I pick up a pen and begin,

Paola, 1963

Cara Sorella,

Please forgive me for having allowed the discord between our sons to keep me from being the sister you need me to be. How could I have let it keep me from the one who called me down from heaven? At this twilight time of my life, I realize that everything you and I ever claimed to be true is so: Our love is the kind the muses deliver to the fortunate ones. We are proof that it transcends earthly woes, able to mend the broken wings of hurt to soar again by the One who can fathom the depths of our love because He, in His benevolence, placed it in us. We, as sisters, are the rhapsody he plays whilst his angels dance.

We can be together again, dear Sorella, through our words, in our hearts. Venire nel mio cuore, sorella, come to my heart, sister.

Con Amore,
Arabella

My old friend Signore Pascal's grandson is the mail carrier now. I hear his motor scooter coming up the drive. I greet him and inquire after his family, and then I slip him the letter. There's a sudden glow of angel's light encompassing him. I pause to feel the message of her here, now. Then, automatically, I reach for some lire from my pocket.

I whisper to him, "This letter is our secret, *buono? Good?*"

He nods his head as if he understands what it is like to be a woman. I'm not sure about the secretive nature of this, but I have learned to follow my angel and not question my inner urgings. I am handed two letters. One is about an upcoming visit from Dominic and his daughter, Rosa, and Carla, Vincent's daughter. And the best news of all from Boston: the awful lawsuit is over! Allesandro and Bernardo received a large cash reward as well as, two territories of the Mandarino Brothers Coffee company. Brilliant! Now my nephews can build something of their own. Though my sons feel like they lost, they will get over it, won't they? There is so much wealth to go around.

Later, as I ponder the underlying issues with the business and the boys, shock waves of understanding shatter my sense of peace: it was never about sharing the wealth as it was being the ones in control.

RAFAELLA'S BEEN WITH ME cooking for days—Dominic's favorite *polpetta melanzane*, almond biscotti, peppers and sausage, homemade spaghetti for the girls. It makes me long for Mama and my sister, Filomena, but I know what a gift Rafaella is.

"Arabella, *come va? What's up with you?*"

"Oh, I can't wait to see my son and introduce my granddaughters to their great grandfather, the wonders of Mezzogiorno and . . ."

"*Si*, but I'm speaking of you."

"I'm just a little tired," I say.

She lifts her eyebrow, but I change the subject to Aldo's troubled breathing, which now requires an oxygen machine. Without it, he couldn't breathe on his own. She doesn't press me anymore today about my health, but it's enough to bring it out of the shadows. And once my son and granddaughters arrive and the activities commence, I'm like the four-year-old who needs her afternoon nap. Secretly, I use Aldo's machine for breathing treatments.

Rafaella comes to cook often. "Let me come and stay for just for a while," she offers. I refuse. She has a business to run and doesn't need to babysit me. She sends a darling young lady to assist me with daily chores, cooking, supervising the girls as they make the *lungomare* their playground, and exploring the groves like Antonio and I did when we were children.

Still, I am exhausted. And terribly worried about my sister's decline.

It's been weeks without a word from my sister. Or so I thought. I kept asking myself, why hasn't my sister responded to my letter, and my sister was asking herself the same exact question. Oh, Filomena, how could I answer a letter I never received because my husband and son intercepted your letter, determined to keep us apart? How dare they think they can control us, thwart our sisterhood, our love. Who do they think they are? Obviously, the resentment over the lawsuit is still alive and well with the mamas paying retribution with more pieces of their hearts.

I would never have known you were on your way to Paola, but *grazie* Mary, Mother of God for angels and miracles! I overheard Aldo and Dominic talking while my granddaughters and I were in the garden. The girls were chasing the chickens around when I caught a glimpse of my angel. I moved toward her and thus in earshot of those sneaky men talking through the kitchen window.

"Papa, I don't want Mama to have anything to do with that Compretta family when they are here in Paola."

"*Si, figlio*, there's no reason for your mother to even know they are here."

I decide not to charge them like an angry bull. I gather my wits, and like the sly fox, I ask Aldo if he has heard any word about your visit. He lies, "No, no, I know nothing."

Another day, a different hour, while he is distracted by a task, I ask the date you are coming. Without thinking, he responds, "Sometime this month," and then he begins to backpedal towards another lie, but I plant my feet on truth's ground and stare him down.

"This month then? And don't you dare lie to me."

He mumbles yes, but he's not sure when.

"How could you even dare to think you have the right to keep us apart?" I ask.

A coughing fit begins, and he reaches for the oxygen.

The girls come running in with Dominic. "Nonna, we're all going to Rome, to the Colosseum and the Trevi Fountain!"

"What? When?"

Dominic laughs the easy laugh of someone who holds all the cards. "Tomorrow, Mama. We have business in Rome so we'll all go on a Roman holiday."

"It sounds like a lovely trip for you and the girls, but I'm going to stay here."

"Why?"

"To wait for my sister."

"Oh, Mama," he lies. "We just heard they won't be coming til the end of the month."

"I will not miss her, "I announce.

"No, no, that won't happen," Aldo says.

Would *you* believe them? No, you would not, dear sister, because you know they are lying. You have already come and gone from Paola–and I never knew.

EVERY SPEEDING MILE NORTH on the *autostrada* to Rome adds to my grief and betrayal by those who insist they control me. Will they succeed in keeping my sister and me apart, or will I get to see my sister?

The men will be at meetings all day, so our driver will take the girls sightseeing. And me? First and foremost, I have a date with God. I slip out of the car, place a black lace veil over my head, and enter the sacred dominion of the Basilica di Santa Maria di Maggiore. Perhaps beneath her gilded ceiling made from the first gold Columbus brought back from the New World, I will find strength as lasting as this precious metal. I will pray next to its crimson red columns—the color of the diseased blood of my sister. I'll remember our togetherness in this sacred place. I envision our hearts glued back together like the thousands of chipped mosaic tiles on these massive walls.

With the holy water, I baptize myself in the waters of redemption in the name of the Father and the Son and the Holy Ghost. I slip into a pew in the back of the church, allowing the magnificence of this place to put me in a state of awe. Peace waits for me in the walls, until I am ready to breathe it in like a breath of gentleness from the Mediterranean waters dropping in to radiate serenity. Wrapped in tranquil reverie, I'm reminded that no matter how things appear, there is always love enough to release the pain of mistake, of regret, of judgment—of myself and others.

I remove the crystal rosary from my *figlia*, Lucy. Placing it in my palm is like holding her hand. I join in the rosary, "Holy Mary, Mother of God, pray for us sinners, now and at the hour of our death." This prayer is a steady, rhythmic petition, soothing like the sea.

When the mass ends, I stay seated. People file out—the young mama and her wide-eyed infant, the widower in black, the newly married couple seeking God's continued blessing. Sweet, penetrating peace continues to fill me up to the top like a fountain, cascading through me. The grand basilica doors open, and glaring light slices the darkness. I need to remain, to inhale the presence of all that is good, holy, just. And being here makes me feel the presence of my sister.

There is a tiny, nearly inaudible moan escaping someone's lips in the pew near the altar. *Poverina. Poor thing.* I will pray to ease her pain. She says something else, a tortured sound. I listen more attentively. There's something familiar about it. Perhaps it is just that pain recognizes pain.

Again, comes the thin voice, but this time it is followed by a whispered prayer, "*Sorella, dove vai? Sister, where are you?*"

My heart stops. Flutters. Settles. Jumpstarts.

"I'm right here," I tentatively answer. "Filomena?"

She turns. Frail, worn, sickly, but it is my sister.

"Arabella?"

Sprinting on legs charged with the memory of youth, hearts, transparent and light as dragonfly wings, into each other's arms, we fall back through the years—before there was sickness, hurt, husbands, or sons. We cannot release each other except to stare into each other's faces and laugh and cry and laugh some more.

Time and again, ad infinitum, we are saved by the sheer, indisputable grace of love. We sisters know that and bask in the miracle of it—our last time together on this Earth. We forgive ourselves first, then one another. Together, we absolve the fearful. We luxuriate in the presence of redeemed love, one that transcends everything—even the scheming folly of misguided men.

RESTORED PHONE LINES HAVE helped me learn of Filomena's status these past weeks. Lucy is my soundboard as I deliberate a host of emotions regarding Filomena's impending death and the betrayal of my son and husband. I think I will keep it all to myself, not bother to say anything because what is done is done. In the end, love won. Through our bond and divine intervention, the sisters could not be kept apart.

But I am unable to remain silent. The men will hear from me.

While drinking some Mandarino Brothers Coffee this morning with Aldo and Dominic, I announce, "The girls are going to the beach today with their cousin, and the three of us will share a meal at 1pm."

"Mama, I have a . . ."

"Whatever it is, cancel it," I order before walking out of the kitchen. Peeking back, I see puzzlement erupt on their faces. Good, let them stew in uncertainty and perhaps, worry, for a while. It will prime the ground.

While I'm cooking the pasta primavera and coating the fish in cornmeal, I deliberate exactly what it is I want them to hear. What's the essence of the message I'll impart? I explore *How dare you* lectures and *Let me help you understand your actions* speeches. I take a lot of deep breaths and call on my angel. *Please help me. I don't want to squander this opportunity by letting my anger lead the way.* Their ears and hearts will shut down faster than a car engine without any gasoline.

"Take your plate from the table and go fill them at the stove," I order. I will not serve them today.

They look from one to the other. I feel the dynamic presence of my angel, and that both calms me and emboldens me.

"I have some things I wish to express, so please be silent, attentive, and do not interrupt me. `E chiaro? Is that clear?"

"Um, yes Mama, sure."

"Well, okay," Aldo manages.

When they return to the table, I take a breath and look squarely into their faces. "No one, and I mean no one, *ever* has the right to interfere with love—not papas, brothers, sons." I pick up momentum. "No one, and damn it, I mean, no one—including either of you, should ever think that you have the power to sabotage love." I take a deep breath.

"Mama, I . . ."

"*Silenzio! Be quiet!* And take this straight to your hearts: do not *ever* fool yourselves into thinking that you can control others—especially me. And here's something else you may have forgotten: *Love always wins.*"

Aldo swallows hard and clears his throat. Dominic hangs his head.
"Now, if you'll excuse me, I am going to call my sister."
I leave them to be together, their pasta turning cold.

DAYS LATER, I AWOKE IN THE NIGHT with a burning sensation in my back and a throb in my jaw. I was certain I knew the cause. Marco drove me on the new autostrada to Cosenza's hospital.

"Arabella?" my worried brother inquired. "Have these symptoms been going on long?"

"Yes, for a while, but they were mild."

"Arabella! How could take excellent care of others but not yourself?"

"It's going to be all right," I assured him.

A stent to open the heart is a new medical breakthrough procedure. I was home in a few days with strict instructions to rest. It made a kind of psychological sense that my heart required aid to open it a little wider, allowing more flow. The betrayal of my husband and son may have squeezed it shut, as well as, the fact that my sister will be gone from this earth very soon. Lucy reports that Filomena has begun calling to me, waiting for me to go to her so she can depart this life. Because my heart is healing, I cannot get on an airplane. It seems cruel, but the timing of it all is beyond my control—another hard lesson in acceptance of the way things are.

So, I do what brings me the closest to God, myself, others. I commune with nature among the dahlias, peonies, the sweet peas, and the chamomile. I speak into each petal, infusing them with love to be carried on the winds to *mia sorella*. In each color-filled bloom, I picture her in the clothes she adored—the periwinkle silk gown she wore to Alessandro's wedding, the fuchsia flouncy skirt she danced the bassa nova to in Rio, the embroidered violet-red sweater I gave her one Christmas. I sing to her in the chorus of the birds' orchestra, chant the songs of our childhood. I even perform my silly imitation of Tonino Bennett for her to recall our humor. I pray the rosary out on my garden bench, incanting both our voices, both of our souls (and that of my unborn daughter buried in this garden). I snap a cucumber from the vine, bite into its cool crispness, whispering, "Remember the good things, sister. Taste only the sweetness of your life." I talk to her in an endless circle of the language of sisters.

Lucy calls today to tell me Filomena is so near the end, but the doctor says, "She is waiting for her sister." Though eaten by unimaginable pain, she waits, murmuring only my name.

I take a breath that could lift a thousand swans to flight. "Lucy, listen to me, please. You tell Filomena . . ." I falter, choke. "I am coming."

"But Mama, your heart . . ."

"Luciana, *basta. Stop.* Nothing matters now except Filomena's peace of mind. We've got to help her let go," I manage. It is Filomena's strength I feel now as my angel's light covers me like a soft blanket. "She cannot go home to God unless she thinks that I am there with her. So, *you go, figlia. You. You go for me.* Do you understand? *Capisce?*"

Something is transferred in that moment, in those words, through blood and cells, through wires and dials, across those ocean and city miles. Something powerful, unseen, something only the most vulnerable would accept. I hang up, trembling, shredded, raw. *I come to you, Filomena. I come to you so that you can go home to God, to your Gregorio, to Mama. Non ti preoccupare, mia sorella. Do not worry. I come now.*

That evening, my daughter entered the hospital room where Filomena, somewhere between this world and the next, opened her eyes, turned her withered mouth to smile, and declared, "Arabella, *la mia sorella.* I knew you would come."

Filomena's daughters and mine held her hands as she left this Earth. In the form and blood of my daughter, *I was with her,* our *famiglia* together, holding the future. The prevailing promise of love is like that, you know. It leaves its imprint on the heart, and therefore, endures forever.

Paola, 1965

THE *RAGAZZI* STROLL ARM AND arm around the piazza, laughing, Mediterranean sunlight kissing their white throats. The young men jostle one another, hoping for recognition. This game of female and male is as old as the mountains.

Antonio and I sit contentedly, admiring youth and the ancient wisdom of the cosmos. He takes my hand. "*Allora, guarda the ragazzi.*" He laughs. "Teeming with future promise."

"Ah, youth, wasted on the young," I answer with just a tinge of jealousy at the ease of their saunter.

"No, Arabella, nothing is wasted unless you take it for granted." He looks at me with utter devotion. "Here we are, Arabella, *together,* and I think Aldo and Stephanie, God bless their souls, would be at peace with that."

"Dottore Arabella." A young mother with a babe in her arms approaches me. "May we come see you in the morning? My other *figlia* has a terrible cough."

"Of course," is my response.

"*Grazie, dottore.*" She almost curtsies and walks away.

He looks into my eyes and runs his thumb across my crinkled cheek. I know our bones are old and our hair gray, but a sizzling current of delight runs up and down my spine.

"Did you ever imagine we would be here, together in our beloved Italia?" I ask.

"I dreamed of it—you the doctor, me the lazy, retired one." He laughs.

"I don't think I ever let go of the dream of us," I profess.

"What's meant to be is worth waiting a lifetime for." He squeezes my hand.

"Not that you stood on the sidelines waiting for me," I tease. "You seized life by the horns and swung it to the moon."

We giggle like we know each enthralling secret of life. And, well, come to think of it, we do. Hand in hand, we make our way down to the *lungomare* beneath the indigo velvet of twilight.

Stay committed to love for
love transcends everything—
the regret of decades past,
the thousands of miles that separate,
the millions of harbors of illusion,
the billions of flames that engulf the mind—
even death itself.
Yes, love transcends all.

ACKNOWLEDGEMENTS

Though writing a novel is a solitary endeavor, it could not be completed without the bountiful support of others.

To all those "*sorelle*" *sisters* who read early drafts of this book and offered insight/input: My Nancy-Old Same, Vinaya, Ann, Dorcas, and the Sisterhood of Encouragement: Ellen 1 and 2, Lise, Sue, Jann, Cindy, Stacy, Paula, and my Unseen Friends, *grazie mille, a million thanks.*

Dad, Lester Edward Przewlocki, what a shining example of intellect and perseverance you modeled, my extraordinary mom, Lynn Italia Przewlocki, a trailblazing beacon of strength, wisdom and courage, my sister, Debbie Fontaine, I know what it is to be and have the gift of a sister because of you; and *fratelli brothers*, Steve, Roberto, Ron, Davey Ray, and Michael, just like the song says: "*we are family*"!

Simpatico Agent, Trisha Telep, you knew when to push, when to pull, when to nudge, when to encourage me to take risks, and eke the door of my writerly self open a little wider.

Patient, affirmative Kim Coghlan, Senior Editor, and the able staff of TouchPoint Press, thank you for giving *La Mia Sorella, My Sister*, wings to fly. *Sono grato, I am grateful.*

To my husband, Jim Thibodeaux, unfailing vessel of boundless promotion, my heart is yours.

To each of you who supports another in her seemingly impossible pursuit, please know, we couldn't do it without you.

Author's Notes

This work of fiction began as a short story for my mother one Mother's Day about a decade ago. The original version told the "true story" of my grandmother and great aunt, legendary for their devotion and love to/for each other. My short story began later in their lives, as one married sister and her family emigrated to America, leaving the other sister and her family behind in Italy. The sisters could not accept living so far apart. They successfully schemed and plotted to get the other sister and her family from Italy to America! Readers of that short story wanted to know more about the early lives of the sisters; how they came to be so close (perhaps looking for the secret code of how to achieve such a bond). No one alive knew the early days of the sisters' relationship; I was unable to interview the sisters, per se, but it seemed that when I began to craft this fictionary tale, they "spoke" to me in dreams and images. I drew on my own relationships with my sister and family members, husbands, cousins, and many others who revealed the complexities and confluences of relationships.

The metamorphosis from short story to novel has also been my metamorphosis from songwriter and poet to novelist. As per usual of the way I have lived my life, I jumped into the deep end with gut and gumption, learning to craft a novel by kicking, sinking, diving, breathing, and trying, again and again.

The only elements of this novel that remain "real" of my grandmother and great aunt's life are A) they lived in Paola, Italy; B) they emigrated to the USA; C) they were always in the kitchen cooking up something delectable, and most importantly; D) they possessed extraordinary love for one another.

Everything else is pure fiction, including the characters.

My knowledge of the lyrical Italian language is limited, at best, so Italians, *per favore, perdonami, forgive me* for all the mistakes I have made! *Marone!*

For any blurred lines of historical events, dates, places and such, I've used my poetic license to drive this story from my heart to yours.

Grazie, Thank you for being a part of it. You are now *famiglia!*

Made in United States
North Haven, CT
09 March 2022

16965985R00200